Thomas Keneally

Thomas Keneally was born in 1935 and was educated
in Sydney. He trained for several years for the Catholic
priesthood but did not take orders. In a distinguished
writing career he has had four novels shortlisted for the
Booker Prize, which he won in 1982 with SCHINDLER'S
ARK – since made by Steven Spielberg into the
internationally acclaimed film, *Schindler's List*. He has
also written several works of non-fiction, including most
recently HOMEBUSH BOY, a memoir about growing up
in Sydney.

S

SCEPTRE

A River Town

THOMAS KENEALLY

SCEPTRE

First published in 1995 by Hodder and Stoughton
First published in paperback in 1995 by Hodder and Stoughton
A division of Hodder Headline PLC
A Sceptre Paperback

10 9 8 7 6 5 4 3 2 1

British Library Cataloguing in Publication Data

Keneally, Thomas
River Town
I. Title
823 [F]

ISBN 0 340 62474 4

Typeset by Hewer Text Composition Services, Edinburgh
Printed and bound in Great Britain by
Cox and Wyman Ltd, Reading, Berkshire

Hodder and Stoughton
A division of Hodder Headline PLC
338 Euston Road
London NW1 3BH

To the memory of my grandparents,
who kept a store in the Macleay Valley.

'Terrors are turned upon me; my dignity hasteth away as the
wind: and my welfare passeth away as a cloud.'

The Book of Job

On a hot morning in the New Year, a black police wagon went rolling along Kempsey's Belgrave Street from the direction of West Kempsey. All of this in the valley of the Macleay on the lush and humid north coast of New South Wales. The wagon attracted a fair amount of notice from the passers-by and witnesses. Many shopowners and customers in fact came out onto the footpaths to watch this wagon be drawn by, and some of them waved mockingly at the dark, barred window of the thing. Tim Shea of *T. Shea – General Store* stayed behind his counter but looked out with as much fascination as anyone as the wagon passed, two constables on the driver's seat, and Fry the sergeant of police riding behind.

The prisoners inside the wagon were being taken to Central wharf for shipment aboard SS *Burrawong* to their trial in Sydney. They were the abortionist Mrs Mulroney and her husband Merv, both of them about fifty years of age.

Just before Christmas, Mrs Mulroney had been visited by a young woman she did not know and who offered only a first name of convenience for the purpose of their transaction. Mrs Mulroney fed the young woman some of the standard drugs of her trade, but the patient had at some stage, instead of miscarrying her unwanted baby, gone into convulsions and perished.

Panicking, the Mulroneys had cleaned her body, packed her into a large bootbox, and driven her by night upriver to Sherwood, where they had added some stones to the box and released it into the river. The box had perversely floated through, and was found the next day wedged amongst logs on the river bank. It was traced almost immediately to Mrs Mulroney.

But she and her husband were obviously sincere in their inability to give the woman a meaningful name. A number of other citizens were similarly incapable of putting a name to her. She was said by the police to be no more than nineteen years old.

To help in identification, the Commissioner of Police in Sydney, nearly three hundred miles south, authorised one of the Kempsey surgeons – in accordance with long police practice in such affairs – to separate the head from the rest of the body. The remains were then given burial on the edge of the cemetery in West Kempsey, but to assist the police, the head was preserved in a flask of alcohol.

When the Mulroneys were shipped south, the flask remained to torment the dreams of some, and to shock and chasten even the hardened citizens of the Macleay.

The age to some was otherwise hopeful. Hard times were said to be ending. Within a year the six former colonies of Australia would – to suit the new century – fall into line as a new federal Commonwealth. *Commonwealth*. A flowering, bountiful word.

But on hearing of this police severing of the unhappy girl, some may have been seized by the superstition that a new spate of barbarities would be let loose.

Despite and because of himself, Tim Shea was one of these.

Anniversary Day today. The birthday of Australia, as the newspapers liked to say. Today everyone could suit himself and not
fret much about the severed girl.

What Tim Shea loved was to read newspapers in peace. He
used his slight fever as an excuse for not going down with Kitty
and the children to the New Entrance on the Agricultural and
Horticultural Association's chartered steamer for the day. *SS
Terara*. It stuck entirely to the river, poor old *Terara*, unlike the
sea-going *Burrawong*. It would creep down the broad, heat-struck
reaches of the Macleay towards the sandbar marking off the deep
green river from the Pacific's blue glitter. The old tub would take
that peculiar kind of riverine forever to get there too.

It would drift, for example, up to the pier at the Smithtown
Creamery to collect further picnickers, and then edge by Summer Island where dengue fever had been a force throughout
the New Year. Mosquitoes from ashore there would certainly
be able to outpace *Terara*. So keep the veiling down over your
face, Kitty.

Then after another two hours of mudflats and mangroves,
Jerseyville.

Kitty, his beloved stranger and spouse, could look at the pub at
Jerseyville without nostalgia, though he never could. He'd come
close once to getting the licence to sell spirituous liquors there.
The Jerseyville pub brought out the darker feelings so strong in
his character. Whereas Kitty was not touched by nostalgia and
regret. She could be imagined pointing to the pub and saying to
the children, 'That's where Papa and I nearly lived. Then you
would be a Jerseyville kid, Johnny. And you, little sister.'

Last night, he'd taken some influenza mixture provided by Mr Nance, the pharmacist of West. He was still too drowsy when Kitty bustled up to wake the children. And that was the thing, could he have faced it? Could he have faced the Empire Loyalist effusions of the Chairman of the A and H, Mr M. M. Chance? The references to our beloved and gracious Majesty the Queen. God forbid anyone should cut into a picnic pie or open an ale bottle in New South Wales unless some old bugger like Chance consecrated the whole bloody indulgence to Her Majesty.

Yet Kitty would have no trouble with any of that. Watching with a smile while Miss Chance and Dr Erson were persuaded to climb up on the coamings and recite or sing! Kitty could let their references to the perils Britain found herself in in Africa – of Australia's duty in the face of those perils, of New South Wales's responsibilities, and all the rest of it – slide off her. To her all that stuff was just like band music at a picnic. It didn't make a dent in the sunlight. What were matters of private principle to him were matters of what came next to her. A happy, happy soul, that Kitty. Drank stout and farted as unabashedly as a farmhorse, in particular when with child. Melancholy didn't claim her.

He'd begun fretting in his sleep about the idea Constable Hanney would ride up soon with horrible remains in a bottle of ether or alcohol. And he knew his turn to countenance her was coming. But it could not happen today, when Hanney and his wife were on *Terara* with perhaps half the population. Excluding the ill like him, the dusky brethren of the native reservations at Burnt Bridge and Greenhill, and those shingle-cutters who could not afford the one and six for adult, the ninepence for child.

He intended to take a folding camp stool into his back paddock. This was in fact part of the high river bank. One section of his property a yard with a shed for his delivery dray, the other a fenced pasture for his turbulent horse Pee Dee. He intended to sit in the yard under the peppertree shade, hear the river close by, read the *Argus* and the *Chronicle*, and take an idle interest in what Bryant's and Savage's were selling jam and soap for. And try to work up an opinion on whether the *Chronicle* was more democratic than the *Argus* or vice versa.

Anyhow, some consideration of these questions in a camp

chair in the shade. And he'd take a flask of rum. His aloneness in a town emptied of all the grander people. Very welcome. He'd take a blanket with him too, to lie on, in case the stupor of the day got the better of him.

He sat down on the camp stool behind his residence and store. *T. Shea – General Store.* Situated in a corner. Where Belgrave Street ran up to the river and then turned at a right-angle to become the chief waterfront street, named after an earlier landholder called Smith. By looking down the lane beside his store and residence, he could take in the bend in the road, parts of bush-fashionable Smith, a section of nearly-as-fashionable Belgrave.

Some black people wandered past his line of sight. Danggadi was the name of the main tribe here. All barefooted, these visitors to town, the men in bits of suits, one coat bright yellow. Where were they going on such a day, with all the shops closed? Talkative ghosts in a town so solidly defined that most of its population could bugger off on a steamer and return to find everything still in place. No dahlias ripped out by the roots, no windows broken.

The river itself now. Another remaining inhabitant. It reached around a bend amongst willows people had planted here in the last half a century. Low yet still three times wider than old world rivers, and deep and richly green.

Take a glimpse too at the mountains in the west richly blue, the underside of a mallard's wing. So that was it. He'd appreciated his bright surroundings, the unembarrassed light and the blue hills and the deep, navigable Macleay river olive with mud, and the quiescent punt at Central wharf, and then the huge pylons sunk in the water for a coming bridge between Central and East.

And now he could take a mouthful of the rum – ahh, the delicious too-muchness at the back of the throat, the shudder that out-shuddered fever – and then picked up the *Argus*. For though he respected the *Chronicle*, the *Argus* was very generous with its serial by A. A. Druitt, the Dickens of the end-of-century.

The Honourable Delia Hobham was the spirited girl who had made three previous appearances in the serial in the *Argus* throughout January. She came from somewhere in the West

Country of England, since A. A. Druitt made a meal out of what the peasants and servants said to her. 'Auw, Miss Delia, there bain't been no bakin' powder fur cook to gi' the pantry a freshenin' wi'.' A. A. Druitt's Miss Hobham lived in Hobham Hall with her mother and father, and every day she rode out amongst the villagers and tenant farmers, who called down blessings on her father's head. Silly buggers!

The father never seemed to turf any tenants off their land. That's how you knew this was fiction. For the Allbrights at home, landowners of Newmarket in Duhallow, North Cork, took every chance to evict people for their own good and recommend them to emigrate to Massachusetts or Australia. But no one ever mentioned emigration from the Hobham estate. Too busy being grateful to bloody Squire Hobham. So the world was fine if you had a good squire and foul if you had a bad one. What about having none at all? This tale, however, was suitable old world pap to serve up in a place like Kempsey, New South Wales.

The male Danggadi blacks had been followed by a string of women now, and children. Gluey ears and blighted eyes on the young ones. Searching for a bloody carnival in a carnival-less town. From looking at them a man got the momentary, mad, missionary urge to live amongst their humpies and pass away with them. Everyone said they were passing. Poor buggers!

He watched them loping for a time down towards the butter factory near Central wharf.

Out in Belgrave Street – broad because surveyed more than seventy years past by a British army officer from Port Macquarie – the younger Habash brother rode past at a mad pace on a grey. He was of a family of licensed hawkers and herbalists. He'd taken advantage of the empty town to get involved in such riding in the two chief commercial thoroughfares. The bloody little brown-complexioned hawker, in a broad felt hat and black waistcoat and trousers, leaning forward in the saddle. Where were the Habashes from? Somewhere east of bloody Suez for a start. India maybe.

'Bloody slow down!' Tim cried, but not too loudly. Habash's golden dust hung in the air, held up there by the day's humidity.

'Jesus,' Tim asked the Honourable Delia, who sat there on

the page of the *Argus*, 'where's the bloody Nuisance Inspector?'

On the *Terara* probably. Under the awnings. Within sight of Kitty who wore her gossamer veil let down over her pink little oval of a face. Annie his daughter sedate on the forehatch. Such a staid child all the time. Johnny of course wild as buggery at six and a half years, climbing things, threatening to hurl himself over the gunwales.

Holy Christ, that bugger Habash was galloping back *down* Belgrave Street now! You could see him fleet through the neck of the laneway between *T. Shea – General Store* and *E. Coleman – Bootmaker*. Thundering back into the dust he'd already made.

'Do you want me to knock you out of the bloody saddle?' Tim asked of the top branches of the peppertree.

Britain's griefs in Africa filled the papers. From them the New South Wales Mounted Rifles, recently embarked for Natal, had not yet had time to deliver the mother nation. However ... on the masthead page of the *Argus*, he noticed, flipping backwards and forwards between the sweet, ridiculous drama of the Honourable Delia Hobham and the pages full of harder intelligence, Mr Baylor, Treasurer of the Patriotic Fund, raised the idea of a Macleay Valley lancer regiment being recruited to send off. To sort out Britain's African affairs. The Australians would pull the fat out of the fire.

Tim reached out of his chair and picked up the *Macleay Chronicle*. Tim's favourite the good old Offhand, editor and chief columnist. No one ever called him by his real name. Through his column he'd become Offhand to everyone. He'd have sent off one of the junior journalists to write of the *Terara* and would be drinking somewhere indoors today, somewhere dark and cool. Maybe with the skinny little widow, Mrs Drake, he visited in West.

There was the Offhand on page nine. 'The factors of the British Army in India, on their visit to the Macleay Valley last August, could find from a total of one hundred Macleay horses offered for their perusal only five that were suitable for active service. It would seem that only the most rigorous and widespread breeding programme would produce enough mounts here to save Macleay Valley volunteers from the disgrace of being infantry.'

One in the eye for Mr Baylor with his plans for a public meeting to raise a regiment. Bloody good for you, son!

Bloody hell, that Afghan or Punjabi hawker was flogging the grey back down Belgrave Street again. He'd been fined just six months back for thrashing some other poor piece of horsemeat down Kemp Street. Then fined again by the Macleay police magistrate for using raucous language with Mrs Clair, standing on her front steps and accusing her of not paying for cloth he'd ordered especially.

In heavy air, Tim folded his papers and laid them on his camp stool. Somewhere on earth a wind was blowing, and somewhere sleet cutting the faces of men and women. But here it was hard to believe that. The Macleay air at mid-summer was gravid, a first class paperweight. Tim got up and walked past the gate behind which his own eccentric and leaden-footed horse, Pee Dee, stood grazing and ignoring him, and out into Belgrave Street. Down by Worthington's butchery, the hawker was recklessly yanking the grey around for another assault on Kempsey's stolid atmosphere. He was lightly whacking the poor beast's sides, but with such a smile that you thought he must believe the horse was enjoying all this as much as he was.

Tim waited a while in the shade of his storefront. Only when Habash was well-launched did he step forward. Thinking in his dark way, *Let the bugger run me down and see what the police magistrate makes of that!*

When Tim presented himself in the middle of the road, he saw Habash's face filled with sudden and innocent alarm. Yes, Tim thought. Yes, I do find myself taking strange risks. He saw Habash reining the horse in crazily to avoid running him down. But the hawker must have put unequal weight on the bridle. The grey slipped and threw the young rider backwards into the street. Tim felt the thud of the falling hawker in his own teeth. Grateful the madness was over, the grey strolled into the shade of Savage's Emporium, and began to drink from the trough there.

Habash got up laughing and with his neat hands brushing brown dust from his black trousers.

'Bad show eh? I thought everyone but the darkies was down the river.'

He spoke exact English, every word presented as its own unit. It made Tim think of a conjuror, smilingly offering one card after another, but face up. They let too many kinds of different people into Australia for its own good.

Habash swung his right arm to test his shoulder. 'Oh God,' he said. 'I was putting the grey mare through its paces, you know. I have a notorious weakness for speed and horse-flesh, Mr Shea.'

'I know,' said Tim, not yielding. 'You're on a good behaviour bond. Here you are bloody breaking it.'

Habash made a noise with his teeth and lowered his head and swung it in an arc. This was some bloody fake act of contrition.

'If I'd known you were there, sir . . . for I do know the sort of man you are. I have often camped on your sister-in-law's property upriver.'

Kitty's younger sister, this was. Molly. She'd emigrated here just five years ago, come up the coast to her sister on *SS Burrawong*, that floating shame of the North Coast Steamship Navigation Company. Lots of very nice-looking, plump, sisterly hugging on the Central wharf. A half-pint like Kitty, actually skinnier than Kitty though, and with a little more restraint. Molly began her Australian career sleeping in the canvassed-off part of the back verandah, near the cookhouse.

A man named Old Burke owned Pee Dee Station, where Tim's own useless nag came from. Far up in the most beautiful reaches of the river. Old Burke rode in one day with his fourteen-year-old motherless daughter Ellen, and gave Molly Kenna a grocery order to fill out while he went and saw M. M. Chance, the stock and estate agent, and then to complain and drink with other farmers in the Commercial. His daughter was still shopping at Savage's or drinking cordial at the Greeks' cafe in Smith Street, pretending this was the big life, and Old Burke had come back into the store with a glow on and thought Molly was a pretty bright girl. What you needed to cheer up a grim homestead and the lonely seasons up at Pee Dee. Rich pastures there, but a bugger of a way up the Macleay!

So now it turned out Habash carried his fabrics and his medical mixtures way up there to Molly.

Tim liked Mrs Molly Burke and usually said so. She was a

natural democrat and put on no airs. And Jesus, what the people thought of her back in the Doneraile area when they found out – without understanding what sort of place New South Wales was – that she'd married thirty-one hundred and fifty acres!

Tim said nothing now though. He wasn't going to share his enthusiasms for his sister-in-law with the hawker.

'What she says,' Habash continued, 'is that you are generous to a fault. So how fortunate I am that it is you who blocked my path.'

'Don't expect the bloody advantage of me, Mr Habab.'

'Not Habab if I dare say so, sir. Habash. My father is Saffy Habash of Forth Street, and I am Saffy Bandy Habash, Bandy to acquaintances. You may know my father.'

'An old feller. On a stick.'

'Yes. On a stick.' Bandy let the wistfulness of that penetrate. 'He is indeed our patriarch. Founded our business in the Macleay twenty years ago. Soon after my mother perished, and my father swallowed his grief and kept at work. Now my brother Mouma and myself have taken the load. Mouma does the settlements north to Macksville and south to Kundabung. I take the valley itself from Comara to the New Entrance. We are hawkers and sellers of medicines to every remote acre of the region. We are the servants of the valley and we rarely see each other. From Arakoon and the wives of the prison officers at Trial Bay to far-off Taylor's Arm. And, of course, to your esteemed sister-in-law at Pee Dee Station.'

'I've seen your wagons,' Tim conceded. 'Moving about the place.'

'As we all do, I get tired of plodding in a wagon, and I want to gallop like my ancestors in the Punjab, horsemen – if I dare say so – to rival the horsemen of the New South Wales contingent.'

Habash's grey was still drinking heartily from the trough outside Savage's two-storey emporium. Habash, admiring it, didn't move however to take its reins and stop it from gorging on the water. 'I paid eleven pounds for it. Its dam is Finisterre, who won the cup at Port Macquarie.'

Tim said, 'You wrench the poor beast around a bit for such an expensive one. Why don't you race it? That would get you out of having to use Belgrave Street as your bloody track.'

'Sir, I was foolish enough to try racing it. But the Kempsey Race Committee pooh-bahs don't wish to see races run by a hawker's grey.'

Tim experienced a second's sympathy for this little Muslim. 'The buggers are utter bloody pooh-bahs, you're right about that.'

'My father says not to waste money on such a thing. And I am an obedient child. That is in our tradition.'

'It's in every bugger's tradition,' said Tim, sharply remembering old Jeremiah Shea, his father, left behind childless in another hemisphere. 'You don't have to come from east of Suez to have a tradition like that.'

'But you do not have the honour to have your father with you here in New South Wales,' said Habash.

'That's exactly right. *My* father lives in a rainy place called Newmarket. It would take me only two months there and two months back and an expenditure of two hundred pounds to visit him and see if he's aged. As the poor old feller must have. All his children are in New South Wales or in America. Nothing for them in Newmarket. A small tenant holding. Laughable land. No bloody dignity.'

Habash shook his head and tested his shoulder again. 'Life is hard for so many in such a lot of places.'

Jeremiah Shea, a literate Irish farmer who rented fifteen acres from a man named Forester. He did part-time clerking in the town of Newcastle for the Board of Works. Knew his Latin but had nothing to give his children. That was for Jeremiah Shea, *pater*, the saddest thing. *In hic valle lacrimarum*. In this vale of tears.

Speaking of Newmarket this way, idly in the Australian dust, revived Tim's joy in having come here. The heat, the sky, the place: all tokens that he wouldn't need to leave Johnny and Annie with dismal prospects.

Behind Habash, like a phantom of the sort of orphaned hope Tim had been reflecting on, a small child in a torn white dress staggered around the corner by Worthington's butchery. Her head twisted back for air, and a keening plea coming from her lips. Tim ran to her and Habash collected his grey by the reins and followed. Her sharp little face was red, and she couldn't understand or tolerate the silent town. Tim rushed up to her and asked her, 'What? What, dear?'

'Papa,' she told him, pointing north towards the farms in that direction. Her dress was all marred with red clay. 'Papa and Hector. The sulky tipped.'

Her face clenched up. Habash asked, 'Where, miss?'

The child said Glenrock near O'Riordan's, and that was a mile and a half. Tim saw the light in Habash's eye. The supreme license to gallop.

'Come on, little miss,' Habash cried and fetched the grey and swung the small girl, who may have been ten but was slight for her age, onto the neck of the horse, arranging her sidesaddle, fixing her small hands around the pommel. His own delicate brown hands on the reins would encase her and keep her from falling.

'Go,' said Tim. 'I'll be ten seconds behind.'

He ran down the street and turned into the laneway beyond his store and so to the gate of the paddock where Pee Dee, a bay with white markings, was still grazing and trying to pretend Tim would make no demands. An old Macleay racehorse himself, Pee Dee, a gelding of promise but of erratic temperament. Tim bought him two years ago and had a obstinate affection for the brute. He served Tim and Kitty both as a dray horse and occasionally as a fairly stylish hack. Only four years old, but his previous owner Mr Milner had given up on him early. Too chancy in behaviour to race. He took to the shafts of the cart with disdain and only after lots of assurance. But he didn't make quite the same outstanding objection to being ridden. Especially if you did not go to the trouble of bridle and reins and all that leather. Tim took one of the stacked sugar bags from the back verandah, grabbed a rope halter and mouthpiece from the shed, eased himself through the fence and approached Pee Dee with it all.

'Here we go, boy.'

He slung the sugar bag well forward on Pee Dee's shoulders and worked the rope halter over his head. He led the unwilling and yet strangely tolerated horse to the gate and opened it. Then he took a handful of the beast's mane with his left hand and clung as best he could to its withers with his right, and so hauled himself onto Pee Dee's back, stomach first. Leaning low over the horse's neck and with his arms extended a long way down the beast's shoulders, he trotted Pee Dee out of the paddock and around the corner of the residence. Hitting Belgrave Street, Pee Dee fell into an apparently eager gait.

'OK,' said Tim leaning forward. 'We'll show that bloody Asiatic something, eh.'

In the street Habash was still waiting, wheeling his horse, impatient as a bloody chasseur of some kind.

But it became apparent as they set out that Habash's mare was quite clearly tired now from all the racing Bandy had given it, and Pee Dee went frolicking after her, and they rounded the corner by Worthington's butchery in tight convoy. They galloped leftwards into Forth Street, past the gardens of cottages whose owners were absent, steamer-picnicking townspeople. Pee Dee ahead, as he'd so rarely been on the racecourse, and relishing it. A few dogs chased them. Looking back, Tim saw the little wizened child with the bloody leg and the torn dress leaning back confidingly into Habash. She may even have fallen asleep. Tim felt Pee Dee's backbone cut into his groin like a blade.

The Macleay River, renowned in its own shire, contained most of the town in a half circle. First, hilly West built up high above its steep-cut bank. Some of the better houses there, and – out beyond the last houses on the hard upriver road to Armidale – the Greenhill blacks' reservation. Then low Central where the Sheas lived, convenient to wharfs but likely to flood. East then of course lay across the water from Central, reached by punt. Its own place, and not party to the dash Habash and Tim were now engaged on. They were making for the farmlands between West and Central, where the river had flowed earlier in its history and had left some fairly good soil for corn and cane-growing and for dairy cattle. Amongst the country fences and the milking sheds, Pee Dee drew enthusiastically clear of the grey. Mad and unpredictable bugger, he was! Showing the way up past Cochrane Street and over a low hill.

Ahead then you could see something, a terrible mess, a sulky pitched sideways over the edge of the road. Tim had to fight an urge to yank on the reins for fear of nearing the catastrophe on his own and seeing unguessable things. But you could not manage such subtle changes anyhow on Pee Dee and, given the primitive rope halter and reins, it was now a case of bloody Pee Dee surging on, performing well only when it was least suitable.

Thus he was first at the mess. 'Oh merciful Jesus!' he said, jumping down, feeling light as a wafer, delivered of his heavy horse.

Seated wailing on the edge of the road, picking up handfuls of gravel and throwing them towards the wreckage down the slope, was a little boy of perhaps four. His targets seemed to be three pigs grazing down there.

Below lay an awfully wounded horse and the ruins of the sulky. One of the shafts had snapped and was stuck deep in the horse's flank. The beast was writhing very weakly to work the stake loose. Impaled and lying on its side, it looked over its shoulder occasionally to get a glimpse of its injury. The hopeless wound did not invite close consideration and Tim did not give it any. A man in a suit lay on his back. He looked intact, even his clothes looked fresh, but O'Riordan's three robust pigs were feeding on his head.

Tim slid down the claggy embankment. He did not necessarily want to do it but had to, couldn't leave it to Habash. White man's bloody burden in a year already tainted with woman-slaughter.

The poor bastard lay on rain-softened earth and even had a white flower in his buttonhole. Worn but clean white shirt, an eloquent, well-sewn button on the neck. No tie. A cow-cocky coming to town on the holiday. His head had been broken somehow, perhaps by the wheel, and the pigs had come in and eaten at his forehead and his nose. Cruel, cruel bloody world. Beheaded girls, defaced men. Jesus! The gravel thrown by the little boy had no impact at all upon the swine.

Bandy Habash was now descending from his grey, and lifted the small girl down.

Tim began kicking the pigs away. He wished he was armed to state his revulsion with more force. He lifted handfuls of shale to throw at them. But, squealing, they only retreated a certain distance, to see if his passionate objections would last. He felt the man's wrist with his dusty hands. There seemed to be no life there but how could he tell? Tim's hands were thickened by the rope reins and his brain clotted with the awfulness.

He heard a huge exhaling, a hiss, a brief gallop of the sulky horse's breath. Turning, he saw that Habash, bloodied knife in hand, had cut into the side of the horse's neck and found some decisive vein. Habash stood back delicately to avoid dirtying his boots. From the road, Pee Dee objected loudly to the released smell of horse blood.

'Yes,' Tim said to the hawker. 'The right thing.'

The poor horse continued to thrash his legs very feebly but for a few seconds only.

Tim told the hawker, 'Go and find one of the doctors.'

Bandy Habash cleaned his knife by plunging it into soft earth. He sighed, 'No, old chap. My horse is tired out. You must go with this poor fellow. I shall take the children to your residence, sir, following behind.'

'How can I take him?' asked Tim. 'His head such a bloody mess!'

But he knew how already and ran up the muddy slope again to the road.

'Papa, papa?' both the children were asking.

'I'm going to get him, darlings,' said Tim. He took the sugar bag saddle from Pee Dee's back and descended the slope again with it. He asked Habash to hold the man upright by the shoulders, and then he placed the sugar bag over his head. Together, Habash by the armpits and he by the ankles, they got the man up to the horse while the children wailed.

'Now you know, Mr Shea,' hissed Habash under the weight, 'why we, like the Jews, think pigs unclean. Oh yes, unclean. Over the withers or over the rump?'

'Oh, Jesus,' said Tim. 'Give me your saddle at least, and I'll carry him over the shoulders.'

They put the man down for a while and found Pee Dee strangely tractable while the saddle was swapped and the girth adjusted. Kitty always said the horse was human. Then the man was lifted and balanced over Pee Dee's very broad withers. The bag, despite the amounts of muck which affixed it in place, threatened to fall off his head. Habash produced string and tied it loosely around the man's neck.

'I don't think he'll smother, poor fellow,' said Tim, fighting the shudders.

'Mr Shea,' said Habash, straightening. 'The man is quite dead. God has received his soul.'

'Oh Jesus,' said Tim. 'But we'll see.'

He could afford no more than a second to steel himself for sharing the horse with the man almost certainly gone. Then he got up decisively into the saddle. It felt unbalanced to have a fine saddle and rope reins, and between those two the lean man. But no delay to be permitted. He kicked Pee Dee's flanks and made decent progress towards town. The man pressed back against his thighs like a living thing.

What doctor? Dr Erson was singing operetta on the *Terara*. Dr Casement, he knew from a notice in the *Argus*, had taken Keogh's coach to the beaches of Port Macquarie. Dr Gabriel was perhaps at home across the river in East, and it would be a nightmare waiting for the punt to come across. It was therefore a matter of the district hospital.

Pee Dee kept up a surprisingly brave canter towards town. You could go on the better roads through West, or more directly over the bush tracks towards the hospital. Through West was the supposedly civilised way, but there would be a few people around the shooting gallery beside the Post Office. Yahoos who couldn't afford the boat fare or who thought such normal country diversions beneath them.

'What do you have there, Tim?' they would call, and the damaged man deserved better, both softer and more urgent enquiries. The Armenian who ran the eyesore of a shooting gallery would grin out from under the shade of the awning and hand one of the would-be Macleay sharpshooters a rifle loaded with pellets.

These sorts of possibilities steered Tim right, along the bush tracks across country to the hill above West Kempsey and the hospital.

'Quick along,' Tim kept urging Pee Dee. He was a much better mount than he was a carthorse, the mad bugger.

The path took him through humid, fly-ridden bush and past the Warwick racecourse the Race Club wouldn't admit Habash to. Heat was pretty dense under these scraggy gumtrees. At last the Macleay could be seen ahead, broad and set low in a wide bed. The heedless river was a pathetic blue here.

'Look, look,' said Tim to the jolting man. 'Did you come to town for a holiday? Look, look, you poor feller.'

Pee Dee, just to be unpredictable, still trotted briskly as they entered the hospital driveway and stopped by the large Morton Bay fig tree. Tim tethered him to the hospital railing. On the verandah, he noticed, a frail child in a nightdress sat in a big wicker chair. Beginning to weep, Tim eased the man down by the shoulders, the feet being the last heavily to flop off Pee Dee's neck, but both boots staying on – for which Tim was somehow grateful. Tim laid the man in the shade of the verandah and ran inside. A pleasant-faced, full-breasted nurse saw him and cried, 'Yes?'

It was the long dusk. In the cookhouse at the back of the store, he lit the range and the heat it gave off reacted more pleasantly than you'd expect on the warmth trapped in the room. Sweating, he made tea and slabs of white bread and honey for the little girl who waited inside in the dining room and whose brother had fallen asleep on the sofa in the drawing room.

This will be an awful year, he knew in spite of knowing better. The omens were so terrible. He shook his head, not wanting to think that way. Wanting to think like a modern fellow, not a bloody peasant. But this will be an awful year.

When he brought the food and drink to the girl, she seemed lost at the head of the table in his large-backed chair. He had earlier bathed her leg with iodine, and this little ritual against sepsis had done them both some good, making her cry out in a plain iodine anguish, proving to him that there were still simple human services to be supplied.

It occurred to Tim now and then that her father was in the room of the dead in the hospital above the river in West, keeping company with a thirteen-year-old boy from Collombattye who had perished from lockjaw. Tim had helped the nurses place him there after they had washed the corpse.

This awareness of her father's location seemed to overtake the small girl too, because sometimes she would put her bread down, appetite fled, and weep purely and privately like a brave grown woman.

She was an orphan now. Her name was Lucy Rochester. Her sleeping brother was Hector. Her father was or had been Albert. Tim knew him – he'd sometimes come into the store on Friday afternoons. A good type. The industrious cow-cocky who rises at four for milking and ends his days in terrible muteness. His children with him milking through every dawn of his life. You could tell it from Lucy Rochester's hands as they held the bread. They were creased from the milking, the butter churn, and from cranking the chaff-cutter. And then, no doubt, her feet hardened by walking into school from Glenrock. Falling asleep in the mathematics class. Smartalec children from town laughing at that. He knew what she didn't. The history of her hard little hands. In the Old Testament-style flood of '92, the maize crops had been wiped out when the water swept over the lowlands and lapped against that embankment where Mr Albert Rochester had this morning suffered his accident. Great hardships at that time. Farms going broke. The prices of produce in Sussex Street, Sydney's bourse of all farm products, being squeezed and squeezed. And authoritative men from the New South Wales Agriculture Department and all manner of dairy enthusiasts, some of them from Sydney University, had come and delivered the dairy message. The Jersey cow. Unlike the maize crops, it could walk to high ground in time of flood, and the dumped mud from upriver would soon be fertilised and would feed herds in coming seasons.

And yet now men were enslaved to the dairy farms, and their women were taken by chills in the predawn, and their children grew hard-handed and sleepy and thus ignorant. He would not be a dairy farmer unless, like the Burkes of Pee Dee, he could hire hands to do the dawn milking.

In the Macleay, men like Rochester were owned by their Jersey cattle.

'Why were you coming to town?' Tim asked the child.

'Seeing Mrs Sutter,' said the little girl. She had a strange grown way of addressing him. People spoke of little women. She was one. 'Mama's best friend, Mrs Sutter. We would stay till night. Papa got the Coleman boys to do the afternoon milking.'

A cow-cocky's holiday, and he's killed while it's all still in anticipation! Was Mrs Sutter to be the second Mrs Rochester?

The glass in the store door was being rattled.

He went through the living room, past the sleeping boy. Through a tasselled doorway. The shop was full of its pent-up special smell today, a smell of tin and tea, sugar and sisal, candles and methylated spirits. A slight honeying of the air from the cans of treacle resting on the shelves. A hint of shortbread, a manly reek of kerosene. Goods supplied to him on two months' credit, unlike the three months' credit he gave his best clients, the Malcolms say and, of course, Old Burke from up the river. And how could you dun a nice man like the Offhand, who needed his scribe's salary to pay for his habits? Miss Myra Howard's theatrical company had run up a bill during their stay at the Commercial, tinned sausages and peas, tea and lemonade. That bill six months unpaid. Miss Howard's agent in Sydney said that he would draw it to her attention as soon as she returned to Sydney from a tour of Far North Queensland at the end of the summer. As a result of such experiences, he no longer looked at the shelves with the undoubting sense of ownership which had, until recently, been one of his vanities.

Rangy Constable Hanney was rattling the glass. He'd tied up his horse and trap to one of the posts which held up the awning of *T. Shea – General Store*.

When Tim opened the door, the constable stepped straight in; a matter of habit. His hat was off, his brushy hair glittering with sweat.

'I thought you were on *Terara*,' said Tim. Don't let him show me the murdered girl's face, on top of everything else!

'No. Sergeants go off on steamers. Mug coppers stay at home. Got to get that statement from you, Shea. You have the children? Good. I need to talk to the girl. Poor bastard. Might have got his leg over with Mrs Sutter. Not now though.'

Tim led him into the dining room. The girl put her bread down and observed the policeman.

'Oh dearie,' said Constable Hanney. 'Dr Gabriel says your papa died straight off. He did not feel any of the pigs. In heaven he's got everything.' Hanney made a sort of inventory with his fingers of his own forehead, his eyes, his nose, his cheeks. 'Your papa is a glorious young fellow in heaven.'

She opened her mouth but did not weep. She rubbed her jaw with her seamed little hand.

She said, 'The horse shied at a heap of gravel. Hector fell out when the wheel went off the edge. My dress got caught on the footboard and I cut my leg. Papa fell too. I saw the wheel go over his head.'

Hanney took notes and questioned Tim, who felt grateful for the constable's official compassion.

The child had gone back to her bread. Hanney and Tim could have been speaking of a separate tragedy from hers.

Hanney said at the end, 'You should see if Mrs Sutter will take them. She's got an income, you know. Her husband left her land upriver, and she sold it and lives off the interest. She and Rochester spoke of buying a pub somewhere, Kew I think, by the bridge there. We have not here a lasting bloody city, eh. Did that bloody ruffian Habash behave himself?'

'He behaved well,' said Tim at once. 'He fixed up Rochester's horse very humanely. Then brought the children here while I took the father . . .'

Why such a defence of the hawker? he asked himself. The bugger had flogged the grey. Yet Tim didn't want him punished for that any more. The horror of the forenoon had been enough punishment.

'You couldn't have the kids go with him,' said Hanney. 'Not into a Mohammedan household. Do you have any brandy?'

Tim admitted he did.

'What if you get one for yourself and one for me?'

'Do you think I need it? I don't think I need it.'

This request for a stimulant was faintly surprising to Tim. Hanney did not look like a cadger of drinks. He lowered his voice. 'I brought the *young woman* with me. Saves me coming back tomorrow.'

'Oh God,' said Tim, getting up. He went and took the Old Toby brandy out of the encyclopedia bookcase in the living room. He poured two hefty glassfuls.

'Whoa!' cried Constable Hanney, smiling slightly. 'I don't have much of a head for liquor.'

The little girl had finished eating and had folded her arms. 'To your papa,' Hanney told her, hitching his glass up and beginning to sip. The child watched him with indifference or lack of forgiveness.

'Yes,' was all Tim could think to say. He drank in uneven gulps. He did not savour it like Hanney did. He noticed though, as the liquor went trembling through him, that his fever was gone.

'But you didn't know him,' said the girl evenly.

Hanney half-smiled but Tim thought Lucy Rochester should be answered. 'We know you and Hector,' he said. 'We feel for you.'

He put his glass down and went and got a bound volume of the *Sydney Mail* of ten years past out of the front room. He brought it back in to Lucy Rochester.

'You might find that interesting to look through,' he said. She began to do it. With her yellowed, seamy, little fingers.

In front of Tim, Hanney walked a bit unsteadily but like a man mellowed. Out through the store, opening the front door for himself. The day had settled sweetly and thickly in Belgrave and Smith Streets, and there was a hint of blueness, of the advancing satin of the wide-open night. The populous frogs of the Macleay had already started up.

Hanney inexactly gestured him around to the passenger side of the trap. A fruit basket lay under the seat there, holding something wrapped in blue and white cloth.

'All right then!' he said, closing his eyes for a second and shaking his head. 'This is the woman they found in the bootbox washed up at Sherwood.'

'I know, I know,' said Tim.

'We call her Missy. She was only young. Just go easy with it, Shea. You'll see, she was lovely in life.'

The empty town's air spoke of all the lovely dead, including Mr Albert Rochester who showed his young man's face forth now only in heaven. Tim gripped one of the handlebars on the trap and Hanney dragged the basket forth and lifted the cloth. Inside was a huge preserving jar. Hanney raised it with care, his great hand with fist and fingers spread wide to keep it steady.

The head of a girl of perhaps twenty years sat crookedly in there. How piteous that crookedness, as if the surgeon hadn't taken enough pains. Barely a complaint on that face, the eyes nearly shut, the lips of what had been a small mouth slightly parted. The docked but trailing hair was light brown. No shallow, no vulgar plea there, in the way she presented herself. This was a serious child, making serious claims. Tim felt them at first sight.

'Nothing but heads today,' he said in confusion. 'Bert's and hers.'

'Steady, old chap,' said Hanney, who didn't seem steady himself. 'Someone must know her. She must have a mother or father somewhere. Or of more interest to me, she's got to have had a lover. Probably here – I bet she got Mrs Mulroney's name from *him*. He could settle the matter. Then she wouldn't need to be called *Unnamed Female* in court.'

No question this was at once the chief question. Bigger than raising regiments. The girl or young woman not to be *Unnamed Female*. Her unnamed state was the shadow over things. The shadow over him.

Tim swallowed and looked away at the violet evening settling on the river. So bloody hard to make any easy connection between the dusk splendour and that face separated from its heart.

'See I thought she might've made a purchase, Shea. The day it happened. She may have had a craving say. Wanted chocolate. Have a good look.'

Tim drew his eyes down again from the lavender southeast, the bluest quarter of the evening, and took a further stare. The demand on him was still there behind the lowered lids. And why not? Such useless and terrible beauty, beauty lopped from its roots. And in new and desperate alliance with him. Begging for the mercy of an identification. Aching for his word. 'Yes, I *did* see her.' Or the supremely exorcising sentence, 'Yes, that's . . .' Waiting to be liberated from the constable's fluid.

Tim would have made a name up right then if it could have helped her.

Hanney said, 'Showed her to Captain Reid of the *Burrawong*, but he swore she hadn't travelled with him. I showed it to the people at Keogh's and Naylor's coaches, thinking she might have come into town on them.'

Hanney staring at him. Was this stare totally kind?

Tim said, 'Never seen her. I wish I could put a name to her. I'd be very damn happy to.'

Hanney took the flask into the crook of his right arm and whacked his police trousers sharply with his left hand. He still looked calm enough though.

'Bloody all beats me,' said Hanney. 'If we can't identify her here, I'll have to go on the road with her.'

'For God's sake,' Tim asked, 'why in the age of the photograph wasn't a picture taken?'

'There was one. And a sketch. But the Commissioner in Sydney says nothing has ever worked like this method. Pierces the imagination, see. Gingers up the memory. It's an old Scottish method.'

'Holy bloody hell,' said Tim.

Hanney had at last covered the jar again, returned it to the basket, said good afternoon without any discernible disappointment, climbed shakily aboard and rode away. Tim knew at once that in sleep his vacant brain would be taken up with the features of the mute, dissected woman.

Still no sign of the *Terara* downriver. A long, long, long way to the New Entrance which the river had found for itself in the awful flood of eight years past.

Entertaining the orphans in these waiting, intervening hours seemed such a huge ordeal. Back through the store, he turned his eyes from the jars on the higher shelves, the bland faces of peaches and pears. In the dining room he told the girl, 'A bit later, we'll go to Mrs Sutter's when I have Pee Dee in his traces.' She looked up briefly and returned her head to the page. Wanting to know what had her engrossed, Tim stepped around the table and looked over her bony shoulder.

It was an engraving marked, *View of the Kimberley Goldfields, Cape Colony, Southern Africa.*

'You look at that then,' he advised her, and decided he must not seem to be rushing the orphans to their father's woman friend, particularly not now, at this most threatening time, as the light faded.

From the meat safe on the back verandah he took two pounds of Knauer's sausages bought fresh a few days before, and in the hot cookhouse re-kindled the fire and began to cook them up with potatoes and sliced onion in a huge frying pan.

When they were fully cooked, he took them inside and dished out a plateful to the girl. She watched him.

'If papa and Hector and I were in a sulky in South Africa,' she asked him, not like a trick question, 'would it've all fallen over like that?'

Unanswerable questions from Missy and now from the waif!

'Sad thing is,' he told her, 'we are where we are.'

He put a hand on her wrist, to still her mind. Then he woke the little boy and took him to the outhouse, waiting in the stillness until he was done. Back at the table, Hector ate fitfully, not speaking at all however of his horrible morning. The girl proved a ferocious eater of her tea. Stick-thin but a real forager.

'Hold hard, Lucy,' he laughed, reloading her plate, refilling her tea cup. Sugar very good for grief. He shovelled four spoonfuls into her cup. She looked up at him without a smile, planting on him his part of the blame for Albert Rochester and his children being here and not in some level place in Africa.

Unlike his industrious diner of a sister, the boy had sat back after devouring half a snag and seemed to be taking pretty judicious thought about his future. Almost for his own comfort, Tim lit a kerosene lamp on the first evening of their fatherlessness.

Crickets had set up madly in the paddock. The evening full of frog-thunder and insect-chirping, and he began to feel orphaned himself.

'Are you tired?' he asked the boy hopefully. But the boy did not answer, and the girl still had her mind on Africa.

The hoot of the river boat *Terara* was at last heard. No august hoot, like that of the *Burrawong*. No memory of New South Wales's long coastline in its bleat. Slower than a cripple, it was bearing Kitty home.

'Do you want to see the *Terara* come in?' Tim asked the children, and they immediately slipped from their chairs as if they'd been threatened, and stood ready to go. He must have been pretty good at getting orders obeyed, poor Albert Rochester.

Tim got his coat and old brown hat off a peg on the wall, and led the children through the shop and out beneath the awning, across the neck of Belgrave Street whose dust had got a churning from the hawker and his grey, and down Smith Street past the Greek cafe and so to the landing. Missy and the day's tragedy receded a little. For a while all felt restored to him. A man in an average season. Across the kindly waters he could hear the picnickers, the returning townspeople, all talking at once.

'See!' he told the orphans. 'Mrs Shea and Johnny and Annie are on that ship.'

He saw his lanky six-and-a-half year old son Johnny hanging over the gunwales. Just his arms and shoulders and head. Unruly little bugger! And Kitty and sedate little Annie waiting on the edge of the ruck of would-be disembarkers. Kitty with veil up and basket in hand. From this distance, she looked somehow more pregnant than when she had left that morning. Not possible, of course. Just that you did not often see your wife distanced in this way. Separated by elements. You on earth. She on water.

The black flank of *Terara* touched the great hempen buffers on the wharf, gates opened amidships and the gangplank came down. People streamed down it pretty much in order of social eminence. Dr Erson with his lush theatrical moustache, his thin wife. Mr Chance, the natty livestock and property agent, his musical daughter . . .

Here were men Tim envied not for their better income but for being at home in the world. No sense of being exiled at all. Erson one of them. Reputed to be the best doctor in the Macleay, though some swore by Doctors Gabriel and Casement. Which of them had separated Missy from her body though?

Women and children milling on deck to descend. Couldn't wait for land after the slow steamer excursion. His wife among them. He felt calmer to watch her, she looked in such control. There should be at least one of those in every family. Someone anchored. Hanney's woman in the jar would be more apprised of all this next time around. She would play things safe and cosy and join the Macleay Valley Theatrical and Operatic Society.

Some of those descending the gangplank with their mild, dazed picnickers' smiles halted for a second wondering what Mr Tim Shea was doing there with children not his own.

Mr Sheridan the solicitor and his wife. Sheridan very much the young statesman and destined for politics, one or other of the two Parliaments which would soon be available, the parliament of Australia-wide or the old parliament of New South Wales.

Then the accountant Mr Malcolm, a beefy man, very jovial, representing earth, and his lovely dark-haired ivory-skinned wife. Slender and – for a woman – tall, Mrs Malcolm. White dress, huge pink hat with a rucked-up veil. She was his finest customer, the only one who occasionally used couplets of Tennyson while buying groceries. But not in a flashy way. As naturally as breathing. Poetry the mist from a noble soul.

Once when dropping off an order in the store, a few young men on horseback had ridden wildly by, yahooing and being fools. A look of genuine defeat crossed Winnie Malcolm's face and one drop of sweat made its way from the direction of her ear down her cheek. Tim had felt a burning pity for her at that second. But she gathered herself and wiped the sweat with a handkerchief.

'We have to remember, Mr Shea, that the Saxons themselves were once unruly tribes. Australia will one day become something more august.'

Did she hope the same thing about Ernie, who was so fortunate to have such a jewel yet didn't seem overwhelmed by his luck? On top of everything, he didn't know that the very air had been mortgaged to Missy, to naming Missy, to giving her rest. She stopped by Tim and her husband waited there too, with his blowsy holiday grin fixed in place and some kind of cheroot carried negligently in the corner of his gob. A customer of *T. Shea – General Store, Belgrave Street, Kempsey*. He had drunk a lot, judging from his hoppy smell, and he was on his way home to eat and drink more, and then he'd probably want to jump on the divine Mrs Malcolm. Lucky, lucky bugger! And that would be the rape of spirit by flesh, yet Mrs Malcolm didn't seem fearful. Her upper lip formed its delicate bow while the lower kept its place, glossy and static.

Native-born Australians were like that. Never used both lips at once. He was beginning to see it this early in his children, and it was there in the little Rochester girl and helped make her sentences like those of a sleepwalker.

'What children are these, Tim?'

'They're the Rochester children, Mrs Malcolm.'

Here in sight of Kitty and his own children, he kept a curb on his pleasure in Mrs Malcolm's normal sentences. And as if to show all was fair and above board, he turned to bovine Mr Ernie Malcolm. What a bush aristocrat! Yet he stood just behind M. M. Chance as a leader of the community.

'They're Mr Albert Rochester's children,' said Tim. 'Poor feller had an accident this morning.'

'Oh dear,' said Mrs Malcolm. She had noble, long features. 'Where is he put . . .?'

'It was a mortal accident, Mrs Malcolm.'

Mrs Malcolm looked at the small, level-gazing Rochester girl who stared so judiciously back at her that now she had to fling her eyes to the sky and say, 'Poor darlings.'

'Here,' said Mr Malcolm. He didn't have any sense that this little kid expected him to help her lift the whole disaster to another continent, and then smooth over any tears in the fabrics of place and of time. He kept the cigarette-ish thing in the bunched corner of his mouth as he threw his head back too and began fumbling in the pockets of his vest. He took out two shillings, and offered one in his left hand and one in his right to each of the Rochester children. He did it too as if this were the spacious limit of his charity.

The children frowned at him. So Malcolm reached down now and opened Hector's hand and put the shilling in there and closed the fingers for him, and then he did the same with Lucy's small, grained hand. He was pretty pleased with himself. He was their gift-horse.

'His head was broken,' Tim whispered to Mrs Malcolm. 'An accident on the road.'

'Dear God!' she said in a low voice back. 'Let me know if there is anything I can do . . .'

Was this a token offer? Tim wondered. Tim didn't like the way, dragging his wife, Mr Malcolm moved off as soon as Kitty arrived on the wharf. Was she a person beneath his bloody attention?

'Hello there,' cried Kitty. Her long mouth split in the plainest and most personable of smiles. How could a fellow not like women with their kindnesses so varied?

'Good evening to you, Mrs Malcolm,' she called after the Malcolms, and winked at Tim.

Mrs Malcolm said over her shoulder almost nervously, 'Yes, Mrs Shea, we met in the store. Didn't we?'

And Kitty murmured, 'We did, and is that the reason you're disappearing like a rat down a drain now?'

How hard his daughter Annie stared at the Rochester child. Tim nudged her round cheek with a knuckle. 'Come on, Duchess. Don't be grim.'

Kitty said, 'She did ask me from the very deck what is papa doing with those children?'

A trace of chastisement in Kitty's voice. As if she thought he'd wilfully gone out and collected two children.

Tim, inhibited by the listening Rochester children, gave a brief summary of the disaster.

'Their horse dragged their sulky off the edge at O'Riordan's at Glenrock this morning. Their father Albert Rochester is finished. These infants are on their own now.'

'Then come, come,' said Kitty when he finished. 'Let's feed you all.'

'Done already,' he told her with the small pride of a male who manages to put a meal together.

Johnny performed a cartwheel on the splintery boards of Central landing to show Lucy Rochester it was possible.

Tipsy excursionists, having crossed the wharf, were struggling now up the ramp to Smith Street and getting up on their parked sulkies and carts. Mr Malcolm, by now having helped his wife into their trap, unhitched his horse and took some heaving to get himself up. He shook out the reins energetically.

'I hope the horse is soberer than he is,' Kitty told Tim. 'What's to do with these waifs would you say, Tim?'

'Careful now,' Tim called to Johnny, who was running into Smith Street and its backing carts and its resentful bucking horses. 'Careful there, John.'

For Johnny had a crazy look in his eye, put there by meeting another child and recognising some answering lunacy there. Soulmates, it seemed. And the steamer trip hadn't taken all the ginger and stampede out of the boy.

As they walked along, Smith Street cleared though the dust

of others hung still in the air. Old Tapley, who was believed to have once been a London pickpocket and to have been sent to Port Macquarie for it in *those* days, puttered out of Belgrave Street with his little ladder and his tapers and began lighting up the lamps in front of the draper's, on a slant across from *T. Shea – General Store*.

Kitty said, 'You did not have your day of solitude then?'

'No chance.'

He felt restored though for the moment. He had that wonderful feeling of being married, and of heading home to a place marked with his name in blue and yellow. He took Kitty's basket, and in reaching across her to do it, picked up the malty aroma of stout she gave off. *Recommended for Carrying and Nursing Mothers*.

When Tim took the basket, letting go of Hector's hand, Hector immediately walked around and claimed Kitty's right hand.

'There you are, darling,' she told him.

But it sounded a little brisk and offhand to Tim. She didn't want to make any promises.

She said, 'I've been choosing the moment to tell you. I had a letter from the last visit of *Burrawong*. My young sister Mamie has already arranged to come here and has been accepted by New South Wales. You'd think the bloody Macleay was the centre of the universe, wouldn't you?'

'Jesus!' said Tim.

'Thought you'd say that.' She'd left the 'h' out of words as everyone did in the part of North Cork they came from. He'd tried to put it into his diction, since that lost 'h' was something the bigots used to beat you on the head with, or at least to justify derision. Kitty however was never going to try. He'd both admired and regretted her for that.

'I've only known myself about Mamie since Thursday,' she said. 'The awful little tart didn't even tell me. Presumed! Presumed we're always open for emigrants. Since last Thursday is all I knew!'

Which she'd pronounced now and ever would, *Tursdy*.

'Don't get cranky, Tim,' she pleaded.

Old Red Kenna, a little rooster of a man, had begotten eleven children along the lines of Kitty. They were a raucous mob. And very earthy. Were they going to come to the Macleay one by one, the arrival of the next one all the more guaranteed by the success of the last? Australia as famous as New York at Red Kenna's hearth and in that corner of North Cork. The same story had already happened in another direction with Tim's own more sedate clan. His eldest sister had gone to Brooklyn and married a newspaper editor – married the *Brooklyn Advocate*, in fact. And so, one by one, two others of his older sisters had crossed the Atlantic on the strength of that founding bit of emigrant luck. One of these follow-the-leader sisters was now a housekeeper to a family of Jewish haberdashers, the other had married a stevedore. He, Tim, had been expected to join his sister in Brooklyn, his important sister, the newspaper editor's wife. From the age of sixteen he'd always said in public that he would, and yet knew in his water he was lying. In the Cork papers were weekly advertisements saying, *Attractive Terms of Emigration to New South Wales*.

Of course, no one really understood what distances were involved. You could return from Brooklyn. The emigrant's return was one of the staple bright hopes of all parties. But who could return from New South Wales?

The thing was the idea of being on his own, away from the maternal manners of sisters. That interested him more than he could properly utter even to himself. And now, what Brooklyn was to the Sheas, his own little store in Belgrave Street was to Red Kenna's squat, charming children.

Kitty said, 'You can't beat Mamie. Went all the way to the Agent-General in the Strand to get a special rate. Imagine!'

'And we'll put Mamie on the verandah like Molly?' asked Tim.

'Out there under a mosquito net while the summer lasts. She should be settled in somewhere by winter. She makes her way, that one. Not at all shy like me!'

'No room in the inn then for some small people,' murmured Tim.

Annie was working herself in between the two of them from behind, saying, 'Mama, mama.'

'You'd think those Rochester children had friends and relatives, wouldn't you?'

'Well, we surely bloody well do,' said Tim.

She dug him with her elbow. 'Don't get sullen there, Tim.'

He flinched. 'I saw Hanney's woman too.'

'Holy God, the little woman they murdered. Did you? Could you see her features and everything else?'

'You could.'

'Anyone we know, would you say?'

'No one. No one.'

'Mama, mama,' yelled Annie.

'She's such a jealous little creature,' said Kitty.

Jealous little creature. Missy the true jealous little creature. Resenting his idle hours, hanging on his shoulders, pending on all events. Wanting her name back.

'Let me alone,' he muttered.

'What did you say?' asked Kitty. But idly. She did not demand an answer.

2

Before you went to the trouble of putting a collar on Pee Dee and harnessing him up, it was best to check the *Argus* to see if any circuses or any large herds of cattle were due to come down Belgrave Street. He didn't even like the teams of bullocks which brought the big cedars down to the timber mill. He would back in the traces, pigroot, buck.

There were no circuses on the morning after the holiday, however. No reason to delay taking the Rochester children up to Mrs Sutter's house by the showground.

The Macleay so flood-prone that everyone thought of the Showground Hill primarily as 'above flood level'. Tim's place was not. In still hours when he woke, he asked himself about the wisdom of living as close to the spirited Macleay River as he did. Flood eight years past had drowned Belgrave Street to the awnings and filled the stores with mud. Tight as a bloody nougat. He knew because he'd helped old Carlton shovel mud out of what was now his place. In those days, he'd not been a shopkeeper but – after working three years for Kiley's haulage – had hopes of the Jerseyville pub. He'd shovelled up the mud and heard Carlton complain. Tim in the last of his four years of bachelorhood in New South Wales. He wanted the licence to the Jerseyville pub, but the pub didn't eventuate – Kitty could not reach New South Wales to marry him in time. Just the same, looking to get into business, and flood was a good season to begin, to trade on Carlton's weariness, to write to the wholesalers in Sydney, sending along your references.

That flood had been a flood out of a prophecy. A chastisement unlikely to recur. So forceful that the river found a new way into the sea near Trial Bay. The New Entrance. Such had been the vigour of the Macleay. It had negotiated a new arrangement, dictating terms of its own with the Pacific Ocean. Kitty, arriving later, didn't understand how bloody strenuous the huge event had been. 'Flood, flood,' she'd complained. 'All you hear on every side is *flood*.'

For she hadn't seen the way young Wooderson and he rowed out from their moorage, which happened to be the upper floor of the Commercial Hotel, to rescue the Kerridges from the roof of their house in Elbow Street. The current terrible to push against, and on the way back with Kerridge and his wife and two children, they'd seen a chest of drawers sail past. Wooderson, being such a good swimmer, had actually got into the flood and attached a rope to it, and the flow of water had swept it and the boat and them back to the Commercial.

In case the *Book of Floods Part Two* struck Kempsey, he had acquired a rowboat, in which he sometimes took the children out on the river. When not so used, it was kept tethered on a long lead, like a goat, in the yard. A prayer against further floods. A child, he knew, was a wafer before the force of the water. And Lucy, the wafer of a child beside him, had been through that, would have been an infant in Glenrock, would have been taken onto the iron roof by her mother and father to wait things out. The range of perils which surrounded young flesh. This was what astounded Tim more than he could ever express.

He hoped she still wasn't pushing Africa round in her head: the possible locale where Albert Rochester might have been safe.

'Do you like Mrs Sutter's place?' he asked.

As ever, she answered in the way she chose. 'Mrs Sutter was mama's and papa's best friend of all.'

For relief from the features of Hanney's Missy, he'd happily clung to Kitty last night, but it had been so hot she did not welcome that. For some hours before going to bed, he had known that once he put his head on the pillow and turned the wick down on the storm lantern, he would feel lost in a particular way. And it had happened. He had felt too nakedly what he was: the lost man on the furtherest river bank of the remotest province. But terrible to apprehend it, awful to feel wadded away under distance. A sort of – what was it? – twelve or thirteen thousand mile high column of distance under which he had managed to pin himself.

Now poor Rochester could nearly be safely thought of in the dark. In this sense: Rochester lived, Rochester perished in a fall from his sulky and while insensible was attacked by beasts. It was different with the girl who'd been cut about by someone who could smile. She was dreadfully everywhere, a face begging its name back.

Predictable dreams of her followed, of course, and their pungency remained by daylight and flavoured the act of getting rid of Lucy.

On the tranquil hill, Mrs Sutter the widow had two gates, one canopied, and another one at the side marked *Tradesmen's Entrance*. Her late husband himself probably put it there. So much nonsense under the gumtrees. A gate for the afternoon tea gentry to enter, and a gate for others to deliver wood and ice and groceries.

You'd think by that label on the gate that beyond Mrs Sutter's bungalow lay hundreds of villagers, dozens of tenant-farmers. And in Kempsey the main gate and tradesmen's gate lay within a short spit of each other. He was buggered if he was going to take Mrs Sutter's suitor's orphans in by the side gate.

Palm off Lucy and Hector to make a place for Kitty's sister. Kitty would have had to have nominated her. A form would have come from the New South Wales Department of Immigration, and she would have needed to sign it. But it had taken the sudden arrival of orphans to make her mention it. Jesus, the slyness!

And at the moment he seemed to get, from the direction of Mrs Sutter's bungalow, a whiff of slyness too. Widowed once, she had now been widowed in a certain sense again. She'd had none of the joy of drinking tea with, none of the secure married talk with poor Rochester. But now she would be offered his children.

He heard the noise of her children inside now, and holding the little boy's hand, he knocked on the yellow front door with its panels of pebbled glass. No one came for some time, and then a boy of about eleven opened the door, grabbed the Rochester children in by the hand and told Tim, 'Mama's round the back.' The door was closed in his face. Tim went around the flank of the yellow house. You could smell the hot, moist odour of the spaces under the house. The Sutter residence had the honour of standing on brick piers. The idea of air circulating beneath the floor had seemed an odd one to him when he first arrived. On top of the moist earth smell there was a tang of sweet corruption from the garbage tip of the yard, but between him and that rankness lay the smell and then the sight of soap-cleansed sheets blowing on a breeze.

A woman wore boots amongst the great flags of bedclothing. Mrs Sutter, dark-haired and tall, narrow in the shoulders, well-set in the hips. An occasional customer of his. A lot of people worked on the principle of spreading custom around, because you never knew when you'd need to spread your debts out a bit as well.

She came forward to him, her hands out, pallid from the soap and water.

'Oh,' she said. 'Oh, you were so brave, Mr Shea.'

He didn't know what she was talking about.

'You relieved poor Bert's last moments, a friendly face bending over him. Constable Hanney told me.'

She began to weep. She smoothed her tears sideways with big, lovely, soapy hands.

'There was another man there,' said Tim.

'Yes, the hawker. God Almighty, that wouldn't have been a particular comfort to Bert.'

He found himself in defence of Bandy Habash. 'He behaved very, very well, Mrs Sutter.' For one damn thing, he dealt with the horse who would have still been thrashing and heaving out there if he hadn't. 'He's not a bad little chap.'

'Yes, but I know that you directed the rescue,' she said.

She didn't know what a pitiable state Bert had been in. Bert in his ending needed the help of all parties.

Tim said, 'I brought his two children with me. Both of them are indoors with yours. The girl Lucy. More presence than a judge, that Lucy. And then the poor little boy.'

He saw tall Mrs Sutter, whose face poor de-faced Rochester

had dwelt on, look away. He knew it was bad news. It astounded him the way women could set limits. The mothers and the motherers, and yet they always had definite ideas about what could be done with ease, and what the boundaries of content were.

Mrs Sutter inhaled and was gathering herself for an answer when three or four children burst from the back steps. A boy, three girls and the children with whom he was now as familiar as if they had emigrated with him. Lucy, Hector. The oldest Sutter boy had proposed some sort of roughhouse, some racing around. Lucy stood back, weighing what it meant. Sharp-featured and calm. What a daughter! She did not blunder into things like the boy Hector. Every course she took a chosen one.

They all went shrilling off around the side of the house towards the front. Towards the Tradesmen's Entrance. Lucy ran behind them, inspecting the Sutter yard as if she'd never seen it before.

Mrs Sutter took a pair of child's bloomers out of a basket, pegged them to the line, but then seemed to need to hang onto them for a sort of support. She stared very hard at the wet fabric.

'I'll take the boy. But Bert wouldn't have expected me to take the girl. She hates me. I've got no affection for her.'

'Is there someone else then?' asked Tim. 'Who can take her? I have a third child on its way, and then my sister-in-law is emigrating, due here on the Aberdeen Line . . .'

'There's no one else I can think of. I wondered would the nuns take her? Get somewhere with her? You know the nuns, don't you? Wonderful music-teachers.'

He waited for her to say she could help with the expense. He was damned if he would mention it and draw her grudgingly into some undertaking. She let go of the bloomers and stood up and looked at him directly.

'*She* was the problem with Bert and me. She didn't like me and did brutal things to the other children. Just to keep me in my place. She's a brutal little thing.'

'I hadn't noticed that.'

Mrs Sutter looked away across her well-ordered backyard. Her garbage heap far off at the back fence. Her woodheap in order against the side fence. You could bet Bert had cut the wood and stacked it for her a week back, on some visit. The palpable benefits of marriage. Stacked wood, cut in regular sizes. A mound of kindling and a tidy little wall of split softwood. Tears appeared on Mrs Sutter's long lashes.

'But for her I would have been widowed twice, I suppose. I can't live with her. Take her to the nuns. She is a destroying little soul. You'd think they would extend their charity to her and do her some benefit. I'm sorry about all this when you've already been so good . . .'

But however sorry she might be, Mrs Sutter was implacable. She went on pegging her clothes.

'It occurred to me though,' said Tim. 'Whether you'd buy the farm.'

'Oh no. No, there's nothing for me in the farm. There's something for the bank.'

Five minutes later, out the front by Tim's wagon, the two Rochester children were making a supervised farewell to each other.

Hector cried, but Mrs Sutter's son and four girls began to distract him. Mrs Sutter herself issued formal instructions from a distance. 'Kiss good-bye to your sister now.'

Tim began offering Lucy consideration. 'I'll bring you to see him on the weekends.'

'Yes,' said Mrs Sutter. 'Perhaps for tea on Sundays.'

Limited to such a small set of future reunions, Lucy gave her tear-stained brother an embrace more muscular than emotional. It was a hug which carried a sort of promise of return in it. Lucy climbed up into the cart without being asked to – she seemed to be too proud to face being directed as her brother had. Tim took the reins and turned Pee Dee's head. Rolling downhill at last from Hector's sadness, he could hear the widow and her children kindly turning young Hector's attention to the Sutters' aged dog.

'Well,' Tim said, shaking Pee Dee into a trot. 'Your brother has a good billet there, eh. For you we might need to see the nuns. It's good there I hear. Girls the one age as you. In from the farms. Friends to make. And no milking. Mind you, the nuns *do* have a cow or two, and the boarders take it in turns to milk. But that's not every morning, is it?'

She said calmly, 'I don't mind milking. I have a poddy calf called Chuckles.' Her tough little hands were folded in her lap.

'You understand . . . there might be others who have a claim on the farm.'

She said nothing. Was she thinking of farms elsewhere that could be held on to?

'My own boy, Johnny. I'm sending him to the nuns from May. Sooner if the little ruffian gets into trouble. The boarding students down there . . . they complain about food. Well, you'll have no need to. I'll make sure you've got ham and chocolate, and a regular supply of cocoa.'

So these were items of the world's trade to a doubting little orphaned heart. A full can of Fry's Cocoa. She didn't seem to take notice. Too busy tasting the world, gauging what it would do to her, doubtful of what he said to explain it to her.

'The Sisters of Mercy,' he muttered, more for his own comfort than hers.

'But I'll need my clothes,' she told him suddenly.

'Of course you will, of course.'

'Hector will need his too. Mrs Sutter'll wash his, I suppose.'

Tim turned Pee Dee's head towards Glenrock.

'Look,' lied Tim. 'No one has anything against you.'

He knew she saw through that.

'I don't have a thing against you. You're a fine little woman. I wish there was room.'

'Your place is very small,' she stated. Letting him off the hook. Putting him on it.

Albert Rochester's little farmhouse on a slope in Glenrock was the standard one they gave you a diagram of in *A Guide for Immigrants and Settlers*. It was supported not on piers of brick like Mrs Sutter's but on stumps of trees capped with a plate of zinc to defeat termites. It was unpainted, and the door had no lock. The inside walls, Tim found when he and Lucy entered, were not lined, but pasted over with old *Heralds* and *Chronicles* and *Arguses*. The energetic North Coast spiders had filled in every panel of the wall frames with misty web.

There was a note on the scrubbed kitchen table which said,

'Every condolense will keep up milking til further arangements and final notice
                    Jim Coleman.'

Some shirts and underwear hanging from a string by the dead fire. They were Bert's and the boy's and a chemise of the girl's. Let Mrs Sutter, Bert's near-wife, sort Bert's stuff out. But the girl went over and took the chemise and folded it up and put it in a sugar bag which had till now lain on a chair. She took the bag into the other room, and he could see her through the open door putting other things in it. He noticed a picture of thin Bert and his pinched wife on the deal dresser at the end of the room. A wedding picture. Mrs Rochester stood up to her wedding day wearing a hat, and the little hands she was to give Lucy were meekly folded in front of her. Blessed was she meek and hers was the kingdom of heaven these days, where, if what was taken as gospel had any value, she had got Bert back and was consoling him again.

It was nearly out of his mouth to tell Lucy to take the photo. He was close to saying, 'While you're here you'll want to . . .' But then he knew he'd be ashamed to see it in her hands, the reproach of her departed parents. It could be collected at another time. At the time of the final notice kindly Jim Coleman spoke of. If from anyone, the notice would probably come from the British Australia and New Zealand Bank. They would want to sell for certain. Mrs Sutter had already said she wouldn't buy Bert's hard little hillside. She needed something like a pub instead, to feed all her children.

Tim talked the child into leaving Hector's clothes for collection by Mrs Sutter. The woman should come here for the task – that much was owed to Bert.

He was pleased the girl was finished and they got out again and left Bert's herds to the neighbour. She didn't ask for the poddy-calf. She knew that attachment was at an end. Chuckles belonged to the bank too.

They followed the route back to town they had taken the day before, past the accident scene again. It had been all cleared away, the horse taken, the wreckage removed, the blood sunk numbly into a wet earth. The next flood would find it there. Bert would rise with the water. 'We saw a man out there walking on the flood. His face shining.' That sort of thing commonly reported both in North Cork and the Macleay . . .

At last around the corner into Belgrave Street, home of the living land of pubs and emporia, of *Nance's Chemist*, of *Philip Sheridan Solicitor*, *Joss Walker Tailor*, *Taylor's Book Office*, and *Tibbett's Ladies' Wear*. And modestly at the end, where Smith and Belgrave made a right-angle, in the blue and gold awning paint, his own store.

Crossing from the *Chronicle* office to the Commercial Hotel for purposes the whole town knew of was the Offhand, a little ferrety bloke with an ironic face and a frightful pallor. He wore a grey suit and a stained collar. A blueness marked his jowls. Editor-in-chief of the Macleay *Chronicle*. Employed by the owner Hinton to pursue definite editorial policies. They were free trade and the Federation of the Australian colonies. Offhand confessed to being a former parson of the Diocese of Southwark. He poked fun at those who were always writing from New South Wales to the Queen or the Archbishop of Canterbury, warning them that Papist symbols and rituals were creeping into the liturgy of the Church of England in New South Wales. He'd never married, at least not in New South Wales; though he had a friend. Poor fellow a dipsomaniac. A good, democratic Englishman though.

The democracy and irony endeared him to Tim, who reached now for the rim of his own hat to greet him.

'Whoa Tim!' cried the Offhand, and Tim reined Pee Dee in successfully in the middle of Belgrave Street. The Offhand caught up to him with a shuffling walk.

'Tim,' he said a second time.

He had traces of a jaunty kind of cockney accent.

'Just to say we are all in admiration of your bravery and compassion *in re* Rochester. One Mr Bandy Habash has been in our office extolling your rescue, and your taking in one of the children. Is this young lady here one of Mr Rochester's?'

'This one is Lucy,' said Tim. He was not at ease. He'd felt threatened by the Offhand's exorbitant praise. 'Habash did a first class job, too. He brought peace to the horse with the trace in its poor bloody entrails.'

'Tuppence,' murmured Lucy.

'What?'

'Tuppence,' said Lucy. 'Our horse Tuppence.'

'Yes.'

'Is young Lucy going to live at the store?' asked Offhand.

'I'm going to see the nuns,' said Tim.

'Then you're a fine fellow,' said the Offhand. 'Those nuns are expensive.'

Tim didn't want to be called that just then. Going to the nuns was callousness in his book, not fineness.

The Offhand said, 'Young Habash even told me that you beat his thoroughbred there . . .'

What did Habash want? Enough reflected glory to get him in the bloody Turf Club?

'His thoroughbred was knackered. Too much buggerising around in Smith Street . . .'

'And you then carried the deceased on your own horse all the way to the Macleay District Hospital.'

'Ditto,' said Tim, almost to himself. 'His horse was knackered, for dear God's sake.'

The Offhand smiled and rubbed his jaw in a way which bespoke relentless thirst.

'Mr Malcolm of the Royal Humane Society is sufficiently impressed,' he said. 'Mr Habash has been to see him too.'

'My God,' said Tim.

The Offhand reached out and patted Pee Dee's haunches as if the conversation were now nearly at its end.

'If you want your valour or compassion cut back in any way, you've spoken to me too late, Tim. The tale as relayed by Habash and by Sister Raymond at the hospital is already set in print.'

'Then why in God's name didn't you consult me?'

The Offhand laughed. 'The gallant Hibernian speaks. Dislike of public praise is the mark of true heroes, Tim.'

'Any news though of that girl?' asked Tim, since that was about the only news that could matter. He had felt Missy pressing him, insisting through all his helpless dreams.

'A bad thing to have lying around,' agreed Offhand. He wasn't anguished, of course. Why should he be? All the bereavements of the world washed up through the cable laid under seas and over mountains and ended up grounded in the *Chronicle*'s pages. 'Meanwhile I'm off for my morning tea.'

The Offhand started on his way. *That* was the trouble with him: he was too quirky. People made more of his contrariness as a columnist than they did of his opinions.

On top of that he had a three weeks overdue account at *T. Shea – General Store*. So he was lucky he hadn't met Kitty.

Dumpling Kitty in the store was seated in a chair behind the counter. Johnny was drawing with chalk on the blackbutt boards which made the floor.

'Holy Christ, woman. I've told you not to let the boy do his art in the middle of the store.'

Lucy Rochester looked at the boy, who raised his head and stared back blankly without malice and with keen interest. His son. He could turn out to be a great lop-eared Australian – few opinions, few ideas. If they weren't careful with him.

'Mrs Sutter wasn't disposed towards the girl?' asked Kitty.

'She took the boy in.'

Tim was partly shamed to be talking like this in front of Lucy Rochester, who stood there with her leg injury still wrapped in the neutral mercy of white rag.

'Well, there's no advantage to Mrs Sutter any more,' asked Kitty fiercely, 'is there?'

He hated her tightened mouth at such times, as right as she might be. He hated her to carry her face in those lines. When he had had their wedding picture taken by Josh Hendy and sent a copy each of two different poses to his parents, his father had written back to him. 'To hand, the photos of your admirable wife and yourself, and all the arbiters of beauty and elegance here around proclaimed her to be as supreme in excellence as could scarcely be described . . .' The poor old fellow had never met her, of course. She'd come to Tim, in answer to his letter of proposal, direct from Red Kenna's hearth, and had never got round to visiting Newmarket during their courtship.

And on the right day, smiling at Josh Hendy's dicky bird in the camera, she justified the judgement of those North Cork arbiters. But she could turn off at will the generous gleam behind her eyes.

'Johnny,' he told his son, 'take Lucy out to the kitchen

and show her where the lemonade is.' And to the girl, 'You know how to slip the stopper off the lemonade do you, darling? Good.'

Johnny wilfully did not hear and went on with his chalkwork.

'Holy Christ, Johnny, will you do it!'

Kitty put another tuck in her mouth and he heard her murmur, 'So, of course, it's the boy who has to pay for the world's grief.'

Johnny dropped his chalk and got up and flapped his arms like wings, a gesture Tim would remember at later dates.

'Come on, come on,' he told the girl.

'So how's trade?' Tim asked when the children had gone.

'Old Crashaw's left an order. And Mrs Malcolm was in.' She put on a fake ceremonial voice to say that. 'I think she was disappointed not to find you here, you know. You're her golden boy.'

'What stupid talk!' he said.

'She tells me you're a hero. I told her in return that you weren't game enough to face up to the nuns.'

'Holy God! We would have had room for people like this girl at the pub, if you'd been prompter.'

The old grievance. Kitty'd been booked to come to Sydney aboard the *Persic*, and he'd told the New South Wales Licensing Board that she would be in the Macleay in time to help him take up the Jerseyville Hotel. Then her oldest sister decided to be married and so Kitty chose to stay on at home until that event, changing her steamer booking to the *Runic* a month later. You had to be a married man to be a pub licensee in New South Wales. The licence went to the married Whelans by default. Just for a Kenna marriage feast.

'One day I'll bloody kill you for saying that,' she told him. 'I won't take endless blame for the Jerseyville hotel. What a bloody hole Jerseyville is anyhow. And what sort of publican would you have been? A mark for every sponger! I didn't understand what I was doing when I changed the steamer. But I tell you it was a mercy. Someone was watching over us. Because you can hardly manage the supply of food and kerosene let alone grog. And the silly desire to keep your hands clean of lucre. Well, look at this!'

She took from her pocket an account from a Sydney supply house, Staines and Gould. He could read their Gothic-printed name on the top.

'You give three months' terms to people and the Sydney houses want to be paid in two. This is our disaster, Tim. Not that I went to a wedding. Nor have a sister coming here. The fact that you have some mad scruple about asking people to pay you for what you've already supplied.'

'Then I'll ask people.'

'You'd better do it or we'll end in some bloody hole by the roadside!'

'That only happens in Ireland,' he protested, and went through into the residence. In the dining room, the girl and Annie were drinking lemonade from large glasses. Lucy sat in a chair, and Annie had climbed up there and seated herself beside her, checking on her sideways, and then mimicking her posture exactly.

'We must go now, Lucy,' he said, and the severity of the sentence startled both girl children. Johnny should be here to say goodbye but was missing somewhere, a bloody ragamuffin. Up a tree, or under the back of the residence, terrifying the wobbegong spiders.

'You'll see her again,' he said then to Annie, in a voice out of which he took all the sting which came from the direction of Staines and Gould, Mother Imelda, Kitty.

Little Kitty, five feet and no inches, followed him and Lucy out to Pee Dee and the wagon. Kitty had a wad of dockets in her hand. She gave them to him.

'Show that old nun these, all unpaid. She's only a woman, you know, she's got armpits like the rest.'

'Christ, you know I can't push dockets at Imelda.'

She took them from his hand again and began to push them into the pockets of his vest.

On the way to the convent, no one rushed up to acclaim him, and he felt all the better for that. He was able to feel, therefore, an ordinary citizen, which was half of his secretly desired condition. The other half of the desired condition was for people to say, 'There goes Mr Shea. Generous man.' Not for such definitions to appear in print, but for them to recur in the mouths of Macleay citizens. This was the vanity Kitty mistrusted in him.

Bryson of West had different ideas. He had a storekeeper's meanness, and delighted in people saying, 'Shrewd old bastard!' He had farmers put up land as guarantee against his supplying them credit on jam and flour. The way to wealth and property in the new land. Hard to imagine the mean and continuous effort of the brain needed for enterprises like that. To Tim it was like an effort of extreme mathematics. Why make it? So customary was all this in the bush, though, that farmers had come to Tim and offered to sign letters of agreement for credit. Pride wouldn't let him enforce them.

As the big convent in Kemp Street loomed up, he said to the girl as another inducement, 'I will come and take you on a visit to Crescent Head with Mrs Shea and the children. Have to get up early in the morning to get to Crescent Head!'

The memory of Crescent Head's ozone and surf hissed in the summer street. A favoured place.

But it was a silly gesture against the numb, grave fact. She was nobody's child.

Tim knocked on the large, glass-panelled door at the front of the convent. Very strange, the smell of convents. Brass polish, bees' wax, a lingering scent of extinguished candles.

The youngest nun answered the door. Only eighteen months off the boat. All that black serge these women wore. Welcome in frozen Ireland. How did it feel here? What did they sleep in, these poor women, in this heat? How did they make their peace with the thick night in New South Wales?

A pleasant-looking young woman, some farmer's lost child from Offaly or Kerry. A native elegance in her despite the pigshit in her family farmyard. Her noble-faced mother – Tim could just imagine her – carrying her bitter secrets in her face, the secrets of her womb, the secrets of short funds and high rent. Dragged down by the gravity of things. And the child thinks, I can get above this! The sacrifice of earthly love a small thing, since the rewards of earthly love were so quickly diminished and brought to bugger-all.

And here she was answering a door in the Macleay. In a place which had once been a rumour but was now too solid, and its sun so high.

She seemed happy though. At least she harboured that young intention to have the joy of the Lord shine forth from her face.

She said, 'It's Mr Shea isn't it?'

The consecrated woman showed them through into the front parlour. Here stood a big dresser and a bees-waxed table and upright chairs. On the wall the lean, amiable-looking Pope Leo XIII, and the visage of Bishop Eugene Skelton, Bishop of Lismore, New South Wales. On a pedestal in the corner a plaster Saint Vincent de Paul. On a pedestal by the window the Virgin Mary in blue and white crushed the serpent with her foot.

Tim and Lucy did not sit at the table. It had very much the air of being reserved for higher events. They sat instead on a settee of severe lines, covered with maroon cloth.

The young nun went to fetch her superior.

'These are just women, you know,' Tim told Lucy. 'Women like Mrs Sutter. Women like my wife. They dress in that way. Tradition. But they have instincts of care, like all other women.'

For he seemed to remember Albert Rochester was a Primitive Methodist, and all these nunnish robes and furnitures would have been accursed in his eyes. His wizened daughter, though, took them as they came.

Mother Imelda could be heard thumping up the corridor and now burst into the room. A big woman, her beads clicking against her unimaginable thighs.

'Well, Mr Shea!' she cried out, closing the door for herself. She'd once told him that her father had owned a warehouse in Waterford, but he had wondered in that case what she was doing here in her Order's remotest province. Surely, unless he'd gone broke, her father could have swung her a grander appointment than commanding Christ's outpost amongst the bush-flash children of cow-cockies in the Macleay. Of course, maybe adventure called, as it had with him – if adventure was the dream of separateness, of not seeking out the common landfalls of your clans: Boston, Brooklyn. These matters weren't accessible to thought or to measurement.

The Primitive Methodist waif had stood up too, though her closed demeanour gave nothing away. 'Sit, sit,' said Mother Imelda, dragging one of the chairs out from under the solemn table and sitting on it, the black cloth of her thumping big hips and thighs dominating the small child on the sofa.

Tim now said who this was. The Rochester child. Mother Imelda may have heard of the accident . . . Now Mrs Shea had both a child and sister on the way, hence it was impossible . . . The Sisters of Mercy were the only boarding school in the valley . . . Mrs Shea and I wanted her well looked after . . . Of course, her dead father's wishes must be respected, and her own as a child who has reached the age of reason. So she is a Protestant, and that must be observed.

Mother Imelda laughed and patted the polished surface of the table. 'We don't lack here for children who are Protestant.'

'Then I would like to see her taken on by you, Mother.'

Mother Imelda looked out past the picture of the Supreme Pontiff and through the lace at the window towards the huge glare outside. Often Tim looked into the nullity of Australian air and wondered what it meant for the existence of a living God. All that light a question put to the sorts of things people believed in dimmer regions, twelve thousand miles away. But it did not seem to wither Mother Imelda's certainty. It did not seem to put a crease in it.

'Lucy, do you think you would like to join us here? We put a large stress on cleanliness and on obedience. We do not countenance backchat. Did you have backchat at home?'

Tim said, 'I've found that little Miss Rochester rarely engages in forward chat let alone the back variety.'

Somehow Mother Imelda did not quite relish the little joke.

'Well, Mr Shea. Given your domestic arrangements, I understand that you would want Miss Rochester to be a year-round boarder.'

Tim felt himself colour with shame. It was a question he had not thought of; was the child to have her Christmasses and her Easters in the convent or was there a place for her at his table?

He said, prickling, 'We would, of course, take the child for outings and the larger holidays. But it seems this will be . . . this will be where she lives. I can't think of better.'

Mother Imelda put her hand cursorily to Lucy Rochester's small chin. 'Are those your clothes there. In the bag?'

'I will provide a better port for her, Mother,' said Tim.

'You should go outside and sit on the verandah. I want you to tell me how many magpies you count in the trees about.'

The small girl rose, keeping her eyes on Tim, and went, opening and closing the door so smoothly.

Now Tim knew he must make a proposal. Imelda would say how much a week. She advertised in the *Argus*, day pupils thrippence a week. How much for boarders? They ate of his groceries, half his anyhow. The other half from Doolan's in West. Keep the two good Irish tradesmen happy. Happy about what? Since the goods were supplied for what could loosely be called the love of God. He hoped Imelda informed the Deity of the way she stretched him.

She stared at his chest. He was aware of the dockets in his breast pocket. He imagined they still had the faint warmth of Kitty's firm hand on them. He would need to make a deal . . . only good sense. Imelda herself was that sort of practical woman. He was underwriting the convent's edibles and useables to the tune of twenty pounds a year wholesale, and that was over thirty pounds retail. What was so blasphemous about her taking the child's boarding fees out in jam and cheese?

Yet he was flinching within. He wasn't scared of the woman. Rather he did not want her to shame him, or the thoroughness of Albert's tragedy, with haggling.

So he started first. He wanted to be able to tell Kitty that. *I started first.*

He managed to say, 'So, Mother Imelda, we must come to an accommodation I suppose.'

He recognised at once in Imelda that dangerous blitheness of someone about to frame the best transaction they can for themselves. 'It is thrippence a day to the day school. We add on ninepence a week for boarders. For year-round boarders – we have one other – we give a two week discount, and so that is fifty shillings a year. Can you afford that, Mr Shea?'

The question affronted him. His hand was already in his vest pocket. He would lay all the causes why he should get special consideration down in front of her.

'I was hoping,' he said, 'that since the child is not mine, and in view of some of my offerings to your community here, you might meet me part of the way.'

'Does Mr Rochester have an estate?'

'There may be a shilling or two left when the bank's finished. It's a matter of doubt, though.'

'You know how we are placed, Mr Shea. From some parents we have to beg. We have expenses too, legal expenses, for instance. The town clerk is a member of the Orange Lodge and we are subject to more inspections and interference and legal argument than any of the hotels in town. We are the hotel of God, that's why. We can't and won't soften him with a bottle of whisky every fortnight. The way things are now it would be in all frankness hard for us to take Lucy, even though the situation cries out to mercy. We have to give our preferences to the Catholic poor, who unhappily abound and are in many cases themselves orphans.'

Bugger it. Going against his nature, he had already debased himself enough and to no good effect.

'Of course I can meet the child's fees then,' he told her.

Generosity the chief revenge. He had his now. He felt a serenity at such a moment which he could not obtain by any other means.

'It is payable at a term in advance,' said Imelda, a miser for Jesus' sake. 'That's sixteen shillings and sixpence ha'penny for the first term, Tim.'

Tim hunted in the other pocket of his vest and found two ten shilling notes. He handed her both notes.

'Perhaps you could give me a receipt at some stage, Mother.'

'Your are always in our prayers, Mr Shea, and your lovely little wife.'

Bloody sight littler than you anyhow, Imelda. Just the same, what a bloody grocer this woman would have been! Savage's Emporium wouldn't have touched her. She would have pursued debtors along the riverflats of Euroka, into the cedar camps of the Hastings Range and amongst the swamps of the lower Macleay. Men coming out of the scrub with grime on their foreheads and an axe on their shoulders to be bushwhacked by big Imelda with her cashbook.

'You may want to give Lucy a few shillings too for expenses,' Imelda suggested.

'I hadn't thought of that,' said Tim, going for his pocket again. He hoped that from the point of view of some abstract critic, which was partly himself and partly a subscriber to a progressive age, he did not look too much like a willing peasant, being sucked dry by a hungry Faith. He wanted this unseen critic to accept that he was acceding to Imelda as a matter of grandeur, of style. Because he did not want to live meanly.

Largely drained of cash, he said good-bye to the child in the corridor. No kisses. He opened her hand, then clasped it in both his, and when she opened it, she found five shillings in it.

'Take good care of that, Miss,' said Imelda looking on. 'It will be quite safe, Mr Shea. We expel without fear or favour for theft.'

She opened the front door for Tim, but as soon as he was through she shut it softly, and the conventual silence closed like an ocean over Lucy Rochester's mute head.

So now, lighter and prouder, he still had to face Kitty. Pee Dee was bending his head down and stealing some grass through the convent's picket fence.

'Get it into you there, Pee Dee old son,' Tim told him. 'Eat her grass. Fifty bobs' worth.'

Missy, just like Lucy, made her claims on him through silence, and now for the sake of Missy's uncertain and omnipresent spirit he must top off the day's berserk largesse. He left Pee Dee to benefit from thief Imelda, and walked to the door of the presbytery. One of the larger houses in town. Just like at home, they comforted themselves pretty well for keeping to lonely beds.

The ancient widow who cooked for the priests answered the door.

'Is Father Bruggy in?' he asked.

'Wait,' said the woman liquidly. 'I will see.'

Her accent. He'd heard she was a Belgian. Closing the door then. It wasn't right she did that, as if he were a supplicant or a thief. It was said that the seminarians who were the sons of the poorer Irish farmers were sent to New South Wales as priests. Yet someone had taught them to behave like people of high class.

The tall, very pale priest named Bruggy was suddenly at the door. He'd had consumption. That may have been why he'd signed on for a subtropic diocese. But didn't the humid air also weigh on the lungs? It often weighed on his own.

'Hello there, Tim.'

The man sounded weary, as always saddened and thinned down at finding humanity's tricks so standard, pole to pole. For it might cross the minds of priests and nuns in Ireland that if they travelled twelve thousand miles, they might outrun original sin, slip aboard their steamers into the island chains of innocence. Not so though. The old Adam was already waiting for them on the new shores. Met every damned boat.

'I wondered could I have a word,' said Tim in a hush, to convey it was not a normal theological matter.

'Yes,' the priest agreed, but without much hope of hearing anything new. He motioned Tim to a green-painted garden seat on the verandah. The parlour would have been offered for others. It would be the parlour for the lawyer Sheridan.

Tim wished those things didn't worry him so much.

'There is a young woman who died here, and Constable Hanney has possession of her head and is showing it to people, hoping they can name her.'

The priest coughed a little into his hand. 'I was shown her also. In case she had been to us for counsel, or to the church for a visit. I told the constable it would be exceptional for one of our faith to seek the death of her child in that way.'

Tim said, 'But she was just a child herself. I found her face pitiful. I'd like a Mass said for her repose.'

Rich people offered a crown for a Mass for the repose. Some as little as two bob. Hard-up cow-cockies sometimes put up a shamefaced shilling for a Mass of remembrance, though anyone would want to do better than that for their dead. Tim offered his crown coin by putting it down on one of the green slats of the chair.

The priest looked at it and grimaced. He coughed a bit and said, 'Hugely generous of you, Tim.' But perhaps he meant *hugely odd*. 'I'll give you a Mass card. But I don't think her chances are too good.' He meant by that the only chances worth anything: eternal chances. 'Perhaps you should apply your offering to broader purposes, including this unfortunate girl as one element?'

'Well there is a broader purpose. I'd like her name discovered so *she can rest*.'

The priest wheezed slowly, and you could smell his shaving soap and his camphor-soaked handkerchief.

'She was murdered making a murder,' he said.

'Yes, but a normal girl's face, Father. In a sense, anyhow.'

Tim beginning to rankle. These people were always telling you parables about the poor and despised coming amongst you, Christ in another guise. Why did they never suspect this girl might have been sent to sort them out?

He should have given the old bugger ten bob. It would have given him greater freedom to express his ideas.

Bruggy said, 'These need to be read out from the pulpit, Tim. The Mass intentions. Why don't I say, *For a Secret Intention*? Anything more flamboyant might excite and distract the Faithful.'

'That's fine with me. A secret intention.'

'You need to resist the village rubbish they believe at home, Tim. Don't for a moment consider yourself haunted.'

Easy to bloody say.

'Of course, when Constable Hanney came here, I realised I might be haunted myself if I let it happen . . . But don't be superstitious about it.'

'Somebody's child, Father,' said Tim.

'Exactly,' said the priest. 'But everyone's child goes to judgment.'

Now Tim stood up. 'Not to keep you any further . . .'

'Hold hard, Tim. I'll write you that Mass card. A sort of divine receipt if you like.'

He didn't want anything like that lying around the house to provoke Kitty.

'No need for a card,' he said.

The priest coughed and considered him. 'Tim, you didn't happen to know this girl, did you?'

'No. Wish I had, in fact. Set her to rest.'

As he left the priest picked up the crown from the verandah seat absent-mindedly. A non-avaricious man. Could afford to be, of course.

Tim found that with his energetic nibbling Pee Dee had dislodged a fence paling.

'You bloody blackguard!' Tim genially told the horse.

He untethered the beast and led the dray quickly down the street, not getting up on the board until they were well past the Australia Hotel on the corner of Kemp and Elbow. Safe in the heart of secular Kempsey.

3

Two dozen deliveries to make now.

Coming out of Mrs Curran's in River Street with the empty butter box he'd delivered goods in, he spotted old Dwyer on his horse, with the hessian saddlebags hung over its neck crammed with *Chronicles*. He saw women come to front fences and buy. And as he delivered goods further up the hill, he found that women smiled as they handed their money over for the delivered biscuits and treacle, sugar and tea. From the back doors, he saw the *Chronicle* was as often as not opened on their kitchen tables. One of his customers told him, 'You're a really decent chap, Mr Shea.' Their cash had no reluctance to it today. None of them mentioned the scandalous prices of things. The few who asked for a week's credit seemed ashamed to do it.

One of life's mysteries. That ordinary people paid well, and the bloody bush aristocrats with their Tradesman's Entrances drained credit to its limit. Even Ernie and Winnie Malcolm who were so keen to nominate him for valour.

Back at last to the junction of Belgrave and Smith, Pee Dee restive, himself yearning for black tea. He spotted his son Johnny swimming like a water rat around the pylons of the unbuilt bridge. The *Argus* and the *Chronicle* went to some lengths to explain to ratepayers that the most important work was the sinking of foundations, using a huge diving bell lowered by crane from a lighter. Men from Sydney who were used to that sort of work stood in that bubble of air at the bottom of the green river and worked the digging and dredging machinery and sank the pylons in place. These men took their butter and chops at Allen's Boarding House in East, as if they were ordinary fellows engaged in ordinary work. Johnny hung round them if given a whisper of encouragement.

Tim got down from the cart on the embankment just past the store, and held Pee Dee's head and called for his son. 'Come out now. Don't be a town ruffian. Come out!'

The child sat bolt upright in the water, like a bloody weasel. Then he swam to shore and found his shirt. The trousers he'd swum in were all discoloured with the river's alluvium, the rich soil which it picked up upstream. Kitty didn't seem to mind any of this, or the idea of a six-year-old swimming about in that massive river.

'You aren't cold?' he asked the boy.

The boy said, 'No.'

Tim shook him by the shoulder. 'You are to keep out of the river, sir. I'll give you a bloody great whack.'

'That's right,' said the boy. He mimed a bloody great whack with one open hand against the other.

'It won't be as funny when it happens,' said Tim. 'Go to the back of the house and dry. Don't come into the store in that condition.'

'Whatever you say,' said the boy.

He didn't sound like his parents. It was as if the sun had got inside his nose and throat and dried all the cords. His *say* sounded like *sigh*. This is what it is to be an emigrant. Your children won't speak like you. He'd never thought of it till it happened.

As a consolation, he took the boy by the hand and together they led Pee Dee and the cart around the back.

When he came into the store, Kitty looked up from the *Chronicle* and smiled at him.

'So you *are* a hero, darling Tim.'

'You shouldn't believe it. I collected over twenty-three shillings this morning.'

'Just as well since we owe the wholesalers twenty-seven. This Bandy Habash is a good talker, isn't he? Speaks so highly of you.'

'I wonder where he thinks he gets the right from?'

'Well,' she said, reaching for his upper arm. 'You are what is reported, *you are*.'

'Kitty, why don't you get some strong tea and have a rest?'

She was willing to do it. He cried after her, 'I just tore that bloody rascal Johnny out of the river!'

Going, she murmured, 'That's him. He isn't frightened of a thing in the known world, the little bugger . . .'

Now he was able to read the paper himself.

'*GLENROCK TRAGEDY*.'

The Rochester accident was then detailed.

'Mr Timothy Shea, grocer of Belgrave Street, and Mr Bandy Habash, hawker of West Kempsey, had been alerted to the accident by Lucy Rochester, and had galloped together to O'Riordan's in Glenrock where they had found . . . Mr Bandy Habash has since visited the offices of the *Chronicle* to praise the behaviour of Mr Timothy Shea . . . carried the remains of the unfortunate Mr Rochester on the back of his horse . . .'

But it was the front. And Albert's back visible all the way.

'. . . to the Macleay District Hospital . . . took in the two unfortunate orphans until suitable places . . . Mr Habash's account of Mr Shea's attempts to revive the unfortunate Mr Rochester have interested the Secretary of the Macleay Valley Branch of the Royal Humane Society, Mr E. V. Malcolm, who has forwarded to Sydney a recommendation that Mr Shea's acts of courage and generosity be recognised by an award.'

His client, Ernie Malcolm, carried on his fob watch chain the bright medallions of at least a dozen civic bodies: Patriotic Fund, Shipwreck Society, Empire Day Committee, Australian Wesleyan Missionary Society, the Australian National Defence League, the Free Trade Association, the New South Wales Typographical Association, the Christian Endeavour Union, the New South Wales Cricket Association. A correspondent of all of them, a convenor of meetings to assess public interest. On top of that an attender of Masonic meetings at the Good Templars. A life spent all in public, sometimes with lovely, tall, fine-drawn Winnie Malcolm beside him, but frequently not. A woman made for private adoration married to a fellow always on a rostrum or at a committee table.

And cracked about bravery and the Humane Society. Inspector of courage and acts of mercy. He had talked in the past as if he saw the Macleay as some valley of pre-eminent valour. Where that impulse came from Tim couldn't understand, since he seemed an ordinary fellow, a man designed for homely things. It frightened Tim to be Ernie's target. It was a sign of the disorder he had sensed as Missy's slaughterers were led to Central wharf.

After Anniversary Day his dreams grew more arduous, more stubborn. Threw their shadow too into the light of morning. Constant presences: Albert for a bloody but ordinary start. But more, more present was Missy. She had so quietly burrowed into his head, like an Oriental bug one heard of in the *Argus*, which sent planters in Malaya screaming out into the jungle.

A dream recurred set aboard the *Burrawong* – a very bright day, and threatening the way Australian brightness can be. An awful quantity of azure and ozone all around this boat which in different years had brought him and Kitty to the Macleay. Tim at the gunwale and the girl, Hanney's Missy, indefinitely dressed in blackish clothes, approached him and pointed downwards into the water, where a very clearly perceived porpoise was rippling like silk in the water.

She said, 'The captain tells me it's the slops they follow us for. But no. They prefer the company of humans.'

She had some English country accent. That was not unexpected.

Waking, he took account of all the men of the Macleay. Timber-getters and small farmers from far up the river. The sort of places where mountains began to squeeze the valley in. Fellows from Taylor's Arm, Hickey's Creek, from Nulla Nulla, Five Day, Stockyard, Kookaburra and Mount Banda Banda. They lived in slab huts. They cut railway sleepers for shipment to Sydney on *Burrawong*. They brought great thews of cedar to town on jinkers dragged by teams of bullocks. Or else their blackbutt planking, cut to provide the decking of the future Kempsey bridge. Perhaps only once every two or three months did these men come to town to meet a woman.

A usual visit: they would park their drays on the river bank, turn in their orders for bacon, split peas, tea and sugar (and even sometimes soap), and then go to the Commercial or the Royal or Kelty's and get drunk. Tim would fill their orders, place each one in the appropriate dray, and then late, late at night, when he and Kitty were asleep, the bachelor owners of the drays would come out, haranguing their own phantoms, would generally take the right vehicle, and head off up the river. Out of the dark streets into the sadder darkness of the bush. Sometimes they fell from the wagon and were found the next morning sleeping on some embankment as their horse cropped grass nearby. Sometimes they simply pitched themselves backwards into the tray of the wagon and slept with the reins in their hands. The sober horses knew the way to whatever far-off acreage these fellows were working.

None of these men from the bush, owners of knowlegeable horses, could be imagined as the lover of Hanney's fine-faced girl. Townsmen though. Some townsman then. Some townsman was it.

One humbler townsman of his acquaintance came to the store at the hottest hour of the afternoon. Wooderson. With whom Tim had shared a dinghy in the great flood, when they were very young and husky.

Wooderson said, 'Tim, I read of your heroism. Bloody good!'

The humid air filled up again with this silly, vaporous rumour from bloody Habash.

'It's all a put-up.'

Big Wooderson laughed. He still worked as a haulier, was easy with life, uninflamed by ambitions. An Australian. Very suntanned and muscular, and his big hands were a map of small, hurtful accidents to do with loading and unloading wagons.

'And I remembered anyhow, Tim, as I read it all. You were, I seem to remember, a first class rough batsman, a walloper. Hook shots I believe. Whack! There's to be the Married versus Single Men Cricket game at Toorooka up the river. I'm the Marrieds' captain. Clarrie Bertram's got the damn meningitis. Would you join us at the wickets, son?'

Tim growled, 'Never respected that bloody English-gentleman game.'

'I've heard that speech before,' said Wooderson, laughing. 'There's a throwing at the stumps contest at lunchtime. Bob to enter. Three quid first prize.'

More than boarding school fees for a small orphan.

Wooderson said, 'You've got a bloody good eye, Tim. The *Terara* will take us up to Toorooka for the game.'

'Quicker to bloody crawl there on hands and knee, wouldn't it be?'

'Yes, but a steamer trip! Nothing like it for novelty. Bring Kitty and the kids, Tim. Lovely day.'

'I see that New South Wales has Victoria in great trouble at the Sydney Cricket Ground,' said Tim, finding the place in the *Chronicle*. New South Wales First Innings, 7–385, Victoria 8–187. Put the bloody Victorians in their place! Sydney people liked to do that.

'Clyde's done the damage,' Tim remarked further. 'Took six wickets for 37 runs.'

'Ah,' said Wooderson. 'An English game eh, Tim? Except when New South Wales is dishing Victoria.'

Tim grinned behind his moustache. 'Go to buggery, Wooderson. But I will play for you if you really require it.'

Wooderson was lucky to get him at the right hour. The secret truth was that the good fellowship was mere playing at fraternity. Were grocery stores and stock agencies and lawyers' offices really run according to the laws of social cricket, where to lose your wicket in a comic runout could actually increase your social standing, if you took it well and joined in the laughter? Whereas to lose at commerce . . . another matter utterly.

He would rather read the latest Victor Daley poem in the *Bulletin* under the peppertree than go out pretending to love the ten other cricketers on his side, and – over beer – the eleven opponents. The Singles. What a cracked concept to base teams on!

All this solemnity he got from his own father Jeremiah, who'd always mistrusted over-easy sociability. Jerry Shea, small land-holder of great style. Too educated for the purposes of a fifteen acre farm and seven pigs. Too literary to be a part-time clerk. He'd loved the English writers – Hood and Lamb and Hazlitt and Pope – and neglected his native Gaelic. He'd spent just one charity term with the Jesuits in Mallow and they'd talked him into betting definitely on English, as if that could give him the place he'd wanted in the world. It was another instance: no one connived at their own destruction the way the Irish did. And yet the newspapers cast them as totally dangerous to others. The thousands of the poor Paddy bastards who were perishing at Spionkopf and other Cape Colony and Natal battlefields weren't dangerous to anyone any more. But they got little bloody credit for it.

As he complicated the impending cricket match at Toorooka with these thoughts, an astonishing realisation struck him. I am playing in Marrieds versus Singles from some mongrel of an idea that the girl's lover might be a square leg or in the covers or at mid-wicket.

Wooderson was watching him, looking amused.

'Have you seen that blackguard Habash on your route?' Tim asked to distract himself. 'The son. The younger one.'

Wooderson grinned. 'The one with the horses. The reckless rider?'

'That's the blackguard.'

'He's working out at Pola Creek, I believe.' Wooderson really started to laugh now. 'I take it you want to thank him.'

'Thank the bastard? It's more murder.'

4

Tim put his hat on the back pew of the Primitive Methodist church in Euroka. A church utterly humble in its unadornment. He could see the appeals of humility, the Christianity of plainness.

He pointed Lucy forward towards the coffin, and the pew where Mrs Sutter sat with her four children and young Hector, who looked as brightly kept as the rest.

'You go and sit with your brother,' Tim said.

Pews, and a lectern. Plain frosted glass in the windows behind. No single aid to the remembrance of God. No stained glass, no statues, no intercessors. The plain act.

A man wasn't supposed to be here. Meant to get the permission of your parish priest, tra-lah, for the deaths and marriages of your heretical and dissenting neighbours. If he was damned for sitting in a back pew, then the clergy were welcome to heaven. Poor coughing Bruggy. Welcome to coughless paradise.

But Jesus this was as bare as the South Pole when put beside the rich, coloured jungles of the Catholic piety he was bred in and Kitty savoured. All its beings, its saints more brilliant than a tiger and more potent. This little Methodist place was something different: on this ice you could be God's Eskimo, in this desert God's Arab. The vacancy spoke. Part of the deranged season was that he could imagine himself a Primitive Methodist, going for this cleanness, condemning the overdone other. Heretical thought. But there was a tendency in him to respect traditions more austere. If he were raised to it, this Euroka Methodist sort of thing would suit his character, his mistrust of stagey things. Whereas Kitty needed the forests of devotion, the scarlet martyrs, the bright blue intercessors.

In this underdecorated, scoured air, Kitty's scapulars to Saint Anthony and special devotion to Saint Blanche, the saint of goitres, a condition to which the Kenna family were susceptible, could look pagan as blazes.

She could forget Saint Blanche anyhow, said Mr Nance the chemist. There was plenty of iodine in the Macleay water. Tim didn't know how it got there. Into the rain-fed tanks at backdoors. Did Nance and other benefactors go around pouring it into household water supplies? The river rich in it too. Go swimming and swallow one mouthful, and you swallowed most of the minerals and chemicals. That rich, broad, healthy, muddy river his son tried to live in.

The Colemans from Glenrock in the second row, with their big bony hands which had kept Albert's herd milked. An official from the Good Templars, Mr Gittoes – Albert Rochester must have been a lodge member. All there to hold back the waters of eternity and oblivion from washing poor Albert's face utterly away. What remained of it.

Lucy had by now sat beside her brother, who'd tried to tell her something. Like a good convent school girl, she hushed him. She didn't seem to want his domestic news. She pointed towards the coffin, fixed Hector's attention on it. Not hard to do. The young child's head did not move any more. All the churches had this one big mystery, free of charge, without debate. Death.

Mr Fyser the minister came up the aisle of the church, wearing a suit. No brocaded vestments, of course. He stopped and spoke to Mrs Sutter. He shook his head a little. 'Expecting to marry you rather than bury Bert,' he could be heard saying.

Then he went to the rostrum and read the 'Our Father' and uttered his confidence that Albert Rochester had been saved. Well, that was different. Here in the plain Methodism of Euroka, the story was ended when it ended. Judgment had already been made, redemption already received. No five bob Masses for the dead. No writhing crowds of the imperfect in Purgatory to be relieved by prayer and sacrifice, by going without rum! A great deal of fuss saved. Except you had to ask what could Mr Fyser, grey suit and little dicky collar, do if haunted by the face in

Hanney's bottle? Where was there something in this purity to combat the more luxuriant ghosts?

'Albert Rochester,' Fyser told the mourners, 'was a member of the brethren of this church. He was as sober and restrained in his habits as one could wish. Dead cruelly and at a younger age than he should have been. But look at the children, brother and sister, from Summer Island who were buried late last year. Wounded by prongs of the same rake, *both* succumbing to lockjaw. The young Queenslanders whose deaths were reported in yesterday's *Argus*. Fighting the Boer in a far place. How can we face these mysteries? The ant looks up from his antheap and sees man and thinks, that must be God. But God is larger and larger by far, and his purposes larger and larger by far. Better to ask of a bucket that it contain the huge Pacific Ocean than to ask the human mind that it contain the extent of God's purpose. To one single part of that purpose have we been made privy. Redemption. The consciousness of having been saved, as Albert Rochester opened himself to his Saviour and was numbered amongst the saved . . .'

Tim felt a hand on his shoulder. A large one. Hanney was there, in uniform, expressing his reverence. For the corpse and – bloody hell – for Tim himself. Hanney murmured, 'Did all you could, old feller.'

Carr the undertaker's men carried Albert Rochester out and placed him in the black lacquered hearse with its black plumes and two fat white horses. Albert had, of course, never travelled so plushly between Glenrock and town.

A long way to the cemetery in West where the grave of Lucy's and Hector's mother was located. Tim chose not to be part of the procession for fear people would point to him as well as at the hearse and shame him by nodding in approval that he should be there. He crossed back to town on an earlier punt than the one the hearse caught and called instead into the store, did brief business, then made his own way to the grave, arriving as the hearse did.

From here you could look across the river to the far mudflats of Euroka and Dongdingalong, where families maintained their hopeful ways growing maize and milking dairy cattle. And then the mountains, which sent a thundershower every summer afternoon, and from which those others of his customers dragged down the great stalks of cedar. Geography of the sweet world seen from a graveside. It looked a world sufficient to itself. Why did it need all its feverishness about Boers and Empire, the threat of Papism, the fear of the Jewish financiers who held the Queen's son in their thrall? Why the bloody need to raise lancers or hussars or mounted rifles? Albert Rochester had joined the real regiment. The army that had the numbers.

Mrs Malcolm, Tennyson lover, looked down on Victor Daley, a Sydney poet Tim loved. Daley wrote an incomparable elegy to humankind. A sensible Australian name to it too. *The Woman at the Wash Tub*, old Victor's best. He had learnt it by heart for the unlikely eventuality of having to recite. As he did now for funerary purposes to himself, while Carr's men stumbled across the hill with Albert's plain coffin.

'I saw a line with banners,' Tim grumbled into his moustache,

> 'Hung forth in proud array –
> The banner of old battles
> From Cain to Judgement Day.
> And they were stiff with slaughter
> And blood from hem to hem,
> And they were red with glory,
> And she was washing them . . .
>
> I rocked him in his cradle,
> I washed him for his tomb,
> I claim his soul and body,
> And I will share his doom.'

In the approaching group, it was Lucy who seemed to be fitted more as the eternal washer, the cleaner-up of disaster. More than wary Mrs Sutter, who looked cautious, shying clear of such a comprehensive role.

Prayers had begun when a sulky pulled up and two people got down from it. Late comers for Albert. Ernie Malcolm and Mrs Malcolm. Getting down from her seat, Winnie Malcolm looked unfamiliar, at odds with what he knew of her. She looked flushed and bleared. She was a being of air. Earth had now somehow entered her long, luscious bones.

Ernie Malcolm guided her over uneven ground amongst the gravestones. The broken columns which were popular and one of Des Kerridge's, the stonemason's, standard items.

And Kerridge did the things suitable for Tim's clan too. Celtic crosses. They and broken columns covered most needs.

> 'How linked in Life and Death –
> The shamrock and the cross.'

Victor Daley again, Australian poet. The vanity of that. Of being Mrs Malcolm's grocer, secretly harbouring verses by the Bard of Enfield, that suburb in the west of Sydney which Daley honoured by living there. But the pleasure and savour of all this now overshadowed and reduced by the poor appearance of Winnie. Fair play, how bleared and uncertain she was. On the plainest level, that bloody public buffoon Ernie had privately upset her. Or something had. Didn't Hanney say he wasn't showing Missy to townswomen? Not that. Just loutish unworthy Ernie. Jesus Almighty Christ!

The Malcolms stood behind a mound of grave dirt and were dressed very well for Albert's funeral. He had a black tie around his stand-up collar, and she was in bombazine so lustrously black that it seemed to attract flies. Within the cloth her body like that of nuns and other goddesses would be pink with the heat. But she had always dressed formally. Her Melbourne origins.

Ernie Malcolm nodded to Tim and then composed himself to listen to Mr Fyser's burial prayers.

They were quickly done, and Hector's hand was contained by Lucy's as Albert made his eternal descent. Tim prayed his pagan *Ave* within sight of Mr Fyser, an heretical utterance for the repose of Bert who, according to Fyser, was already in the Kingdom anyhow. As the coffin hit the bottom of the pit, Tim betrayed himself with the sign of the cross. Mr Fyser observed him coolly. As an insult did it rank beside what the pigs had done?

Mrs Sutter now encouraged the two children forward, and Lucy, demonstrating for her brother what should be done, picked up a red clod and threw it in. Hector did it then, reaching over the hole with the dirt held between his thumb and forefinger. Farewell, chieftain and father. Fountain of kindnesses, maker of chastisements. In Mr Fyser's presence, the chance of an ecstatic reunion of the Rochesters at some redeemed date didn't quite seem a starter.

Mrs Malcolm looked out at the children with ponderous and darkly plush reflection from beneath her lashes. She was still concerned with whatever grief had delayed Ernie and herself. No children of her own, though Ernie looked like a lusty bugger.

Hector raised his arm and said aloud, 'Heaven, heaven.' Lucy re-gathered his hand, pulling him back into the ranks of the Sutter children. Maybe to ensure there was still a place for him there. Tim himself couldn't refrain from looking regularly at unquiet Mrs Malcolm. Images of consoling her too readily came to mind.

One Friday afternoon she had asked him where he had come from, and he had told her. And yourself, Mrs Malcolm? he'd asked. Melbourne born-and-bred, she'd told him, with that robust pride which typified Melbourne people. 'It's a far more refined city than Sydney, isn't it?' she enquired of him. 'If you wanted a city to represent young Australia before the world, Melbourne would be the one, Mr Shea, wouldn't it? Sydney's so rough at the edges. When you land at Darling Harbour, you take your life in your hands getting to the Hotel Australia. And a cab's the only form of transport open to you. Even the tram conductors are rough and ready and likely to swear. And there's far too much of the spirit of Sydney in the Macleay, isn't there?'

There were lots of *Isn't-its* and *Wouldn't-its* in Mrs Malcolm's charming discourse.

'You know, I think it might be the humidity,' Tim suggested. 'The closer you get to the tropics, the more irregular personal behaviour grows.'

That was scientific fact as reported in all the papers. The *Argus* and *Chronicle* agreed on that one.

'Yes,' she agreed. 'Humidity *is* a great ally of barbarism.'

'You agree with me all the way and in each bloody particular, Mr Shea, don't you?' Kitty later mocked. He needed to be grateful she found his conversations with Mrs Malcolm more a cause for poking fun than the other, the jealous stuff.

He found out a little more about Mrs Malcolm at each visit. 'It's so pleasant to find a storekeeper who can carry a proper conversation, Mr Shea,' she told him once, and he felt his face blaze with the compliment. And in the course of conversations, it came out that she was an only child and that her father had been an umbrella manufacturer and an alderman of Brighton Council, a municipality of the city of Melbourne. She had grown up in the shadow of a public-spirited man, and perhaps that was why she'd taken to Ernie.

Her favourite poem, she said, was Tennyson's grand *In Memoriam*.

'Ring out a slowly dying cause,
And ancient forms of party strife:
Ring in the nobler modes of life,
With sweeter manners, purer laws . . .'

She looked down from the tenebral heights of *In Memoriam* at the efforts of the men Tim liked – Henry Lawson, the revolutionary of the *Bulletin*, and Victor Daley of both the *Bulletin* and the *Freeman's Journal*. The greater of these being Victor.

But today at Albert's grave, her face bleared and all at once giving itself up to puffiness, she didn't look like a Tennyson woman. It made you wonder, was she really well?

The filling in began. One of the diggers was Causley, who'd had all his money invested in a cream-separating business. Everything lost when the small patented separating machines every farmer could own had come in. Reduced now to restoring earth to Albert Rochester's grave.

By the cemetery gate Mr Fyser bade Mrs Sutter and the children good-bye. Constable Hanney waited by his sulky. Dear God, if Mrs Malcolm hadn't seen it, let him not spring that thing on her. She and Ernie had caught up with Tim now and she uttered a liquid, 'Mr Shea,' and passed on. Ernie himself stopped.

'Well,' said Mr Malcolm rubbing his jawline. 'Some things even valour can't attend to. I salute you though, Mr Shea.'

'For dear God's sake, don't do that,' said Tim.

Tim couldn't be too raw though in his methods of telling

Malcolm to give away the idea of heroic rescue. Malcolm was a customer, even if he did have three months' terms, and had normally to be spoken to gently. But this fiction of bravery had to be trampled on.

'You might as well give Bandy a medal,' Tim said.

Ernie began fanning himself with his hat. 'Him? Sooner decorate the bloody Mahdi for killing General Gordon!'

'Then reward neither of us.'

'Imagine this, Tim. The opening of the bridge, Central to East. Imagine a line of men, women, even children, receiving medals and certificates for valour. Young Shaw who lifted a fallen tree from his uncle's leg and carried him sixteen miles to rescue. Tessie Venables who rescued a grown youth from the surf at South West Rocks. Yourself. With yourself, Tim, we begin to get an array of appropriate acts of gallantry. I see you standing at the mouth of the bridge, at the mouth of a new century. Standing for our community.'

You also see yourself, Tim might have said if he didn't fear losing Malcolm as a customer, as commanding officer of the brave. You see your words reproduced in the *Sydney Morning Herald*. Mr Malcolm, accountant, brave by association, and quoted verbatim.

Ernie said, 'I have been waiting some time for the third appropriate act to report to the main committee in Sydney. With proper respect, Tim, I can identify it when I see it. Mr Habash tells me that you were endless in your attempts at resuscitation, even though poor Albert had become a thing of revulsion.'

Ahead of them, in the street, Winnie Malcolm had baulked by the stirrup-step up to her sulky, as if the idea of the climb was too much to be faced. Then, shakily, she tried it. One of her less graceful ascents. If Malcolm hadn't been a customer, he might have said, 'Why don't you be brave yourself and go and look after your wife?'

'It is a time in the Empire's history,' Malcolm – with something almost like desperation – confided in him, 'when in each community an exemplar, a paladin, is very much looked for.' He rubbed some sweat into his upper lip. 'I know you agree.'

At least, Tim noticed, Hanney had untethered the police horse and sulky and trotted away on his sombre business.

Tim put a restraining hand on Malcolm's arm. That was what he had been driven to.

'Please,' he said. 'Please, Ernie. We are all being made a mockery of by that dark little jockey, Habash. Please.'

Stepping back, Ernie looked up at the great sky.

'Tim, what do we have in this world to go on except the accounts of witnesses? The British army itself . . .'

'But they don't listen to just one unreliable bugger of a hawker.'

'Ah, you're a bloody Jesuit, aren't you, Tim? I spoke to the child too at the convent. And to the duty sister at the hospital up there.'

'No, look! Any fool could carry a poor dead bastard to hospital. It wasn't a rush to mercy, Ernie. He was past mercy.'

Ernie laughed again. 'I hope to Jesus you make a better speech than that when they give you the medal and make us in the Macleay famous.'

Make Ernie famous, that meant.

Now Mrs Malcolm sat uncertain in the sulky, shoulder turned, considering her situation. As if Ernie could see what Tim was seeing he now remembered his wife. 'Must go, Tim,' he said, making a chastened face.

Mrs Sutter walked up holding Hector's hand and accompanied by Lucy. 'Thank you for coming, Mr Shea. I take it you'll drop Lucy back at the convent.'

'I have a business you know, Mrs Sutter,' he said. Then for Lucy's sake repented. It did not cause even a shadow on Lucy's sharp little face. But for fatal tact he'd say, share the cost of her schooling, you miserable old jade! Or at least buy all your stores from me.

'I have the care of six children,' she said. 'I know you understand.'

Her children by the late Mr Sutter were playing loudly amongst the graves, clutching at broken columns, grazing their fingers in the apertures of Celtic crosses.

'I suppose I must understand.' He cupped a hand around Lucy's head. 'My wife and I . . . I ought to tell you . . . are very fond of Lucy. She plays well with our children and gives us no problem.'

'I'm very pleased.'

Yet she seemed barely tolerant as Lucy and Hector made their farewells. Dawn milkings and hardships had consumed the childhoods of Albert's boy and girl. They were like an aged sister caressing an aged brother.

In his pocket he had a chocolate for Lucy, especially for the post-burial, to distract her from the knowledge of Mrs Sutter's disregard of her, and of his own neglect as well. The heat had softened it in its silver wrapping.

He gave it to her as they sat on the board of the dray. 'Keep it till the cool of evening, Lucy,' he told her. 'It will get more solid then.'

She said, 'We have Benediction tonight.'

'But you as a Protestant don't need to go.'

'I like it. Sometimes I see papa's face there.'

In the great gilt orb of the monstrance the priest lifted.

Tim had some customers across the river, in East. People who'd fallen out with the storekeeper Corbett there, an argumentative Orangeman and high pricer. A number took the trouble to come across to Central in the punt, to buy from *T. Shea – General Store*. Or children would come over on Mondays or Tuesdays with their mothers' requirements written on notes in their hands, spend a while playing with Johnny and Annie, tending to end up messing about in the river with Johnny, while Annie sat barefoot at the very edge, plying the rich silt with her fingers. He hoped Johnny wouldn't put his customers' children, who were often blackguards themselves, in any harm.

'How's old Corbett?' he would ask of the customers in East, and a number would say, 'I hope the old bastard dies!'

Naturally, to make the deliveries, Tim needed to coax Pee Dee onto the punt. If there were other conveyances and horses getting off, Pee Dee would often shy sideways, wilfully feigning fright. Pee Dee really didn't like it when there were cattle aboard, or when pigs harried him, running between his legs. One day he was going to shy right over the embankment and cover the river banks in sugar, flour, baking soda, oatmeal, tapioca, tea and broken biscuit.

People disembarking from East sometimes cried, 'Why don't

you get rid of the old nag, Tim?' It was in a sense a sane question. 'Pee Dee's my bloody horse,' he answered. Part of T. Shea's terms of trade. Sometimes louts cried that sentence back at him as he and Pee Dee clopped past making the deliveries.

Recently Tim had taken to avoiding embarrassment by waiting with Pee Dee in the butter factory lane, not approaching the ramp to the punt until all the traffic from East had dispersed itself. Then lead him down onto the punt apron, hoping he wouldn't make a display. And so with the stutter of the steam engine, out into the current. No great sea journey, but in Tim's mind the crossing of water always significant.

Out there today Daley still with him. No apparent ghosts out here on the bright river, but Daley had the lines for the season of Albert's tragedy:

'O dead men, long-outthrust
From light and life and song –
O kinsmen in the dust . . .'

The sunk pylons for the new Macleay bridge, which would make the punt unnecessary by the start of winter, rose from the green river like columns from a sunk civilisation.

Some time later that day, he was delivering in Rudder Street, East Kempsey, when he saw a covered hawker's wagon swaying up the road out of the Dock Flat swamp. One of the Habashes. He reined Pee Dee in to the side and got down from the dray. He could see bloody Bandy at the reins of his green wagon all right. Coming back to town after palavering the poor women of Pola Creek.

A bracing anger rose in Tim at the sight of that failed Punjabi jockey. He walked out and waited in the middle of the road. He raised his arms and couldn't help calling out, 'Get round me if you can, you little ruffian!'

Bandy Habash waved joyously at this prospect of reunion. He drew up, and Tim walked to the side of the green wagon with its tin canopy and stared up at him.

'I wanted to know . . . What in the bloody hell are you doing telling these lies about me?'

Bandy put on a wonderful, melodramatic frown.

'This stuff about Albert is all rubbish and flummery, and it makes me ashamed. What in God's name were you doing going to Ernie bloody Malcolm?'

'Mr Shea, after our adventure I was simply full of admiration . . .'

'What bloody for? Might as well admire a man for making the tea or emptying a jerry. You've made a bloody fool of me!'

Tim kicked one of the wheels of the hawker's wagon.

'My dear old chap, may I get down and talk to you?'

'What do you bloody well think? I'm looking for an explanation.'

Bandy worked himself trimly out of his seat and fell gracefully to the road. Wholly and neatly in front of Tim.

'I watched you in your movements, Mr Shea. In all respects I thought they were the movements of a hero.'

'I was not anything in my movements. I hung back. *You* were the person who fixed his horse!'

'I was well-educated in the English language, Mr Shea. I have read Scott, Dickens and Thackeray, in all of whom such sentiments as I expressed to Mr Malcolm are common.'

'But I ask you! Why land me, a poor bloody grocer, with this stuff?'

Bandy was abashed. Beyond the theatrical manners, a true bewilderment could be seen. He lowered his head and shook it.

'I was alarmed by what I saw on approaching the place of the accident, Mr Shea. I would have found it hard to approach such horrifying affairs. Yet I witnessed the heroism of your movements, sir, the decisiveness you showed. This alone made it possible for me to draw near.'

'Bugger it! You were the one who did the real work.'

'Oh, Mr Tim, my dear chap. We both behaved well to be honest, though I yield first place to you. But do you think Mr Malcolm would want to write to the Royal Humane Society about a Punjabi hawker? About the courage of a Muslim? To be the first amongst the brave in the Valley of the Macleay? The world would not be interested in my bravery. They want true British grit.'

'Well, Mr Bandy, I'm an Irishman.'

'Same thing in my book. They are willing to see British grit in your face, you see. We were brave together, Mr Shea, in the face of the tragedy. But my part could not be pushed forward, so I was more than happy to push forward your part. I know about these things. I don't complain. But I do know that if you are honoured as you deserve, I am partially honoured too. In your shadow, as they say, old chap.'

Tim could do little more at first than wave his head from side to side. 'What sort of plan is this? What bloody sort? A prank? Poking mullock at Ernie and the Turf Club? And me as the bait!'

'No, no, no, no! I am above all an admirer of yours, Mr Shea, and wish your family well. When I had heard of you from Mrs Burke at Pee Dee, your sister by marriage, for some reason I thought, I want that good man as a friend in town. And now, as an honoured friend.'

Now that it was all explained Tim in fact felt quite awed by the scale of Bandy's intentions. His relentless and always denied desire to race his grey at the Warwick Course. So he raced his grey up and down empty streets, a sort of audition for greater things. Showing the indifferent vicinity how worthy his grey was, while the Turf Club committee picnicked on *Terara*.

Tim had a lurking and undeclared sympathy for such deranged schemes. This one so lunatic, and Bandy deserved to be thumped for it. But it was its scope that slowed you down. Made you understand: this is a really serious little bugger!

Tim said, 'I came here to be an ordinary citizen. I've seen heroes and don't like them.'

His Uncle Johnny of Glenlara transported to Western Australia more than thirty years back for being a Fenian organiser in Cork. Did no one good. Made his mother prematurely aged so that the young Tim had to be silent in her presence.

'I came here to be an ordinary citizen,' Tim repeated. 'This is all a vanity on Ernie Malcolm's part.'

Bandy murmured, 'Mr Shea, you cannot expect me, can you, to go to Mr Malcolm now and tell him I was mistaken. I was *not* mistaken. You deserve to be considered a true man. Again, Mrs Burke tells me you are a giver of alms and feed half the valley. I as your friend would like you to be publicly acclaimed.'

Since all this smelt of excess, Tim – in protest and not without fear – took hold of the lapel of Bandy's coat.

'Listen, you're using the wrong bloody methods, my dear Indian friend. I am not here to be the sort of feller that suits you. I have a hard time enough being the sort of feller that suits me.'

'But I know, Mr Shea, that what I've done doesn't displease your charming wife.'

'What do you know about Kitty?'

'I came to the store two nights past. I saw Mrs Shea. She said to me that it was grand for you to be praised like this, and thanked me for bringing it to the notice of the public. Look for wisdom to the women. For they know all our faces, don't they? The face of the hero. The face of the coward as well. The face of the brute and the face of the beloved.'

So how to work up a consuming rage when even now, with Bandy intruding on the question of Kitty, he had to strain to achieve it. What he really felt was fear. Fear of being dragged down and marred by this little hawker's efforts to exalt him.

Tim felt the burden of this defeat. No one could be dissuaded from the fable of brave Shea. And the man so artful. He had the approaches to this lie of his ratified by all parties except Tim, and covered from every angle. Habash couldn't be defeated by an average good talking-to and a flick in the ear.

'Don't discount that I can take you to court,' Tim impotently told the hawker. 'I can talk to the solicitor Sheridan about this, and I bloody will. I'll leave it at that for now. We don't have anything more to say from this point.'

But he felt he'd fallen into the overstating trap, and his summing-up had already erred by being too long. He turned away sharply and walked back to Pee Dee, deliberately using an urgent gait that suggested he might punch the horse. He heard Bandy murmur something. It sounded like, 'I am already part of your family.' Yet it could just be Mohammedan incantations or curses. He decided to ignore it, but within five yards of Pee Dee he adopted a less menacing stance – for Pee Dee might have taken the excuse to rear in the traces if he hadn't softened his approach – and waited there by his dray, his back to the hawker, his face to the river, until Bandy drew level and passed him. He watched the faded green and yellow paint on the pressed-tin walls of Bandy's wagon.

S. B. HABASH AND SONS – MATERIALS AND REMEDIES
Licensed Hawkers.

People on the lonely farms, with little else to swear by, swearing by the Habash herbal remedies. As always, people preferred to be poisoned in hope than to live sanely and know the strict limits of the world.

'Remember,' Tim cried after him, but it sounded a fairly limp command.

5

Though it had no railway, the Macleay Valley was full of railway
sleeper cutters. The railways were far away, had reached the
Hunter River a hundred and fifty miles south, but not further.
The country between the Hunter and the Macleay was so
mountainous, so full of terrifying grades, that only those who
profoundly feared the sea or were profoundly attracted to steam
engines travelled down there by a succession of coaches to the
distant steel tracks on the Hunter.

So for the moment it was a matter of ironic reflection that the
right trees for railway sleepers grew here. *Burrawong* frequently
went to Sydney loaded with them, as with maize and pigs. People
who got visionary would look out south across the great, green
face of the Macleay and say, 'The railway will one day arrive and
let me tell you it'll make this bloody place.' One of the sleeper
cutters was a Kerry man called Curran, who came in at intervals
to buy plug tobacco.

'Jesus, Tim!' he'd say, raving away. 'They're catching it now!
They're catching more than we ever threw their way. Those
Boer boys are throwing more the way of the bloody English
than they ever saw before this, on any battlefield. It's one thing
to fight and beat niggers. Another to face up to white men with
decent rifles.'

It was a glorious thing to see fellers like Curran work with their
string and pencil and adze, turning a mere log or branch into an
exactly shaped oblong, fit and beautiful enough to hold up the
rails on which the enormity of locomotive engines progressed.
A man like Curran was all grace at work. Clean cuts, and great
florid, generous motions.

'Modder River, eh? Majersfontein! The punishment they've been looking for all this century they're getting now, the bloody Saxons!'

'A lot of Scotties though,' Tim reminded him. 'A lot of Paddies too!'

'I say *more fool them*,' Curran cried, his eyes alight.

'Lads looking for a wage, you know,' said Tim. 'A fellow could imagine himself in the ranks if it weren't for emigration.'

Tim also imagined Curran, in his shack on the mudflats, haranguing his wife and her brood. A primitive Wolfe Tone of the bush. Looking in the *Argus* and the *Chronicle*, in the *Freeman's Journal*, for clues to the Empire's death.

Curran's propositions of vengeance had a certain dark appeal to Tim. But the old trouble was – as people of any mental discrimination at all knew – that the price was always paid by the wrong people. Not one course was deducted from the table of the rulers. They moaned and bleated, but their wine was still in its bottle, and their gloved servants still brought the plate. Curran, full of native wit, kept himself determinedly innocent enough to believe in the fairy story of thorough vengeance.

With an air of gloating, Curran went off with his tobacco. He received no regular deliveries of supplies from Tim. The Offhand also received no regular deliveries of groceries, and bought things as he needed them. He ate only occasionally and when he remembered to, breakfast at Mottee's Greek cafe, dinners at the Commercial. Soap for his toilet and tea for his painful mornings, however, he got at *T. Shea*.

Breathlessness could overcome the Offhand and he might need to hitch his lean thigh onto a stool which had come from Swallow and Ariel, Biscuit Makers, with the first large order Tim had made eight years ago.

While in this posture one day he said, 'This meeting to form our battalion the Empire so badly needs.'

'Yes, I read about it.'

'General Roberts will say, Who is that battalion we gallantly slaughtered in the past ten minutes? And his aides will say, They're the Macleay Mounted Farters, milord. And General Roberts will say, If only we had more of that calibre! Where in the name of God did you say they're from?'

Tim laughed, relishing the Offhand nearly as fully in the flesh as in print.

'That's a fable if you like,' said Tim. 'That's M. M. Chance's fable.'

'Absolutely right,' groaned the Offhand.

The consumption he'd suffered as a young man and theological student still had at least a second mortgage on his flesh.

'This meeting of Baylor's and M. M. Chance's then. In the flatulent minds of some, anti-war and pro-Boer are the same thing of course. So I wonder might it not be politic for you to attend that meeting? You need donate nothing to the Patriotic Fund, but you could treat the question with solemnity. No one would resent your saying nothing – they all have enough inflated concepts of their own to fill up a good evening.'

Tim didn't like the idea. Having been forced into heroic mould against his wishes, he was now advised by the Offhand it was good business to show himself off in the guise of a devout Briton.

'And I suppose to end the evening I would have to listen to Dr Erson singing "Soldiers of the Queen".' That seemed the final item he would not be able to bear. Dr Erson's loyal tenor.

'Not too big a price, Tim. Yes, "Soldiers of the Queen" with rich Scottish vigour. But you will also hear me speak. The benefits, you see!'

Some of Curran's hot, heedless anger sizzled in him.

'I can't be bullied by Baylor or Chance into standing up for some belief I don't have. As far as I'm concerned, the Boers are entitled to manage their own affairs in Transvaal without intrusion. And there are men in the House of Commons itself who agree with me, especially the Liberals. Imagine if the French landed here now and muscled into New South Wales. There'd be Froggy versions of M. M. Chance back in country towns in France approving of it all and making their bloody loyal lists. I won't waste an evening on this, Offhand. They can go to buggery!'

The Offhand looked away and up at the rafters of the shop. He seemed to be scared out of his irony.

'Well, of course, the depth of your feeling . . . and a pungent argument you put forward . . . one which accords with my own. I don't ask you to act against your principles. I ask you to trip them up in theirs. They are fair enough democratic men in most matters, but in this area of jingoism . . . well, they seem to believe all the Monarch thinks of is them, here, on the banks of the Macleay. Never mind. You'll read about the whole pompous affair in the *Chronicle*. Dealt with according to the lesser Muse of whimsy, the only Muse to give yours truly the time of any day.'

The Offhand grinned, nearly wistful, and got down from his stool, gathering himself for a return to his newspaper. Whereas Tim had the eternal deliveries to do, which were the office of the grocer. The counterpart of milking the cows.

As he crested the top of River Street in West, Constable Hanney was blurred by heat haze. He came from the direction of the upriver settlements, and in the afternoon humidity he and his horse made no show of liveliness.

The dead hour of the afternoon, quarter to three, and every westward blind in River Street drawn against a sun still evilly high above lavender-coloured mountains to the west. Women who came to the back doors to take Tim's orders, made up to their request, looked stewed and wiped their upper lips with handkerchiefs and asked Tim when it would end, this calm, deadly heat.

Now, at the sight of Hanney, it seemed to Tim that Missy was instantly back with him, standing sideways at Mrs Catton's front fence. Her features were more sharply defined in apparition than were Kitty's and Winnie Malcolm's in memory.

'Quiet for Jesus's sake!' said Tim. He made himself appear busy by moving butterboxes around in the back of the dray.

When Hanney drew nearer and clearer, out of the haze, Tim saw that his navy collar was undone. He wore an old pair of white breeches tucked into his boots, and a white pith helmet on his head. The breeches had streaks of reddish dust on them. Work at the washing tub for Mrs Hanney. He rode a big-bellied police mount, and that implied he had been to the remoter parts, up the Armidale Road, where the hard mountain terraces of the track to New England did lots of damage to carriage work.

Tim finished with the cart and now waited as he had recently waited for Bandy, though this time waving one arm slowly and without the tension of threat. Hanney hardly had to rein in to make the police horse stop.

'Comara, that's where,' said Hanney out of stubbled jaw and in answer to the question Tim didn't need to ask. 'I've been on patrol all the way to bloody Comara.'

'Holy God,' said Tim. Comara more than fifty rough miles up the Macleay. Tim looked at the nearer of the policeman's big saddlebags. Was she there, enduring her hard journey? And still unnamed?

Hanney said, 'Christ, I'm fed up, Tim!' His big rectangular face was pink, and there was a coating of sweat or prickly heat under his chin, and down the V of his unbuttoned shirt. Poor big lump.

Tim said, 'You'd think there aren't many that could possibly know her at a place like Comara.'

'You'd be surprised. Some of the pastoralists' sons . . . never fully buttoned up! Some of the pastoralists for that matter . . . It was thought, too, that maybe she came down the road from Armidale by coach. If someone said, *Yes, we saw her stop here* then I could send her to Armidale. The blokes up there could have the pleasure . . .'

He scratched his under-chin and looked so piteous.

'Are you able to drink a beer while in the Queen's uniform?' asked Tim on a mad impulse. Once he'd uttered the idea, he remembered how Hanney had been unsteady from brandy on the holiday when Bert Rochester died.

'No bugger would mind after the journey I've had. I drank my last beer in Willawarrin last night. Dismal little town.'

'I'm at the end of deliveries. I could shout you.'

'You're a bloody white man, Shea. Make it fast as you can.'

Yet they were a mile from the nearest pub.

'My shout then,' said Tim.

'Thank you, son!'

It was strange though to be exercising the muscles of male joviality. Promising to shout. There was a small social cost in being seen drinking with a policeman. Cattle theft was a regular enterprise of the frequenters of some Kempsey pubs, and they did not like policemen in the bar. But he would not be back there to hear the regulars cry, 'Drinking with a trap, Tim?'

Tim went to his cart and turned Pee Dee and it about in River Street's torpid dust. The tired policeman travelled at his side down the hill. Hope no bugger thinks I've been arrested! But the ill-shaven policeman, with his big rectangular face in shadow and hung at an angle which had nothing to do with authority, looked himself under arrest.

The constable said, 'I've even been to the blacks' camps at Greenhill and Burnt Bridge. When I took out the flask, the black gins screamed pretty awful and threw up handfuls of dust in the air. An off-chance, of course, them knowing her. But I've always found them very honest in that regard. They don't like to lie about the dead, the dusky brethren.'

'I reckon they know the dead have too much bloody power,' said Tim.

'Jesus! Especially in the form I have to present things.'

The way he shook his head, he looked more defeated than a officer of public order ever should. He showed Missy to black women. Did he show her to any white ones? Kitty hadn't seen her, Tim was pretty sure.

There was a bakery at the bottom of River Street, and they rode through the pool of fragrance it made as the road turned, copying the bend in the river. Now they were in aptly named Elbow Street, the long low verandah of Kelty's Hotel could be seen beyond Bryant's store. It had a reputation as a rough house but no noise escaped today from beneath its low eaves. Everything in sight spoke of eternal life and fixity. Tim was in a mood to like the idea of the world having stopped under the day's fierce hand. The sun never to go down. The river, set like a pudding in its banks, never to rise. The bread always fragrant. The award for false bravery never given. But then . . . Missy never named or delivered!

Some cream and butter haulage carts and a scatter of horses were tethered in the street, very still as if to prove the day's point. Tim let the dismounted Constable Hanney go down the steps to Kelty's low-slung verandah and so pass into the dark, fuggy warmth of Kelty's public bar. As the policeman walked he rolled his spine to get the saddle soreness out. A few of the men in the public bar looked up at the strange company that had entered. Tim heard one of them murmur, 'Come in, why don't you bloody well?' Another muttered, 'Commercial, bugger it!'

The Commercial in Central was better suited for talk between a constable and a grocer.

At the bar with the travel-dazed constable, Tim ordered two schooners which pale Mrs Kelty poured, and he and Hanney took them to a table rather than stand at the bar. In one draft, Hanney drank half the schooner down.

'Oh, that's fine,' he said at the end of the process, his eyes misting with the delight.

In the meantime, Tim found he'd rashly uttered aloud what was meant to be a private surmise. 'You haven't shown the girl to my wife, have you?'

Tim had never asked Kitty straight out. He would have been ashamed to give her a hint of the grasp Missy had on him.

'I don't show it to respectable women,' said Hanney. 'They would not have had contact with her after all. Except the Mulroney woman.'

'But women may have spoken with her.'

Hanney laughed, and wiped his long, doggy face. 'Are you a bush lawyer or something, Tim? Let me tell you, whoever I'm looking for as witness is a fellow with a standing prick and no conscience.'

'You show it to the black gins though.'

'Well, it's a good warning for them.'

Holy hell. Did the Police Commissioner in Sydney know the random and illogical way Hanney was carrying out his orders? Should he be told?

The policeman drank down the rest of his pot. Tim had barely sipped of the sour, heavy brew from kegs shipped up aboard *Burrawong*. He liked rum better than ale anyhow.

'I'm getting another,' said Hanney. 'You?'

Tim said no, he would hold what he had for a while. He noticed that when Mrs Kelty refilled Hanney's pot, there was no exchange of cash. Hanney did not expect to pay; Mrs Kelty to receive payment. His transaction however, or lack of transaction, changed him. He came back with a strange, frank gleam on his face, and sat down. Tim no longer felt as safe with him. What sort of fellow, forced to travel to Comara in awesome heat, missed out on trying to solve his puzzle by showing Missy's features to women?

Hanney drank again and then stared at Tim from beneath a lowered brow.

'Look, you're very interested in this, aren't you? Strikes me you've got a load of interest in this Missy. I have to wonder. Why do you keep quizzing me? A man no sooner back from Comara . . .'

'I have a normal desire to see the poor child finished with.'

'A normal desire, eh?'

Tim felt now an unwelcome panic in his blood. How fast a uniform would turn on a person! How it divided man from man.

Deciding not to take a step back, Tim said, 'Bugger it, constable. I claim to have no more pity than other fellers. But the girl's face struck me very hard.'

'Enough to buy a constable a bloody ale,' commented Hanney pretty much to himself. 'I've never known anyone to take so much interest. Upriver, you show Missy and they hold their heads on the side and say no, and that's the end, she's forgotten, the little slut. But not you, Tim. It's the big interest of your bloody life.'

By now the new tack had enlivened Hanney. Tim wondered how he'd not noticed before how large the man's hands were. Shall I be able to break such a grasp?

'You have something to tell me, Paddy?'

'My name's not bloody Paddy. I was Tim when I bought you a drink.'

The constable raised his chin and drained his glass the second time. He had a good, defiant swallow. He put the nearly finished schooner down.

'And you can buy me a drink a second time, Tim.'

Tim said, 'But then I'm going to leave. Back to the store. My wife . . .'

'Do you think I am a leper?'

'Not on the strength of a few jars. But you've already started to rave.'

Men at the bar were frankly turning around now to sneer at the argument between the policeman with his poor capacity for liquor and the grocer from Central.

'If I took you in for some long questioning on the matter . . . do you think that would do your business any good?'

'You know it wouldn't.'

'Well, I won't yet anyhow. I'm too buggered.'

A blowfly distracted Hanney by swimming noisily in a little pond of ale on the table. Hanney's gaze got stuck on that area of standing liquor, and the insect's agitated desire to stupefy and drown itself there.

'You know, you're a tall feller to be married to such a short woman,' he said, still watching the fly. 'I'd say you've probably got other women. Taller girls. Missy was taller.'

'As a matter of fact, I don't have any interest in other women.'

Almost true. Mrs Malcolm an exception. An Australian incarnation of Tennyson's heavenly girls.

'He said, "She has a lovely face;
God in his mercy give her grace,
The Lady of Shallot."'

'Get me that beer though,' said Hanney. He did not seem capable now of raising his eyes from the small lake of spilled beer and the fly. Tim took both pots up to the bar. He put down a two shilling piece in front of Mrs Kelty and said nothing.

'Mad bastard,' she said without moving her lips.

'Me or the copper?' muttered Tim. No one could hear that. 'Make mine a smaller one.'

She nodded minutely, her stewed-looking brow. She was used to muttered arrangements. Kelty himself lay in the cool cellar most of the day, asleep amongst all the fermentation. Where had liquor got its reputation from, its name for joviality? Tim felt a genuine but enlarged dread taking the beer back to big Hanney, who had managed now to loll back and take thought about the ceiling. His white breeches and black boots seemed to take up a lot of space between the few tables.

'Truth is I'm like you, you hapless bastard,' Hanney said. He sat forward, applied himself and drank some more, but his mouth was sour when it rose again from the rim of the glass. He drank far too fast, but Tim wasn't going to tell him that.

He covered his eyes with both great hands which could just as easily have taken hold of Tim and forced him into custody. Tim could hear him groaning from behind the fingers. It was a short little session of gasps, and it ended soon.

'Aaah,' said the constable, clearing his hands away from his face now. 'No decent sleep, that's the problem.'

In fact he stretched his arms straight across the table and laid his head on them and got ready to sleep.

'Dear God,' said Tim. 'We must get you home.'

'Home's not home,' Hanney murmured.

This was said not necessarily for Tim's instruction.

The drinkers at the bar, and Mrs Kelty herself, laughed to see the grocer trying to help the constable to his feet.

'Put the bastard in charge, Tim,' one of the men called. 'Charge him with all the bloody heifers gone missing!'

It was a relief to push Hanney outside, let down the tailboard of the cart, sit the constable on the tray, jump up yourself, haul him along so that he lay flat. Bugger, his hat was still inside. Tim jumped down and walked in again and took it from the table, and that made the drinkers double up with hilarity. Tim and the hat, Victoria's laughed-at crown on the front of it.

'Your hat,' said Tim outside again, putting it in beside prone Constable Hanney.

Then tether the weary police horse to the tailboard. No mockery echoed out here, in this silent, stolid air.

Now they started off for Hanney's house in Cochrane Street. Slow, slow. No quick pace likely. They waded through swamps of light towards Central but turned left then. And there in Kemp Street, Habash's wagon parked. Habash labouring out of a house carrying three bolts of linen he'd taken in there for some wife's consideration. Habash stood still with his eyes lit.

'Mr Shea,' he called tentatively.

Tim shook the reins. Pee Dee increased his pace a little. Gracious of the bugger!

Habash of course saw the prone constable in the back.

'But what are you doing, Mr Shea?'

'Taking Constable Hanney home. He grew sick upriver.'

'Ever the man of mercy, old chap,' Habash yelled after him. 'You see. Ever the man!'

'Go to buggery!' Tim called.

They rounded the corner of Cochrane and he pulled up outside the right house. A dreary little weatherboard place, with a low-slung verandah, the designated house for New South Wales constables of police.

Missy's unreliable constable. Missy's berserk officer of peace. Who showed her to some, protected her from others. Ease him down and prop him up and take the side gate. Then there could be at the front door no problem or scene observable from the street. Let it be backyard drama, if there had to be a drama. Backyard smells – shit and creosote from the jakes, a sourness from the refuse pile, a fragrance of split wood from the pyramidal woodheap.

Tim didn't have to knock. Large Mrs Hanney appeared at the door and advanced down the steps. She had delicate shoulders, spacious hips, and wore the broiled complexion which suited the season and which all citizens were wearing. Macleay fashions.

'Oh God!' she said. 'Did you give him drink?'

Laden with the constable's enormous weight, Tim could barely get an answer together before she said, 'Every damned fool knows he can't take drink. Hell and damnation, who are you? You're that grocer, aren't you?'

'I met your husband on the edge of town. Coming back from Comara. Pretty down, missus. Pretty thirsty.'

'Everyone knows it!' she accused Tim again.

'Missus, I didn't know. It's not written up in *Chambers' Encyclopedia*.'

She had picked up a broom from inside the door. It was possible she intended an attack.

'No, but it's written on his forehead, isn't it? You can all bloody tell. He's a butt. Sergeant Fry sends him around with a head in a bottle. Damned great laugh! And you get him drunk pretty cheaply and drop him back so *I* have to tidy up his misery.'

'Madame, I'm not in a plot with anyone. I don't know Sergeant Fry. Could I lay your husband down somewhere?'

Mrs Hanney squeezed her eyes shut and raised her face, complaining to the eaves.

'I have no life. I have no damned life. All right. Bring him in.'

But at least she put the broom down. It proved nearly impossible to get big Hanney up the steps. Mrs Hanney had to help in the end. Struggling with the bulky policeman, Tim wondered would either of them have it in for him over this. Want his head. Forevermore.

6

On Sundays when Tim had her home for dinner, Lucy Rochester
ate it with the rest of them in the silence Tim required. The
same silence which had been ordained by his father at table in
Glenlara, a townland of Newmarket, County Cork, in Munster
of the kings and the Kingdom of Ireland. A fellow of standards.
Dear Jerry Shea.

But it seemed that behind the august silence of Sunday dinner,
Lucy kept an extra, secretive silence of her own. He would have
liked her to say she liked life in boarding school, or even to weep
and beg him to get her out. She seemed cautious to give him
neither one version nor the other.

Comfort could be taken from observing little Annie, who
examined gristle in her fingers exactly like a scientist making
up a picture in his head of a whole beast out of one of the
fragments. Silence suited Annie's style. Early in courtship he'd
told Kitty he preferred silent tables, their ceremony. That was
fine by her though it hadn't been the way things were done
at Red Kenna's. She'd travelled fourteen thousand miles on
the White Star Line from Red's disordered board to the Shea
Sunday table in the Macleay. Jeremiah Shea's little triumph at
the limits of the Empire was the silence maintained here in the
shop residence.

A penny chocolate for all hands at the end of the meal. By
these normal exercises he kept at length an idea which plagued
him by night: that he should perhaps for Missy's sake press
sergeants and commissioners to put her into the hands of
someone of greater strength of spirit than Constable Hanney.

He greased the axle on Sunday afternoons, a soothing Sabbath task. Meanwhile the river drew the children. He kept an eye on them. They would be no more than poor bloody little leaves on the surface of its powerful charm. One time, looking up, he saw Lucy and Annie and Johnny all together in a rowing boat. How had the little buggers managed that? A silent plan carried out between them. Lucy on one oar, Johnny on the other, an uneven match. Tim heard Annie begin shrilling with fright or pleasure, you couldn't tell which. Saw the boat swirling in a lazy current, downriver towards the great black pylons of the still largely imaginary, unbuilt bridge.

'Bring that bloody thing back in here!' Tim yelled.

The girls would float in their pinafores. Flapping their hands. But it would be Lucy who would come to shore, and Annie's sedate spirit that would be likely to sink.

Kitty was lax about the river, philosophic, leaving the children to luck. To the Angel of God. My guardian dear, to whom God's care commits me here, ever this day be up to my side to light and guard, to rule and guide. Amen. A more regular kick in the ass for Johnny was certainly called for, yet his puzzled, animal watchfulness turned away wrath.

The children got the oars working together and brought the boat back to the river bank. Lucy piggy-backing Annie ashore.

And after Lucy had been taken back to the care of the Mercy nuns, Annie says, when she's in her night dress and he is about to read to her from her *Funny Picture Book*, 'Lucy pulls the bung out from the boat.'

'What?'

'Lucy lets the water in the boat. That's why I screamed *Papa*!'

'Well, don't you go into the boat with her.'

He would discuss this with Kitty except she would take it as a final reason to limit Lucy to the boarding school and not let her into the house. Bung-pulling would go to warrant the lack of room for the orphan in the shop residence.

Tim in the storeroom later in the week when the postmaster's son turned up on a bicycle and rang the bell on the counter. Tim came out from making up the orders, from that lovely odour of kerosene and shortbread, candles and tea-leaves, and saw the peculiar envelope in the boy's hand.

'Is that a telegram there?' asked Tim. It evoked the first one he'd ever encountered, the one which said REGRET NOT ARRIVING BY *SS PERSIC* IN VIEW MARRIAGE OF SISTER STOP TRAVELLING NEXT MONTH BY *SS RUNIC*.

'For Mrs Kitty Shea,' said the boy.

Characteristic: Kitty a casual client of the wonders of the age.

'Would you sign my book?'

Tim did. He found Kitty at the dining room table drinking tea with one hand and feeling her back with the other. Such a squat frame to take the full weight of maternity, to carry a reasonably tall fellow's children.

It struck him as he handed it over: Could it be something dismal about Red Kenna or her mother? But somehow he could not envisage even one of those wild children rushing into Doneraile to a telegraph office, instead of writing a more kindly letter. Rowdy at table, yes, yet they liked to talk and explain at length. So they would have thought of sea mail as the proper organ for sad, detailed news. He hoped he could swear to that.

'Have you ever received a telegram before?' he asked as cheerily as he could. 'You've got one today, Mrs Kitty Shea.'

She was eager at once. 'Wouldn't it astound you?' she murmured.

When she had it in her hands and had opened and begun to read it, she broke out in laughter. Her laugh delightful to him; unless directed to someone like Bandy Habash, or joined in with the relentless chorus of her loud family.

'Isn't this Mamie to the nearest square inch? It's from a ship at sea. Who'd think of sending a cable from a ship at sea? She must have been drinking.'

Kitty stood up to read it. '*ARRIVE MELBOURNE TUESDAY 10th* – Holy God, that's just tomorrow! *STAYING WITH MAGS PHELAN MIGRANT WOMENS HOSTEL ONE WEEK EMBARK* SS IRIS *TO SYDNEY ON TUESDAY 18 EXCITED SISTERLY LOVE – MAMIE.*'

When she'd finished reading, Kitty's breath escaped her. 'Oh huh!' She sat down at the table, and began to laugh again. 'Of all the people you'd pick as likely to send cables from a ship at sea!'

He smiled too, but was thinking with a new clarity, my God another one of them. One more robust woman to feed. As long as the two Kenna boys didn't decide to come. Powerful, little mottled men with gappy smiles. Devout drinkers like their father. Although the bush, the reaches of Euroka and Toorooka, would in the end absorb their rowdiness.

He heard Kitty still laughing. 'You've got to watch that Mamie. Go through you for a short cut!'

The fact was Mamie already ashore and laughing in Melbourne. The Kenna girls bracketing the great east coast of the continent of Australia with their hectic laughter. It was to be hoped she didn't laugh too much with some unreliable fellow.

Tim himself had never seen Mrs Malcolm's great gold city of Melbourne, except from a distance. He'd had to stay aboard his ship with influenza. Had walked the low foreshores of Fremantle, the ones that made you wonder what you'd let yourself in for. But not Melbourne. Melbourne had this august, distant aura in his mind.

He'd landed in Sydney still fevered and hoped for clerk's work, but the clerks were out of work here too. So it was the truth: hard times all over the globe. He'd been a little surprised at that. He hadn't got out of the hard times latitudes. At the Migrant Settlement Office, they were advertising for carters for the Macleay.

HAULIERS REQUIRED, MACLEAY VALLEY HAULAGE, KEMPSEY, NEW SOUTH WALES. PRIME WAGES IN A MOST PROMISING LOCALITY.

Sydney seemed a close, warm, seedy city of rough and casual manners – out of key with his normal way of doing business. But the tone . . . something in the tone of the place suited him. He would have stayed if the job had been there.

He remembered liking the huge noisy pubs where you could be quiet and unknown, and make a shy friendship with another newcomer and share crumbs of information you had picked up from this landfall.

These days Molly Kenna, the first arriving sister, reverted to form only in Kitty's company. For example, Tim could hear Kenna laughter surging from the residence as he arrived at the storefront one afternoon after deliveries. He left Pee Dee tethered outside, still in the traces, meditating in his chaff bag, and came in through the store. It was women's laughter he could hear. Kitty's ringing in the midst of it.

He went through the store into the residence out the back and came upon the visitors seated at the crowded table set with the Stafford china, a silver cake stand glittering, and the plate with shepherds painted on it laden with shortbread.

First in view, long-faced Old Burke smoking his aromatic and temperamental pipe. Husband of Molly Kenna. He'd come here before Molly was even born. A twenty-year-old timber cutter. There had still been at that time convict shipwrights and labourers working around the river for Enoch Rudder, the town's founder, a West Country Englishman who'd built small launches and tried everything from maize to vineyards. A long time ago, Burke moved far upriver and selected a little land at Pee Dee. Always a very frugal fellow. A lot of sheep up the river in those days, but the rich pasturage devoted now to cattle. Burke owned steeper slopes too, covered with a bountiful native growth of blackbutt and other hardwoods.

Buying up the land of other small selectors, and fragments here and there of the original land grants to English gentlemen, this canny Antrim labourer had taken on and still possessed the gravity which land gives a person.

At Tim's dinner table now he was smoking his aromatic pipe, and sat a little separate from his wife, Molly Burke. Molly had acquired the Burke gravity too, though you could see she was letting it slip a bit today. She'd been enough like a Kenna when she'd first arrived on *Burrawong* and worked in the store. Some of the smaller dairy farmers who were bachelors hung around a lot to joke with her and to be melodiously laughed at.

Old Burke's daughter Ellen – by his first, deceased wife – sat at the table today too. A tall girl, and would be a big one later in life. Sixteen or was it seventeen years? She had pretty features – Burke's features in fact transmuted and graced. According to what Kitty said, she had no cross words at all for her stepmother, Molly. Ellen Burke had been one of Mother Imelda's students too until two years ago. She could play the piano for occasional visitors to Pee Dee – Constable Hanney, Mr Chance the stock and station agent, Dr Erson,

Father Bruggy. Bandy Habash? Was Bandy allowed into the homestead for recitals?

Tim said, 'Hello to all.'

Young Ellen rose and politely laid a place for him at the table, saving pregnant Kitty the trouble.

You could see, despite Molly's new respectability, the glimmer of a kind of conspiracy between the two sisters. Even Ellen Burke was in it too.

Tim asked the expected questions – why they were in town, how their two-horse cart had stood up to the hilly grades upriver. (Old Burke believed in getting himself to town without spending cash on the Armidale stage.) A good run it seemed to have been for them. Up the first morning before four – Old Burke's normal rising hour anyhow. First a long day to the pub at Willawarrin where they put up. Then making good time from Willawarrin at dawn to Kempsey late afternoon. Ellen read to them a large part of the way. Charles White's *History of Australian Bushranging*. 'Lawless rubbish!' said Burke, 'and glorified cattle-duffing. But it stimulates the women.'

'We said the Rosary too,' said Molly. 'The whole fifteen decades spaced out throughout the day. Made the time pass.'

Following the long river down, the Joyful, Sorrowful and Glorious Mysteries, the incense of those old prayers rising amongst the heathen eucalypts. But they seemed to Tim to be delighted to have made the journey, the Burkes. Old Burke said with lenient disapproval that the women had been after him to come to town for months. But the real reason he was here was to go to court.

He complained sepulchrally, 'Bloody man has cattle duffed by some scoundrel, and has to travel two days there and back to give evidence of it.'

'Well,' said Molly, winking across the table, 'this is one of those cases where Mohammed has to come to the mountain.'

All the women laughed. They were ready for it.

Working to keep his pipe going, struggling with the damned thing, re-packing it, re-lighting it, strewing his plate with used matches, Old Burke told the story. A dairy farmer called Stevens from Clybucca was found in possession of a heifer bearing Burke's brand which was a BB. Stevens was a bloody Scot and he might as well have been talking Gaelic for all you could understand him. 'But he's a cute bastard,' Old Burke added.

Tim noticed the women were beginning to clear, a dish of this and a cup of that, and trail out to the kitchen. Soon you could hear them talking out there, saying loud bird-like things. They'd obviously heard enough about Old Burke and Stevens.

'. . . so when Sergeant Fry asks him why he has my poley heifer in his back paddock, the crafty old bugger says, *But I sent seven pounds with Ferguson the bullocky who goes up to Pee Dee for timber. Hasn't bloody Ferguson given it to Mr Burke?*'

'My God!' said Tim, sounding appalled because Old Burke wanted him to. 'How would a Clybucca dairy farmer be, putting shoes on his children's feet? What with paying seven quid for one of your heifers?'

'That's the right bloody question to ask. But you see, under our justice, all stories stand up. But not before a man had to travel two bloody days and put up with that drunken cook at the Willawarrin Hotel on the way through.'

Burke did even further sucking and tending of the pipe. Yet he wasn't really upset about his journey to town. An old man content with his grievances. He's be pretty disgusted, of course, if Stevens the dairy farmer got away with his story. He'd be a two-day misery for the women all the way back to Pee Dee.

Thinking of where Old Burke came from at the start, and so daring him to exercise the sort of pity Old Burke himself would once have welcomed, Tim said, 'The smaller cockies always say they duff cattle to feed their families.'

Old Burke groaned. 'They duff cattle to cosset their habits and buy liquor.'

Gales of woman-laughter from the kitchen.

'Listen to them,' murmured Old Burke. 'This is very good for Molly and Ellen.'

'You should take them to Sydney next summer,' Tim suggested for mischief's sake. 'Cooler than here. And that's where the celebrations will be.'

According to all the papers, Sir William Lyne, who'd once opposed the Federation of the Australian states, had now decided it represented the future, and he was full of suggestions and edicts to do with the coming Commonwealth of Australia. He had urged that Tumbarumba should be considered for the national capital! (He must need votes in Tumbarumba.) And his decision was that the chief Federation celebrations should be in Sydney. A nice arrangement for the big town and its businesses. From this enormous state almost too large to be imagined, encompassed, travelled, old Sir William wanted everyone with the rail or boat fare, with a reliable string of horses, to come all that way and so behold the founding of the Federation he had so determinedly fought.

'I wouldn't grace the event, Tim,' said Old Burke. 'Humans bloody astound me. Change for change's sake. And Sir William Lyne, who used to be a decent feller and against the Federal idea . . . now in consort with the Sydney Jews and pub-keepers. Trying to conscript people to a festival! Just to watch some hopeless, chinless, English bugger in a cocked hat saying *I declare* . . . And can you imagine the bloody footpads and the mashers and the razor gangs everywhere, running round in derby hats. I say, no bloody thanks, Sir William.' Still more pipe-work. 'I voted against Federation. You realise we'll need to have bloody taxes spent on keeping hopeless Tasmania afloat. Ever been to Tasmania, Tim? Awful bloody hole! Full of tattooed criminals. And the weather frightful. Like bloody Donegal with gum trees.'

Tim was pleased with the rise he'd got from Old Burke. Now he kept his voice soft so that he could cause greater annoyance still. Something about Old Burke set him off.

'I think there is a vision in it all, you know. I think there is something of the future to it too. A federal Australia.'

'Sentimentality,' Old Burke grunted. 'This is nothing about Australia. This is all to do with Britain, Tim. They would have us raise a Federal army. And where would that army fight? Like the Irish, like the Scots, like the poor, bloody niggers of India and Africa, this army would die for British enterprises. Read the *Freeman's Journal* on this. No, I won't go to Sydney to honour that kind of arrangement. Not at Billy Lyne's word. He can go to the whores and lawyers in Phillip Street and order them around! Not me!'

Tim said, 'I weighed it up but voted in favour. Do you know why? For the sake of my children.'

'It's a keen mind that can see a connection between the matter of Federation and his children.'

'I wanted Johnny and Annie, if they chose, to live in South Australia or Western Australia on the same terms as the locals.'

'Why would you want your children to live in West Australia? It's a desert shore of totally no value.'

'We can't tell the future.'

'That's the very cause why I voted no. *No*, the first time, and still *no* the second. You're not telling me you voted yes the first referendum as well as the second?'

'After serious thought,' said Tim.

The truth was that there was something which excited him in the idea of the unity of such immense spaces of earth.

'Well, Tim, I gave you credit for a more sensible fellow.'

'When you have men like Barton in favour,' Tim argued, 'and when a feller like George Reid comes around.'

'Puppets,' said Burke. 'Look how Barton switched over from Free Trade to Protection once the Jews and the British spoke. And Yes-No Reid. *Yes, I want Federation!* one day, *No, I oppose it!* the next. Besides, he's a lunatic for the women and riddled with social disease.'

Tim smiled. 'But has he duffed anyone's cattle?'

Old Burke took it well. 'All jokes aside, I can see a Federal tyranny behind this whole move, and I can see lots of blood in the end. The Americans had their grand bloody federation, and look what blood was spilt at Gettysburg!'

But the huge spaces still sang in Tim's mind.

The women came in whispering, tamping their laughter down their throats with their pleasing, splayed fingers. Plump Kenna fingers in the case of Kitty and Molly. How these Burke women must run rings around Old Burke's simple and fixed ideas.

In the residue of the teaparty, for some reason, Kitty kept pressing Annie and Johnny – whenever you could get the latter little bugger in from the paddock out the back – on Ellen Burke, and they all took to each other. Annie ending by sitting on Ellen Burke's knee. To Tim it all seemed to have a purpose not yet revealed.

Then Tim minded the store while in the dusk Kitty and

the children walked the Burkes down Belgrave Street to the Commercial. Good to see Old Burke go, taking the assumptions that went with all his acreage back with him to the Commercial. In the Macleay's lavender dusk, Tim could see Johnny doing cartwheels for the Burke women in Smith Street's reddish dust. It was his way of communicating with people.

Kitty and Ellen leaning together, he noticed. What conspiracy?

A bit of swank catching the *Terara* to Toorooka. Because you could ride by cart there easily cross-country. Even Tim could see the limits of that, though. Going on the river itself, in numbers, was appropriate to Marrieds versus Singles cricket match. A more thorough relief too from amounts owed, spirits unappeased, coppers offended. A day of undistinguished enjoyment in a paddock upriver awaited all passengers.

After an early Mass though. The tales of childhood, after all, were salted with stories of the faithful who missed Mass once for a river excursion, and drowned with their omission screaming to Heaven.

Tim at the presbytery early to renew yet again and for another last time the five bob offering. The secret, relentless intention. 'They prefer the company of humans,' Missy still insisted in his dreams. Since he kept delaying writing to the Commissioner of Police (signed 'Concerned, Kempsey') and doubted it might do much good anyhow, he was reduced to more ancient magics at five bob a pop.

The boarding school pupils left the church in two long lines, Lucy at the back, just in front of Imelda and the other nuns. Keeping the heretics close to the sisters. No rosary in Lucy's hands, no missal. Outside, Tim extracted her from the shadow of Mother Imelda, took her to Kitty and the others in the dray and rode home with her. There, full of an unusual exhilaration and sense of the plenteousness of the world, he took Pee Dee out of his traces and let him loose in his paddock – the horse wouldn't have been happy with a day spent standing round at Central wharf with a chaff bag round his neck. He would have done his best to get loose and kick buggery out of the buckboards.

And now a sweet walk to the *Terara*, Kitty on one arm, and

a picnic in hand, 'Carry me,' aristocratic Annie saying. Tim had bought canvas sandshoes for himself and Johnny, but before they reached the gangplank, bloody Johnny had them off and hung by the laces around his neck. If Tim and Kitty had been born here, the boy still couldn't have turned out a more thorough colonial urchin.

Big Wooderson, captain of the Marrieds, waited with young Curnow at the head of the gangplank, each greeting his team aboard. Young Curnow wore the whole rig – a straw hat, a blazer and flannels, and a business-like handkerchief tied around his neck to protect him during what he intended to be a long time at the wicket.

'We've got Tim,' called Wooderson, spotting the Sheas. 'The other fellers are doomed.'

Curnow was a bank clerk and half the women in town were crazy to marry him. Bank clerks happened to be such bloody aristocrats in piss-ant towns at the world's end. Free of counts and marquis and all that clap, the Macleay citizens made their own tin-pot version. People devoted their energies and waking hours to trying to ensure Kempsey was as caste-ridden as anywhere else on earth. The only saving grace: democracy did break out everywhere and wasn't punished like at home. The castes were fragile too. One bad season could get rid of the bush aristocrats, one flood, one unwise investment, one reckless act. *That* could be said. The word *hereditary* didn't count for much.

So pretension frayed pretty readily, even if not fast enough. And it didn't have battalions to support it. A far, far from terrible universe on *Terara*, under the universal shell of blue. Not yet the heat which would creep up at mid-morning to stupefy those who drank ale too early, nor a prophecy of the afternoon, sure-thing thunderstorm from the mountains.

He was surprised and yet not surprised to see Ernie Malcolm on board, standing by a forward hatch, half in the shade of the awnings, laughing with some of the Singles. This was not a *serious* Cricket Association game. Yet no social event, planned and advertised, got past Ernie's attention. You had to give it to him.

On a canvas chair under the awning sat Mrs Malcolm herself. She was dressed in white for the day, and her white straw hat was loaded with gossamer she could pull down to keep out the flies and wasps of Toorooka. She had at base a divine, willowy shape and yet was somehow tightly bundled up. As if to signal that the world was not to touch. Or was she trying to curb and punish her own beauty? That happened with particular kinds of women.

No whisper of the birth of little Ernies. She often carried a cat in her arms whenever Tim called. A not very distinguished-looking cat. In the ordinary way she stroked it, there seemed to be a prospect of the ordinary offices of motherhood. If so she had better get a move on. About thirty-five years, Tim would guess.

Tim tipped his flannel hat to her. To be a lover to her, even if he were sure he wished to be, could not even be imagined. Like the idea of walking on the moon, in both splendour and reality it evaded all speculation.

'Mr Shea,' she called in a tired voice. 'With your whole family!'

'Mrs bloody Shea too,' murmured Kitty at his side. 'There's room in the back.' Kitty pointed in the opposite direction to the Malcolms, past *Terara*'s quaint amidships castle to the stern where another awning had been stretched and canvas chairs set out.

So by Kitty's decree the Shea family moved on out of sight of Mrs Malcolm's half of *Terara*. 'Holy Christ,' whispered Kitty to him, secure in her own squat beauty. 'That Mrs Malcolm's straight up and down like a yard of pump water. Ernie should feed her up on stout.'

He and Kitty and Annie found three chairs beneath the awning. Nearby two young men were already broaching a keg. Boys would drink too fast and be sick after lunch in Toorooka's thick grass. He wondered was Hanney, who couldn't handle enquiries or ale, on board, and the wife who'd been ready to toss blame round so bitterly? Not in sight, thank Christ!

Someone had brought a banjo which could be heard forward. A few bars of 'Nellie the Flower of the Bower'. Lucy and Johnny already tearing around the place. She too had ditched her shoes somewhere.

'Why doesn't Johnny sit still in the cool?' asked Annie in that voice, as if she were raising one of the universe's most broadly debated questions.

What an august and sturdy thing a river is. *Terara* pulled away and began its turn in midstream, and at once you felt the tension between the current and *Terara*'s old iron. Huge forces: the river, *Terara*'s much-laughed-at engines. But you only laughed at them ashore.

There was an old excitement you couldn't help in leaving a wharf. Always hard to keep seated during the experience. The banjo rattling away in full spate now. 'Lilly of the Glade', 'My Old Kentucky Home', 'Mister, Give Me a Bob'.

Anyone could foretell the notice the day would get in the *Argus*: 'A gleeful party of cricketers, spectators and their families departed the Central Wharf at 8:30 in the morning.'

Ernie Malcolm came wandering down towards the taffrail in his very sporty light-blue suit. His tie was undone, his eyes lively. You wondered what it meant. That the Humane Society had not yet told him to cease being a fool. Or that they'd said yes to him, had agreed, and had false honours in store for Timothy Shea, storekeeper, Belgrave Street, Kempsey, and a number of others.

Terara shuddered and set itself against the current, gentle though it was today. The old tub eked its way around the new curve the river had taken in '92, when it had shown them all its easy, unanswerable force.

Tim took off his coat and let the expansive surroundings influence him.

Rich pastures on the western side. Euroka, where dairy farmers lived, rich and poor, with some of them taking occasional recourse to cattle-duffing. They thought they were remote from police scrutiny, those people, since the river had chosen to set a barrier between them and the law. Lavender mountains ran forever to the north behind those emerald mudflats.

Aboard, young men were earnestly drinking now. Tim hoped they were the Singles batsmen blurring their sight. 'I can hit drunk, balls other fellers can't hit sober!' Marriage would educate them on what their limits were.

'The willows,' said Kitty, pointing to the shoreline from her chair. 'They are so lovely. No wonder the Chinamen put them on their plates.'

Both to port and starboard river mullet leapt. 'Fish leppin' out of the rivers at you there,' an old man had told Tim before emigration. Old fool had never seen Australia, but had been right by either accident or vision. If his own father could see this – the spacious sky, the violet mountains, the potent river enriched with fertile silt – he'd be reconciled to the loss of children. Raucous little Red Kenna would be pleased to yield up three daughters to such a splendid place.

The great hill of West Kempsey bore up. It looked so wooded that an uninformed traveller wouldn't know there were houses and graves, a hospital and Greenhill blackfellers' camp up there.

'D'you know, we could be explorers,' said Kitty.

He reached his hand to her shoulder. 'You would be the first child-carrying explorer there was.'

She laughed that quick chuckle.

'Shea, you'll find me telling people that you've got this sense of humour. But you don't do it when others are around.'

'I do it,' said Tim, 'for Bandy Habash when I'm telling him to get to buggery!'

'So, there you are. It takes love or anger.'

She stood up urgently and grabbed his arm.

'My God, Tim. What's that little ruffian doing?'

As Kitty had, he looked to the stern and was at once appalled. Johnny in his knee pants and Lucy Rochester in her muslin dress. Both barefoot, they had climbed up on the taffrail and were standing on the stern looking down into the river. You could see their bodies jolting with every shudder of *Terara*. They had this air of having decided to do it by spontaneous mental messages, without any words passing between them. All they had to keep them in place was a hand each attached to the flag pole which rose up the middle of the railing. They were staring down into the wonderful surf of *Terara*'s wake.

'Get down from there!' he yelled, sounding predictable to himself and therefore negligible to the brats on the railing. Others were moving towards the children too, a couple of the young Singles team who made amused noises. It seemed to him that

Lucy and Johnny jumped by common and wilful consent, but again without words. His son and Lucy were simply gone in an instant. The Singles cricketers screamed, 'Children overboard!'

Kitty stood behind Tim gasping and crying out in terror. Tim knew that the playful Singles were no use to him, nor overdressed Ernie. A simple and dreadful thing to act. Rushing aft, he climbed the taffrail and launched himself, sandshoes first, into the turbulence behind *Terara*, where the children could be seen bobbing and apparently enjoying themselves.

He was no more than a social swimmer, he remembered on the way down. He'd have swum a few strokes at a beach in Capetown and another few in Ceylon. He'd swum sometimes in the creek at Crescent Head and, observing the style of Wooderson, in the river. Then during the great floods, small distances, down Belgrave Street, from the dinghy to a given rooftop say, from one hotel upstairs verandah to another, or to put a rope on an item of floating furniture. Assisting Wooderson who was the sublime, unbeatable swimmer. Now here he was going alone into the ferment of water behind *Terara*.

Before Tim's white shoes broke the tumbled surface, he confusedly saw Johnny swimming free of the wake with short choppy strokes. But Lucy on her back, her pinafore blossoming, flapping casually at the water with her hands.

A shock to hit the river and go down into that dark, bubbling mess and get at once the tang of mud on your tongue and the pinching fullness of water in your nose. And so long under, yearning for the fall to cease, for the ascent to light. And who bloody said the ascent *was* to happen, who guaranteed he would rise? Was it physics or just occasional good luck that brought people up for a last look at a known world?

Keep your mouth shut; you silly bugger.

Dark water choked him. But he came up and while biting off his first breath found the recovered universe busy as blazes. *Terara*, more massive than he ever believed it to be, was turned abeam of him. He watched Jim Wooderson commence a lovely swallow dive from amidships. The captain shouting through a bullhorn. 'All wait where you are! Help at hand! Help at hand!' Lifebuoys came arching through the air.

Johnny swam towards Tim as he stayed upright, pedalling

in the water, dragging himself along, using his arms as oars. Johnny, bush humourist as he was, began imitating him. Or perhaps it was honest filial imitation. Who had time to tell?

'What are you at?' Tim asked the boy, and the boy actually scooped water up and pushed it towards Tim and had leisure to laugh.

There was a rope within grabbing distance and they both grabbed it. Aboard, he could see even from water level, a crewman and some of the cricketers took energetic hold, and someone shouted, 'Willing Hands!' The slight speed of the boat combined with the vigour of the men on the rope meant that Tim and Johnny were hauled through the water more speedily than Tim would have liked. The river had settled though, and Tim could see that Jim Wooderson had meanwhile swum to the girl, who still gave every sign of enjoying her floating exercises.

'I'm going to give you something when we're aboard!' Tim cried to his son. The captain was letting down a ladder, and the hauled rope brought Tim and Johnny to its base. Johnny leapt from the water and was up it, deft as something inhuman. As Tim pulled himself out of the river and up the rungs, leaving the water and becoming heavy, the full weight of his shock returned to him. He had to pause halfway up and then continue after deep breaths, but when he reached the top, a dozen hands pulled him over the steely rim of the ship, and two dozen others tried to. There was applause and whistles. 'Don't go hard on the boy, Tim!' people called.

In the water, Jim Wooderson was dragging the girl along with great brave strokes of his big, fast-bowler arms. No nonsense from Lucy. She was coming quietly. Tim turned and reached out to cuff Johnny's ear and someone put a beer in his hand. Yes, he thought, delightful. He drank. Wonderful. Kitty was there to cuff and shake the boy anyhow. Then she clung to Tim and looked up at him. There was such terror in her little peasant pan of a face.

She said, 'That bloody Lucy. What in the name of all holy is she about?'

'I will find out,' said Tim softly in her ear.

'Thank Christ I didn't let her into the house!'

After drinking, he no longer had the breath to tell her, 'That might be why she did it.'

On top of the bluff at Toorooka, some local cricketers had mown the grass and raised a bit of a tent. People had placed a chair solicitously for Mrs Kitty Shea in the shade at the edge of the field. Fearful maybe that her shock might cause a premature birth. The children sat at her feet, Annie without having to be ordered to do it, Johnny and Lucy in their silt-stiff, drying picnic clothes. Under the severest orders of the entire company not to move.

'Of course, I'll bloody play,' Tim had to keep reassuring the group. Wooderson, wrapped in a fresh shirt and someone's huge towel, was already twirling the bat in his hand, playing strokes at phantom balls. Since he was an utter tower of a fellow, no one asked *him* was he fit to play.

Tim himself wore a jacket and trousers. His shirt was drying, laid out on the grass. He'd lost a sandshoe to the river. A fresh pair from Savage's. Three and sixpence worth. He would have to field and bat barefoot.

He'd taken Lucy aside after they had landed at the bottom of the lane which led up to the cricket pitch. Young men, singing, carried the blanco-ed bag of cricket gear past them.

'Tell me why you'd try to drown my son?'

'No,' she said, looking calmly down the hill at the river. 'No, I didn't try it. He wanted to jump. I jumped with him.'

'No, you're older, miss. What did you tell him to get him up on the rail? You say nothing to me. What did you tell him?'

'He went up there. I went up there too.'

'Him first?'

'Yes. It was being like the birds.'

'I don't believe you, that he went up before you.'

'No,' she said. 'Him first.'

There was a small flexing of the mouth and her eyes filled, but only a moistening. No bawling from flinty little Lucy.

'And you jumped? I saw that. You jumped exactly together. Why?'

'Men screamed at us. That's why we jumped.'

God, men *had* screamed.

'Mother Imelda might hear of this.'

She said nothing.

'Tell me straight,' he asked, pursuing old suspicions. 'Are you happy at the nuns?'

'Yes.'

'Do you think I killed your father? I didn't kill your father, you know. I carried him to hospital. He had already gone. Do you understand?'

She looked straight back at him. No evasion in the eyes. She was the most astounding child, nor could she be reached.

'Thank you for bringing me the condensed milk,' she said, her eyes creasing against the light. 'It's lovely in the tea.'

'Well, any more fuss with water, and that'll be the stony end of condensed milk. Will you for sweet Christ's sake please tell me are you happy? Are you at peace?'

He lay at the centre of a universe of women who generally went less than satisfied. Particularly this one. Particularly Missy. The others, kindlier stars, smiled on him.

'I like it when you bring me chocolate too,' she said.

'And the nuns let you keep it?'

'Yes.'

'And they don't make you say the Hail Mary.'

'Only if I want.'

He put his hand on her shoulder. He could feel her tiny bones there.

'So no one wishes you any harm. Don't try to drown my son.'

'No,' she said. 'But he does it on his own too.'

'I can scare him out of it. But don't you betray me, Lucy.'

'No,' she said. She still went on looking west. Towards the smokier reaches of the Macleay.

In the centre of the mown sward, Wooderson and Curnow were tossing for the right to bat first, while the last of the Singles were breasting the hill carrying a keg jovially between them. Players in white flannel pants, held up by striped ties worn as belts, were pacing out a twenty-two-yard pitch in the middle of the mown space and then hammering in the the three stumps and setting the bails atop them. This scene gave Tim a sense of event, and for the first time it struck him intimately that he would have within an hour or so to face some ferocious young bowler, defend his wicket and try to score runs.

'Marrieds are batting,' cried Wooderson, strolling back towards the shade where Kitty and Mrs Malcolm sat, though not exactly together. With them, all the docile children, including the temporarily docile Lucy and Johnny. Two tall young dairy farmers, each with a pad on his left leg and bat in hand, were stroking at imaginary balls. The Marrieds' openers, blocking, sweeping, pushing away. Were these two boys really old enough to be married? Men were leaning over the scorer's chair, wanting to see where Wooderson had put them in the batting order. Tim sauntered across. Someone said, 'You're fourth wicket down, Tim. Give your clothes time to dry out. Unless all the other buggers get ducks.'

Everyone, the women too, concentrated on the tall, dark-haired young Aldavilla farmer who would open the bowling for the Singles. He stood near the stumps at the northern end of the paddock, swinging his giant arm in its big shoulder. You could see the machinery of all this shoulder-exercise working under his shirt. Curnow the bank clerk placed his fieldsmen wide of the wicket. In the spirit of the day, he expected lots of flaying of the ball, hoiks and hooks and spoonings-up. Slashes high and wide.

The first ball from the fast bowler wasn't hit at all. It went through to the wicket-keeper who fumbled with his gloves and managed to stop it. But the next ball, the young Married farmer hit straight down the wicket past the bowler, and the runs began. The cricket match was thus initiated, and everyone relaxed and began to talk and by and large ignore the progress of the game. Such was the strange rite of cricket.

On his blanket, Tim sat like a child by Kitty's chair. She put a hand on his shoulder. 'Are you well, darling?' she asked.

'Perfectly so,' he assured her.

He wished the others would stop fussing, but he liked it in her, the plump hand on his shoulder by which she reassured herself of his substance.

She gave out a little stutter of laughter. 'Can't that little ruffian swim though?' She nodded towards Johnny. 'An utter water rat. In his bath, I look between his toes for the webs, you know.'

She laughed. She'd really tickled herself with this image of her son as a water animal.

He was going to tell her to watch the bony little girl while he was batting, but the picture of Lucy paddling backwards, buoyed by air trapped in her pinafore, rose and was all at once too pitiable to be spoken about.

Kitty said, 'Might as well get all the surprises over in one bundle. I've come to the conclusion – I'd like to go and meet Mamie in Sydney.'

For a time he felt ambushed, but then he said, 'In your state?'

'I'm never stronger than when carrying,' she said. 'I would be gone five days. Bring Mamie back with me on *Burrawong*, you see.'

'Dear Jesus,' he murmured. 'It's a rat tub, that *Burrawong*.' He could see Missy approaching her at the railing as, plump and defenceless, she faced both New Zealand and infinity. 'You'd have to travel saloon, and we can't afford it.'

She said dreamily, 'Well, we can only afford to send the children of strangers to bloody old Imelda. And who says *saloon*? Everyone sleeps on deck anyhow, this time of year.'

'Sleeping on deck is fine if you're seventeen and there's no storm. What if you're seasick up in that focsle with the rats and the drunks?'

'Then I'll know it'll end in two and a half days. Two and a half day's misery never hurt anyone.'

'Forty-five bob return in saloon.'

Kitty winked at him. 'Oh, dear God, he's suddenly got the gift to count money!'

'Think, Kitty. In violent weather you could miscarry.'

'Not this one! This one's like Annie! Not like the water rat. This one sticks with Mama.'

There was a yell from the field. One of the batsmen had failed to connect cleanly, and the ball had risen lazily and was falling slowly towards the hand of the Singles fielder at square leg. There was some hope that he may have drunk too much from the keg, but no, he held the ball secure and raised it above his head. Mr Malcolm, who was acting as umpire at the bowler's end, dramatically signalled *out*.

The man in the straw hat who was doing the scoring cried out to the people who were sitting in the shade. 'One wicket for fourteen. The rot has set in.'

Tim had seen few of the recent runs scored. His mind had been taken up with images of the *Burrawong* out on the Pacific, with over-bright days at sea, stormy nights.

'Ellen Burke will look to the children if you agree,' said Kitty. 'It's been arranged.'

'Jesus, I thought all that tittering the other day stood for something.'

'She's staying on in town. Old Burke's in a mood to afford that now he's won the case. You get on well enough with Ellen Burke, don't you now?'

'Will you be safe though? Those Walsh Bay wharves . . . Darling Harbour?'

'Dear Lord, observe the wonder! His concern for his little wife!'

She put her hand to his shoulder again. If they had not been in public, he would have kissed it for fear of losing it. Even though her gesture was purest irony.

'Dear God,' he said, 'it looks like I can't hammer you in place.'

Out in the field, another hopeful batsman was caught out swiping.

'Here we go,' said Wooderson, the incoming batsman. He would hold the bowling attack. But what am I doing here, an Irishman playing an English game in so far off a place, listening to my wife propose the *Burrawong*?

He saw Ernie Malcolm surrender his umpiring job to a farmer. Ernie advanced towards the keg, rubbing his dry lips. A confession of a sizable thirst. Very soon, Ernie – glass of ale in hand – came and squatted near Tim and Kitty. The accountant hunched by the storekeeper! If only this were business. Ernie took a long pull on the savagely needed glass of beer. To look at his pruney face made Tim understand how hot it was out on the field.

'Tim,' said Ernie, panting. 'I have to tell you that what I saw this morning confirms me in my opinion as much as what I heard before. As to your quality as a man. Your unquestioning response. Straight over the rail and into the river!'

'For Jesus' sake, Ernie, it was my son in the river.'

'No hesitation, Tim.'

Tim said helplessly, 'It should not be counted in with the other matter. And as you saw, I might as well have stayed on deck. The boy had already saved himself. Treading water easier than me.'

'I would anticipate,' said Ernie, dragging in another huge mouthful of ale and managing to get it down, 'that you would say such a thing. When bravery is habitual, the hero cannot understand what other people see in it.'

'That's nonsense,' said Tim. Bugger clientele like Ernie!

'Tim, you are a credit to your kind. It is a mark of the new country, where one citizen has as much at stake in the society as the next, that valour should gradually become universal. The point we want to emphasise as the Macleay is spanned later this year. And you have proven the point.'

Tim had taken enough. His son in the river, his wife going to sea, and these further unwelcome accusations of gallantry.

Ernie chose to laugh and to jostle Tim's shoulder.

'Well, you're a remarkable fellow, Tim, and I see your gallantry in that vigorous Australian son of yours.'

Then he grew pensive.

'I've noted Wooderson's bravery. There's a fellow. He'll be in my correspondence too.'

Ask him about Missy, said an impulse in Tim. If he's such a letter-writer. So public-spirited. A letter from him on accounting stationery, and the Commissioner would sit up.

But he couldn't manage it in time. Johnny and other boys ran past and distracted Ernie. He took Tim's elbow and grew solemn. 'Mrs Malcolm and I cannot achieve any such reflection of ourselves. Problems, you see . . . This is why I like to think of myself as being related to the entire *civis* of the Macleay. And, of course, not only the valley. My organisations. These are some of the means by which a life of a childless man is fulfilled, Mr Shea.'

'And by umpiring cricket matches,' suggested Tim, for the sake of good humour.

'That also,' Mr Malcolm assented, and as he did so a third

wicket fell to the Singles' rangy fast bowler. Someone brought a cricket pad to Tim.

'Better put that on, Tim.'

Wooderson was out there at the moment. An athlete from his mother's womb. He traipsed down the wicket to play their slower bowler on the full. Whack! The red pellet came singing like a wasp towards the wives, and there were cries of alarm and then clapping. The little red orb sizzled in amongst the picnic baskets but rolled away into long grass.

'Stroke!' called Ernie Malcolm by way of applause. 'How much now, scorer?'

'Wooderson 47 not out, MacKenzie 29 not out. Three wickets for 123.'

Ernie Malcolm whistled. 'Fast scoring!'

Tim hadn't noticed most of Wooderson's rapid earning of runs.

But then MacKenzie slashed at square leg and Curnow caught him.

'You're in there, Tim.'

Tim rose, barefoot, a pad on one leg.

'There you go now, Tim,' Kitty whispered. How strange to advance towards the centre of the mown area. A sort of electric otherness to it, of being outside yourself. The kind of actor you were in your dreams of the theatre. Unsure of your lines. MacKenzie coming towards you yields up the bat, its handle clammy. 'I went too much for the slash, Tim! Should have been more careful.'

'Here he is!' yelled one of the inner fieldsmen joyfully, as if they expected Tim to be easy game. An edge to what the boy said too. *Here comes a tyke, an Irishman, a Papist. No good at honest British games.* But Tim decided to be jovial, a mere batsman and not a token of divine debate.

'I want some mullygrubbers, thank you, boys!' he called, to show that he could face his fate with irony. 'Right along the ground if you don't mind.'

His fellow batsman Wooderson came up to Tim's end of the wicket. 'If we can have twenty-five runs from you, then I think it'll be dead easy. Get 'em well and truly pissed at lunchtime. They won't see our bowlers on this pitch.'

At the stumps, Tim went through the ritual he'd seen other men engage in at cricket matches, moving his bat about on the crease until the umpire at the bowler's end assured him that it now covered his middle stump. He settled into a stance copied from cricketers' pictures in the Sydney *Mail*. The big dairy farmer-cum-bowler thundered in, and the faces on the fielders became intent, their hands stretched out to take a catch. He thought he saw the ball coming and made a swipe, but there was no connection. The ball went through to the keeper. Some of the fieldsmen whistled to show how close it had been to the wicket. Tim hated that whistle, the idea of his coming victimhood that went with it.

'Watch the bloody thing, Tim,' he told himself aloud.

The big bugger running in again. But on to it this time. Whack! The vibration from the willow bat up into the arms. The ball rising up to the left of him and towards the river. Flying down past mid-bloody-glorious-wicket! Wooderson has already begun running, and Tim starts too. They are co-conspirators as in the flood of '92.

One of the men who whistled when I missed the last ball is chasing like buggery after it. Yes, turn and run again. Wooderson is. Bloody bindi-eye sticking in my bare foot. Damn the thing. Cast not your seed on barren ground for the tares and thistles will rise up and cripple the Jesus out of you!

The over ended, and he had time to stand by his wicket and feel like a man in possession. What must Kitty think of him? Diving in the river before ten o'clock. Defending his stumps at noon. A gentleman batsman, three not out.

He bent and picked the bindi-eye out of his foot. A small irritant. He hoped that his son the river rat was watching. This was how you behaved. You were nonchalant between threats.

The other bowler now, not as tall as the dairy farmer, came in and bowled to Wooderson, who gave the ball a little nudge into the covers, and the two of them ran one – another bloody bindi-eye in the pad of his foot. Tim facing the bowler again. Medium speed. Oh, he span the ball, but that was all right. Tim could not read fast bowling, but he could read a spinning ball. Again the beautiful contact. In the arms, the sweet echo of a full-bladed hit.

The ball had disappeared around the back of the wicket – to the field position they called deep fine leg. Square leg umpire was signalling four runs. This makes me a bloody citizen, Tim thought. He and Wooderson didn't even have to move. Dear God, he had the sudden eminence of a man now seven not out. Batting amongst the furtherest English. The English of New South Wales. Batting at their best game. Seven not out!

Next ball he didn't hit clean. It dribbled off the bat. But Wooderson thought they should run, and so he and Tim were running. One run. And the pressure off him.

Wooderson in command of the bowler, and the bowler seemed to know it and bowl in a defeated way. Way out across the mown grass the red ball flew. One hop, two hops. Into the wilderness. Four more runs. Applaud at your end by knocking the palm of your left hand casually with the bat held in your right.

Another Wooderson slice then. A run in it. The tares and bindi-eyes were a distant rumour in his flesh. He and Wooderson casually crossed in mid-pitch and changed ends. The cavalry of cricket. The mounted bloody bushmen.

A fat young man, Tim noticed, had begun supplying glasses of beer to the outer fringe of fielders. Accepting the amber glasses, the fielders laughed, but each had to put his glass down as Tim knocked the ball off through square leg again. Set the bloody Singles running with froth on their mouths to cut off the ball. A poor throw-back from a beer-blurred Single. He and Wooderson ran three. 'Seeing them, Tim!' Wooderson called to him in commendation as they passed each other in the middle of the wicket.

The sun had started to burn his scalp through his flannel hat. The Macleay partook of the same latitude as did parts of Africa, and the sun had an African sort of bite. Tim was delirious for lack of breath. The tall dairy farmer came on and bowled again, but both he and Wooderson had their eye in now and kept cracking him away for runs.

The medium pacer back on, Tim sent the ball off untrammelled and high in the direction of the river.

But one of the Singles, a wholesome teetotal boy perhaps, who had not been vitiated by the beer, was running for the ball like a terrier. He had an appointment with that ball, and

Wooderson kept running, and Tim had his back to the boy when he heard the scream of triumph, and over his shoulder saw that the boy was flat on his back holding up in one hand the safely taken catch. Tim was exceptionally *out*. Patting his left hand with the blade of his bat, Wooderson applauded him as he left the paddock. Johnny came running towards him. 'Dada, you scored thirty-seven runs.' The boy stood on his hands and remained like that for a time. A sign that he had all his unruliness back and would need to be watched.

Approaching Kitty, Tim could hear the patter of applause from wives and spectators. He yielded up his sweaty bat to the next batsman in, who said, 'Can't match you, Tim.'

'Here he is,' called Kitty to him. He noticed she had a glass of stout sitting thickly by her chair. *Ideal for expectant and nursing mothers* . . . Deep in the shade he saw pale Mrs Malcolm clapping, though in a distracted way. As he knelt to unclasp the pad on his right leg, he saw his large white feet stained with grass and dirt. He wished he'd been wearing shoes for his cricketing performance. The river, by taking one of his new canvas shoes, had rendered him into a yokel.

'Sturdy chap, Tim!' called Ernie Malcolm. As if a score of 37 runs confirmed everything he'd ever known.

Someone put some warm ale into his hand, and as he drank it down he felt its amber pressure in his bladder. He waved to Kitty, and then off to the bushes for one of the great male delights. The open air piddle. A lion of cricket marking the open ground. Knees bent. Looking up at the rugged filigree tops of eucalypts. And 37 runs. Bugger me! Wondrous number.

In returning to Kitty he passed the keg. Two young men were standing there. One of them held his ale glass in his left hand, and in his right had raised up for viewing by himself and his friend a photograph of a young woman. One of those photographs taken by what they flashly called a studio. The photo was stiffly backed in cardboard. Passing behind them, Tim had no reason not to glance at it. The endless fascination of the twinning of souls. This kind of photograph commonly celebrated in photographic studies with the photographer's name and address embossed on the edge of the object of desire and tenderness.

So he glanced. And oh Jesus it was Missy. Quite clearly so.

Missy with her throat and shoulders shown off by a summer blouse. She stared indirectly at the viewer. Her head was turned down towards the bottom corner of the photograph, but her eyes held the centre of his gaze.

'What is this?' he asked the young man urgently. They turned to him, but the one with the photograph did not lower it.

'A dear friend of mine,' said the young man holding the photograph.

'Dear God,' said Tim. 'Do you not bloody know . . .?'

'Know what?' asked the young man.

Tim's face felt insanely hot. The sun had burned him by its massive stealth, and he was aware of the fact now.

'What is her name?' he asked the young man. 'What is her name?'

The young man winked at his mate.

'Afraid she's spoken for, Tim,' said the mate.

'For God's sake, don't play around. Give her name!'

'Go to hell, Tim,' said the boy with the photograph, lowering it now.

'Don't you know?' asked Tim. 'Don't you even know that Constable Hanney is riding around with her head in a bottle?'

The first young man, the owner of the photograph, stepped forward.

'What're you saying? What sort of bloody insult is that?'

'The sun's got to him,' said the second young man, holding back his friend.

'Bloody hope so!' said the first one. He had however decided now not to attack Tim. He was looking around for his blazer to put the photograph away in it. Tim stepped out though and grabbed him by the arm. 'For dear Christ's sake, son, give me her name.'

'Miss Millie Holmes,' the young man yelled at him. 'Miss Millie Holmes of Summer Island. Not in any bloody bottle, I can tell you, and I resent the idea like blazes.'

To prove the point, the young man ran at Tim and pushed him away. Trying to keep balance, Tim found he had no legs. He fell hard on his back under a bare, blue, circling sky. He saw the young man's face swing like an errant star across his vision, and felt in his skull the urgent tread of many people on the earth close by. Wooderson's voice crying, 'Hold hard there!'

'Bloody disgrace, bloody disgrace,' he heard the friend of Millie Holmes say. A man's voice asked, 'Has he been drinking?' Kitty's face and Wooderson's swung into his vision, both massive. Welcome stars descended.

'It's shock,' said Wooderson.

'And the heat,' said Kitty. 'Poor Tim. Get him up, will you?' Of course Kitty could not bend forward. Wooderson could, and helped sit him up.

'He was ranting on about Millie Holmes,' Millie's admirer's well-liquored, easily-angered mate said. But he sounded uncertain.

'Don't be a bloody fool,' Wooderson told the tipsy boy, and Kitty from her lesser height made soothing noises with her lips. Mrs Malcolm had appeared with a glass of lemonade, and she was able to bend also. Tim was very careful to make all these observations, comparisons and calculations about people's movements. He wasn't sure which pieces of knowledge would be of help to him later. 'Mr Shea,' Mrs Malcolm said in her lovely, serious, fey manner. 'I knew this morning would prove altogether too much for you.'

Tennyson's *Maude*. 'On either side the river lie,' Tim told her, 'long fields of barley and of rye.'

'Well, that is correct,' said Mrs Malcolm, but Tim could tell she didn't get the message.

Wooderson on his haunches now right beside him.

'Ask them please to show me the girl's photograph,' Tim pleaded with Wooderson.

'Why, dear, do you want to see it?' murmured Kitty over Wooderson's shoulder. She was frowning, and fearful too. She spoke softly. 'Who do you think it is?'

'It's Hanney's Missy,' he told her. He had begun to shudder. He was fevered.

'That's sunstroke talking,' said Wooderson to Kitty.

Kitty walked straight to the young man who owned the photograph.

'Let my husband see the picture,' she said commandingly. 'Come on, give the thing up! He's not going to eat it.'

And the boy did, defeated by little Kitty, who brought it over and lowered it towards Tim and said, 'There!'

But when Tim inspected it the photograph had changed to something normal. All the lightning had gone from it. He saw there an altered, ordinary young woman who would see old age. A woman with an ordered life ahead. It could be told just by looking at her that she would not be hauled around the country by a bewildered constable. Hard for Tim to know now how the mistake had been made.

'I'm sorry,' he told Kitty, shivering. 'I made an awful mistake. I'm sorry.'

Wooderson said. 'No, don't give it a thought. It's heat prostration and the shock.'

'He's sensitive to these things,' Kitty explained to Wooderson and Mrs Malcolm. 'To a fault, you know. Too much of a poet.'

Tim saw Winnie Malcolm's rose-pink lips purse, going along with Kitty's judgment.

The young admirer received his photograph back from Kitty, and went and put it away in his jacket with scarcely any show of grievance.

Someone – not Kitty – brought a cushion for Tim's head. Perhaps it was Mrs Malcolm again, but he could not be sure.

'No need for you to field, Tim,' said Wooderson. 'You've done the brave task with your batting.'

Tim lay back on the utterly comfortable earth now of New South Wales. People drifted away from him, as if from a kind of respect. He felt very much at one with this ground, with the way it harboured him beneath branches.

'There's been surprises, eh?' he heard Kitty say, the words trailing over his face like fingers. 'But it's sweet here. Take a rest, Mr Shea.'

He drowsed. Of course, he'd made a fool of himself and been punished for inaction by Missy. Yet under the sun, she receded from his mind now. The whole farce of it, her face jumping out at him from a usual photo. But chastised now, he *could* have a licensed break in the shade. His wife beside him, hands folded, in a canvas chair she'd dragged over for the sake of being near.

Jesus, he and Kitty would rest here in the absolute end as well. This fact struck him for the first intimate time. No going back to reclaim soggier ground in Duhallow. This was the earth which would take them. And they would feed this ground. He lay close down to it, and it seemed to him to yield slightly as if it were in on the realisation too.

'Mother of God,' Kitty told him after a time. 'They are having a tossing-the-ball-at-the-stumps contest out there. And that bloody scamp Johnny's involved. Crikey, he has an arm on him! Where did he get that from?'

And she recounted to him as it happened, how their son kept hitting the wicket from all angles and from thirty yards out, then forty yards out. The men were whistling Johnny for his sure eye. He and some great lump of a farmer were left in the contest at the end, and the farmer won. But it seemed to Tim that Johnny had made a claim on things, on Australia itself, with his true eye. As he himself now made the same claim by his tranquil lying-down, his New South Wales holiday in the shade.

'Couldn't you just see him playing the toff's game? That Johnny. Wearing creams. You know, I won't be going on *Burrawong* unless you're well.'

'Don't be ridiculous, woman. Of course I'm bloody well, and you'll travel saloon. And your sister too.'

Mamie Kenna travelling saloon. Poshly into the valley of plenty.

7

You would think a fellow's reputation as a cricketer would pause the pace of the world for him for at least a few weeks. But it wasn't so, and he knew it wouldn't be either. The question of attending the loyal meeting to do with Macleay lancers or bush battalions had had a certain light thrown on it by the mail arrived from *Burrawong*. Amongst a shovelful of accounts and catalogues, a letter written the previous November by his father, Jeremiah.

Tim was still pensive from the seizure he'd taken at the cricket, and was fit to receive the patriarchal letter. Distance too, of course, gave it more force, and Jeremiah wrote with such graciousness as well. Famous for it in his locality and amongst his family.

'We have got photos, how lovely, how grand. You appear thin, but apparently in good health, and all the connoisseurs of beauty and taste to have the privilege of seeing your amiable wife's photo pronounce her as being far in excellence as could scarcely be seen. On that subject there is a deed of separation. I fear an eternal decree that during my life I shall never again see you or any of my exiled children – which is painful to endure on your part and on ours.

'In the meantime, it is pleasing to hear and know that your brothers and sisters are well. We have lately heard from them one and all, particularly from the New York contingent with encouraging prospects. May God continue His Graces to us all.

'The mere fact of the photos so joyfully received was near putting out of my mind thanks for the two sovereigns so gratefully received last August. And though much money may be valued, the photos far exceed as an endearing, everlasting memorial. What would I give if I could only gaze on your lovely wife and children for one moment.'

Thanks for the two sovereigns so gratefully received.

Tim was all at once turned into a staid citizen by a sentence like that. If ruined, he could always go back to hauling to support Kitty and the children. But then where would the two sovereigns so gratefully received be found? On top of the fifty bob he was paying Imelda for the child?

So where was the harm in a man turning his face for a second towards the oratory of such city fathers as Baylor and Chance, Good Templars and patriots to something or other?

In the same batch of letters, one from Truscott and Lowe saying how much they had valued his custom, but that his account with them was in arrears by in excess of seventeen pounds. From the cash box in the store, he had perhaps enough to send them a soothing tenner, and ask them to bear with him two weeks for the rest. But keep enough to hold off his other chief supplier, Staines and Gould. If people like Imelda paid an occasional token and the Malcolms and others paid two monthly instead of three, he could meet Truscott and Lowe's account in full. He would need to go out to rattle the tin at his customers.

Kitty of course found and read the Truscott and Lowe account. Other men were able to sequester that sort of correspondence from their wives. No bloody chance with Kitty.

And government interference in the business of keeping a store! NOTICE TO STOREKEEPERS ran in all the papers. Trading hours to be enforced by exemplary fines. Selling after six o'clock: fifteen pounds! The government of New South Wales trying to keep people off the streets after dark. Don't put troops on the corners – that didn't suit the temper of Australian life. But close the shops and fine the poor shopkeepers.

In any case, in this complicated world, he resolved he would go to the Patriotic Fund meeting for safety's sake, just to observe. The Offhand would be surprised when he appeared. But the fact was there was no reason, in a land where he had considerable freedoms, why a fellow like him couldn't attach himself to the same drama as true Britons like Chance. To feel for a short time *right in* with the drama – the grieving loss of a glaring battle here and there. The joyous winning of trudging wars.

The afternoon of the meeting, back from deliveries, he saw Hanney just sitting a horse outside the Commercial Hotel.

In the back, releasing Pee Dee from the traces and taking him into his pasture, he saw his four-year-old daughter Annie rise in a white pinafore of sacking from where she was sitting on the back step, and come with her hand out to fetch him. Her solidly composed face looked as though she had a complaint. He could hear Kitty singing in the dining room.

'Oh kind Providence, won't you sent me to a weddin'.

And it's oh dearie me, how will it be

If I die an old maid in a garret?'

He could tell that Annie, who got her air of reserve from him, thought that singing immoderate. A rough but resonant voice. Girlish in some of its register, full and mature in others. The voice of someone from a comic variety show.

In wonder at what he might find, he led the child inside. She was clinging though. So in they went. Observing herself in a handheld mirror, Kitty stood by the sand-soaped table, swathed in yellow cloth. It ran crookedly around her legs, her hips, her upper body, and made a cowl over her head. She looked splendid but alien, like an Indian, or the women he had seen in Colombo when coming out on the *SS Ayrshire*.

'Oh, Tim,' she said lightly.

'What are you doing in that bloody cloth?' he asked, trying to sound half-amused. 'Where did you get it?'

Still regarding herself but at least dropping the cloth back from her head, Kitty said, 'Mr Habash, you know. The hawker. I invited him in to show me material.'

'Show you? Smother you in the stuff!'

'Don't you understand? After the child, I'll be needing new clothes. You know that. I've let the old out as far as they'll go.' She patted her abdomen. 'Don't you see I have to prepare for the little scoundrel. You were keen enough on the making of him.'

Had the hawker bedecked her? Or had his visit made her flighty enough to do it herself? Tim was frightened by the strangeness Bandy Habash had brought into Kitty's behaviour, and angry he was not still there to be expelled from the premises.

'What if a customer came in and heard all that hooting out here in yellow cloth?'

'I'd say that I owe him the supply of kerosene and butter and soap. But nothing says I can't sing as much as I bloody like!'

She ran her stubby little fingers over the cloth. He wouldn't mind betting she had also bought a fresh bottle of some mad Punjabi elixir as well. He'd found the bottles in the past. Now he walked up, held her by the shoulder and unwrapped her. Beneath the golden extravagance, she wore a dress of white muslin. He let the swathes fall on the floor. 'How many yards is this?' he asked.

'I needed four,' she told him, unabashed, firm. 'I can use it for Anne's dresses too.'

'There are other bloody hawkers, you know.'

'And I have regard for what they cost. Do you want me to run up a bill? I can certainly manage that but normally leave it to you.'

Again, a blow delivered. Kitty was landing all of them. He had no chance of successful rage, since the bloody little Punjabi was gone.

'You should understand,' he told her, 'I've already warned Mr Habash off.'

'And I'm supposed to know. Read it in the *Argus* I suppose.'

The bell in the shop began to ring. Someone had come in wanting something. Kitty processed out, her small hands joined in front of the bulge beneath her breasts.

Tim was restless with this slow, uneasy rage. To help contain and diffuse it he sat down at the table and read the *Chronicle*. Habash made all a man's Britishness rise in him. You were going pretty well to do that in an Irishman. Bandy made you think of regiments, flashes of scarlet, take that you Dervish dogs! Such feelings came in handy for spiking up his enthusiasm for tonight's meeting.

Good Templars' Hall, Smith Street, Kempsey: centre of civic enthusiasms. Of sandstone quarried by the prisoners at Trial

Bay, it rose two storeys and had a Greek architrave in which the symbol of masonry, the compass, had its place.

Approaching it by the gas lanterns lit by Tapley, who had once done the Empire's time, you couldn't see stars, and you felt you were a squat, solid citizen in a low-ceilinged world. You forgot your half-shameful, half-just rancour against the hawker and fixed on other questions. Whether to wear a tie and dress as a player in that world, or an open collar as a spectator, a contemplative observer of tonight's argument? He'd decided on a tie, but worn casually, the top button undone. And please don't ask me for a donation to the Patriotic Fund! I gave all I had to Imelda. The Irish Empire. The British Empire needs to get in line.

'Sure you want to go?' Kitty asked. 'Look a bit weird you being there.'

'I'm going to hear the Offhand,' he said, telling part of the truth.

'Don't you dare enlist,' she warned him as a joke. As if the Macleay's contingent would be enlisted by the end of the meeting and marched straight past the enthusiastic citizens of the Shire to embark on the *Burrawong* for Cape Town or Durban!

An immense crowd inside, barely a seat left. The Offhand was already there, flushed with his evening's drink, and holding very visibly a notebook and shorthand pencil, recording names. The names of people whose ties were done up, the names of the well-suited. Constable Hanney patrolling a side aisle, sober and unburdened tonight, without Missy, without a bewildered spouse. And on the platform, dapper M. M. Chance, and old Mr Baylor, father of a tormented chemist in West who – the year before – had killed himself by accident, through drinking laudanum. Now Mr Baylor was all suited up to show the Boers he meant business. To give them indirectly the hell which would be delivered in person through the hands of sleeper-cutters and dairy farmers' sons. Why not go himself and bully them into becoming opium-eaters like his poor son?

Chance had a pleasant, smooth face, and the capacity to dress up his ideas in very appeasing language. He was a widower with two daughters everyone called brilliant. One sang duets with

Dr Erson, the second was a famous painter of the East Kempsey swamp and of the river. Chance was supporting her now as she painted in Paris, which as a city was, according to the *Argus*, very pro-Boer.

Everywhere, members of the Farmer's Union wearing blue ribbons to show their high calling as owners of cattle and growers of corn. Feeders of swine as well. Willing now to discuss the form in which boys were to be sent to the cannon, to the bullet, or – even more likely – to the fevers of the encampment. One little louse, after all, more potent than a sniper. One tiny and impartial louse.

Ernie Malcolm came in from the edge of the stage. Treasurer.

At five past eight Baylor got up and called for silence and read some unintelligible minutes, which someone on the floor moved the acceptance of. Ernie Malcolm presented a financial statement and tendered various minor bills for settlement. Then Chance rose and initiated the debate on the major item of that evening's agenda. Speaking first, moustache jutting and gleaming with wax, a hand hooked on a watch chain, easy command of the gift of oratory.

'The underpinning proposition of our existence is that we live in a robust dominion of British citizens, in a smiling land whose safety is dependent on the British fleet and on British military force. Thus, if the centre of the Empire is under threat, we are by that fact ourselves under threat. Britain stands between our smiling society and the prospect of our becoming a mongrelised province of Asia. For that reason it behoves us to help Britain in every season of her distress.'

A tall dairy farmer named Borger stood up and asked whether it were possible for Australia to depend on itself for safety?

Though there were catcalls, Mr Chance himself seemed neither affronted nor threatened by Borger's interjection.

'Sir, I believe the answer is obvious. We are six fledgling colonies, just now contemplating a unity of self-defence. We are dependent upon the protection of the parent. But like a maturing child, we are able to come to the mother's defence.'

Borger would not sit down, even though people groaned. Tim thought him in a way an admirable but dangerous fellow. Like Uncle Johnny, his own *political* uncle from Glenlara, a Shea family secret. Uncle Johnny was Fenian 'Centre' – they said at his trial in Tim's infancy – for the whole of Cork. Denied absolution by most priests. Broke his aging mother, whom Tim remembered from funerals and weddings in the old days. Uncle Johnny harried in the newspapers. Stuck by his ideas, like Borger, and was shipped on the last convict ship to Western Australia. Ultimately pardoned, the last Tim had heard of him. Johnny named in his honour and having the same dangerous edge. Uncle Johnny now old and living in California somewhere, according to old Jerry Shea. A soul like Borger's. A soul Tim didn't want to have.

'Great Britain took it into its head to commit aggression against the Boers of the Transvaal, purely for the sake of British gold mining interests there. And look at it – an army so pathetic, generals so pathetic, they can't get within coo-ee of their goal.'

There were now cries of 'Fenian!' and 'Papist bastard!' But despite the accusations of being fatally Irish, Borger was native-born of the Macleay and had the accent to go with it.

'This war is being fought for gold, and for Jewish gold interests! Read the *Bulletin* and have the scales fall from your eyes. I tell you!'

Borger pursed his lips and sat down in a welter of hisses.

Old Billy Thurmond, owner of a model farm at Pola Creek, and a scientific sort of farmer, was on his feet with an Antrim voice which Tim thought of as being capable of ripping through ice and disintegrating glaciers.

'There you have, Mr Chairman, the basis, the living reason for a black list for pro-Boer sympathisers. Borger's not the sole one. There are others too in this hall.'

A native Australian voice took it up, the vowels slung like wet washing on a droopy, lazy line. 'Botha the Boer's down there on the river, Billy, in the bilges on *Burrawong*, waiting for word from Borger. He's shitting himself they're going to send the boys from Hickey's Creek.'

Laughter. Joyful laughter. And safe to join in. Great mockers, the Australians. One of their graces. Billy Thurmond held out the fingers of both his hands before him crookedly. 'Don't you worry about that,' he yelled, nodding. What he knew, he knew. He cast his eyes around the hall and they lay a second at a time on all those likely to agree with Borger. The old man's gaze hung, of course, on Tim amongst others.

'Go to buggery,' Tim muttered under his breath.

Tim saw Ernie Malcolm rise immaculate from the Treasurer's chair, a man with a clean domestic and civil plate.

'Mr Chairman,' Ernie said. His medallions glittered on his watch fob, each one of them a token of community service. You had to admire the bugger, and Tim did. Would there be a timetable of fêtes for Kitty to attend and Tim to stand aside from without fellows like him?

His voice was strong but with an adenoidal timbre. From it, you could bet he was a snorer. There he would lie beside darkly well-ordered Mrs Malcolm snorting like a mastiff with a bone.

'We are an equestrian nation,' said Ernie. 'From childhood we think nothing of travelling huge distances on horseback.'

Kempsey to Comara and back, like Constable Hanney.

'There would be no better form for our boys to make their entry onto the world's scene than as mounted cavalry. I would like to move a motion that a light cavalry regiment be raised from the Macleay. Its fibre would far outshine that of recruits drawn from the slums of Birmingham or Manchester.'

Ernie's wide-set eyes shone. He was pre-awarding the medals and preparing his speech for the *Argus*, the *Chronicle*, the *Sydney Morning Herald*.

'I move too, that the Macleay's willingness to recruit such a body of men be communicated, if necessary by a delegation of citizens, to Sir William Lyne, Premier of New South Wales.'

'Seconded!' shouted Billy Thurmond. There was a lot of applause and a few whistles which could have stood for votes either way. But the clapping was a sign that you never went wrong congratulating Australians on their horsemanship.

In the mêlée of general approval for Ernie's gallantry, the tall Scot Dr Erson had risen to his feet.

'I would like to inform the company that my brother-in-law, who is a surgeon to a company of Natal mounted gentlemen . . .'

This unfinished sentence itself brought a round of cheers for the popular physician's brother, who was no doubt a charming, sportive bloke like Erson himself.

'He informs me, gentlemen, that irregular formations do well against the Boer. Men who can dismount to take shelter, then mount again quickly and be in pursuit. Marksmanship a premium, horsemanship essential. How do you describe these sorts of men? You describe them as mounted bushmen. With the greatest respect to our treasurer, Mr Malcolm, I urge that the motion be amended and that the Premier be informed of our willingness to enlist a battalion of mounted bushmen.'

'Exactly, exactly!' men were crying.

'Well why not send bloody both?' remarked a tie-less satirical young farmer at Tim's side. 'And a bloody navy as well.'

Tim noticed with a pulse of excitement that the Offhand was amongst those who had risen now and had their arm up. There seemed to be a reluctance in dapper M. M. Chance as, knowing the press could not safely be ignored, he gestured towards the journalist. Sad to see the Offhand's flushed face and purple gills. Tuberculosis, liquor or both. Would have made a British statesman if not for the drink.

'Sir,' said the Offhand in his cockneyish accent, redeemed a little by oratory lessons in an Anglican school of divinity. 'Sir, I take both Mr Ernie Malcolm's point about young Australians spending their childhood on horseback, and likewise Dr Erson's observation that an irregular horse unit would best suit the moral temperament of the young men of Northern New South Wales. We would first, of course, need to find foreign horses for them, since there aren't enough up-to-scratch military horses in the Macleay.'

There was a stutter of laughter. The Offhand raised his eyes to the ceiling and smiled with charming, lax lips. 'I ask, what is the most common relationship between man and horse in this valley? What is the most universal competence and trade which the men of the Macleay demonstrate?'

There were cries of, 'Boozing!' or, 'Gin jockeying.'

Oh the black camps. The mineral spirits drunk there! Who rode out there stealthily on horseback to beget on the black gins the half-white little bastards of Greenhill or Burnt Bridge? The gin jockeys.

The Offhand picked up again in the lee of everyone's hilarity.

'The men of this valley are above all hauliers and carters. The men of this valley, above all, know how to grease an axle, and how to get a wagon out of a bog. The men of this valley are not easily defeated by dust or mud, like – to quote Mr Malcolm – the children of the slums of Manchester and Birmingham. I believe that we can raise from the Macleay a transportation unit unparalleled in the Empire. And since the armies of Generals Buller and Roberts and French are faced above all with this problem – the problem of supply, and problems of hygienic facilities – let the Macleay come to the party with the finest company of wagoneers imaginable under any dispensation!'

The Offhand held his arms out as if to invite applause, yet there was utter silence in the hall.

'Come, sirs,' he cried. 'Men languish for want of bandage and biscuit and bullet! I refer you to the figures for deaths from camp fever. A single set of de-lousing equipment carried to the front by wagon would itself save hundreds of lives. In that sense, one Macleay Valley haulier would be worth a battalion. Given our already-expressed debt to, our dependence upon Britain Our Mother, would we not wish to make the most effective contribution? Or would we prefer merely to make the one which suits our municipal vanity?'

M. M. Chance said evenly, 'Sir, Offhand, we are all used to your notorious sense of caprice.'

Offhand however was being careful to show no sign of any caprice at all. 'Mr Chance, if you consider the skills which are invested daily in bringing down to Kempsey the large timber from Kookaburra, and likewise all the daily cleverness which goes into the delivery of cream to the dairy co-operatives, then I'm sure that like me you would be struck by a seamless admiration for the craft of haulage as exercised in the Macleay.'

'I think we may be looking for a more directly martial expression,' Mr Chance admitted.

Tim's long, thin moustache, falling in fronds over his lips due to recent growth, was a good veil to smile behind. And so he did smile. Bravo to blazes, Offhand!

Meanwhile, old Thurmond's patriarchal stance and the curious sense that his red-grey beard was on fire with the force of vision meant he was certain to be called on to thunder yet again. And Mr Chance, to stop him from combusting on the spot, pointed to him.

'I'm dead against this Casual fellow's proposal . . .' said Mr Thurmond.

Men hooted, and Billy corrected himself.

'. . . All right, Offhand then. I don't read his rag. But I think you are too kind to him by far, Mr Chance. Damn him is what I say! Damn the power of his column! I stick by the mounted bushmen resolution which I seconded earlier, and I add to it a second wing, which I shall back with an immediate donation of five pounds.'

He took a scarlet five pound note from his fob pocket, where he must have already placed it in readiness for this scene, and held it extended between his first two fingers for all the room to see . . .

'I have long been of the opinion too readily dismissed by your committee that every member of this meeting be asked to take the following oath. *That as a loyal subject of Her Majesty, I support without equivocation the aims of the British Empire in Southern Africa, including the extinction of all Boer pretensions of sovereignty in Transvaal and Orange Free State. So help me God.*'

'Is that a motion?' asked Mr Chance, in whose nature good sense and not frenzy was so dominant, and who seemed shocked by Billy Thurmond's fervour.

'That is a motion, sir. It is a voluntary oath, but we know what to make of those who will not take it.'

'Yes,' the farmer Borger called out in his urgent accent. 'We'll know that they're honest men, careful about swearing oaths at the drop of a bloody hat!'

A loud furore, ranging from whistles to groans to some applause! In a baritone voice Chance demanded and slowly got a little control back, and could at last speak. 'Yours will need to be a separate motion, Mr Thurmond. At the moment we are considering the matter of the Macleay contingent.'

Tim understood he should have foreseen the direction of the meeting: That there would be a publicly observed vote. Those who did not raise their hands would be counted and listed by people like Billy. There a philo-Boer. There a disloyalist. There an Empire-hater. Bloody awful for a man's business, such a perception. Yet how in hell's name could you vote casually for the death of the young?

Though he was willing to risk being poor for the sake of everyone thinking him openhanded, he didn't want to risk it for the sake of politics.

But when the motion was put, Tim sat with both hands planted on his knees. Make of it what you bloody want, old Billy. Chance counted the room and said, 'A majority, I believe.' But not sweeping. Sir William Lyne would not be able to be told that the Macleay was unanimous in its militant intentions. Chance enclosed his jaw with his hand, and then took it away, his moustache flattened a little.

The Offhand called, 'I think many men would have committed themselves to the fray, Mr Chance. But not necessarily others.'

'Thank you, Offhand. Is that intended to be a comfort or a reproach?'

The Offhand didn't answer, but nodded ambiguously, approving of Mr Chance's subtlety. A great fellow, the Offhand. Crafty defender of small men, of complicated thought.

Though now Billy Thurmond was enraged in a new way, far above his average level of rancour.

'In view of this disgusting display, Mr Chairman, I suggest that loyal members of the community be placed at the doors to administer the oath to the members of this meeting.'

Borger yelled. 'Men placed on doors? Haven't you heard of *habeas corpus*, you silly old bugger?'

Taking his hands from his knees, Tim applauded Borger. It was the first public display he had given, and he could feel the blood prickling its way along his arms and legs. For there was some rare gesture building in him. He was excited by such occasional rushes of courage, but loathed them too, the way they exposed him. He could never have been a willing rebel, for the reason that rebels put themselves willingly at the centre of the picture. All society's glare and mistrust was turned on them.

Yet Jesus, he was on his own feet, and Chance, out of a desperate desire for a new voice amongst all the repetitious ones, pointed to him.

'Mr Chance,' Tim resonated out of a throat which felt fragile to him. Bloody hell! Even Billy Thurmond was turned to him with something like a neutral face. 'Mr Chance, we were invited here for a discussion on suitable troops. We were not told that we had to have oaths administered to us. An oath is a solemn declaration, and ought to be reserved for the most serious civil occasions.'

Where in the bloody hell was this speech coming from? His great-uncle John the rebel, in his days as a travelling drapery salesman, calling at Glenlara to punch him on the arm and say, 'Are we up to the big life, Tim?' And that little nudge of the knuckle now emerging, after a quarter of a century underground, as a speech. 'It seems to me that so serious a matter should have been notified to us in the public advice and advertisements.'

Billy Thurmond talking still and waving his free hand dismissively. Did his maize grow so well because he harangued it? Did the cows yield their cream to get away from his cowshed lectures? Wouldn't mind having the five quid which sat in Billy's other hand. Two years board and tuition for Lucy Rochester with hard-handed Imelda.

Faces were however turned approvingly to Tim. Grateful frowns above moustaches. There was something they found alien in Billy's extreme proposal. The Uncle Johnny speech had seized up in Tim now, quenched by so much approval. By instinct he looked to the Offhand to finish it for him, and the Offhand casually responded, speaking while still seated. 'I can imagine men, Mr Chance, who supported the content of the oath, but not the air of social coercion which surrounds it.'

Tim sat. Look at them. They are nodding. And not all of them readers of the *Freeman's Journal*.

On the platform, Ernie Malcolm admitted, 'I can see the speaker's point. In addition, there is a New South Wales Oaths Act we may contravene by recklessly requiring citizens to swear.'

Billy Thurmond couldn't disapprove of Ernie. Too much social standing there. But he said he wanted his loyal motion to be put on the agenda of the next meeting of the Patriotic Fund. One of Billy's big sons seconded that.

'Then you won't get too much of a crowd here,' sang Borger.

Offhand took the final and not quite logical word. 'Let's not forget,' he said poetically, 'that our cream all comes in hygienic buckets. And our butter all is salted.'

*   *   *

On the steps as they all left, Billy Thurmond accosted Offhand, Tim saw, and said, 'Just look at what our bloody cream will be like if Britannia no longer rules our waves, sonny! We will be mongrelised by Jews and Kanakas and Chinks. An enjoyable prospect, Mr Scribbler?'

The Offhand started chuckling at that.

Ernie Malcolm touched Tim's elbow in passing. 'Shea,' he murmured. 'In view of your origins and persuasions, it might be more politic not to say anything when zealots like Billy get going.'

Ernie perhaps meant to be a friend, but there was coldness there as well. The civic merit Tim had got together through his big cricket innings with Wooderson had now somehow been cancelled.

Tim cried out, 'Ernie.' And Ernie turned and looked at him and returned close up, as if he really knew what Tim was going to say and didn't want others to hear it.

'Ernie, I'm not haunted by any of this. I'm haunted by that child in the bottle. The girl, you know. Missy.'

Ernie stared as men jostled past.

'Are you haunted too?' Tim asked. Across the lines of class and politics, Tim wanted to know, are we united in a brotherhood of concern? 'Hanney is not doing a good job with this. If someone of your authority told the Commissioner . . .'

No smiling valley till this is attended to, Tim meant to make clear. No valley of heroes. No safe bridge from this shore to the other.

Ernie said, 'What are you trying to say?'

'I would write myself but what would my complaint be worth? Constable Hanney is not properly pursuing the question.'

'Some would say,' said Ernie in a narrow voice, not playful at all, 'it's not worth pursuing. If it were important a sergeant of police would be put on the job. What does it matter? Best dropped.'

One could imagine though. Missy. Adrift in fluid, nameless female. On a bench in some police museum. Far into a new century.

'Aren't you tormented too, Ernie? Isn't every man tormented by this?'

And there was a glimmer there, in Ernie's face. Or it was more like a telltale lack of a glimmer. All night Ernie'd been playing the civic father, but it was Missy who secretly plagued him. That was a conclusion which now tempted Tim.

'Don't you go round uttering this bullshit. We are together in nothing, Shea. Don't try dragging me down to your level, or I'll show you what dragging down is.'

He didn't wait for Tim to explain himself. He went off fuming and definitely haunted, Tim knew. But certain of his power and so twice as dangerous.

8

For what it's worth, select a nondescript page of ruled letter paper and a nondescript plain envelope such as any cow-cocky might employ. And begin, printing in large letters, using a different slant of the hand from that you normally employ.

'Dear Sir,
    It may be important for you to know that many citizens in the Macleay are concerned at the partial and intermittent way in which the search for the name of the unknown Female in the Mulroney case is being conducted. This may be due to the fact the enquiry has been entrusted to a very junior officer when perhaps a more senior one would pursue the matter in a better way. The Mulroney business distressed many citizens who wish to see the matter cleared up, and I urge you to treat it with continuing seriousness.
                    A CITIZEN'

Once he'd taken this letter to the post office and dropped it into a box when no one was around, he felt he had done everything he could for Missy in both the temporal and spiritual realm.

Now he found himself reading shipping reports more closely than was usual. There were so many bomboras and reefs off the New South Wales coast, and onto one of them the North Coast Steamship Navigation Company's *SS Burrawong* might some foul night blunder with his spouse.

An hour before sailing, when Tim was loading up the dray with Kitty's trunk, Ellen Burke strolled across from old Mrs Manion's, a cousin of Old Burke's, where she'd been staying since her father and stepmother left town. She carried an emu egg for Johnny and a knitted doll for Annie. She was well pleased with herself – this business of watching the Shea children had been her reason to remain on in Central. She had wanted to stay at the Commercial at her father's expense, like her own woman. Like an actress on tour. Old Burke did not permit that.

'Do you like stews, Uncle Tim?' she asked Tim, smiling up from her place at the table where the children made a fuss of her. She had dark hair and fine brown eyes and a big-framed build, which all put the banal question: was she a beautiful young woman, or was she what people called *arresting*?

Kitty's trunk still had things that were stuck on it in Cobh. Traces of her great exodus from the hearth of Red Kenna. An uneasy feeling to see it on the dray again, a place it hadn't been in for the past seven or so years, since she arrived in the Macleay for good. Looking at it, he felt a baseless fear that perhaps a reverse migration might be on the cards. Why did she need such a big trunk? Half of it filled with food. She was going to sustain, build up and cosset her sister in the big port of Sydney, as well as having gifts for her relatives, the Rooneys of Randwick. That was another thing he knew only now to have been arranged. She had written to the Rooneys and got a reply. This had all been long-planned. A man should complain more.

So strange to drive her down Smith Street, the children and young Ellen Burke excited in the back, though Annie was cautious like him about proceeding so merrily to the ship and yielding up Kitty as if it were a festive matter.

Tim went aboard and paid one of the deckhands a shilling to help him get the trunk onto the deck. From the main deck he saw tall Captain Reid, whiskered like a parody of a coastal captain, leaning over the edge of the bridge. Tim and the sailor lifted the trunk, one on the front, one on the back.

'Christ, mister,' said the deckhand. 'The normal load of boulders!'

'It's the weight of absence,' Tim could have told him, but didn't. Edging the great load aft past the crowd on deck, he knew that there would be no adequate or calm goodbyes. Mr Alfred Howe's Travelling Variety were all – he was horrified to see – on board, returning to Sydney to pick up a train or ship

to some other bush community. Some of the performers had
yellow waistcoats, and others wore plaid, just like the Sydney
swells, the pushers of the Rocks. The women had flouncey skirts
and looked as if they'd been drinking to ready themselves for the
voyage. Thank God he'd insisted on paying for the saloon. Kitty
would have had to share steerage with smartalec commercial
travellers, tumblers, and mandolin-players. And might have
enjoyed it too much.

By the time he and the deckhand got the trunk below decks,
the space in her cabin seemed full of Annie, Ellen Burke, Johnny
who was somehow barefoot again, and dear dumpling Kitty
herself. The cabin white and panelled with Macleay cedar. A
middle-aged man and woman in there too, along with the
two bunks and the hinged washing basin and fairly spacious
portholes through which the vivid Pacific Ocean would glitter.
The man stood side-on, and the woman sat on the bunk she had
already chosen, the one aft as it turned out.

Both these people were well-dressed. He recognised them.
Mr and Mrs Arnold from Sherwood upriver. Mrs Arnold off
to her niece's wedding in Sydney, said Mr Arnold, with an Old
Burke haughtiness which said, 'You wouldn't get me leaving the
Macleay for some flippant Sydney wedding.'

What he said in fact was, 'I hope those damn aerialists and
jugglers don't keep you ladies awake all night.'

Later, deep in the night's meat, *Burrawong* would need to pass
over the Macleay bar at the New Entrance. In his temperamen-
tally anxious mind, Tim could envisage a scene of disaster: the
ship stuck there on the bar of sand which cramped the entry.
The vessel then ground about by waves until beam-on to the
crashing open sea. Seas fizzing over the decks. Mrs Arnold and
Kitty flying out of their bunks, colliding in the space between,
struggling in darkness up a canting floor.

Annie and Johnny experimentally worked the hinge to the
sink in which their mother would wash tomorrow morning in
open sea. Ellen got some marks with Tim by saying, 'Come up
with me on deck, you kids.' Of course, that left the old Arnolds
in place still. So he could only say the usual solicitous things said
by husbands when overheard. 'Well, you'll be right here then?'
If the thing named *Burrawong* twisted on the bar at the New

Entrance, how could she be right? Her brown, lively, peasant eyes glimmered. For she was a traveller. He could tell she had by no means made her last journey.

On impulse he whispered, 'If anything evil happened to you, I'd be no good for anything at all. Who would I find to go to for instruction?'

'Yes,' she grinned, very brisk. 'You'd mistake the faces of girls in pictures, and there'd be no one to sort you out.'

She winked at him. He kissed her, aiming for her forehead but, because she moved, getting her cheek. She stood calmly in his embrace and patted his upper arm.

'You're a good fellow,' she said.

'Bloody good batsman,' he murmured, and they laughed together.

A cockney steward came in and palavered all over Kitty and Mrs Arnold. He and Kitty took to the corridor to get away from him.

'There,' said Kitty pointing up and down the panelled passage-way. 'That doesn't look too rat-infested, does it?'

Out on deck, a clear night, no sign of storms. But the sea was a real meander away down the course of the Macleay. He would need to inspect the sky, to read its face, for some hours yet to know how the night would go.

Ellen and the children down in the bows, watching a drunken acrobat do pretty well with somersaults. There was some sad hooting from the direction of the bridge and the cockney steward came around the deck ringing a bell. Kitty pushed Tim gently.

'There you are. There you go now. You'll find on the second shelf behind the counter a list of the three-month-old accounts. You need to say a word to a few of them.'

'Remember me to your relatives in Randwick,' said Tim.

'Remember you? You've never met them.'

'Then you can bloody introduce me by photograph. The one with the straggly moustache. The masher one.'

'Taken to impress them by the village-load back home. *Look at our Tim doing so well in the new world!*'

'That's the very one.'

He had the strangest, unsettling yet admiring feeling that she had become so easily separate from him and the children. A woman sailing on her own behalf. There were a few caresses which afterwards he barely remembered. Exiled in his own town, he went ashore with Ellen and the children. *Burrawong* creaked and growled out of Central wharf, and there on the dark river, seen by the lanterns on the mast, stood Kitty with her elbows on the rails! Various of Mr Howe's Variety's local friends were hooting and whistling from the wharf, but the hugeness of the river and the night absorbed them all at a gradual but relentless rate. Performers and wives alike. The lantern on the mast was very soon all that could be seen.

'Oh, well,' Mr Arnold said beside him on the wharf. He sounded like a man delivered from a social duty, a civil event or even a funeral, who could now go and take a drink in peace.

'They'll be fine, they'll be fine,' murmured Tim like a prayer.

'It's very crowded,' said Arnold in parting. 'Must be seven dozen passengers at least. The bloody North Coast Steamship Company has a cheek!'

And then, the complaint hanging, he was gone.

How he felt, Tim understood, was an echo of how his parents had felt seeing them all go. A jealousy of the size of the earth and the enormity of the night. The idea that the sea holds, caresses, owns the travellers intimately.

During the walk home, Annie and he on more or less the same lines as each other remained wisely suspicious of events. Ellen Burke and Johnny had the holiday fevers. The little bugger went all the way down Smith Street walking on his hands. Howe's Variety had had a dangerous influence on him.

At home, and just to deepen his mood, Tim went into the store while Ellen Burke washed the children and readied them for their motherless night. He sorted through the pile of overdues which Kitty had left for him to deal with. Amongst them was a politely wrathful letter from Truscott and Lowe acknowledging receipt of part payment of their account but pointing out the remainder was overdue, and that he should be prompt to avoid legal action.

These clients of his owed him the amounts Truscott and Lowe were dunning him for. Holy God, the Malcolms with nearly four months unpaid. Ernie would want to give you an award for bravery rather than pay you for sardines! Others. Grant the pharmacist, more than two months. Things not good in that household. Like young Baylor a pleasant man, but said to be another opium-eater – or drinker rather. Draughts of laudanum for some pain he didn't state.

Well, these were two, Malcolm and Grant, to give a nudge to.

Midnight. Making reasonable time on a calm night, Kitty should now be safely over the bar, prone in her bunk, blinking at the dark.

That night, to reduce the world to size, he drank some of the brandy he had last broached with Constable Hanney the day Missy had been presented. He lay down with a sugary, thick head. Deep in the night he saw *Burrawong* in a sunlit sea which reason said it could not yet have reached. He yearned to be aboard the vessel, so happy did her situation seem to be with the ocean. For a better view he sat on the side of his bed.

Not unreasonably the door opened and his father, Jeremiah Shea of Glenlara via Newmarket, Duhallow, brought the girl Missy into Tim's bedroom by the hand. His father creaking along in a rare mood of levity.

'There you are,' he said. 'Dear God, what a lord! In your big wifeless bed in New South Wales.'

He gestured to the girl, who wore a veil as protection from the glare.

'Man could not have a better fellow pilgrim.' And, as never happened in the years before immigration, his father prattled on. 'Miss, here's my son?' old Jeremiah said. A social creature now, a rabid introducer all at once.

Missy lifted her veil the better to inspect Tim. The gaze was level and yet properly restrained. She was the sober person, whereas Old Jeremiah would have fitted in with the half-stewed boys around the keg at the cricket match, or with Howe's Variety.

'She knows your face,' said Jeremiah. 'We all wonder about the name.'

What was his name? And he wondered why did she think it important?

'Bandy Habash,' he told Jeremiah and Missy as a ploy. He kept his real name from them, and turned the heat of their attention towards the hawker.

She said, 'I'll put the veil back down. I get my blemishes from being watched.'

Tim said, 'I'm sorry.' But he saw that no blemishes marked her face.

'No,' she assured him. 'Not your fault.'

'I've overdone the staring business myself,' his old man shamelessly admitted. 'Well, the day goes on . . .'

Missy took the hint and turned to leave.

'You came by ship,' said Tim, staring past his father out into the broad sea and *Burrawong* set eternally in it.

'Well,' said Missy, who by her tone was used to being mistrusted. 'You can ask them.'

She turned and vanished around a corner of darkness within which the blinding sea was framed.

His father remained to say, 'How is it? Tell me.'

'I could be happy,' Tim meant to tell him. But the father did not wait for that answer.

Ernie Malcolm's big plum-red brick place in West Kempsey had broad verandahs where, according to the builder's fancy, Ernie and Mrs Malcolm could sit on spacious rattan chairs and get the air off the river. Neither of them, of course, were ever seen at leisure out there. As Tim arrived, summer light slanted across the unfrequented boards of the wide porch. But that was not the trade entrance, the entrance to take when begging for money. Tim went to the back of the house to make his delivery. He hoped Ernie had not yet left for his office, for after the angry scene in front of the Good Templars he wished to see Ernie again, to gauge him, to have him accept and acknowledge an honest claim for payment.

At the same time, somewhere, at the core of the house, in an unimaginable cool place, pale and lovely Mrs Malcolm waited for the summer to complete its course.

They had a maid, an old half-caste lady named Primrose, and she was the one who always took the deliveries. Primrose shuffled to the back door when he knocked. He asked her kindly to fetch Mr or Mrs Malcolm.

Old Primrose said Mr Malcolm was already at the office. (Bloody Ernie so industrious!) She would have to go and see how Missus was.

She was gone so long that Tim thought – with some relief Kitty wouldn't have approved of – that today he would not need after all to ask for payment, and put Ernie and his wife to any test. In daylight the demand was mitigated . . . He could well wait a day or so before putting the hard word on anyone. He didn't want people, especially an admirer of Alfred Lord Tennyson, to call him *hungry*, to lump him in and say, 'They've always got their hands out, those fellows.'

But Mrs Malcolm did all at once appear in the back area, near the kitchen and the curtained-off space where Primrose slept. Strands of her hair were coming loose from their ribbons, and though he had never imagined such a thing, it was understandable on a day like this, when any sane woman not on extreme personal display would feel entitled to let her hair stray. And yet there was something heightened about her. This was the further stage of the bewilderment she'd shown first at Bert Rochester's funeral. He had never seen her face exactly like this though. It wasn't a colour that could be explained by the heat.

'Tim,' she said, licking her pale lips. 'Hello.'

She did not normally call him Tim. She was in fact as far out of her normal character as his father had been in the dream.

'Come into the dining room. Come! Come!'

He obeyed her, entering through the curtain she held aside and standing by her varnished table while she swayed by the hallway door.

'Would you like tea?'

Her head weaved about as if to cast up the possibility of tea.

'I don't need any, thank you kindly,' said Tim, since he did not want to turn his shame at finding her like this into a social event.

'But Primrose,' Mrs Malcolm called, 'Mr Shea must have at least a glass of water.'

Primrose appeared, went to the tap which came into the house from the water tanks, and poured Tim a lean tumbler of tank water. She held it up to the light.

'The wrigglers still in it, Mrs Malcolm,' she told Mrs Malcolm, inspecting the larvae which flickered in the water like tiny, luminous eels.

Mrs Malcolm laughed greatly, walked up to inspect the glass, then sat at one of the chairs by the kitchen table.

'A man like Tim won't mind those. A solid fellow and such a good batsman. You won't mind them. Will you?'

He said not at all. He wondered aloud could he have a word. At an inexact nod from Mrs Malcolm, Primrose disappeared out of the dining room and then through the outer door into the heat-hazed back yard and the cookhouse.

Tim reached into a pocket in his coat and brought out the Malcolm account.

'I hope you won't mind this, Mrs Malcolm. Your account is nearly four months overdue now. I just wondered if you could take the time to raise the matter with Mr Malcolm. You see, it's not me. But the Sydney business houses demand payment within three months at the latest. I'm very happy to extend good credit to you and Mr Malcolm and I value . . .'

Mrs Malcolm held up his explanations by raising her hand. She said, 'I can get no remedy against this consumption of the purse:

Borrowing only lingers it out, but the disease is incurable . . .'

He must have been frowning and she laughed sharply. '*Henry IV*. We did both Parts I and II at the Brighton Town Hall on successive nights . . . Rather . . . rather neglected in the Shakespearian repertoire.'

'Oh yes. I've never actually heard the quotation before. But you always surprise me, Mrs Malcolm.'

Never more than now.

'Don't worry. I know your clients in the Macleay play on your good nature, Tim. I see it. I have an eye for it. It's happened to me too. But I am abashed . . . abashed . . .'

She lowered her head and swung it from side to side. This was bad to see. He was certain that this was drink. Though at the cricket she had not taken even a sip of ale.

'Ernie should be doing this,' she stated. 'Hell and damnation, Tim. He's an accountant.' She started beating the table with the palm of her hand. 'He should come to *account*.'

She stood up with a jerky suddenness.

'I shall get you the sum, Tim. What is it again?'

Ashamed, he read the amount of the bill.

'At once, at once,' said Mrs Malcolm.

But she seemed hit by bewilderment or loss of memory, and so did not move. She made a whimpering, and raised her hand and put her forehead against the back of the palm.

Tim touched her elbow to get her moving, to bring her back to earth. 'Please, don't go to any trouble or be upset. I should have gone perhaps to Mr Malcolm's office.'

'Oh,' she said, 'you don't know what Ernie's offices are. I, Mr Shea, have been the object of them, and know well his offices.' She raised an index finger to her lips and let out a long sustained, theatrical shush. 'I believe the petty cash is in the tea caddy. Pound notes with your name on them, so to speak. Housekeeping money. A second, Tim.'

She disappeared through the kitchen door, and he heard her stop for a while in the corridor, confused again. He could not follow her there though. 'Oh well,' he heard her say.

He disliked anyhow the stillness of kitchens in the meat of summer days, when a woman had gone to count and get money, sometimes sighing as she came back with it. At these moments he felt that smallness threatened his heart. A commercial boredom drenched the air, and he felt he'd lost and betrayed the better part of his vocation in life.

It had been cleaner and more suitable when he had worked as a haulier. Everyone expected to pay hauliers.

Mrs Malcolm tottered back with an antique tea caddy in her hands. She opened it and inspected the bank notes within. Then she selected and took out a five pound note and gave it to Tim.

'This is more than is owed,' said Tim, appalled.

Mrs Malcolm's head swayed again.

'No. We've put you to the inconvenience. We should now give you in simple decency an advance against our next account.'

'No, I'll give you change.' He began to search in the leather bag in which he carried his delivery money. Mrs Malcolm held out her hand, palm forward. It was pretty dramatic. Isabella telling the grandees to let Columbus have a go with his three little boats. Helen of Troy refusing to go home. Elizabeth the First rebuffing a gesture of affection from the Queen of Scots.

Mrs Malcolm uttered noises of denial too, which sounded like 'Chut, chut!'

'But I didn't ask for more than is on the bill.'

'I understand that. But I will be very offended if you try to slip the change to Primrose. That won't be tolerated, Tim.'

'Then I'll give you a receipt,' said Tim.

She did not object, and he got the receipt book from the pouch he carried and began to write. At the bottom of the receipt, he showed the credit of more than one pound, and underlined the sum. He tore out the page and gave it to Mrs Malcolm.

'You will point out that receipt to your husband. A credit, see.'

'I can't guarantee he'll take notice,' she told Tim, an ordinary woman with the ordinary sourness she'd been forced to. 'He has had a number of preoccupations.'

'I'm very grateful,' said Tim, straightening up from his work in the receipt book.

Mrs Malcolm put her hand out temporarily, seeking an invisible object.

'You have three children to feed, Mr Shea?'

'I have the third on the way, Mrs Malcolm. April perhaps.'

'Ah, what a creation we are! Cattle for instance can't state, do not know the terms of their pregnancies. They have to be told by the farmer.'

Tim did not know what to make of that. 'I suppose that's right, Mrs Malcolm. What a work we are.'

But with the plain exchange of pleaded-for money done, he didn't feel like much of a work of anything.

'We don't have children, but as Ernie says we have the Masonic Lodge and the Good Templars, and the Macleay District Hospital Board, and the Board of the Cricket Club, and, of course, the Turf Club and the Patriotic Fund and the Royal Humane Society. And we keep accounts at as many stores as we can. Spread the wealth, eh. I suppose that in a way the storekeepers' children are our children. By an indirect route. So we must be happy, I suppose.'

Ernie had talked like that at the cricket. It must be an article of faith of the Malcolm household.

'That's a fair way of looking at it, Mrs Malcolm,' said Tim.

Now he wanted to escape, to take his embarrassment out to old Pee Dee, his confessor nag to whom he could mutter away as he drove.

She grabbed his wrist. Frantic suddenness. 'I'd be grateful if you would look at it that way.'

'Of course,' he said. He would make any pledges if she'd let him go.

'Good,' said Mrs Malcolm. 'That's guaranteed then.'

'Could I call Primrose for you, Mrs Malcolm?'

She laughed at this. 'I can find my way around my own house, thank you.'

'Of course.'

But she stood there, did not move further into the house, did not release him to the working day, the hard outside light.

'If you'll excuse me, Mrs Malcolm,' he said.

'Yes, I suppose you've done your business, haven't you, Tim?'

It sounded as if he were again being cast as a storekeeper in a variety sketch. Meanness, the vice you found in everyone, and everywhere in the hard-up bush. The copper tedium of coins coloured the soul.

'Far beyond the price of any grocery bill, there's the friendship with yourself and Mr Malcolm.'

'Oh,' she said. 'Very well. Then you might as well go.'

He thanked her in a normal voice and took his hat and left. Outside, in heat like a blow on the back of the head, he passed the sterile verandahs where the dream of elegant Winnie and devoted Ernie sitting together in childless serenity on hot evenings had soured and gone stale. He passed out the *Tradesman's Entrance*, untethered the cart and got aboard, Pee Dee waving his head from side to side in complaint. Tim spoke in the huge afternoon, into which longed-for thunderclouds had now come massing from the west. 'Five pounds, you bugger! Gratefully received.'

Back to the wifeless store and hearth. Ellen Burke cooked a better bush-style breakfast than Kitty, and sandsoaped the kitchen table afterwards as a matter of course. So he would have been an ungrateful fellow indeed to complain. But the tidiness felt like the tidiness of someone else's house, and the food like food from a stranger's kitchen.

The store felt his, and so he minded it while Ellen exercised his permission to take the children for a walk.

An Aboriginal man, in a blue shirt and trousers tied with rope, appeared as the afternoon storms began and lightning reduced Belgrave Street to size. He looked around to be sure where he was. His feet had left on the boards the faintest trace of soft yellow dust. He had that damaged look: his eyes at odds with his face and with each other. A bad case. People sold them any old poison to drink.

'Mr Shea,' the man said in a sharp-edged accent, half-cockney, half something left from before whites came to the Macleay. 'I'd like a pint of methylated for cleaning things. And you got some of that rosehip syrup?'

They were barred from the pubs, and so they drank methylated spirits sweetened with syrup. That's why the man had that look, as if his eyes were not part of his body but were floating, without reference to one another.

Tim said, 'Not here, Jack. I don't sell methylated for those purposes.'

Every other bugger did, so why should he be so fastidious and not a practical man?

'Mate, be a good feller to me!' the man pleaded. The thunder high above and wide out in the cow pastures seemed to jolt his head.

'No. Don't you come in here asking for White Lady. I tell you that every time.'

The man went out muttering, and stood under the awning, looking to the left up Belgrave Street, to the right up Smith. His White Lady beckoned. His love. Visiting circuses always went out there, to the blacks' camp. The circus midgets with their liquor to trade. The huge men with beards and breasts like women. Some townsmen too. Cheap delights. *Black velvet*, they were reputed to call it. God knows why. Such a luscious name for wretched townships of hessian and bark and iron sheeting. But how must it be for a fellow to see the half-castes trailing into town and see your features on the brown faces of the Greenhill children?

'White Lady, mate,' the natives said lovingly. It had brought quick ruin to blackfellers who hadn't even seen white men until three score and ten years ago. The first of them a few convicts escaped out this way from Port Macquarie. They'd begun the long mix of blood. And the torment. And now everyone said the blacks would die out, that that was the world's way.

The Offhand cheered one of his wifeless midmornings by coming in for Woodbines. A sparing smoker, he lit one shakingly in the shop and very politely went outside to hurl the spent match into Smith Street. Then he returned, puffing and trembling.

'A second great rescue for you, Tim. This time from the decks of *Terara*. The *Chronicle* reports many a bush cricket match, but this one will stand out in the telling. Children overboard! The two highest scoring batsmen dive in to save said children overboard! And one of the children saved is then runner-up in the wicket-hitting competition. Sublime!'

Tim began to laugh. 'That's Johnny. Born athlete. Only drawback is the little bugger seems to want to kill his father.'

'And then,' said the Offhand, 'going on to a new topic. The courage of Mr Artillery, Lancer, Mounted-Bushman, Light-Infantry, Horse-Guards Chance. It was good to have a few sane men there to say otherwise to him and his brethren.'

Tim felt a spurt of unrest. All right for the Offhand to volunteer to be sane or mocking or whatever he'd been. The mighty feared his powers of satire.

'I would have been better not to go,' said Tim. 'It always comes back to loyal vows I would rather not take.'

The Offhand shook his head. 'Tim, they will find it very hard to get up a loyal list or a disloyal list or whatever it is they want to get up. The civilised British value of free speech takes precedence over monarchs in my book, and I shall be saying so.'

They both watched through the glass as a white horse drawing a sulky pig-rooted while turning into Smith Street outside *T. Shea – General Store*. The horse did not send up much dust since the road was baked hard now, and after the intense storms it had grown quite hot again. They saw Meagher, a publican, beefy but with very fine, good-looking features, fighting with the reins, looking too heavy for his sulky.

'Ah,' said the Offhand, puffing away. 'Tim, there's a parable for you. How decency brings its own ruin!'

Meagher managed to wrench his horse and buggy around the corner, heading towards the Wharf Hotel, which he owned.

'He still walks with a limp you know,' said the Offhand.

Tim knew.

'No good deed goes without its proper punishment,' said the Offhand, smiling at that truth.

The events they were reflecting on concerned a man called Slater, who had been a heavy client of Meagher's Wharf Hotel. The drink, as people curiously say, had got him. Mr Meagher was a scrupulous man, and concerned for Slater's wife and children. He'd begun returning money to the wife at her house in West Kempsey, saying that Mr Slater had accidentally left it behind. Such delicacy of feeling on Meagher's part was fabled. It was believed he'd done similar things before. Mrs Slater had been revived by Meagher's kindness. They had begun a romance.

Impossible for these things to happen in the Macleay without people finding out. When Mrs Meagher discovered it, she took their son and daughter and went to live in Sydney. When drunken Slater found out, he attended the Wharf Hotel with an axe and hacked poor Meagher in the ribs and the hip. Arrested, of course, Slater was tried and shipped on *Burrawong* to Darlinghurst jail. Mrs Slater moved away from the Macleay in acute shame, and Meagher was left with his pub. He limped around the bar, weary of the whispered jokes of drinkers. And whatever people paid him now, he kept. He did not try any straight-out refunds to the widows and orphans of those men good-as-dead who lived for grog. Because he had grief of his own, one good leg left, and barely half a life.

Dragging these mysteries behind him in tiny puffs of sun-glinting grit from the hard pavement, Meagher vanished out of sight and pretty much out of light, bound for his dark front bar.

'He's been to Corrigan's funeral,' said the Offhand. 'Cousin of his. Does Meagher still take the Catholic sacraments, would you say?'

'He goes to Communion, but people point him out.'

'Well, where would this town be without pointings-out?

And makings of loyal lists. It's enough to make a scribe turn mischievous. I came to tell you. Look out for some mischief in tomorrow's paper, Tim.'

The Offhand finished his Woodbine and stubbed out the nose of it and put it in his side pocket. He always did that. You'd see him handing them out by the fistful to this or that blackfellow from Greenhill. Charitable according to his means. Like poor bloody Meagher.

He could hear his children out the back, playing around the shed and paddock. Well-married, well-fathering Tim Shea. But without Kitty today. Dear God, the little buggers were making a noise. Even Annie shouting out some ditty. He'd go out the back and see what was exciting them.

In the shade of the shed, Bandy Habash and Ellen Burke sat together applauding a song Annie was singing in a reedy voice. Johnny doing his normal stuff, hand-walking and somersaults to entertain the hawker.

Here was a fellow he refused to be charmed by, the man he'd warned off so frequently. Yet the children had behind their father's back been mesmerised into performing for the bugger. Here too the protector of his children laughed in the man's company. Tim felt not only the anger of being betrayed but as well the instant fury Habash seemed always and at an instant to call forth in him. Certainly it was that Habash was a brown man, but most of all that he was an *insinuator* of himself into places, into roles, where Tim resented finding him. The image of Kitty in yellow cloth recurred to him as flaming proof of this.

Tim did not want his children to hear the full force of his anger. They were not at fault. Ellen was. Johnny sensed a change in his audience, saw his father, and stood upright and still.

'You and Annie go to the shop. Go on, go on. Tell any people that your papa's coming. Go on!'

Annie stopped her singing, inspected him, frowned, and placed her hand in her brother's. They went together. The duchess and the bloody vagabond. Bandy had risen from the log and looked crestfallen already, his face as smooth and as pausable as an infant's. No flashiness to him though. An ordinary brown suit and an open collar. The girl displayed pursed, full lips and her brow was flushed as she stood. But she looked for her age a bit defiant as well. Her hands folded, but not contritely. Seventeen-year-olds were meant to be easily made contrite.

'You have been put in my charge by your parents,' Tim told her, 'and I've put my children in your charge.'

Ellen Burke worked her tongue inside her jaws. Was she getting together the spit for an argument?

'Mr Habash is a great friend of my family's, uncle,' she said.

So that part of Bandy's oft-repeated argument was correct.

'When he comes to Pee Dee, he's allowed to camp in the home paddock.'

'Then,' Tim argued, 'he's got a better sight reputation at Pee Dee than he has here in town.'

Bandy stepped in between Ellen and Tim. 'It is the case, Mr Shea. I am not here on business. I am here renewing friendship.'

'You're like the bloody hydra, Bandy. Kick one head and another arises to take you in the backside. And besides, you, Ellen! He wasn't a hundred yards from the bloody door in the home paddock. He was beside you on a log.'

Tim again expected her to step back or turn away enraged, leaving him alone to chastise Bandy Habash if it were possible. But she stood up to him. She was ferocious.

She said, 'We girls from the bush have an easier manner than women do in that terrible old place you all talk about all the time. I'm pleased I'm an Australian, and let me tell you, Ellen and Kitty came here to have an easier manner without being shouted at! I think you're trying to suggest something else than manners though, Uncle Tim. And since you think I'm that sort of person, I'll see the children fed, go to Mrs Manion's tonight, and wait there till the Friday coach up the river.'

'Jesus, you won't! On your own responsibility? No.'

Ellen Burke marched off down the yard. Tim turned on Habash.

'Will you go?'

Bandy stood straight, spreading his fingers at his sides and then drawing them back into a fist.

'Mr Shea,' he said pleadingly. 'It seems I cannot do anything to suit you.'

'All the more reason to clear out to blazes. I don't look to be pleased by you. I don't look for you to break the bloody horizon more than is necessary.'

Bandy swallowed. 'Yet the rest of your clan likes me, old chap. You think you do not need to look at me. But you are not ignorant like others. You understand that my God is your God and my prophets your prophets. And you can see that you and I are in the same club. For even amongst Christians there are the despised and the despisers. I would remind you of that.'

Ah. Cunning, cunning little bastard.

And he continued. 'I may be a jockey the Turf Club won't license, but it may happen, since these things *do* happen, that you will one day need *me* for a friend. What am I then to make of your hostility, Mr Shea? Even a man of my equable nature can be tested too far.'

'Believe me to the limit, Habash! I won't want anything you have.'

Bandy reflected on him a while and started to go, but Tim knew in his water that it wasn't final. That the departure wouldn't take. He knew it in fact before Bandy seemed to. And Bandy *did* turn.

'The fault is mine,' he said. 'Miss Burke was not aware that there was any lack of amity between you and me.'

'Yes, but you knew it bloody well, and should have told her.'

'Miss Burke is faultless, and should be treated in those terms.'

He turned and stared at Ellen Burke, whose back was to him. She stood on the shady, eastern side of the cookhouse.

'We don't punish women,' said Tim, proud of his manners, shipped from Europe and to the bush.

When Ellen would not return Bandy's gaze, he walked defeated off down the lane beside the residence towards his wagon, which Tim could remotely see parked near Central wharf. A perverse image of their joint endeavours with poor Albert Rochester arose, and Tim felt regretful.

Ellen Burke stood between himself and the house and now turned, her cheeks plumped out with rage.

Trying to be conciliatory, Tim said, 'Very well, you were not to know. But would your father and stepmother want the familiarity of a shared log? That's all I'm saying.'

She went on regarding him from beneath the dark eyebrows her dead mother had given her.

'Naturally, it won't go further,' he promised.

'But,' she said, not pointedly, not testy in a girlish way. Like a woman ten years older perhaps. 'You'll hold this over me.'

'It's not my mode of doing business,' he murmured. She looked away but seemed to believe him. 'Except, if you go back to Mrs Manion's, your father would know there had been an argument, and ask me about the cause.'

'So you *will* hold it over me.'

'No, but stay till Friday. If you like, stay till next week and meet Kitty's other sister.'

She said, 'You can't turn it into a tea party as easily as that.'

'All right, don't damn well stay.'

'You swear too much!'

'It's an Irish failing.'

'Not only swearing, if you ask me!'

'You shouldn't bloody sneer, miss. Your father came here without anything but a pair of hands.'

She said, 'I have to see to the children.' And to show she was still arguing like an equal, 'And you still have half an hour before closing.'

Though he intended to walk with her towards the residence, she made an officious and aggrieved detour towards the cook-house. Feeling hollow now after his flaring display of anger, Tim turned through the residence and into the store where Johnny was, of course, chalking a wildly rendered tree on the floorboards, and Annie had climbed on the stool to extract cans of peaches from the shelf and fixedly build a pyramid with them on the counter. Tim didn't have the steam left for an argument with blithe Johnny. He pushed the boy's shoulder. 'That again. You are a colonial ruffian who can't be reformed!'

Annie stared at him, seeking with raised chin his permission to continue with her peach-tin construction. He smiled.

Kitty was on the sea off the Hunter River, and Sydney still a huge way south on a coastline of submerged ledges. She watched the sunset with Mrs Arnold and perhaps drank for health and fortitude some stout brought to her by the Pommy steward on a tin tray.

The children stayed in the store, and he let them pursue their works. When the Central post office clock rang six, he closed the door, as the distant Parliament in Macquarie Street decreed. A curious thing – the power of such far-off authority. He was further from the New South Wales Parliament than the outmost Atlantic isle was from Dublin. How strange the consent of the citizen to government notices posted in the *Argus*. Rebellion was in his opinion not the mystery. Civic agreement was the mystery. Uncle Johnny and the other transported Fenians had misunderstood such things.

The door closed. He faced the house, the evening. Ellen Burke's stew, whose smell warmly penetrated from the cook-house, came like a pledge as far as the store, and would aid him. Stews made a man sleepy and served as a signal of the close of things. Ambition and industry unclenched themselves, were etherised by stew-aroma.

'How do you think that smells, eh?' he asked the children, who looked up at him in some wonder, some puzzlement, as if he were speaking to them in French. They took their stew when it came. Why mention it, though, while there were still peach pyramids to be built, boards to be profaned with chalk?

Tonight he was tempted to suggest to Ellen Burke that they ought all to talk at table as if it was Christmas. But perhaps that would increase Johnny's giddiness, license his desire to be an entertainer. Tim could envisage how he might walk down the table on his hands, avoiding the vinegar cruets and the salt and pepper cellars by great concentration on the task.

Afterwards, settling with a somewhat water-stained volume of the *London Illustrated News 1891* bought at the auction in Chance's auctioneering offices from old Miller's deceased estate. He liked these books, since they had the marks of the great flood upon them. The flood waters had read these pages too. The great brown, snaky Australian flood waters invading the genteel magazine. The news utterly out of date, of course, even by the standards of the Macleay. South Africa nine years back a minor cloud on the Empire's remote horizon.

In fact in this volume, views of Uganda, newly ceded by Germany to Great Britain in return for Heligoland. Looked a bit like views of western New South Wales – wheat and sheep country.

Ellen Burke was settling the children in their bedroom. Later she would sleep in the screened-off bed on the back verandah. At the moment she did not seem to be punishing his son and daughter at all for the quarrel he'd had with her and bloody Bandy.

Someone was rattling and banging on the door of the store. He unlatched the storm lantern from its hook on the wall and walked out of the sitting-room to see to it.

At the door a man of ordinary height in an aged but well-tended suit waited. The cluster of rare acetylene street lamps at the junction of Smith and Belgrave Streets threw bright light on his right shoulder, but his square, hatted head was obscured.

'Yes?' Tim called through the glass.

'I wonder could you help me, old fellow,' the man said loudly, but then he lowered his voice so that it could not really get through the door glass. Tim therefore opened the door.

'Do I know you?' asked Tim.

'Perhaps. I just moved here with the bank. My wife's having an important tea and – if the truth were told – gin party. To meet the locals. She's out of biscuits and petit-fours and low on sugar. Does everyone on the Macleay eat like a bloody grasshopper?'

'It's almost seven. Strange enough time to be having a tea party.'

'Know how it is. We're a bit of a novelty and the guests won't go home, and being newcomers who are we to tell them to?'

'You're aware there's a new law?'

'It's a pretty poor state of human freedom when a man can't get some shortbread and sugar for his wife's party. Can a fellow come in?'

Tim opened the door just enough to admit the man. The man entered, pleasant-faced, smiling. Could of course be a first-class customer to have. Would no doubt want extended credit.

Tim asked him how much sugar and how many pounds of biscuits? Then stealthily weighed out the sugar from a bag beneath the counter into the scales. He went into the back storeroom where the biscuits were kept in their rectangular, insect- and water-proof tin cases. He weighed out the amount on the scales in there, put them in a paper bag, and then came out to the smiling man and weighed them on the counter scales as well. A conscientious storekeeper. Then he did a sum in his head and announced the amount the man owed him.

Without changing demeanour, the man produced an ornamental badge from the fob of his vest. He said, 'I am an officer from the Department of Colonial Secretary. Our instructions have been to warn storekeepers of the new regulations via notice in local papers and then to enact punitive fines for violations. The fine as advertised is fifteen pounds.'

Tim leaned for a while against his counter. 'Sweet Jesus!' he protested. 'What a pernicious way of going about it! What was I to do?'

'You were to refuse to serve me. You may send the fine by telegraphic money transfer through any post office to the address on this form.'

The man handed him a penalty form already filled out. The name Timothy Shea was on it already, and the address.

'You had me as a bloody target!' Tim protested.

'Someone in the Commercial told me you were a pretty sentimental fellow, so I immediately put you down. It saves me time to fill out the summons first, and then *you* don't have the aggravation of my presence in your store for longer than necessary. You can, of course, contest the summons in court, but it will be expensive, and I have the evidence.'

He lifted the sugar and biscuits and shook them by the necks of the bags which contained them.

'You could bloody pay me for them then.'

'No, these are forfeit. You should read the Act. Any sensible storekeeper would have it framed on the premises like butcher shops which have the Health Act on the wall. Then when plausible buggers like me come knocking, the storekeeper can point to the Act and say sorry.'

'I say bloody sorry all right,' said Tim fervently. He wished Kitty was here to give this fellow her style of treatment. Men were frightened of her contempt.

Bereft of her, Tim went to the door, opened it, and gestured the inspector out into the night. The man collected himself to leave.

'Do you ever ask yourself, if this is a fit way for a man to make a living?' asked Tim.

'You can put that question to a magistrate, old feller. And he'll tell you that it's quite fit. Show me a society that does not need regulation.' The man was actually smiling broadly. 'Consider this as a living act of affection from the government of New South Wales. People hate it when they are made an example of. But there have to be examples, now wouldn't you agree?' He saluted by touching the brim of his hat. 'I don't object at all if you relate your experiences to the other storekeepers in town.'

And he sauntered off to the Commercial, having brought down the hugest and most exemplary debt upon the household of Shea.

'I bet you consulted the Lodge at the Good Templars on who to hit!' Tim muttered for his own comfort before closing up.

The teeth marks of authority were on him. How they stung! He was reminded by a familiar spurt of panic of the manner in which Constable Hanney had also shown power's teeth in Kelty's pub. You were left by Hanney and the man from the Colonial Secretary's, both of them clanging on about civilisation and authority, with a fearful awareness of the crust-thinness of the civilised world.

Fifteen pounds just about cleaned him out. Spiritually as well as otherwise. And now without a spouse to tether him to living flesh and the named world, he knew he faced more visitations.

From his bedroom he could hear Ellen Burke leaving the sleeping children, creeping out the back to the privy and then back to an aggrieved bed. As long as she wasn't dreaming of that little hawker. The idea that she might be doing so rankled with him.

Turn on his side. Turn towards the south-east and its mountains, away from the tricky town, away from the deadly ocean eastwards downriver.

Yet that didn't save him. His marriage bed sat in the bright sea, and he trembled to see Kitty and Mrs Arnold walking the deck staring over the gunwales. There was terrible Missy. In the sea, afloat Ophelia-wise, a bridal veil drifting out widely around her head. She paddled like a calm character. Like a child of

Albert Rochester's playing tranquilly in the Macleay at joining her father in his deep purgatory in West Kempsey cemetery.

'Can't you make things go faster?' he cried out to Kitty. Pleading with his callous wife. For he wanted to leave Ophelia and Missy behind. Kitty nudged Mrs Arnold, one woman nudging another in sisterly wisdom. Men have no patience. Wanting everything at once. If they bore children, they'd want to give birth within two days and God how they'd whinge about the endless wait!

So Kitty excluded him in front of her cabin-mate, old Mrs Arnold. So Kitty ignored his fear. Like a judgment, Missy rose up on a rope ladder. When her head struck the over-vivid sky, there would be lightning. He began to yell in protest, and anger and terror woke him.

Oh Jesus. He got up and walked around trembling for a while. Despite the fifteen pounds, the smiling inspector so proud of the impact of good order on the storekeepers in the Macleay, Tim knew he must now clearly authorise another five-bob Mass. For the unnamed intention.

9

So well did Ellen Burke give off that air of resentful efficiency that Tim sheltered from it for hours at a time in the store. The *Chronicle* or *Argus* spread as if for wrapping goods, but in fact to comfort and illumine the day. *Argus* carrying a demented report that in Africa the New South Wales and New Zealand contingents bravely participated in a gymkhana on the Modder River in spite of shelling. Then Queen Natalie of Servia retains her beauty by a diet of buttermilk and by washing her face in it. Exactly what the Macleay storekeeper needs to know. Some plague reported in the French Pacific in January. Cases in Noumea.

'Mr John McDonald is leaving Coopernook for the Transvaal.' Coopernook a very quiet place, beside which Kempsey was London, Vienna, New York. So it went on – papers a great chaotic puzzle omniscient as God but not in as orderly a manner. Queen Natalie's cheeks shoved up against Chinese silkworms and sick Kanakas in Noumea.

Amongst these drifts of information, Tim remotely heard one forenoon sudden wild laughter and whistles from Smith and Belgrave Streets. From the direction of the river appeared a strange bolt of colour and jolting, interrupted light flickered past the windows of the store. Mad, barefoot Johnny aboard mad pig-rooting, barebacked Pee Dee! Not so quickly did they flash by that Tim couldn't tell Johnny had a rope halter on Pee Dee, but only that. Not even a saddle cloth. A pretty fragile means of containing all the flight there was in Pee Dee.

Running from behind the counter, one still hoped, even in a state of alarm, for Johnny's continued life. His wiriness encouraged that margin of hope which edged the all-but-consuming alarm. Even in mid-rush for the door, with the known chance Pee Dee might make all decisions unnecessary by driving a hoof through the child's head, Tim resolved at once that this flash beyond the glass meant it was time to send Johnny to Imelda. Yet fear choked a man and made him slow. The boards of the floor on which Johnny had sometimes been at least a placid artist canted up and delayed him.

Getting into the street, Tim saw almost at once far up Belgrave Street beyond Pee Dee and Johnny that, oh dear Jesus, there was a mob of cattle coming down from the direction of West. Pee Dee could not tolerate cattle. And on the footpaths of Belgrave, callous men and boys whistled and cat-called as the abominable horse went juddering and flicking and bucking down towards the cattle. What a frenzy when their beefy, pissy scent got to Pee Dee!

His flour-bag apron still wrapped around him, Tim went running after the horse. In a valley of heroes or mounted bushmen or whatever they were to be, there was no one of the criminal pedestrian cowards up Belgrave Street to run out and grap the mad horse's halter. They whistled, and called, 'Wild horses!'

Pee Dee had not even seen the cattle yet.

But the drovers had seen him. They sent their dogs out in front of the herd, which were all over the road and footpaths, and rode hard themselves to wheel them, stop them and see what developed with the crazed Pee Dee.

Pee Dee at last scented the cattle.

He stood on his hind legs as upright as some flash stallion from Aroni's Circus. Johnny simply hung free and swung by the halter. Then a sideways contortion and Johnny was hurled against one of the posts of the Commercial Hotel. Shoulder and head. Tim saw Johnny's brown-red hair flick out with the shock of the thing.

This impact cut off all the cat-calls and whistles. Men who had a second before been hooting at Johnny's peril came running up to him. Drinkers appeared from the Commercial's front bar. Miss Dynes, the barmaid, appeared while Tim still ran towards the boy. She had towels in her hands, and she began mopping at Johnny's head and ordering the spectators. Complaining to

God and to Johnny, Tim scooped the boy up and began to run, and wizened Miss Dynes kept pace with him, holding the bloody towels in place as Tim ran towards Dr Erson's rooms in Forth Street.

Tim could see some wiry little man soothing Pee Dee and leading him off to tether him.

Along the footpath, into Dr Erson the songbird's garden, up the steps and into the front room where Mrs Erson, a pale-skinned goddess used to bloody events, opened the door of the doctor's inner office for Tim and Miss Dynes to carry the slug-grey, bloodied child indoors. Erson, so often mocked by Tim as an over-active tenor, now gloriously present here when needed! Packing his bag to visit Macleay District Hospital, where women patients always found him so knightly and such a darling fellow.

'Oh doctor!' Tim yelled, so grateful that forever more when he heard Erson start up with, 'We are tenting tonight on the old camp ground,' he would greet it as a wonderful, strange, divinely generous sound.

Erson called, 'Here! here!' Patting the leather of his surgical couch like a doctor in a crisis in a play. No more than half a degree away from being a Thespian at most times.

But now he became all business.

'Is Johnny dead?' Tim asked repeatedly. Dr Erson did not say so, and yet did not seem to be ignoring the question for the sake of theatrical suspense either. He was checking pulse and raising Johnny's eyelids to see the pole-axed eyes beneath, and he and his wife had bowls of water and iodine, and Mrs Erson went to a cabinet and got needle and thread and catgut.

'He is not dead, Mr Shea,' said Dr Erson. 'My God, a good skull. Where are you and your wife from?'

'Newmarket and Doneraile. Near Mallow. You know it? In North Cork.'

'Oh, God, yes,' said Erson enthusiastically. 'Utterly characteristic. A well-formed Celtic scone, this one of your son's. Fortified by a little Norman interbreeding. A fortunate shape. If he had a squarer Germanic skull, your concerns might be justified.'

Mrs Erson washed around the wound and dribbled iodine and

water in it. Erson himself threaded the needle and began sewing together the living flesh of Johnny's scalp.

'You must watch him,' the doctor told Tim. 'He may swallow his tongue and may fit.'

Erson went on with brisk sutures, sewing life back into the boy.

At last he asked Tim what had happened. Tim recounted the sudden accident. Miss Dynes, the ugliest and loveliest barmaid of any valley, stood by the door smoothing the alarm out of her cheeks with both hands.

'You will kill a horse as mad as that, I suppose,' said Dr Erson, pulling a stitch.

Johnny began to murmur to himself. 'Hold hard,' pleaded Johnny.

'He is an old racehorse,' said Tim. 'Temperamental by nature.'
My dear God, he thought, I am pleading for my cart horse!

'Temperament is not worth putting up with,' said Dr Erson. 'My God, what a beautiful skull your boy has. Where my grandparents come from, in Saxony, a skull like this would be a relic from a much earlier age.'

'I thought you were Scottish,' said Tim, watching carefully. And after all, didn't they call the English Saxons?

'My grandparents went to Scotland in the wool trade,' said Dr Erson, distractedly, tugging on the thread. 'But the horse . . .?'

'He is all right if you obey certain rules with him,' said Tim. To himself it sounded hollow.

'I thought we were the rule-makers,' said Dr Erson. 'When it comes to beasts.'

Tim thought of Bandy Habash in that instant. Wanting the Turf Club to consider the merits of his grey. The question formed beneath his ribs. So, Bandy was suspect for his horse-passion. Yet what excuse can be made for the sort of man who expects his own issue, the bone of his bone, scalp of scalp, to obey the rules of a broken-down thoroughbred like Pee Dee? Who was this bloody horse, after all?

'I'll certainly consider selling him,' said Tim.

The doctor laughed. 'So that I can be mending someone else's head. Well, this boy may, as I said, have convulsions and will need to be sat with all night. Can that be arranged? By the way, a bruising on his shoulder but no fracture. And he's young, so I'm sure no memory loss. He'll recall his adventure. Which might not be a bad thing.'

'I'm going to send him to school after this,' pledged Tim. 'But how can I thank you?'

Dr Erson began tenderly to wash Johnny's scalp a last time. The water in the bowl pinkened as he proceeded. He flapped one hand.

'Oh, this is nothing. This is gross medicine. This is carpentry. I was prepared for far more momentous things in the School of Medicine at Edinburgh.'

He finished the laving of Johnny's head suddenly. He said he had to be off to the Macleay District Hospital. He left his wife to wrap Johnny in a blanket and put the boy murmuring into Tim's arms.

'I shall post you an account,' she whispered. Tim began to weep, walking out with the boy. Miss Dynes accompanied him.

'You are going to kill that bloody horse, aren't you, Tim?' she asked him. 'He's always backing and pig-rooting. The wrong type.'

You couldn't argue with her. But my comrade, thought Tim. My fellow campaigner.

Not all the blame was Pee Dee's.

It quietened Ellen Burke down to see Johnny and to keep watch at his bedside. He himself, Tim, returned Pee Dee to his paddock, and took the extreme measure of flicking him on his way with a branch of a gum tree.

'You're a bloody scoundrel blackguard,' he told Pee Dee. But the horse had the bearing of a creature who could explain himself adequately to a judge of his own distinction. A noble in bloody exile, a remittance man of the horseworld.

In the afternoon Tim found himself making notes on paper as to whether Dr Erson would charge a half-sovereign or a sovereign and putting it against other debts. Dear Christ, the bills were heroic.

By now, as his son lay under the watchfulness of Ellen Burke, plump-with-child Kitty would be at the wharf, seeing SS *Iris* heave into the Semi-Circular Quay over Sydney's bright water.

Kitty innocent, and waving to her sister. Putting on a cockney scream as a joke. 'Oi to you, Mamie!'

When she came back, she might bloody persuade me to shoot my brother, the horse!

And he would meet her at the boat and say, 'I think it's time Johnny began schooling. Can't be trusted around horses or boats or rivers. Needs the Joyful and Sorrowful Mysteries, including an occasional Sorrowful Mystery across the arse from Mother Imelda.'

He'd returned from deliveries to find Johnny a little fevered and muttering – this is what Ellen Burke reported – but nothing too severe. Then into the store to wait the normal afternoon tea rush, on whose tail-end the man from the Colonial Secretary's had craftily tacked himself.

He saw Ernie Malcolm stride out of Smith Street from the direction of his office. Oh, Jesus, Tim thought. I'm going to be given credit for carrying my own bleeding son to Dr Erson's. And yet there was a change in manner here. It made you wonder the way Ernie was walking in his light grey suit. He didn't look as open to any rumour of brave service, any chance for civil pride, as he usually did.

There was a child in the store with a note when Ernie stepped in. Ernie offered no background greeting, but concerned himself with the labels of the biscuit cans, the hams, the treacles and the puddings on the further wall near the storeroom. But Ernie's reading of labels was only a way of banking some urgency he had in him.

The child left. Ernie looked at Tim. His head had an unusual angle. Not the angle of expecting the best of the best of all possible citizens in the best of all possible Empires. It was some other, more private and dangerous angle.

'Mr Malcolm,' said Tim.

'Mr Shea, I take it very badly that you impose yourself on Mrs Malcolm in this way.'

'What way is that?'

'Certainly I am happy to pay my way, and I don't think any man's ever said otherwise. But I find my wife has been in a moment of illness gouged for extra money, more than due. This makes me wonder about my judgment on you. Makes me more disposed, too, to listen to other buggers whose judgment of you isn't as high as mine. If the terms were Cash On Delivery, and you'd made them clear to me, that would have been acceptable. But Cash Before Delivery . . . well, they're terms of trade I haven't heard of before.'

Tim shook his head. 'Oh, God, Ernie,' he said. 'I was uneasy about that extra payment, and I never asked for it.'

'Well, you would say that. And if you do say it, what am I supposed to believe about my wife?'

'I think your wife may have been a bit indisposed that afternoon. That was behind the extra money. But I expect you to believe she didn't pay it at *my* suggestion.'

Of course, he should have taken the extra to Ernie's office, but the man from the Colonial Secretary's had certainly put that idea fair out of his head.

'I'm not going to hang around while you do your sums,' said Mr Ernie Malcolm, flushed. 'But I expect a full accounting of where we stand at the moment and a refund. I think you'll understand if I transfer my account here to some other shop.'

'Oh God, Mr Malcolm.'

The fellow seemed to be pleased to have an excuse for anger though. This was the next step along the road of warnings Ernie began after the loyal meeting. It was more. A punishment for suggesting Ernie write about Missy.

'I have to caution you, there are those who think you are a pretty subtle feller, a cunning paddy. A joker behind it all. I'll be more disposed to listen to them now.'

He tucked the fingers of one hand into the base of his vest, tugged it downwards, and walked for the door, turning at the end of course for the required final word.

'All awards for bravery are in abeyance,' he said.

Then he rushed out.

To hear his social credit cancelled in that way! Tim clutched the counter and groaned. He was in severe trouble now in his chosen place in New South Wales. A damaged son, an absent wife, a significant client, an exemplary fine. Apparitions to be dealt with by night. He was no longer the happy immigrant. The world had pretty thoroughly found him out on the Macleay.

*   *   *

And yet just one more dusk and Kitty and Mamie would board *Burrawong* in Darling Harbour, in the port of Sydney. They would drink stout beforehand in some hotel in Sussex Street and catch a cab down to the boat. *Burrawong* the humble, old iron midwife of all their arrivals and returns. *Burrawong* might plough up the coast in record time for all a man knew. Might put in by midnight Thursday.

Sitting by Johnny's bed, Tim felt the wheels of night turn so minutely. He imagined the dark, slow weight of time seeping into the split in Johnny's scalp. All to the good, all to the good! He kept a wet cloth on the boy's brow. Coolness a known aid against convulsions. Beyond the window, the last light was on the river, which seemed set and inert in its dark green silty mass.

Across the room Annie slept a dignified, unfevered, steadfast sleep.

'England,' he read for consolation in the *Chronicle*, 'pays seventy million pounds a year for Australian butter. The three criteria of good butter, as applied by judges at Agricultural and Horticultural Shows through the civilised world, are flavour, aroma and grain. Lack of farm hygiene and contaminated containers are the great enemy of these three vaunted qualities . . .'

The night air pressing on Johnny's much-praised Celtic scalp was soft and warm and gracious. 'Bless it,' said Tim. 'Bless it!'

At the window however, Missy bowed in, pale-eyed. Tim looked at her not with a sense of terror but with something more familiar.

'Out to sea,' she said genially, though he wondered was it a threat.

He felt the room itself reach down into a trough, like a hearty old steamer taking on the first complexity of the open Pacific beyond the New Entrance. Like an echo of the sea, a spray of air broke over him. The square, unseaworthy room whirled, and again he saw *Burrawong* by day, in the blue Pacific with the two distant Kenna sisters, the known and unknown one, Kitty and Mamie, grinning at the rails. As the room bucked, Annie and Johnny kept solidly to their cots. Anchored. He saw a sky of stars, but then the window took a swing down and caught Red Kenna's loud fire-lit kitchen.

'Well, you don't expect me to take the bugger too seriously,' called Red to him.

Shudder. Another wave taking the room. Albert Rochester galloped through Glenrock up a hill. Serious but intact, carnation in lapel, on his way to Mrs Sutter. Johnny ran with strange Lucy into some surf as three agile rats came over the windowsill, but then couldn't be seen. Missy re-entered from the hallway and passed by Johnny's bed. A normal tread. She hadn't come to point any doomy finger. When the room pitched, she fell in her black dress from the window.

All stopped rolling. Tim stood up in relief and Johnny snorted.

'Dear God,' said Tim, sitting down and picking up the *Chronicle*, which had fallen to the floor from all the room's gyrations.

'Oh, Kitty,' he pleaded.

While his son swam down to profounder sleep.

Tim woke on the floor of the childrens' room in the silken first light. The children slept heroically. Give them a medal, Mr Malcolm, you old bastard.

He remained stiffly where he was and could soon hear energetic hammering from somewhere outside.

Oh he knew! They'd started again the daily work of putting down the planking over the pylons of the bridge. It had happened suddenly after all the work of sinking columns, and now less than seventy yards from his door, the bridge had taken on a surprising reality, making its first small but conclusive flight above the river. Perhaps three dozen men in flannel shirts and big hats hammering and bolting the carriageway to the pylons and joists. Drills and auger bits spun beneath their hands. This was civilisation, and you could foresee the completed physical bridge now from what they had done. East and Central and West being made one by a lot of scrawny men with hammers. The community would come to take this convenient arrangement as a given, putting down its weight with confidence.

He went and got some tea and took it to the storefront to watch the labourers in the high middle distance. Out in Belgrave Street a number of boys appeared, running up with news-sheets in their hands. A *Chronicle* special, Tim could see. No bigger than a poster for a concert. Tim went to the door, opened it, and bought one.

He took it back off the street and into the shade of the store to read.

The news-sheet said, *PLAGUE OUTBREAK IN SYDNEY*.

An epidemic of bubonic plague, Tim read, the terrible Black Death of the Middle Ages, broken out in the port of Sydney. Believed the disease has made its way into the town through infected rats arriving on freighters from a number of Chinese ports . . . the United States vessel *Mindanao* aboard which the first victim, a seaman, perished ten days ago in Sydney Harbour . . .

'Dear God almighty!' murmured Tim to the now awakened street, to the industrious bridge-builders on whose labours he had so recently been congratulating himself and society. Kitty had found infallibly the time and place of greatest peril. Sweat flooding all his pores here in the shade – some sort of sympathetic fever. He was powerless before the lavish distance which lay between Kitty and him.

The news-sheet then alarmed him further by claiming to know who was the first Sydney victim. A Mr Gleason, licensee of the Hunter River Inn in Sussex Street. He had taken ill the previous Thursday, and he and seventeen contacts had been sealed up in the inn. Two members of the Benson-Howard wedding party in the Rocks on Saturday afternoon, a young man of seventeen years and another of nineteen, took sick before midnight and were dead of the most sudden and violent form of plague – pneumonic plague – before the end of church on Sunday. The entire wedding party had been moved to the quarantine station. A woman in Darling Harbour who had sickened on Sunday had been sealed up in her house with nine contacts, and a young wife from a boarding house on Margaret Street with eleven contacts had been taken sick.

A British plague expert, Dr Hugh Mortonson, who had helped combat an outbreak in Calcutta two years before, had been sent for, and Doctor Silver, a Brisbane expert on tropical diseases, had made a long statement about oxygen and the plague. 'Oxygen is a deadly foe of the plague . . .' Fumigating teams were being sent into houses in the Rocks . . . and rats bearing signs of the plague, though few in number, had been found in areas of Darling Harbour. The fur of rats suffering from plague turned grey and then fell out . . . Onset of pneumonic plague was very sudden, beginning with the normal signs of a cold or fever and progressing through extreme temperatures and great difficulty in breathing to an utter collapse of the system . . .

Another collapse of the system. In streets where Kitty walked with Mamie, congratulating her on her Australian landfall!

Inside to the dining room to finish reading of the disaster. Spreading the sheet on Kitty's table. The North Coast Steamship Navigation Company had announced that all its vessels would be fumigated before departure from Sydney. Captains of the steamship company's vessels had been instructed to co-operate fully with the local requirements of the sanitation inspectors of the North Coast settlements serviced by the those vessels . . . *Burrawong* upon arrival at the New Entrance would have its passengers and freight transferred to droghers for the eventual journey downriver. Hence direct contact between *Burrawong* and Kempsey itself would cease.

It had already been decided by the Macleay Shire sanitation officials that passengers arriving from Sydney would be put ashore near the Pilot Station and detained there for a week.

Looking out over Trial Bay and waiting to see if they had plague or not!

With all this information spread on the table before him, Tim could not avoid the crazed suspicion that wilfully Kitty had put herself in the way of such giant dangers from the East! Rather, the North for Australians. The feared, the deadly Asiatic North. Cockpit of every strangeness and disease.

He took the news-sheet one further step, out through the residence and into the back garden where Annie, awakened by now but still in a night dress, was watching a weary Ellen Burke drinking tea. He handed the sheet to Ellen, who could see at once that it stood for something weightier than their squabble over Habash.

'I don't know what this means,' said Tim.

Yet surely Kitty would come back. There was enough oxygen in her even for Dr Silver of Brisbane.

Before Johnny's dizziness fully went, but while he was still reflective, Tim asked Ellen Burke to dress him up, including putting a little pair of oxfords on his feet, which would show he had caring parents. Then, given he was delivering his gratis supplies to Imelda, he took the bandaged Johnny with him on the cart.

Imelda didn't blink, of course. In the big front parlour where bishops had tea – His Lordship lording it – Imelda said thrippence a week as if Tim was a stranger, and hadn't just delivered the next week's food and sandsoap round the back.

Tim sent Johnny outside to wait in the wagon. 'And don't touch the horse!'

When the boy left, Tim said, 'I wanted to know about Lucy. What kind of pupil is she?'

'She's in the better half,' said Imelda. 'And her work is very tidy.'

'She does not talk much to me. Does she talk much here?'

'No. Yet that is always valuable in a student.'

Yes, he could have said. And something strange as buggery too. Lucy's silences were not like Johnny's. They were silences crammed with something pressing to be uttered.

'Does she get herself into danger, Mother? Do you find her climbing things, say.'

'You know we don't let the girls climb or jump off heights. That is what parents are paying the convent for. As well, of course, as communicating the Faith.'

'When she meets up with my son, they both tend to climb things. You may have read they fell together from *Terara*. They must set each other off.' He could too readily imagine Imelda giving Johnny what-for with a cane for this. So he said, 'When they climb things together, you get the clear idea Lucy's not being led. She's a stronger soul altogether than Johnny. But you'd never guess it. Looking at her when she's sitting down drinking tea. I think you could tell the nuns to keep them apart.'

Imelda nodded, her head concedingly on its side. Was her scalp shaven under that great black hood? What a sight that would make!

A great joy for Tim to make these little arrangements today, the day *Burrawong* would be fumigated in Sydney Harbour, Kitty and her sister would be coming aboard laughing once the fumes cleared, the last of the odour twitching at their nostrils.

The fifteen quid writ awaited him and he had another week to pay. Society looked sideways at him. Missy remained in Hanney limbo from which the Commissioner in Sydney must now be giving orders that she be rescued and at least put into the hands of Sergeant Fry. Altogether, given the present cast of the world, it was soothing to be able to arrange a thing or two. To tell the nuns not to let Johnny and Lucy go together on ledges.

10

It was known that Dr Erson and the Macleay Shire Sanitation Officer Mr D. Stevens had visited the quarantine camp, which the citizens of Kempsey had begun to call 'the plague camp', and had reported all quarantined passengers in good condition. The camp conditions were comfortable, they claimed – and Tim now tended to believe Erson's announcements – and passengers' clothing had all been boiled up in camp coppers. Even suits had not been exempt, since lives were at stake. Dr Erson and Mr Stevens had worn white masks during the inspection.

As Dr Erson told the *Chronicle*, the physicians of the Macleay were one in believing, as progressive opinion did, that the disease was caused by the bites of fleas and transmitted by the exhalations of sufferers. After the quarantine period, however, which was hoped to be no longer than ten days if the plague did not manifest itself amongst *Burrawong*'s passengers, the passengers could all be approached without fear and without white masks. The plague, said Erson with his Saxon or Scots good reason, was not a matter of superstition but of sensible behaviour.

After a week of quarantine, during which no bad news came upriver to town, Tim was beginning to feel grudging reliance on Dr Erson's hopeful manner. He stood by his counter and congratulated himself on every passed hour of commerce.

One afternoon, wearing a clean, starched white shirt and a neat grey coat and pants which just the same had plenty of the dust of the Macleay's roads impacted into the weave, Bandy Habash crossed the diagonal from the Post Office to *T. Shea* and then actually entered the store, his thin hand held delicately high to encourage peace.

'I know what you have told me, Mr Shea. But I happen to have some items close to your heart.'

His hand still held up, with the other he took a wadded document out of the left bottom pocket of his jacket.

'These letters have been aired,' he assured Tim and – by displaying them also in the direction of Belgrave Street – anyone unseen who happened to be a witness. Such well-modulated motions, running like silk. His voice was like silk lain over a woman's shoulders.

'The quarantine period is only seven days in true terms. It seems the passengers are all well with that period expired. This is from Mrs Kitty.'

'You've seen her?' Tim asked.

The man was everywhere, and had forestalled him again.

'I was able to trade with people from the plague camp on the South West Rocks Road.'

'I suppose you sell them all sorts of herbal rubbish.'

'I sold some jasmine and camomile tea. But not much. The people are in excellent health and not anticipating an outbreak.'

Tim took the pages from Bandy and felt the slight shock of risk which they possessed. He would not open them in front of the Punjabi. But he could envisage Red Kenna's daughters loudly trading with Bandy at the green wagon parked on a sandy road amongst paperbarks.

Kitty: 'What do you have for the awful tedium of sitting in the bush, Mr Habash? And something for my sister please, so she can get one of the big old blokes upriver crazy for her!'

'Wait by the door there,' Tim told Bandy. He might need to send a reply to Kitty.

Tim took the letter into the storeroom to read it. Safe in the hempen sweet perfume of the sugar bags, which despite everything was a fragrance associated with riches! He sat on a bag of sago and delicately unwrapped the pages.

'Dearest husband,

'What a turnup, would you say. Mamie and self in the utter pink. Mamie calls it an adventure to tell the Kennas about this camping on the banks of Australian rivers! Are the little ones asking? Their mama is just delayed a little time bringing up their new Aunt. I have grown bigger in the ten days, Tim. Will you want a new woman? Ha! Doctor Erson and Sanitation Clerk met the ship and told the captain to take all maskings and facings and lumbers down so that ship could be totally searched for the dead rats. A job bigger than the pyramids say the wits. We were in meantime shipped ashore on a drogher where tents were set up and groceries provided. Some I hope to God from *Timothy Shea – General Store*, but suspect it's the Masons again and that Good Templar crowd looking after their own, so it's probably Bryant's tea and damper we're getting by on. All our luggage is with us, and if yourself were too would be happy to live on here though insects pretty thick and men bringing in brown snakes every ten minutes, the loathsome things. Johnny would scare the venom out of them I imagine.

'Two days time Dr Erson will come back to see if rats found onboard carried the plague. Mamie and self inspected clothes closely and no fleas on us.

'Blessed Mother watch over you and keep you safe from smart merchants like Mrs Malcolm. Blessed Mother keep Johnny from jumping into things.

'Know you don't like Mr Habash. But who else to take a note? So give him fair play.

XXXX Kitty'

He emerged from the storeroom, half-ashamed to face Habash. His desire to see Kitty might be discernible. Bandy seemed to read him anyhow, and nodded.

'I have two fine horses. The grey you remember. My gelding as well. I do not want to make unwelcome offers, though.'

'You're going again?'

'If you are, Mr Shea.'

So easy to see the fellow as an ally now, and Tim barely resisted it.

'I could not go till dusk. And I would need to leave Miss Burke here with the children.'

Bandy screwed up his eyes and took thought. 'It is a safe

township,' he said. 'They would be secure. However, yet again I do not wish to have my gestures mistaken for butting in.'

The little bugger had him on toast.

Tim said, 'I could rent horses, but that would be all over town. And Pee Dee . . . in spite of his bloodlines . . . he's not the horse for a fifty mile round-trip.'

'That's clear to everyone,' said Bandy.

'I will pay you for a horse.'

'Please, sir.'

'No, I'll pay.'

'I intended to go anyhow. I have business. Packages to deliver.'

'Wait then, will you?' he asked. Politeness. He might as well try that, since the hawker seemed to flourish on hostility.

Tim went to see Ellen Burke in the kitchen at the back of the house. He weighed the hard light in her eye as she listened, frowning a little. '. . . and tell people I'll deliver tomorrow afternoon.'

'But how can you after more than twenty miles there and twenty back? You'll rest here and I'll make deliveries.'

'No,' he said. 'No. I'll put in my normal day.'

She looked away across the room, to the wall on which molten light within the oven was reflecting. She was the sort of robust girl who very much liked to think of herself as a possible cartwoman.

'So,' she said. 'Some people are allowed to travel and talk with Mr Habash then?'

'This is a different case, miss,' Tim warned her.

'Is that what it is?' she asked. She began feeding the fire with split wood. 'I'll be very pleased if when I am married seven years, a man will do a mad ride for me just to spend an hour.'

From a seventeen-year-old, this was an astounding observation. Just the same, someone was sure to do it for Ellen, for her big bones and her ironic tongue.

'You're not going to bring us back the plague, are you?' she asked.

'No. The seven days are more than up. There is, thank God, no plague out there.' He smiled at her. 'Do you fight with my sister-in-law, Molly? I bet you fight like blazes.'

'Sometimes. We're like sisters, you see. Putting up with my father. I'll make you a quart of stew to take to Kitty.'

He would take some condensed milk too, in case the quarantine groceries didn't cover that. Kitty liked condensed milk in her tea best of all. She had that in common with Lucy. She would acclaim condensed milk, breathing out through her broad lips.

Back in the store, Tim and Bandy made their arrangements for after closing. 'I shall be back with both horses,' Bandy promised formally.

Johnny's dawdling manner of returning home from school showed he fancied himself as a schoolboy and that Imelda was not a terror to him. It was to be hoped someone would be. His bandage was still in place, but it had ochre dust on it. His eyes looked clear, which was what counted. So don't enquire into the history of his day.

Annie, sipping her own tea, watched Tim narrowly with wide brown eyes.

'Father,' she enquired, 'are *you* going to leave us now?'

At the stove, Ellen Burke covered her mouth with a hand.

'I'm going to see Mama. Back tomorrow. Tell you what, I'll leave that friend of mine with you.' He turned to his right and theatrically pushed towards her that phantom spirit which had attended him in North Cork and supposedly emigrated with him.

'There,' he said. 'Look after Annie, and answer all her questions.'

The child said to the vacancy and to Tim, 'I've got a question then. Will we have treacle duff?'

'It happens I was going to make sago pudding,' said Ellen Burke. 'But something or other told me treacle duff!'

Bandy shamed him by bringing the horses the back way, not down Belgrave Street to the front of the shop, but by laneways across the hip of river bank behind the main thoroughfare. All to save Tim embarrassment. The grey mare, the bay gelding. Two horses neat as skiffs. Not bloated and gone slack with the Macleay's easy grass. All the quiet energy Bandy put into keeping these horses up to the mark!

Seeing him coming from a window, Tim ducked out of the back of the house to greet him. 'You could have come the front,' he called.

'That manner of proceeding leaves people knowing all our business, old chap,' said Bandy, touching his nose with the finger of a hand which still held the grey's reins.

A man could have asked him then, why tell the *Chronicle* about our bumbling rescue of Albert? But who could be so crude to a fellow who had delivered two such wonderful horses to your door?

'Please, come into the kitchen for some tea. Talk to Ellen Burke and wait for me to pack a saddlebag.'

Bandy put his head on the side and closed one eye. 'It will be one or two in the morning before we reach the quarantine camp. If you wanted a rest first or . . .?'

Tim decided to shave and even then found himself hoping that the town, closing for business now, seeing him and Bandy ride together to the river punt, wouldn't use it as an excuse to say, 'There he goes. Fine thing. One day extorting money from Mrs Malcolm, doing business with the hawker the next.'

'The trouble with you,' he told his mirror, the receptor of his discourse, 'is that you're stuck halfway between a madman and a cagey bugger.'

Wrap the stew in a big cloth, then in a sealskin bag. Ignore its then resemblance to Hanney's package. Chocolate and condensed milk and some Norwegian sardines. A copy of the *Messenger of the Sacred Heart*, which Kitty must have ordered at Mass one Sunday, and which had turned up two days after she left – took the lazy buggers at the post office that long to sort and deliver the mail which had come on *Burrawong*. Then he stood in the store, looking about him at the shelves. What else to take Red Kenna's beloved daughter? He used the opportunity of the customerless store to readjust his breeches and privates for the punishing ride.

At last, outside the back door with Pee Dee whickering at the two fine horses from his paddock, Tim drew himself up into his saddle on the gelding. Beside Bandy on the grey. Mounted bushmen. He ignored Pee Dee and he felt the leather creak, so well-oiled, so delicate, accommodating him as precisely as you could hope. Annie watched him from the back verandah like a chronicler, and Ellen Burke kept a good hold on bandaged Johnny. Tim blew kisses. 'Now go inside with Ellen!'

He rode out waving his hand. Then out of the lane into Smith Street. Beyond the part-built bridge, a crowd of end-of-day people were waiting for the punt to return from East. Old Billy Thurmond, the patriotic farmer, was there with his wagon and looked coldly up the embankment at arriving Tim, as if what he saw confirmed something. Maybe something he'd heard from Ernie Malcolm.

Tim took off his hat. 'Mr Thurmond.' But the old man, model farmer, Pola Creek, merely fluttered his lips with a blast of air. You couldn't tell whether it was contempt or hello.

Tim murmured to Bandy, 'Do you call at old Billy's place?'

'His big daughter buys cloth from me, and a remedy for costiveness.'

'Pity Billy himself didn't take some of it,' said Tim.

The punt had left East and was eking its way back over darkening water. Some ducks and then a pelican made late, low flights over the surface, dragging a rumour of light behind them. Yet shadow also fell like a veil from the pelican's big wings. Smelling of its peculiar, cranky old steam engine the punt came into Central wharf. A few wagons and tired-looking horsemen rode ashore. Tim and Bandy led their horses aboard, and the gelding travelled from embankment to punt so easily and without fuss that Tim was reminded of Dr Erson's question: 'Will you shoot that cranky horse of yours?'

Everyone on the Central side was able to crowd aboard, with walking passengers and Billy's dray and the two horsemen, and old Hagan, the punt captain, and his son Boy Hagan, pulled levers and let the thing be swung away from shore, let the current take it and the cable hold it, balancing the drift against the thrust of the engine.

'You're going out selling herbals, are you?' Billy Thurmond called down the length of his wagon to Tim. Tim did not answer.

Some fine enough houses in East, rising up Rudder's Hill. At the end of the journey, Billy Thurmond urged his wagon ashore in East. Bandy and Tim tranquilly led their horses down the ramp, pleased to give Billy a head start, and then mounted and took the hill at an easy trot.

'You keep these horses marvellously,' Tim called across to Bandy. He hoped he sat half as well as Bandy did, but doubted it.

Bandy grinned softly, flicking his head sideways towards the river.

'They are my total passion, old fellow,' he said.

The signpost turning left at Rudder's Hill said *Gladstone*. They swung their horses to it and saw before them the paperbark lowlands of Dock Flat and O'Sullivan's Swamp. A brown, swampy darkness beginning to pool down there, pricked with the kerosene lamp of this and that cottage. Melancholy country, this. The river's abandoned ground. The lonely lights looked as if they'd been set there by survivors of a flood. These were the houses of men who did not do one thing but many: they kept cows, they grew some cane and bananas, they burned charcoal, they cut shingles, and when they had done all that, were still landed with the question of how to feed a family.

Soon, at an easy pace, he and Bandy were at the furtherest point to which he made deliveries – the slopes of Red Hill, where better farms and orchards lay, where prosperous farmers could be found sitting at their tables reading the *Argus* with such a clear, scrupulous eye that you'd think they'd been here two hundred years. Some of the fanciest new ploughing, threshing, winnowing and seeding machines, coming up straight out of the catalogues of the Sydney manufacturers by way of *Burrawong*, were taken to Red Hill whose farmers considered themselves advanced. To Red Hill and Pola Creek too came the agricultural and horticultural journals of the world, and they were read and disseminated. Agriculture sat as science, not as hit-and-miss magic, atop Red Hill.

A long way away to the north, beyond the mudflats and the river, was a perfect bar of golden light, and then violet all the way to the apex of the dusk. And on this side of things the road down to Pola Creek, and night a blue mist. This air, this air. The same air which dealt tenderly with him after his cricketing mistake, which pressed so knowingly on the seam in mad Johnny's scone.

The most wonderful thing to do, to ride recklessly to the supreme woman in a soft night.

At the corner of a laneway amongst corn paddocks in Pola Creek a young woman in a black dress waited, bare-headed. Piled up hair. Just waiting for some cow-cocky's son who'd sent her a note? Seeing Tim and Bandy, she seemed abashed and turned and moved away through corn taller than she was.

'The road downriver used to be so devilish bad when my father first brought us to the Macleay,' Bandy recounted, his voice sounding like a ballad. 'You saw broken-down drays every mile, and men marked the particular mud holes with a cut-down sapling and a rag tied to it, to warn travellers away.'

Austral Eden, wide, low, rich land, beside the track now. The river was somewhere near too. You could smell its muddiness, for all the world like the sweet drag of odour you got from a freshly opened two pound can of plum jam. Austral Eden. What a name! Southern heaven.

But these little reflections swam like petals on the wide, hypnotic movement of Bandy's well-kept horses.

You could hear the river now too. By proxy at least. Drumming away in the throats of those huge emerald bullfrogs Kitty hated to find on the shouse seat. The closer you got to the great body of the river the more urgent the wings of night birds sounded. The moon came up and there were flying foxes in it, creaking their way across the mudflats towards somebody's luscious orchard. Johnny liked to feed those buggers as they hung upside down from branches, bony and natty at the same time, dapper in their fur.

Ah, the bloody river sweeps into sight now. Going to the sea for its salt. Broad between the canebrakes on this side, and the answering canebrakes on the Smithtown shore. Bandy's grey snorted at the river for its size and the authority of its smell. 'Shhhh,' said Bandy. Pacifying it with a small brown hand.

By the bridge at Belmore River, a Macleay tributary, they let the horses drink, and Tim and Bandy swigged cold tea from a billycan and found that it was almost nine o'clock. He was being sucked in well and truly, he knew. Becoming this little brown man's accomplice.

Through the town of Gladstone, drenched by moonlight but unaware of itself. The Divine Presence resting in the big church Father McCambridge had built. The stained glass windows in memory of dairy farmers' beloved spouses. Tim took his hat off for the wakeful divinity of the place, and said a prayer for no plague and Missy's name. The divine mystery: why did Ernie not want to write a letter to cause a proper search? Why was it part of his civic intent to let the Missy question fade?

Bandy had also taken off his hat. Sympathetically, Tim presumed. But his eyes were lustrous as a devotee's in the moonlight.

They waded Kinchela Creek and then, though the river was always a presence, they came upon it only sometimes. They found themselves now amongst melancholy paperbarks that smelled of nearby swamp. They were getting close, he knew. He was so joyous that sometimes he let himself loll in the saddle like a drunkard, slackening and bending his back. He indulged himself this way frequently, at times when Bandy had drawn ahead.

Past the creek at Jerseyville, where the pub which had nearly been Tim's was kept by the Whelans, Bandy by a sudden jerk of his elbows showed it was all right to break the horses into a canter. So fresh they still seemed. Lots of running coiled up in their great big hips.

From the top of the last hill, they could see the camp, with plenty of fires still burning. It was set on the first low, dry piece of shore before the mangrove swamps of the Entrance, and beyond it in the river sat *Burrawong*, whose shape you could read dimly from the storm lantern hanging from the crosstree of its mast.

They left their horses in a patch of lank grass amongst paperbarks, and walked in like two people engaged in approved business. Tim carried with him the twin mercies of the billycan of stew, the condensed milk, and the *Messenger of the Sacred Heart*.

Paperbark trees, grey by day and stark white by night, smelled anciently and remotely sour. Whatever tragedy or fall they'd been involved in had happened in an unrecorded age. Therefrom they took this air: all debts paid, all tears long shed, all decay long concluded. Tim enlivened though by this very quality. Charmed by this bush which didn't try to charm him.

Some parts of the track he and Bandy had to scrape through briary shrubs. This may have been why Bandy had wanted them to leave the well-kept horses behind.

From up the path Tim could hear a banjo plunking at midnight! Joined idly by a fiddle. Didn't the buggers go to bed early for their health?

'Here we are,' Bandy told him in a normal voice.

The paperbarks eased away to right and left to make the New Entrance picnic grounds. Three rows of six or seven bell tents each. A big cooking stove standing in the open with its funnel, and a canvas bathhouse nearby. Light still shone inside the canvas of some tents – a magical look, a tent lit from inside itself. Further along, the men and women who were still up were clustered to the campfire, which was not needed for warmth but for the soul and to keep insects away. This small party were engaged in watching the flames die now. The banjo and the fiddle only a sad strain here and there. A last burst of showiness from their owners, the tag end of brighter, more deliberate stuff performed earlier in the night.

Now Tim heard a familiar little yell of woman-laughter, cut back immediately out of consideration for those who might be sleeping in the tents. Dear God, this was inimitably Kitty's. Kitty sitting up to all hours in the plague camp.

Within the light of the near-dead fire two little women sat on camp stools, with men standing and lolling about them. The banjo player standing close to the women. He was the one who first saw Bandy and Tim coming.

'Keeping you up, are we, gentlemen?' the banjo player asked. This bewildering night! The fellow was talking in a North Cork accent.

Kitty stood up wobblingly. An empty, froth-lined stout glass stood by her chair. An approved, a respectable drink. So why did he resent her for drinking it amongst strangers?

'Dear mother,' she cried, grabbing the arm of the other, like woman. 'It's Timmy!'

Tim looked at his sister-in-law, Mamie, oval-faced, slim, with a bunched little amused mouth. She had been a bit of a child when Tim had first visited the Kennas.

Kitty clung to him, her hard little head, the brownish-red bun of her hair, pulled up into a knot by some hairdresser in Sydney, socketed into the cavity where his shoulder met his chest. And even though there were strangers looking he bent to this red hair, inhaled its decent, vegetable, mothering smell, and kissed it.

'Don't catch any fleas now,' she told him.

'I'll only kiss the bits that aren't plaguey,' he murmured.

'Get my husband and his friend a drink!' Kitty insisted, and a young man who was English by his accent shook out the froth from a used glass and then filled it with warm stout and passed it into Tim's free hand. It tasted divine. The Englishman found another glass, but Bandy called musically, 'No thank you, sir.'

'Water then?'

'Yes, water.'

The young man picked up a water bag and half-delivered it to, half-threw it, jovially, at Bandy.

'Catch there!'

'There are no guards on this camp, eh?' Tim murmured.

'It's an utter joke,' Kitty told him. 'Captain Reid collected all these rats on board two whole days ago, and not a one showed marks of plague.'

'But were you worried?'

'There are city streets roped off and houses sealed. But Sydney is still Sydney.' A soft malty burp fluttered her lips very slightly. 'Now meet Mamie.'

Mamie had risen in her white dress. Very compact. Jesus, what a dangerous smile, and underneath the smile, what? In the bone? He could spot something. Flightiness, a canny soul, a temper. There might be an interest in holding grudges as well.

'Tim,' Mamie said warmly, in a rising tone. She came to him on the other side than the one where Kitty leaned. Brushed his cheeks softly. Again he remembered her somehow, as a partially distinct, largely indefinite part of the Kenna brood. She would have been about eleven, a bit sullen, likely to throw bread across the table. Now she was between kitchens. Red's and the one she might have here in the end. A thing or two would be thrown about in that one as well.

The fairly neatly turned out young banjo player followed every smallest move she made, Tim could see. Every trace of intent in her face. He certainly had hopes of being her future target.

Mamie said, 'Oh! Mr Habash again.'

Seemingly her old friend, Bandy stood a little way off from the reunion, touching his hat.

'I didn't expect to see you travelling with the hawker,' said Kitty, laughing at him.

'I didn't know there'd be bloody plague in Sydney when I had a fight with him,' muttered Tim. 'History is a bugger when you are in it.'

'This thing isn't history. It'll soon be over.' Kitty nodded to the banjo player. 'Here's Joey O'Neill who worked for the cooperage just over the Mitchelstown road. Three or so miles out from home, would you believe? We met him in Sydney and he's going to be joining an uncle farming in Toorooka. Can you believe that one? My sisters went to a dance in Kanturk less than a year ago, and saw him there, and here he is on the Macleay. I think the world is certainly shrinking.'

'How are you, Mr Shea?' said Joey O'Neill, saluting like a soldier, but not normally a shy acker, only because he'd been drinking. You could tell his manner was more restrained at other times, and he was certainly terrified of Mamie.

'If you read it in a novel,' asked Kitty, 'would you even start to believe it? Did *you* know he had an uncle and aunt in Toorooka?'

Under the power of the Kenna sisters' sociability, Tim said he was as amazed as anyone. But he wondered how he was supposed to know of Joey O'Neill's existence down the Mitchelstown road, and so how he was to know that the banjo player had relatives in Toorooka?

They introduced the fiddler, who was a Meath man joining his brother on a dairy farm on Nulla Nulla Creek. And then there was the young Englishman with some washed-out accent – somewhere like Essex – and a couple of Sydney commercial travellers. Decent chaps all of them, no question of that.

'I'm the chaperone for my wild sister,' said Kitty, nuzzling against him once more with an animal insistence. 'Otherwise by now I'd be long asleep. But she bears watching.'

'Who's chaperoning the wild chaperone,' he asked, and everyone laughed. 'Welcome to the Macleay, gentlemen,' he then added anyhow at last, *that* duty devolving on him. 'You're only just inside it, but with any luck you'll get further, and I don't know if it's good or bad news.'

'Rubbish!' called Kitty. 'This is the greatest of lands.'

Still holding the fiddle and bow, the fiddler clapped the more or less formal speech of welcome.

The young men began to excuse themselves. Joey O'Neill thought that Mamie would do the same, and seemed to be alarmed to find himself wandering off alone down the avenues of tents, while Mamie stayed behind with the embers and her sister and the two visitors. He couldn't come back without seeming an idiot, yet loitered in the shadows. The commercial travellers cleared up the stout bottles which lay around and went off themselves to the their camp cots.

Kitty murmured to her sister, 'Joe wants you to walk with him.'

'I've heard everything he has to say,' said Mamie, dismissing the idea. 'Good night, Joe,' she called merrily nonetheless. 'Thanks for the fine music.'

'You're an awful hypocrite,' her sister Kitty whispered to her.

Now the camp was very still, but the river still drummed with frogs. Tim had utterly forgotten Bandy, but then noticed that he remained meekly there, keeping a distance.

'You didn't have to come and see me,' said Kitty. 'I'll be home in two days, they won't be able to keep this up. All this fuss. Boiling up all our underwear in iron drums. They won't be able to do it with every shipload. Captain Reid says, we cannot put such hindrances to commerce.'

Smiling Mamie said, 'Mr Habash, are you a gentleman?'

Bandy shifted lightly on his feet.

'You should be aware, Miss Kenna, that I am a follower of the Prophet.'

'Oh Jesus,' said Mamie. 'We've got prophets and saints to burn, so what does one more matter? But are followers of the Prophet gentlemen?'

'Better than some of the white brethren, if you don't mind my saying.'

'That's not much of a claim,' said Mamie. 'Anyhow, I believe you *are* a gentleman, Mr Habash, and I wonder if you would mind accompanying me down to the shore for a view of *Burrawong* while my sister and her husband spend a fragment of time together.'

'Miss Kenna, I would be honoured and it would be a sacred trust.'

'Dear Mother, Tim,' said Kitty. 'Every bugger here's talking like a play.'

In the moonlight, Mamie put a small but decisive hand out in front of her, signalling Bandy towards the river.

'Now you two just have your conversations,' she said. 'Come on, Mr Habash.'

She walked off, trailing a big straw hat. Bandy turned his eyes to Tim, and spread his hands in front of him to show they were vacant of any intent.

'Go on, Bandy,' Kitty told him. 'If you want to be a bloody gallant, walk in front so it's you who treads on the sleeping brown snakes.'

Again Bandy touched his hat, and caught up with Mamie. They were about the same height, and Mamie inclined a little to him, chatting away.

Kitty said, 'She gives that poor Joe O'Neill an awful time, God help him.'

She stepped back and took Tim by the wrist.

'We can go to the tent. I've been missing you. Sydney's got its points, but it isn't Tim Shea.'

'How can we go to your tent? Mind you, I'd like to see it, of course. But Mamie could be back at any second.'

'Then why do you think she's gone for a walk. She won't be back for at least forty minutes. And if she'd gone with Joey, it'd be all over the camp by breakfast.'

Kitty was leading him amongst the quiet tents, a camp where few lights shone, the canvas itself offering only a night cry here, a brief fragment of snore there.

'How does a girl like that know these things?'

'She's a Kenna, I suppose,' said Kitty.

This was nearly enough explanation. The Kennas knew things which didn't seem to be known in his family. Kitty, for example, always insisted that carrying a child was no hindrance to love. The man needed simply to beware of his weight and take reasonable care. Who had told her that? Had Mrs Kenna bowled right up and told her before she caught the boat? Had her sister told her at the wedding feast which delayed her in her emigration? It wasn't at all unlikely. But could he imagine his mother, Anne, telling such things to any of the Shea girls before they took their American ship? Telling Brooklyn-bound Ellen Shea there was no need to put off further joy till three months after the child was born?

He had already stiffened up enough. A standing prick hath no conscience. One of Kitty's axioms. From whom had she heard *that*? Did the Kennas pass such wisdom around the table?

For some reason, a surmise entered his head. What of Bandy's Muslim prick, smooth as an eel?

In a light summer night dress which left her shoulders bare, Red Kenna's freckles visible on them even by kerosene lamp, Kitty drifted asleep on her side. Tim, fully dressed again to fool the unfoolable Mamie Kenna, stretched atop Mamie's camp cot and went profoundly asleep. Bending over him with pursed, knowing lips, Mamie woke him.

'Mr Habash has returned me in good fettle. I see you put your wife to sleep, Tim! What a good thing!'

He took his fob watch and saw that it was nearing two o'clock. Oh, Jesus, the huge ride! And the air relentless hot!

He rose and kissed Kitty's bare shoulder and she shuddered and said, 'Dear,' but did not wake.

'I suppose young Bandy is raring to go?' he asked Mamie in a whisper.

Mamie watched him with a subtle smile on her lips.

'So it seems I'll be meeting you again before the end of the week,' she said.

'May I just check a thing or two?' he asked, and he went to Kitty's old sea trunk and eased it back by the hinges and inspected her black and white dresses and her undergarments by lamplight, encountering no insect other than a dead tiger moth. Everything in fine order. He repacked the truck, folding things lovingly. 'All clean,' Mamie whispered, 'and no fleas. She airs everything every second day anyhow.'

He felt a surge of love and would have kissed Kitty's shoulder again if they'd been alone. Because Kitty had such a casual air, there was something poignant about her when she took her uncommon care.

'Goodbye then,' he told Mamie, and she brushed his cheek again. 'And welcome to the Macleay.'

'Give my regards to Mr Habash,' she told Tim. 'He's a feller of real charm.'

Outside, some way from the door of the tent, Bandy waited for him by the dead fire.

'Right,' Tim called to him.

Bandy said nothing. Had Mamie staunched his oratorical flow? They fell into step together, tramping back amongst the tea-tree, the melaleuca, the slug-white paperbarks.

'May I say your sister-in-law is a very lively girl, and excellent company.'

'You don't need to tell me about *lively*,' said Tim. 'I'll have her on the premises for at least a few months I suppose!'

'Then you will have three women with you, including your little girl. You are a fortunate man, Mr Shea. My father, my brother and I live in a womanless household. It is not a natural thing at all. But our faith is a problem at the same time as being our glory.'

'Well,' said Tim. 'I respect your attitudes in that regard.'

The Habashes had no reputation for seeking solace either in the blacks' camp. Mind you, a lot of respectable women perversely liked them. Perhaps there was an illicit bit of business sometimes.

They found their horses standing somnolent in the clearing. As Tim climbed aboard he called, 'Wake me if I fall asleep. Otherwise, I'll end up on the ground.'

'The same for me, old chap,' said Bandy, delicately yawning. 'Pigs will come and eat our faces.'

On the at first sandy road back up the Macleay, the night grew stiller and even hotter. Tim would sleep and wake, sleep and wake, and Bandy frankly slept for long stretches of the road, his cheek tucked into the hollow of his collarbone. Tim roused again and again, sweating and startled each time and aware at once of all the catalogue of earthly dangers:

that Johnny would go on seeking chances to crack his skull;

that Ernie Malcolm would malign Tim Shea;

that all customers might leave;

that the plague might after all – surely not through him – come to town.

It was a chafing, starting, restless eon before they crossed Spencer's Creek again. Then he would blink at the broad and blatant river which seemed to stretch off limitlessly from his stirrup into an undetermined and unreachable point between water and sky. Now it looked not like his familiar but a foreign river to him, a bitter one. A Congo. Africa, and he some sort of missionary riding to some hopeless task with the heathen.

Breath of a hot westerly met them as they rode through Gladstone. There were fragments of black grit on that wind. Upriver the bush was burning. You could not see it, but it could be read in the force, heat, the density of that blast. Fragments of blackened gumleaf would be raining in his back yard by the river. A furious, hazy ochre light was up by Pola Creek, where the cattle would be already wandering back satisfied from the milking shed.

Tim was starting to revive.

'A hard life,' he commented to Bandy.

But the horses had been so steady, so sure-footed all night. Again they let them drink from the Belmore River, where it entered the Macleay from the south. The horses began pointedly to sniff the air soon thereafter, as if it gave them grounds for unease, but they were not so impolite as to toss their heads around and back downriver as some horses would. *Noblesse* bloody *oblige*.

From the top of Red Hill, you could see the mountains distantly burning and the valley filling with hot white smoke.

'Oh, dear,' said Bandy. 'It looks like Nulla Creek is ablaze. All my families. A terrible thing. Drought and fire, fire and drought. God's seasons in the Macleay.'

'I wouldn't blame God,' said Tim, but not as belligerently as he would have a week ago.

They rode down into the East Kempsey Swamp, where the air was densest. It must be far more than a hundred degrees already in this syrupy bottom, an inhuman day ahead. A good day for selling Stone's Ginger Beer in its earthenware bottle. Open the top and there's a marble over which the children can fight. A good day for selling the cordials from Sharp's factory in West Kempsey. The creaming soda. He could drink a bucket of it now. It didn't cut the thirst though, not really. Tea. Black and strong. Cut the whistle. Made you sweat.

As they crested Commandant Hill, Constable Hanney and one of the younger constables on police mounts rode into their path.

'May I ask you gentlemen where you have been?' called Hanney through nearly closed lips.

What to say? Visiting the plague camp no more than a technical infringement. But Hanney could make it a massive crime.

Bandy wagged his head significantly to Tim. He seemed to say, I provide the horses but you answer the questions.

At the sight of the uniform, Tim had been unable to prevent himself wondering if Hanney knew somehow of his anonymous letter to the Commissioner. But that was not possible.

'We have been down the river to visit friends.'

'Mohammedan or Christian?' asked Constable Hanney out of his locked jaw.

'I'd take it they were Christian. Why do you ask, constable?'

'Where are these Christian friends of yours located then?'

'Near . . . near Belmore River, more or less.'

'Is that right?' Hanney called to Bandy.

'That's right, constable,' Bandy assured the man.

'The beak's going to ask you the same bloody question,' said Hanney. 'Think twice, and tell the truth, or else I'll stick you with your first answer. The question is: have you been visiting the *Burrawong* passengers?'

'What would make you ask that?' asked Tim. Just the same, he found himself swallowing those bilious inklings which unleashed power produces in its subjects.

'The sanitation officer had a report that Mr Bandy Habash

started trading with the passengers just a few days back. Someone saw you clearing off down the road to the New Entrance last night. He warned us.'

Billy Thurmond. Old bugger. Would've got home and put his son on a horse and sent him to town to complain to Sergeant Fry.

'Those horses of Mr Habash's certainly look knackered enough,' the younger constable said.

'My wife is six months pregnant,' said Tim. 'I was anxious as to how she was.'

'Is this a confession?' asked Constable Hanney.

For the first time, the profound soreness of the ride was entering. He bent forward in the saddle like a cripple. 'Doctor Erson and the sanitation officer are about to release the passengers in any case. I'd come to the conclusion I wasn't putting a soul in any peril.'

Hanney looked at his colleague. Then back to Tim. 'Kind enough to accompany us to the police station?'

It seemed too hot for the execution of the law. Above one hundred and five degrees, who wanted the literal justice whose minister Hanney had decided to be?

'Go easy, constable. I have deliveries to do today.'

'Bugger your deliveries.'

Tim found himself looking at Bandy for directions. Bandy had hung his head. Why not? He had to show himself humble before the ways of superior authority. Tim himself had used them on him.

'There's nothing you can have at the police station which couldn't be had here,' said Tim. 'If you want to charge us for visiting the passengers, you can do it here and leave our day free. I confess that we visited the camp, and that Mr Habash did, though not for trade. Purely out of kindness towards me.'

'You weren't so bloody keen on him the last time we met,' said Hanney.

'Well, I was more ignorant then. Surely you don't want us to follow you through the streets of town?'

'I think that's what we'd like, Mr Shea.'

'I'm a man in business.'

'Something you should have thought about at dusk last night. Follow us, and bloody shut up.'

Fortunately though, even by the time they crossed in the punt with the constables and followed them up Belgrave Street towards West Kempsey, where the Majesty of the Queen abided in the office beside the courthouse, the commercial day had not begun in Kempsey.

The passage through town didn't take so long. A young woman watched them from the upper verandah of the Commercial. She might carry the news. Bandy's horses seemed to keep right up with the police mounts, and to be pleased for the company, and Tim hoped that this implied to onlookers a lack of coercion in the whole arrangement. Arriving in Kemp Street, they all trotted into the police yard together. But Tim had no doubt that the pegged and markered world ceased at the gate, and that as the constables ran their mounts in under the shade of their stables, he and Bandy had placed themselves profoundly under the dominion of power exercised fancifully.

Yet as if they had freedom, Bandy and Tim rode their horses up to a post and rail. Now everyone dismounted. He and Bandy and the constables walked together like friends across the barren yard to the station. As Constable Hanney opened the unlocked door – who would be silly enough to steal from a police station? – and led everyone in, he took it as read that Tim and Bandy would follow. On the doorstep Tim saw in Bandy's eye the intention to decamp. To horse and to buggery! How Hanney would adore that.

'Let's put up with it,' Tim counselled the hawker.

Inside the warm air which reached for Tim smelled of official ink and carbolic. Hanney opened the flap in the counter, and facing to the interior, kept it negligently open with a hand held behind him. Sure of their obedience. The habits necessary to an officer of the law.

'Get yourselves chairs,' he said.

There were three desks in here, in the joyless interior. On the wall the main poster was a paltry ink sketch of Missy marked UNKNOWN FEMALE.

Tim and Bandy fetched two chairs from their place against the back wall and bore them to Hanney's desk, while the senior constable himself wiped his sweaty hands on his tunic, saying, 'God, bound to be a stinker!'

He was looking around for writing materials. He found some sheets of notepaper with V R on the top and the lion and unicorn. Astounding creatures! Their bite as strong here as anywhere.

The younger constable had already sat at his own desk further back in the room, and was engaged at once in documents which seemed to have no bearing at all on Bandy or Tim.

Dipping his pen in the inkwell, Hanney said, 'Bugger this heavy air!' and began to write. He asked Tim what his second name was, and Tim said *Edmund*. Hanney wrote that down. He asked Bandy for his second name.

'I am not aware of any second name,' said Bandy.

Hanney looked up, considering this departure from the given. 'All right then,' he conceded at last.

Reading upside down what the constable wrote, Tim saw Hanney put down *Solus* after the word *Bandy* and before *Habash*. This perhaps to save magistrates asking the question or presuming that Hanney hadn't asked. They were deep in the moils of the thing now. They were being prepared to appear in Court Notes in the *Chronicle*.

'Constable,' said Tim, 'with the greatest respect, I will not be signing any documents before I have spoken to Mr Sheridan.'

The words sounded momentary to Tim, fugitive birds uncaged. Barely a dent made on the air. Hanney looked up at him.

'I'm not accusing you of murder, Tim,' he said with a painful grin. 'I'm accusing you of violating the New South Wales Quarantine Act.'

Bandy watchful beside him, expected something clever of him, just as *he*'d expected a horse of Bandy.

Tim said, 'Isn't that a matter for the sanitation officer to report to you?'

'Jesus, you *are* a bush lawyer, Mr Shea. It's like the bloody Impounding Act, Tim. I can impound wandered cattle and lay a charge, and so can the impounding officer. And now I can impound stray citizens under the Sanitation Ordinance and under the Act.' Hanney shook his head. He found Tim hugely eccentric. 'You've got deliveries to make, Tim, and I have a day's work. Do you mind if I expedite matters?'

He continued writing, muttering, 'You're lucky I caught you. If I was in this game for the sake of persecution, I could keep you buggers here all day, ruin your business, confuse your children, leave you spare of anyone's trust.'

'I have no children,' said Bandy, speaking in defiance for the first time.

'That's what you say, you black bastard.'

'Brown bastard, constable.'

The second policeman laughed in the dimness of the office, of the eucalyptus shade which fell over the back of the police station.

Tim consulted the watch in his fob. Nearing eight o'clock. His schoolboy son would be along soon, going to Imelda.

Hanney turned the document to them at last. It said,

'I, Timothy Edmund Shea, and I, Bandy Solus Habash, freely admit that each in the company of the other in violation of Section 17 of the New South Wales Quarantine Act and of Macleay Shire's Sanitation Ordinance 8 illegally travelled to and entered the quarantine camp at the New Entrance, thereby placing ourselves and the community in peril and making ourselves liable to sentencing and a fine before the Macleay District Police Magistrate's Court.'

He wrote that stuff well, Tim saw. Dressing up a mean intent in flowing terms.

'You both sign at the bottom,' Hanney told them. He turned the inkstand to them so that they could conveniently sign.

Tim said, 'Just charge us and let the magistrate decide. You've said already it's not like we committed murder.'

Hanney tilted his chair back, 'Is that your casual attitude too, Mr Habash?'

'I would rather await the settlement of the question before the court,' said Bandy, grandly but looking away.

'Well, I think you two fellows should know that some of us think that as a whole there's a stink of murder or near-murder about you two. *There* – yes you, Brownie! – there is a fellow, a herbalist, who supplied specifics to Mrs Mulroney the abortionist. We found quarts of his arsenic remedy on Mrs Mulroney's premises.'

Bandy sat forward and his delicate little hands came passionately into play. 'My arsenic tonic is quite harmless, constable, and could not be blamed for anyone's ill-health let alone demise. The same prescription has a renown absolutely everywhere – from the Alps to Turkey, and from Persia to China, as a specific for rheumatism, anaemia and weak nerves. Mrs Mulroney was one of my customers, but used the tonic you refer to for her own purposes.'

The hated look from Hanney, snide in the heavy, heavy way of lesser yet total power. 'Where'd you get him, Tim? Talks like a bloody professor. Look, cases could be bloody made, Habash. I could consider going lenient on you if you sign up here and avoid court squabbles. But if you bloody rile me . . .'

With a dry mouth, Tim said, 'I won't advise my friend to sign a confession for something as silly.'

Bandy had gone as pale as a European, but it was clear he was resolved to stand solid. Tim wondered too how he could have been blind to his fellow prisoner's qualities, the courage and the loyalty. Just the same, there was a sort of plea in Bandy's eye. *Just remember, things will always fall more heavily on me than on you. Police magistrates will believe you more than me.*

But not by too bloody much of a margin, Tim wanted to tell him.

'Let me show you something,' murmured Hanney. Standing, Hanney moved to a storeroom and past the junior policeman's desk. Tim could not think of anything to say to Bandy in the man's absence. After a time, Hanney emerged, oh Jesus, with the basket covered by the checked cloth. The letter Tim had risked writing had been futile. Had it gone astray or been lost by a clerk? Had the Commissioner lost interest in the young woman's name?

He placed it all on the table, removed the great flask, took the checked cloth off it. A glimpse showed Tim that Missy leaned here, brow first, in hostage to Hanney. Tim felt his blood abandon him, fleeing this sight. The fixity of dimmed and barely brown eyes more open than at last viewing. Unblinking. Disconnected from the intent of her heart.

'There you are, you black bastard,' said Hanney. 'Would you like to come clean that this is what your rheumatic mixture did.'

'Untrue, untrue,' cried Bandy. 'My mixture could not achieve this horrible thing. Dear heaven!'

Bandy averted his eyes. You could tell that as much as any North Corker farmer's son, he was seized by Missy's unreleased spirit.

'My mixture is nothing,' said Bandy in a thin voice. 'A tiny, kindly ripple, constable, on the huge ocean of human pain.'

He stood up, his mouth warped.

'Not this,' he said, trembling. 'This is not my tradition or my father's.'

He fell. His legs gave way. One delicate groan as he dropped like a thrown-off garment.

'What do you think that could mean?' Hanney – looking over his desk at the stupefied Bandy – asked Tim.

Tim had begun to rise to assist Bandy . . .

'Leave him. Leave him! Tell me what you think it bloody well means?'

'It means he hasn't seen her before.'

'Well, you wouldn't find a woman like her messing around with a black hawker.'

'But you said you'd shown him! You told me that. You showed it to cow-cockies but not to Bandy!'

'Are you dissatisfied with my investigation, Tim?' Hanney opened his desk and took a letter out. 'Read that, eh.'

It was a letter on the stationery of Ernest Malcolm and Company, Accountants. It was addressed to the Commissioner of Police for New South Wales. 'I would be remiss not to commend to you the work done by way of the present enquiry into the identity of the unfortunate young woman by Constable Hanney . . .' It was signed by Ernie, along with a list of all his secretaryships and posts as treasurer.

Hanney took the letter back. 'Bloody nice to be appreciated by a pillar of the community. Now, tell me what you think it means, this bloody fainting?'

'It's the bloody horror. It's not guilt.' Another glimpse of the child in the flask. 'I feel the same as Habash.'

'So you'd say you are similar characters, would you?'

So tediously Hanney fancied himself as cornering a man whatever way he turned. Were coppers like that as babies? Or did the uniform do it?

'Well?' Hanney insisted. 'Similar types, would you say?'

'Will you let me pick up my friend? Fainted people shouldn't be left lying like that.'

'Just sit there.' Again Hanney craned over his desk and surveyed Bandy. 'Look at him there. You'd be bloody surprised, Mr Shea, by the numbers of women upriver who'd do him favours. The old cow-cockies mistrust him, but the women think he's a bloody darling. They let him camp near the homestead, and when their old man's snoring, they go creeping down to his wagon.'

Why would Ernie praise methods like those of Hanney? 'If Habash is the sort who gets round to the women, why didn't you show him Missy earlier?'

Hanney did not answer, but went back to the matter of Bandy the seducer. 'You'd be astounded. Even your sister-in-law and that step-niece. He's the sort of little bugger women like to take on their knees. Look at that! Hands and arms like a bloody cherub.'

Bandy began to cough. Tim got up now and helped him to his feet, and sat him in his chair again. Bandy fluttering his lips like a man about to be sick. He seemed to be unsure of what had befallen him.

He saw the flask again but closed his eyes then.

'Can't you put that bloody thing away?' Tim asked Constable Hanney. It was not of course a bloody thing. It had a holiness.

The policeman said, 'You keep pestering me. Has she been recognised? Buying me drinks, getting me pissed. Were you her bloke, Tim? Where did you meet her? Was it Sydney on some trip?'

Tim writhed. The copper's profane ideas were a torment.

'I haven't been to Sydney in five years.'

'So why are you so fussy about Missy's name? Hoping it'll come out. Or hoping it won't.'

Try the truth out on him. Defy him with it. 'She's in torment until she's named. Any idiot can tell.'

'How do you know, *in torment*?'

'That's the way it strikes me. Again and again. If it doesn't strike you and spur you on, I bloody pity you!'

'Is this some potato superstition you're into, Tim? Some spuddy thing?'

'I think it's bloody called using your imagination.'

'Ah,' said Hanney, setting his big jaw. 'I'm sorry, my imagination's not up to scratch with yours. But there's something all the old coppers in Sydney used to tell me. That if there is a person who hangs around and ask lots of questions, he's generally the bugger.'

Bandy had placed his hands on the desk.

'And my God,' he murmured. 'Woman's fine features.'

'What do you say, Tim? Don't wait for others to do it. *You* give me her name.'

'Get me a Bible. I'll swear. I just don't bloody know!'

'Sign this then,' said Hanney, sighing in a concluding manner. 'You'll both receive a summons to answer the charge.' He nudged the flask. 'The charge of visiting the quarantine. You do remember that one, don't you?'

'It's hard to remember anything with *that* on the table.'

'You remember some things, son! You couldn't wait for your wife to be home in two days. So you went up the river to get your end in. You remember that.'

Tim burned but leaned forward in his chair.

'There is no plague,' Bandy murmured to reinforce Tim.

'This isn't what all the messages off the wire say, but you two smartalecs know better. Sign the bloody thing here.'

But neither of them moved to sign, so Hanney put on a sour mouth and said, 'Go and sit down the back of the office there, the both of you.'

Tim, still blazing as any man would from that accusation of lust, one he didn't want mentioned in court, stood up, helping Bandy by the elbow and grabbing the backs of the two chairs with his free hand. They passed the younger constable's desk and Tim repositioned the chairs against the back wall and eased Bandy into his.

'Notice, he hasn't put us in cells,' Tim whispered to Bandy.

As well, and at last, Hanney returned the flask to storage. Carrying it, he moved like a tired servant.

Tim tilted his chair and forced the back of his head against the wall. The back legs of his chair provided him with the other half of the leaning equation which would enable him to sleep. Bandy slept too, and at one stage Tim was drowsily aware of the little man slipping from his chair and curling himself on the floor.

At one stage that morning Sergeant Fry, who was bull-necked but had what many people called an intelligent face, came into the office like a man who hardly had the time for it, and Hanney pointed out the two offenders at the rear of the room. Hanney did not use large gestures or try the smart-copper act on his sergeant. Fry murmured brisk things at Hanney, and Hanney nodded.

Don't try to scrutinise or interpret the buggers. Drowse. From nowhere now Tim remembers a music hall song, 'Never Buy a Copper a Drink':

> Never buy a copper a drink,
> It might only make the blighter think.
> He will get all suspicious,
> As you sip the wine delicious,
> So never buy a copper a drink.

Sleep. Waking again, he found Dr Erson in the office, talking energetically to Hanney. Tim now adjusted his chair and sat upright to convince the doctor of his respectability. He watched Hanney begin shrugging, but Erson was a large magician in the Macleay for his medicine and for his singing, and so the ungifted Hanney now looked shorn of power.

Erson came to Tim now, smiling a little as if remembering miscreant Johnny.

'We should have had guards on the Trial Bay road, shouldn't we?'

Tim said, 'My regrets, doctor. But I was anxious about my wife.'

'I was pleased to see in passing the shed that you have a new horse.'

Tim lowered his eyes for the first time since arrested by Hanney. 'Oh, a borrowed, reliable one. I still use the old one for deliveries. But keep Johnny separate from him.'

Erson grinned briefly, considered him and coughed. 'A terrible searing day, Mr Shea.'

'Yes,' said Tim.

Dr Erson reached out and felt the glands under Tim's chin.

Then he asked to see Tim's tongue. Tim let him do whatever he wanted.

Bandy stirred on the floor and sat up.

Dr Erson smiled. 'Mr Habash.'

Bandy stood up now. 'My dear Dr Erson.'

Tim was of course astounded that they greeted each other as friends.

'Sir,' said Bandy, 'forgive my journey, but I know well that the strict quarantine time had expired.'

'Had it?' asked Erson. He still seemed amused, reaching up to Bandy's chin as he had earlier to Tim's. 'You are not to talk about any of this, Bandy, or of going up there. And God help if you do it again. It is not a good precedent. You must both give me an undertaking!'

'I understand,' said Bandy. 'You are such a good friend I have no problem in offering my solemn undertaking.'

'Well, I think in that case you can both go.' The doctor turned to Constable Hanney, who was making himself busy at his desk. 'These fellows are free to go, constable?'

Hanney thought a while, an actor who had forgotten the play's simplest line. 'Yes, doctor,' he managed in the end. He began tearing up the page he had written for them to sign.

Outside the air ferocious, an incoming tide, and they fought their way through it, crossing the yard. It scalded the cheeks. It was so thick and full of flecks of black leaf. Yet Erson had made this blazing day habitable.

Tim murmured, 'What a civilised fellow!'

Bandy said, 'I am a fool for fainting.'

He wavered in the white haze.

'You've never seen her before though?'

'I have not, old fellow.' Bandy shook his head to clear it of apparitions. 'But as to the rest, *they* don't want people to know about us. You noticed what Dr Erson said? We are not a good precedent for people to know about. It is up to them to guard the camp, and we have shown them up.'

'He seemed such friends with you.'

Bandy smiled. 'He visited my father, my brother and myself, looked into our prescriptions to make sure they were safe, and

found they were. As of course he should have expected. We
have been herbalists and chemists from generation to generation,
Mr Shea. Out of our meeting grew a compact with Dr Erson. We
are to urge our clearly ill customers to attend the surgeries of the
doctors in town. We are all brothers in concern for health.'

Tim began to laugh, far too much for the day. But he was
tickled by this unexpected kindly alliance the world harboured.

'Bloody hell!'

The air too ferocious for him to consider other alliances and
their meaning. The alliance between Ernie and Hanney, stated
so fulsomely in Ernie's letter. What did that bloody signify?

Ten past nine, he saw by his fob watch. Unless she was
overtaken by a vengeful mood, Ellen Burke would surely have
opened the store. Though who would buy butter on a day like
this? Butter from the Central or Warneton creameries melting
to a smear in the hands or the back of the cart. Yet he must
make deliveries in this furnace.

They found their horses in the shed. The poor beasts were
snuffling. The air worried them. They knew that fire was
everywhere, downriver and up, out of their control, out of
anyone else's.

Remembering Missy, Bandy continued to shake his head and
climbed onto the grey. He said nothing as they rode the horses
out of the gate, steering them towards the water trough outside
Kelty's where Tim had got his first bad reputation with Constable
Hanney. They found the beasts unwilling, pulling at the reins.
Having been pliable all night, they were now jacking up.

'Oh, dear sir, we could have been in great trouble,' said
Bandy.

'See,' said Tim, 'I told you there was nothing to be gained from
friendship with me. I am just one step away, Bandy, from you. I
am a white nigger. If I'd been an Orangeman or Good Templar,
that old bastard Thurmond would have taken his hat off to us
and wished us a good ride.'

As his horse and Bandy's drank from Kelty's trough, 'How
well a lager would go down,' Tim murmured.

'I must not,' muttered Bandy.

Tim felt a sigh escape him. 'Black tea is always the best.'

'Mr Shea, I saw that woman dressed as a boy.'

'A boy?'

'A boy in a school uniform of the English type. I saw him walking in West. This being at a time early in the summer. I saw him at once and thought, that may surely be a girl in masquerade. A beautiful being, boy or girl. More beautiful than most other beings in the Macleay.'

'A *boy*?' Tim asked.

'That face however,' Bandy murmured. 'The very chin. The very forehead. Europeans are so distinct to me, one at a time.'

In a fever, Tim hauled his horse's head out of Kelty's slimy water and turned it to the river which the day had turned turgid and browner than manure. Bandy obligingly followed.

'You're telling me it's the very girl, are you?'

'Certainly,' said Bandy. 'A memorable child.'

'A child,' said Tim. Bandy had the same word Tim had harboured within himself so long. 'That's right. A child.'

Her name wheeled above him in the air, at the margin of sight. It cast the day's sole shadow.

11

Savouring black tea at last from a big mug in a respite in the living room, the deepest, most shadowy room of the house, Tim in his crazed exhausted wakefulness turned to the *Argus*. Ellen Burke had bought it that morning in between kindly making up the orders in the storeroom and scratching clients' names on them with indelible pencil. What he sought, for relief from all the wakeful tangles of the day, was the normal mismatched bags of bones newspapers, the restful oddments of fiction and items off the wire and cattle sales and distant murders.

He did not get it. He turned a page and at once encountered a startling letter. This was a document so outright that it seemed to Tim to be incised into the great furriness of the heat and the burning air by the sharpness of its tone, its zest for its own argument.

'Sir,' it began.

'In connection with the incidents in the Transvaal, one poetic phrase worthy of a closer look is the one which we hear everywhere now, "When the Empire calls . . ." I haven't particularly heard the Empire calling, yet I seem to be surrounded by people who hear it all the time. Perhaps they know that the Continental press, together with the American journals, have universally condemned the British adventure in South Africa, and these citizens of the Macleay are, therefore, all the more willing volunteers to share in and absorb some of the Empire's shame.

'Whether our Empire calls or not however, and asks us poor Colonials to bear its poor name, we have no say in its counsels regarding the making of these wars. Our government in New South Wales will contribute thousands of pounds to help force a road across the Drakensberg mountains to relieve the British garrisons at Mafeking, Kimberley and Ladysmith, yet cannot spare a mere thousand pounds to push a road into the rich timber resources of the Upper Macleay. It seems that when the Empire calls, it is calling for large quantities of lucre, and not merely for the blood of our poor boys.

'Are we really so servile that we fear that unless we engage in all Mother's follies, she might interfere in the Commonwealth Bill by which we will federate in the new year?

'I urge all my fellow inhabitants of the Macleay to take a more independent and demanding line on all these matters. For the Empire may be saved – with or without shame – and there would still be no roads in the Macleay, and perhaps no Federation according to our desire. We should all think hard on this.

Yours etc.,
Australis,
Central Kempsey'

Tim looked up from the paper and lifted his ear, as if even in this torpid air, the cries of outrage could be heard in Belgrave Street. Australis was out to cause an outcry and the most stir he could, by writing to the more staid *Argus* instead of the jauntier *Chronicle*.

Nothing though to be heard. Nothing. The Empire of Billy Thurmond, M. M. Chance, Mr Malcolm went maligned, and no single protest pierced the walls of heat, the circle of fire, the shower of vegetable ash. In Pompeii-on-the-Macleay, the sentinels had gone to sleep.

In the shade of the peppermint tree outside, Ellen Burke and Annie lay together on a rug, wearing shifts which had been dipped in water. He went out to them and smiled. He approved of this strategem and thought it a clever thing. The whole bloody town should be doing it. He would dearly love to dampen himself and lie there with them. But he needed to lead Pee Dee out and place him in the traces. Pee Dee, of course, in a much higher spirit of protest than Bandy's horses. Dragging his head from side to side. Alarmed by the torrid wind.

Loading the cart at the front of the store, a very slow matter. With one or two people drifting by, one or two broiled ladies of the Macleay entering the store to interrupt his loading, to rant about the criminal day it was and buy some item – lard or flour – their households had run out of.

And then, dear merciful God, finding that amongst what must be loaded there were five butter boxes full of the plenty of the earth and the manufactures of Sydney destined for the Sisters of Mercy. Nothing for the Malcolms, though. Ernie true to his threat!

He put the feed bag on Pee Dee to distract him from the day. Some orders from East could wait till tomorrow. He was not crossing the river. He'd already crossed twice to his peril in less than a day.

At last ready, nearly fainting, to bring people their supplies. Lead Pee Dee, deprived of his feed bag and tossing his head in a way which said, 'Not me, not me. And not today.' Up for a last water fill up at the trough outside Savage's. For himself, a fill up with Sharp's lemonade. The whole bottle down him as quick as half a cup of tea.

And now off! Struggle forth into mid-street, mid-heat. In Belgrave Street, no one doing business, but Pee Dee heading now – with sudden, touching uncomplaint – for West. What must it be like in the camp? But Kitty and Mamie would be lying in moistened white shifts beneath a tree, he hoped, and the sea breeze which would end this madness would reach them first.

Yet Mamie must be repenting of her emigration. Australia presenting her with all its disadvantages on the one day or in the one week. Plague and fire, heat that withered the Celtic skin.

In the haze, the Offhand came loping diagonally from the door of the *Chronicle* office. He wore a suit coat and a vest as always. He might have thought he was running across the street somewhere else, not in a valley in a furious old continent you knew could fry you in a second if it was not so casual.

'Tim, Tim,' said the Offhand. The normal stewed face. The temporary tan of whiskied veins either side of the delicate nose. The pink lips enriched with the thinnest blood. The Reverend Offhand.

'Did you, Tim, happen to see that letter in the *Argus*. Can you imagine them actually publishing such a thing?'

'What is it? . . . *Australis*.'

'That one. A robust, Australian bloody letter, wouldn't you agree, Tim?'

His eyes were dancing away. Even today, it was all excitement and passionate opinion to him. Of course, he didn't have to deliver groceries to West.

'I read it. The argument had a certain virtue.'

'Tim, I do not ask you as a correspondent. I am speaking about literary matters as any man speaks in the streets to a friend.'

'My mind is rather distracted. My wife is up the river in that plague or quarantine camp or whatever it is.'

'Oh, that place is a formality now, Tim.' The Offhand shook his head, but his eyes glittered still. 'But tell me, don't you hope this *Australis* will write again? A fresh voice in a backward place is always most, most welcome! I found it so. A bloody minor miracle, Tim.'

'The fires and the heat are likely to take peoples' minds more,' Tim warned. 'Do you have any news from the Upper Macleay?'

'Oh,' said the Offhand. Offhandedly. 'Hickey's Creek is ablaze, and the Nulla.'

'The wife's sister's at Pee Dee.' Square miles of blaze distant.

'There are no reports of death, Tim. People place their homesteads in clearings for that reason, you might remember.'

'Exactly right,' said Tim. 'But the gumtrees explode like bombs.'

'Will you come into the Commercial with me and toast *Signor Australis*?'

'Is he Italian then? Or Spanish?'

'I use the *Signor* loosely, Tim,' said the Offhand.

'I hope you won't be offended, Offhand. I have all this to deliver.'

He swept his hand towards the crammed tray of the cart. 'I have a fifteen pounds fine to pay off.'

'How is that so, Tim? What did you do?'

'I am reluctant to say.'

'Again, please, as a friend.'

Tim told his tale of the smooth-faced inspector from the Colonial Secretary's.

'This is outrageous in a democracy,' said the Offhand when Tim had finished. It was a true sentiment, but how would it hold up against a magistrate's? And what would be its place amongst the other grievances – Ernie Malcolm, the suggestions of Constable Hanney. The Offhand was taken by the surface glitter of injustices. That was the great fault of writers. Injustice never penetrated their skins too deeply, put them off a meal, or the next drink which waited for them in the bar of the Commercial.

'For God's sake, don't put it in your column. I am in deep enough trouble.'

The Offhand held his hands up. They weren't much bigger than Bandy's.

'But you can be sure that that brute of an inspector checked with the powers of the town to ensure he made no example of one of theirs. Hence the injustice which cannot be defined, but which is everywhere in our community!'

'I shouldn't have sold him the bloody sugar to start with.'

'And he should not have been a *provocateur*,' the Offhand insisted. 'Is the coming Commonwealth of Australia to operate by such principles? By spying and provocation? If it is, we might as well be in Europe!'

'Except that the climate is better,' said Tim, laughing, and to spite the blaze and black grit of the air.

'I shall toast *Australis* on my own then,' said the Offhand. 'I still cannot get over the *Argus* actually putting ink to them. It's bloody rich, Tim. Not you, by any chance?'

'Never,' said Tim.

And the Offhand laughed and passed on his way.

Tim and Pee Dee straggled on a mile and into Kemp Street.

'Tiptoe past the bloody police station,' Tim urged Pee Dee. Everything dormant. Birds vanished from the trees. The trees themselves, between gusts of fiery wind, looking like they were considering the desirability of themselves blossoming into flame.

And yet there was undue movement at St Joseph's Convent. Nuns were running by the wooden scaffolding tower from which the Angelus bell hung. Children were moving, and piercing the white heat with excited cries. My God, the poor little savages will faint if they don't stop! Mad Johnny would run till he dropped. Unless mercifully stopped.

The Angelus tower in front of the convent. It was made of yellow painted struts of hardwood bolted together. Yellow diagonals of timbers rose to the little, corrugated iron roof, beneath which was slung the great crossbeam from which hung the bell. Rung at six o'clock in the morning, twelve noon, six o'clock in the evening. *The Angel of the Lord declared unto Mary*, everyone in the convent prayed as the bell rang out, inviting even the godless New South Wales police down the road to celebrate the Annunciation. Three Hail Marys, one Glory Be. Bandy the Muslim would understand these impulses, these summonses from a tower, better than Constable Hanney. And Missy in her motherless fluid at the cop shop – did redemption call to her thus? Was someone in the town moved secretly to name her, in a bathroom or at the corner of a bar, muttering into his lapel? Daphne or Winnie or Constance. Ellen or Hilda or Dorothea. Naming her on an impulse at hearing the far-off, familiar three-times-a-day bell of the Tykes.

Methodists and the good Wesleyans of South Kempsey didn't go for any of it, yet shared the town with the mystery for which that tower stood in its plain Macleay timbers.

Where was the sense in paying Imelda a bob a week for a full-time boarder? If they were permitted to run themselves mad under a sun and in an air like this one? Drawing nearer, he saw Imelda striking the uprights of the tower with her cane, and then standing back, pointing the cane to the apex where the seemingly white bell stood.

This white bell at the peak of the structure was not the real gun-metal bell at all. Rather it was Lucy. And in brown pants and a blue shirt, with the dirty bandage on his head awaiting removal by Dr Erson, Johnny. Somehow they had climbed the tower to the highest side beam together. He could envisage too clearly Johnny going up with his long, pliable feet, Lucy with her crazy suppleness.

Tim drew up Pee Dee and the cart and ran into the convent garden. Someone's redheaded brat was imitating with hooting sounds the spread-armed balancing pose Johnny took as he walked a little way along his beam and grabbed a corner upright. Tim reached Imelda, who was still whacking the corner of one of the tower's uprights with her cane.

'Come down, you two ruffians!' she yelled. But the diagonals which someone with climbing skills might well shinny up were too steep to shinny down.

Two girls about Lucy's age – in pinafores, strolling together, an arm around each other's shoulder – chattered away, engrossed. To them, time out of the classroom was a gift to amity. Didn't matter to them that there were two pupils who had got themselves to an impossible point in today's bloody murderous sky.

Imelda panted from punishing the tower, but would not give up the practice.

'Don't do that,' Tim called to her. 'Could make them jump.'

Imelda did at least soften and decrease the tempo of her blows. Her face broiling under the black cloth, under the white band which covered her forehead for Christ's sake. No man shall see thy brow . . .

'Tea,' she called to one of the younger nuns, who was standing by, clutching the huge black beads hanging at her waist from the Order's thick black belt. 'Could you ever get me tea, sister? I'm dying of parchment.'

And before the young nun runs off to do it, Tim mentally complained that *parchment* was something you wrote on, an animal skin. *Parched* was thirsty. Was he paying out all this money to a headmistress who didn't know the difference?

Imelda stopped caning the tower altogether.

'I've sent a child for the fire brigade,' she told Tim. 'Mr Crane, you know. And their extension ladder. But God knows, they could be in the bush somewhere battling flames.'

To look directly up the thwarts at the two figures at the apex of the tower was too terrifying a view. He stepped away many paces and tried it from a slightly kinder angle. 'Don't jump!' he yelled. 'We have some men coming. Sit still. Wait for the ladder!'

It was Lucy who looked so light up there, as if she might step out and float to ground on the searing westerly. Johnny looked solider, in possession of himself and the tower, and so more endangered.

'I will see if I can come up,' Tim yelled, pronouncing each word.

He wrenched off his elastic-sided boots.

'Oh, dear Jesus,' he said to himself, looking up again and assessing the task. Johnny always putting him up for awful trials for heroism.

He lifted himself into the angle where a diagonal beam came down and bolted itself to one of the uprights of the tower. This diagonal would take him up to a cross bar perhaps twenty feet from the earth, and then another diagonal would begin. No other way up existed. You had to admire and abhor the little buggers for having managed it in such blazing air!

He forced himself to begin climbing the diagonal. Splayed-out feet. Hauling himself on the harsh, barely-planed, yellow-painted timber. Bowed over like a bloody ape. Everything aching. And bent like this, the idea about not casting your eyes to the earth utterly impossible! He knew to all the nuns and all the children he looked graceless, scrambling and frightened. There were bloody convent urchins mimicking him. Swinging one foot out, as he had to to bypass the one which held him to his previously highest point. Up to the first cross bar. Haul yourself up on it and award yourself a breath, grasping the diagonal which might take you up to the tower's next stage. The thing built in three sections, like the prayers of the Angelus itself. Father, Son, Holy Spirit. Three Hail Marys for your sins and the repose of souls. Some bloody repose up here in a sky abandoned even by the magpies!

'Careful, Mr Shea,' cried a nun from below. Waterford accent.

'Listen to me,' he called to Johnny, who had the grace to stare down, to Lucy who was looking off into the unscannable haze. 'Stay there. The ladder's coming. Papa's coming.'

How would *he* stand up there though, looking out at the seared heavens and the valley full of smoke?

His breath as good as terror would let it be, he began the next diagonal. He found he had a way with it all now. Sailors he had so admired, up in the top mast, feet on one of those ratlines. It can be learned. Ascent. He'd learned to rescue Johnny from the stern of *Terara*. Now in the topmost! Watch below on deck!

Shinnying on further, diagonally to the sky, calling in a voice in which people could hear the quavers. 'Stay there! Stay there!' Since history showed that if *she* jumped for whatever reason of her own, Johnny would step out too, falling like a willing stone and getting joy from it for the instant it lasted.

There was further flutter of activity below. Horses were mixed up in it, and stupid Imelda cried, 'Mr Shea. Save yourself!' Smoky air passed in front of his eyes. Had the tower itself caught alight? One of his feet had slithered away from the diagonal. An awful shin-whack pain in that leg! He fell now and was full of terror for the instant that lasted. The thunder of the ground, punishing him on the soles of the feet. The bastinado punishment, up through the soles.

'Oh Mother,' he said, lying on his side and gulping with pain. Nuns were touching his legs in a spirit of medical experiment.

It turned out it had been another of Imelda's inexact meanings, like *parchment*. In calling, 'Save yourself!' she had meant *Save yourself the trouble*. When he could make sense of things again, he could see she had been informing him that Mr Crane and his big boy Arnold had ridden up to the gate on the fire engine behind its two old draught horses. He had heard it as a warning though, and it had knocked one of his legs from beneath him.

A youngish nun, the Waterford one, had already begun bandaging his swollen ankle, and the pressure of the bandage was the clearest thing he felt. A second nun brought him fully to his senses by pouring iodine on his right shin below the torn and rucked-up trouser leg. Mr Crane and his son had the extension ladder up to the top of the tower, and big Arnold was coming down first with Lucy reserved in his arms. Ladies first, as if she did not have Johnny by the scruff of his bloody will. Mr Crane at the base of the ladder was calling out counsels at Johnny. 'Stay up there, sonny!' And then under his breath, 'You little bastard.'

Arnold was more lenient and brought Johnny down on his shoulders. Through the mist of all his astringent pain, Tim doubted whether this tribute to Johnny's manliness was a wise gesture.

Meanwhile Imelda rapped Lucy once across the upper arm with her cane. Immediately a few tears fell down Lucy's face. They weren't passionate. The jolt of the cane had shaken them out.

'Go to the dormitory and sit on your bed, miss,' Imelda told her.

'Come here!' Tim called as she went off with that deliberateness so dreadful to find in a child.

The little girl turned and walked across, carrying her scatter of tears.

'Tell me, Lucy, what do you want done that hasn't been? I asked you before and now have to ask again. Why do you make my son do these things?'

He knew how silly the question was. Adults always ask these questions of children who would not give the answer for another twenty or thirty years. But this particular trick of muteness could drive an adult to blows. And he could feel the blows rising in him.

She looked at him directly and he saw what she was watching in him: that he could support the idea of her falling, but not the idea of Johnny's plummet. She lacked someone to fear her fall more than his own death. That level stare. She forgave him, she was philosophic. But she knew.

'We thought we could see everything from the top,' she told him. 'Johnny's mother down the river.'

'No. No, it's not high enough. You must know there's no place on earth from which you can see all the rest. There's no height you can get to.'

She bunched her eyes. Another tear emerged under this pressure. 'I know.'

'What do you want? I can't do more.'

She said nothing.

'If you behave like this just once again,' he said, 'I will let go of you for good, Lucy. I swear to Jesus! But if you stop being a mad child, I'll keep you here and take you to Crescent Head for picnics.'

Arnold Crane delivered Johnny now to the base of the tower. Imelda began scourging him with her birch.

'No!' called Tim. 'No! Send him to me.'

Imelda stopped lashing and pointed the boy towards his prone father. The boy, too, had a few stained droplets on his cheeks. They meant nothing under this sun.

'I am suspending your education, you bloody ruffian. You have half killed me. Get the Sisters' boxes out of the cart and take them to the kitchen. I'm too crippled myself.'

So here he was, lamed, reaching up to cuff the boy behind the ear and point him to where Pee Dee stood, tethered to the fence, trying to back away nonetheless from the placid old plough horses who pulled the fire wagon.

'Give Pee Dee a whack for me too and tell him to behave!' Tim roared after the boy.

Two of the nuns were ushering children back towards the classrooms beneath the Celtic cross which stood at the apex of St Joseph's school hall. The young Waterford nun had finished binding up Tim's ankle and was struggling to rise within the great black folds of her habit. A dark, sweat-drenched furze on her upper lip. A plain young woman but beautiful in her own way.

'Can you get up under your own steam now, Mr Shea?' she asked.

Tim rolled onto his good leg and forced himself upright with his palm. She was by his left elbow, assisting. He put his weight on his bound foot but, of course, it would not take it.

'You may need crutches then,' the consecrated Waterford woman told him.

'I have a blackthorn at home,' he told her.

From the direction of the cart came Johnny labouring under a butterbox but doing fairly well. A number of older and larger boys had joined in to help him carry things. You had to admire the little blackguard. As long as Mad Lucy let him live.

Imelda herself struggled over to ask how he was, and without ceremony he said, 'You might remember, Mother. I asked you to keep them apart.'

Imelda angry to be spoken to so outright in front of one of her nuns. 'Well, we are not God Himself, Mr Shea,' she told him. 'We cannot enquire into each one of their seconds. We do our best. I now see what you mean. But I would tell you that there is mischief in the boy too. Children don't have to talk to each other to make up some mad plan. They do things. It is called Original Sin. But their Guardian Angels were with them today.'

He looked at the boxes of groceries making for the convent kitchen on the shoulders of boys large and small. 'I thought that

was what I was paying you one and threepence a week for. So
that Guardian Angels would be saved the trouble.'

She turned away, stung. Yet they always had an answer these
women!

After some dawdling children went Imelda, thrashing the air
with her cane. The flail of the cane, the rattle of her Rosary.
The invisible ministers, the seraphim, the Guardian Angels were
taking a bloody thrashing!

Through all this morning's adventure, while climbing the hard,
painted diagonals of the timbers with splayed feet, he'd had it
in mind.

'Sister,' he asked the Waterford nun. 'Have you heard of the
young woman who died at Mulroney's?'

'Yes, I have, Mr Shea.'

'Do you think it proper to pray for the repose of her soul?'

The questioning made the young nun nervous. She showed
it by being brusque.

'I do. We are all sisters, Mr Shea.'

'Very good. Now do you think there is any way her soul is
running amok? In what we see here. The children run wild.'

'No. I certainly don't believe that. That's theologically unsound,
Mr Shea.'

But you could tell she knew about visitations and was as fearful
now as if she'd had one, had seen Missy inhabiting fiery ground
or glittering sea.

'I am cursed with dreams,' said Tim.

'All human beings are, in this vale of tears,' said the nun. But
now she was all business again. 'You should wear a scapular
for the proper protection, Mr Shea. We must be on our guard
against superstitious belief. Now come and have some tea like
a good fellow.'

At that moment Johnny was back in Tim's vicinity, standing
some paces away. His deliveries done.

'You'll come with me,' said Tim. And to the nun, 'Thank you,
I have water on my cart.'

On the second day of terrible heat, Dr Erson and the sanitation
officer visited the plague camp and declared everyone well, and
clothing clear of infestation. That evening a huge cleansing wind

came from the south, gusting up thunderheads with it. The sky cracked and people covered their mirrors with a cloth lest the lightning have a surface to admire itself by. Men were already going around collecting for the burned-out farms of Nulla Creek. The *Argus* would say that six thousand pigs had been consumed, twelve thousand cattle and as many as a thousand horses. By some startling mercy – no human fatalities.

Tim could have been one if he'd taken an unlucky posture in falling to the earth. The lunatic children could have been if they'd stepped into the air in the way Lucy looked as though she might throughout the enterprise.

On a cleansed and overcast morning, Kitty and Mamie and the other *Burrawong* passengers were loaded on a drogher with *Burrawong*'s cargo and made a slow, long passage up the Macleay. People who saw them coming ran up and down Smith and Belgrave Streets announcing it. Those who needed to meet the drogher came up to Central wharf with a strange reluctance. His foot in a sock, and supporting himself on a blackthorn, so that louts outside the Commercial called, 'Dot and carry one!', Tim took Annie down there to see the drogher berth. Others watched it from their windows and under their eaves, and then pretended they weren't much interested. But of course, you needed to be interested. Even in him an unreasonable voice asked was this slow, blunt vessel the plague's fatal bark?

In both the papers this morning, a letter had appeared from Captain Reid:

'The Captain of *Burrawong* would like to advise the clientele of the North Coast Steamship Navigation Company that following the fumigation of the ship in Darling Harbour, and its arrival at the New Entrance of the Macleay, the vessel was thoroughly searched for rats, living or dead. The limber boards, sparketting and all lumber corners were removed, and dead rats to the number of thirty-five were collected and disposed of. None of these showed any signs of being infested with the plague.

'Following the disposal of the rats, and in expectation of continued passenger custom from the inhabitants of the Macleay Valley, the crew undertook a further thorough disinfecting of the ship. Disinfectant was spread throughout the ceiling, the forepeak and the lazarette of the vessel. Such procedures will be continued regularly throughout the present epidemic. I can assure passengers that every care will be taken. The ship will be fumigated with charcoal and sulphur prior to every departure from Sydney . . .'

The captain's letter however was followed by another from someone who signed himself *Sanitas*, some old cow-cocky from downriver, complaining that there'd been 'various improprieties' in the handling of the *Burrawong* during her time in quarantine at the New Entrance. The droghers which were designated to bring cargo and passengers to Kempsey were permitted to lie beside *Burrawong* at night, and there existed the possibility of rats infected by the plague passing aboard the droghers and thence to settlements along the river. The sanitation officer, said *Sanitas*, had to prevent droghers from lying beside *Burrawong* at night. 'The capacity of the flea to travel is nothing short of prodigious . . .'

So the scholarly farmer continued, pealing his verbal klaxon on the Macleay. No wonder people looked warily as the drogher, laden with provisions and passengers, now neared the wharf.

Telling Annie to be careful, Tim stumbled with her down the embankment towards the river bank itself and, dear God, there was Bandy.

'Mr Shea,' said Bandy, formally bowing, as if again they had become strangers.

'Well then, Bandy.'

'Mr Shea,' said Bandy. 'I thought the women might need help with their baggage.'

They were bound together in Constable Hanney's accusations now, so Tim bowed and said, 'Very thoughtful of you, Bandy.'

Not a dramatic landing for Mamie the emigrant, not from a drogher. At this tide, the gangplank slanted up to the wharf from the hard-laden deck. Mamie and Kitty waving from the deck, and Joe O'Neill smiling wanly too, banjo-less, a little behind them. Still tormented, poor scoundrel, by Mamie. Kitty plumply pointing towards him, tapping her upper leg. Asking what's wrong with his?

Tim making soothing motions with his free hand.

At last, after the commercial travellers had hustled back and forth on the narrow gangplank, landing their bags of samples, the sisters struggled up to the wharf. Not even gallant Bandy could get aboard to help the sisters up such a busy plank. Kitty helped ashore by Mr Joe O'Neill, who then boarded again and came ashore with his and Mamie's bags. He was strong enough in his desire to carry them all the way to West.

'No fuss, I had a fall, I'll tell you,' said Tim as Kitty embraced him. Annie hid her face from Mamie and clung to Kitty's skirts. 'I suppose you'd like presents?' said Kitty, grinning down. The girl would grow up taller than her mother. You could see it already in her four-and-a-half-year-old frame.

'I know you have presents, mama.'

'I do. I have lovely things. They are for nice girls who say hello to their Aunt Mamie.'

So all the greetings were made. 'Say hello to Mr O'Neill who comes from near where Mama and Aunt Mamie come in Cork.'

What did Annie think Cork was? The other side of the moon.

Joe had come ashore with Mamie's sea trunk, and Bandy made certain he went aboard to get Kitty's. As if to keep the honours even. Tim said, 'Didn't bother hitching up the old feller. I'll get Naylor's cab to bring your sea chest down to the residence.'

'Not at all,' said Kitty. 'Mr Habash would do it for us, wouldn't you?'

At this announcement by his wife, Tim felt rising within him a persisting reluctance at being espoused by Habash. Better that honest Joe O'Neill labour down Smith Street with both on his back.

'No, Mr Habash has work to do,' said Tim. 'I will go and hitch up Pee Dee. It's no trouble.'

'Nonsense, nonsense, nonsense,' said Kitty. And knowing who was in charge, O'Neill and Bandy were already setting off up the embankment with one of the sea chests. Up there, unnoticed before by Tim, stood Bandy's green wagon.

'How can you make deliveries with that ankle?' asked Kitty.

'It's difficult just now.'

'Well, Joe'll make them for you while he's waiting for his relatives to turn up.'

Having arranged the muscle power of the men, Kitty took Annie by the hand and mounted the ramp to Smith Street.

Smith Street, where Mamie walked past the banks, the creamery, the Good Templars' Hall with the demeanour of a native. Typical of Red Kenna's children, she took things as they presented. This was, he was sure yet again, a gift.

He did not mar the homecoming, the stories of the voyage, the time in Sydney, the quarantine, by telling Kitty about Johnny's adventure, though Johnny came home from day school looking wary and frightened, suspecting that the tale had been told. He was by now bandage-less, and his hair was growing back, so there was nothing to alert the new arrivals.

Ellen Burke had made another good stew, and its pungency came in from the cookhouse and filled the residence like a solid caress. Bandy had been invited to dinner, and Joe O'Neill was ecstatic to be staying under a roof with Mamie. More or less under a roof anyhow. There was no bed for him in the house but he would spread some blankets outside by the shed. If he had any of the Irishman's normal advanced dread of serpents, he was willing to forget it for Mamie's sake. Big red-bellied blacksnakes had once or twice been found on the verandah, yet were timid unless trodden on. Nonetheless, made a big dent in a fellow's composure. Joey would fight them for Mamie.

Since business proved slow in the afternoon, Tim wondered did people know Kitty had come down on the drogher? Did they fear she'd pass the plague to them along with the crackers and cheese?

Look in the *Argus* for plague-news and the hope of sighting a new letter to grace the day of Kitty's return. And it was there! Page Nine.

'Dear Sir,

'It appears from the casualty figures for Queenslanders and northern New South Welshmen published in your last issue and shown to be due to meningitis [1], enteric fever [5], and ambush of a column of two hundred mounted rifles by Boers [13], that the tactics of General French in the Transvaal have been nothing short of disastrous. Even the Australian bushmen move in column of march, like an outmoded British regiment.

'Is General French characteristic of the men born to rule over us and long to reign over us? I simply ask the question. While we sacrifice our young in South Africa, we are asked also to sacrifice the best concepts of our coming Federation. Our colonial staesmen, led by Mr Alfred Deakin of Victoria, are now asked to take our Bill for the Commonwealth of Australia to Britain, where the political equivalents of General French can peer over them in the offices of the Secretary of State for the Colonies in Whitehall. Not only do we then surrender our young to the incompetence of British generals, but we surrender the best ideas for our future to the supervision and amendment of far-off British Ministers of State who have never seen our shore, and can have no chief and primary interest in our welfare.

'The British will be very ill-informed indeed if they decide to interfere too much with the Australian Commonwealth Act. The sweet clauses we have raised up for a Federal Commonwealth, like the sweet boys we have sent to South Africa, will be mowed down by incompetent men if we do not take care.

I am, etc.
Australis
Central Kempsey'

Tim laid his hand emphatically a number of times on the page. Fair enough, fair enough, *Australis*.

But who had written these letters? A farmer with time to think? Yet the address was Central Kempsey. Was that a mere blind? Who was this Thomas Paine of the Macleay?

He went through a list in his head. Old Burke upriver at Pee Dee had time enough and adequate disgruntlement to write these. But they were not his opinions. He was not *for* Federation. He was in favour purely of running Pee Dee station as he wished under a regime of free trade and low tax. So Old Burke had not written these. Borger, the farmer who had spoken up at the Patriotic Fund meeting in the Good Templars? Certainly Borger, you would think. It was pure *Freeman's Journal* stuff.

Well, good for the lad, though he would suffer. He might take his cream to the butter factory and find it turned back by some fellow worried about far, far South Africa. It was the one thing wrong with the country. People were too in love with other quarters of the globe and not enough with this place itself. To an emigrant, the Macleay was sufficient kingdom. You couldn't tell the women that, of course. Kitty loved reading the Palace news. Didn't see any of it as political. It was purely a matter of tiaras, blood-lines, balls and regattas. If you wanted to be strict about it, as *Australis* obviously did, you could say that the women were abettors of the high loyalism of New South Wales. But then why shouldn't they enjoy themselves, reading about fanciful things?

In late afternoon, more rain to soothe the burnt pastures upriver. Old Kylie from the Good Templars came around under a big black umbrella asking for donations for farmers who had lost their stock, their crops, their outbuildings. Contributions over ten shillings would be published in the list of donations to appear in both the *Argus* and *Chronicle*. Tim went into the storeroom, to the black and red cash box. He opened it with the key from his fob and took out a ten bob banknote. A green pound note beckoned to him. Ten bob contributors would be the lowest on the list. In the face of fines and threats, he would show his open-handedness. He knew the crime of vanity beckoned. People on the way to Mass calling out to him with respect and then muttering to each other that he was a good fellow and always ready to extend credit. He loved to be suspected of generosity beyond his means. Besides, poor buggers had lost their stock, their horses and cattle, and could go broke.

He took the thirty shillings, the one pound ten, out to old Kylie. Lunacy. The old man whistled and wrote him a receipt. 'This is very generous of you, Mr Shea. Not all the tradespeople are as generous as this!'

One in the eye for Ernie Malcolm.

Through the rain *without* an umbrella came Joe O'Neill slightly aglow and his lips a little thick. Stammery. He'd been to the Commercial to meet the natives, and now was coming to dinner carrying bottles of lager and stout cradled in his arms. If the rain kept up he would have to sleep in the cart in the shed.

'I think I'll like this place,' he told Tim, coming into the store and shaking himself. It would have been the Offhand who pumped almost too much grog into Joe, asking him for impressions of recent events in Ireland and the British Isles. Would Ireland ever get Home Rule, or had Home Rule run aground for good on the snowy white breast of Mrs O'Shea (a Kitty like his), mistress of the late, great Parnell? And so on. Ireland suffering mortally from Parnell's mortal lusts, and Joe passing on the news to the Offhand on the Northern Rivers of New South Wales.

Joe had the look of an emigrant who believed he'd settled in already. A few pints with the natives had done it. With the denizens. But there was no chance that he'd make an easy voyager, the way Mamie did. When he got out to his relatives and started to live in his slab hut, the silence and otherness would get to him, and he'd be struck by a big bush melancholy.

At dinner, Joe and Mamie took the chance to tell further tales of the voyage. An extraordinary thing, a voyage of that extent. When you are on it, you think that you would be able to talk by the hour about it afterwards. But there is something you can't convey about the sea's repetitive sunsets and dawns, about the variations of swell, about porpoises seen off the stern, about the ferocity of sea sickness. The other mistake you made was to think that life after you landed would be as varied as that. A frustration that in giving a picture of the voyage, you made it sound as ordinary as the rest of life.

When it came to taking places at table, Mamie insisted on sitting between Kitty and Bandy Habash. Then the children down one side, and Joe O'Neill and Ellen Burke at the foot, looking a little wan together. Tim praised Ellen to Kitty, and recounted now the accidents which had marked her absence.

'Holy Mary,' said Kitty, 'Pee Dee. And Angelus tower! If I'd stayed away another week, you'd all be dead!'

But tonight it seemed a comic rather than fatal possibility. Joe O'Neill flicked Johnny's ear playfully, and even Tim found himself laughing.

A number of bottles of stout and ale had been opened with the soup, and everyone was drinking freely except for Bandy.

'Thank Christ I'm a Catholic,' said Joe, adding to the beer

already in him. 'Drinking's the one thing you're allowed. I would have made a rotten Mohammedan.'

But you could see by the way his eyes moved at the beginnings and ends of sentences and during silences that he was thinking, 'Surely she can't really like this little brown fellow?'

As for Ellen Burke, she kept dashing out to the cookhouse, just like someone covering up with kitchen work her lack of ease.

Tim said, 'Now tell me, Bandy, these remedies of yours. Do they cure anything? What do you put in these things, Bandy, you sell to people?'

Kitty sank back in her chair and looked up at the ceiling; a posture encouraged by her condition. 'Tim is a sort of Doubting Thomas. But I tell you, Tim, the man's main tonic is a grand pick-me-up.'

All eyes then on Bandy. Ellen Burke's dwelling on him from the end of the table.

'Give us a scientific exposition,' called Joe, winking, and sipping again at his beer.

Bandy murmured, 'Where to begin? The chief constituents of the body in Punjabi herbalism are the blood, flesh, fat, bone, marrow, chyle, and semen. One element, when disordered, influences all the others through their connection.'

'Who taught you all this?' Tim asked.

'My father of course. In my homeland, there are a list of more than three hundred vegetables which can be used as cures. Some of those cannot be had here in the Macleay, though some can. We are able to get useful animal and herbal substances brought up also on the *Burrawong* from Sydney.'

'Any cure for plague?' called Joe. Desire and drink had made him mean.

'And then of course,' Bandy continued, 'sometimes a mixture of the mineral and vegetable is required. Take the blood. We make a mixture of rhubarb and iron for our blood tonic.'

'Rhubarb and iron,' murmured Kitty.

'I feed blood tonic now and then to my own horses. For breathing problems I make up a herbal mixture to be burned beside the patient's bed. This is moxa, which we are supplied by the Chinese herbalist of Dixon Street, and some Indian hemp, which grows wild in this valley and can be harvested by penknife. For the illnesses of women in pregnancy and for general liverishness, we use belladonna, which restores the fabric of women and is much appreciated. Mr Nance the pharmacist, you will find, uses the same herb, the foxglove, as in Habash's Heart Tonic.'

'A body of scholarship, Mr Habash,' said Mamie, seemingly in awe. 'A body of scholarship you carry in your head.'

Bandy gave just a margin of a smile but then swallowed it.

'It is true,' he said in a very low voice, which might have been actually beyond the hearing of Ellen Burke and Joe O'Neill, 'that many people tell us that they are grateful for our remedies, more grateful than for some others they receive from chemists.'

'Sure, the chemists and doctors don't know everything,' said Kitty.

Tim found himself treating Bandy's exposition of his craft as a herbalist with greater tolerance now than he might have a month ago. He asked what other remedies. Bandy mentioned rhinoceros horn for older men, and ground quantities of gallstones from bulls mixed with cardamom and cinnamon. Arsenic was excellent for rheumatism and for the complexion.

Tim noticed Mamie had the hawker-cum-herbalist enchanted. The more substances he mentioned, the more his gaze turned to her.

Abruptly Ellen Burke stood up. All she could manage to say was, 'Custard.' She grabbed the apron off the back of her chair and half-rushed, half-staggered out to the cookhouse.

'Oh yes,' said Mamie, rising after a moment. 'I'll help.'

Again, the amazing lack of novelty with which she moved, as if she'd grown up in this house. Her going left a silence.

Kitty whispered to Tim, 'Go and see, Tim. Go on. Something's up.'

Tim rose. Dear God, he was not as steady as he thought. Even on one leg.

'I'm just going out to lend a hand,' he told the other men.

Both Joe and Bandy bounded up. They did not want to see a lame man doing what they could.

'No, gentlemen,' said Kitty from her powerful, seated position. 'You are guests.'

Outside, a light rain, softer than silk, slanted in under the verandah. He hobbled along under the covered way to the cookhouse where the fire was restrained.

From outside the cookhouse he could hear the women speaking, and a certain tightness in Ellen Burke's voice.

'No, put it down. Let me do things, for God's sake.'

'Would you prefer I didn't help at all?' asked Mamie. She sounded half-amused.

'I'd prefer that you didn't come in from nowhere, swing in on a steamer from some bloody damp heap of a place and upset friendships. That's what I'd prefer.'

'Upset friendships. What do you mean?'

'Some things are already set up here. And you blunder in as if everything starts from your arrival. All earlier bets off! Well, that's not the way you'll get on here.'

Tim stepped further back into the shade of the verandah. He did not want to be discovered by them but also did not want to go.

'You're teasing poor Mr Habash,' said Ellen. 'He's a lonely soul, but you make him sit beside you. Only so that Joe O'Neill will pant all the more for you. Well Mr Habash is more than something you can make use of, and he already has his friends. Don't think of that though! Miss Importance from some shitty pigyard in Cork! Queening it in the bloody colonies, for dear God's sweet sake!'

Tim waited through the silence in which Mamie's temper – such to resemble Kitty's – rose. 'What a performance, miss,' Mamie ultimately said. 'I'm not using Mr O'Neill or Mr Habash one way or another. Men *use* themselves and they always have and are happy to do so. Now, do you want me to help you carry in the pud or what do you want?'

But there was no sound of movement from within the cookhouse. It could be sensed that Ellen Burke was on the edge of tears or perhaps in them. She was dealing with an older, archer, and more stubborn woman.

'Your sister isn't going to like it,' Ellen plaintively argued, 'if you come in here interfering with old friendships.'

'Kitty? Kitty seems perfectly happy sitting there with her big stomach. Kitty's troubles are over. Kitty is easy.'

'I don't mean Kitty. Your other sister. Remember? My step-mother. Mrs Molly Burke. A genuine lady.'

'Oh, Molly? Molly isn't just like the rest of us. Always had the airs. All she was looking for was a chance to exercise them. And why would Molly be upset? You don't mean to say *she* has a fancy for the little brown feller?'

This was fierce, close stuff, exactly like Kitty's method of debate. Ellen could be heard frankly weeping. 'We don't want another bloody bitch in this country,' she cried. 'We have a full supply already.'

Mamie turned softer now. 'Stop blubbering and let me take that tray for you. Now come on, Ellen. Listen, do you love the little pagan? Is he your sweetie, is that what this is?'

There was no answer.

'Well, come on, tell a woman for sweet Christ's sake!'

Ellen said, 'You'll marry Joe in the end, so all you're doing is messing Bandy up!'

'It's kind of you to make predictions, Miss Burke. I can tell you that Joe O'Neill can whistle. I don't intend to be shackled to a mopey old bugger like him. I'd like a contest out of life! Come on, give me that bloody tray and dry up!'

'Wait,' Ellen Burke protested through her tears, 'I have to put the plates on.'

With soft rain slanting down onto his shoulders, Tim began retreating up the verandah lest he be overtaken by partly reconciled women carrying pudding and custard and plates.

That night, when all his guests were asleep, worn out by good times or by anguish, as he lay beside Kitty, who was profoundly and noisily asleep, Missy again – and as was to be expected – stepped into the room from the sea. She wore a blazer, a man's shirt and tie. She appeared to have theatrical purposes. You could tell that, since her cheeks were rouged. An overpowering sea, hurtful to the gaze, lay behind her.

Old Bruggy's Masses hadn't soothed away this restive spirit, who brought everything into play, the sea, his father, Bandy's predictions, assertions and suggestions. Depending on him for her salvation and her substantiality, poor bitch. As Imelda had chosen him to supply groceries *gratis*, Missy had looked up through the fluids, seen him as the town's co-operative spirit, the easy mark, the man who would go to proud and tormented trouble.

'In the name of the Father,' he said, 'and of the Son and of the Holy Spirit, Amen.' Then he turned away, onto his side.

This did not, however, mean he wouldn't do something.

In a morning that was still cool, all the smoke blown away or absorbed by rain, the sort of morning which might convince emigrants of the glories of the Macleay, Tim saw Joe O'Neill come in, already washed and shaven, from his billet in the shed. The remorse of booze in him, but determined to look well and reliable.

Meanwhile Kitty lay in, but Mamie was loud and efficient, bringing the big pot into the dining room and pouring lots of tea.

Half past eight. Tim at table taking Joe O'Niell through the cash and credit books he would need to take out with him on deliveries. 'Take no nonsense from the bloody horse either!'

Joe went off, making his deliveries for Mamie's sake. Able to put his foot on the ground and to wear an unlaced shoe, Tim limped down Smith Street towards the offices of the North Coast Steamship Navigation Company. The stairs were hard, but once he'd dragged his lame leg up, he asked after Captain Reid of *Burrawong*, and Miss Hunt who ran the front office stiffly told him that Captain Reid always stayed at the Hotel Kempsey.

Limping back towards Belgrave Street, Tim saw a notice outside the Good Templars.

PATRIOTIC FUND MEETING – FEBRUARY 28

A Special Meeting of the Patriotic Fund has been called to consider the following motion from Mr William Thurmond, JP, Pola Creek:

That in view of certain recent inflammatory and philo-Boer letters published in the Macleay press, and in view of other signs of disloyalty apparent in the community, the Fund authorises its executive to produce a black list of disloyal Businesses and Employees for the guidance of the populace.

This meeting called by the Authority of Mr Arthur Baylor, President and Mr Ernest Malcolm, Secretary.

No sooner read than he heard a voice behind him. 'You see, you see!'

He turned and saw Ernie Malcolm standing there in his going-to-work grey suit and with a cheroot in his mouth. 'This is what it all comes to, Tim, if you keep pushing the boundaries.'

'What does it come to? I've done nothing.'

'A mistake to take us chaps on. Enlightened and tolerant we may be to suit the age, Shea. But what we hold dear we hold dear!'

Ernie did not wait for a reply, though Tim did not have one, being too confounded. Could *he* be the object of such a meeting?

'Mr Malcolm,' Tim called after him.

Ernie barely stopped and did not turn.

'Why did you write a letter praising the work of that hopeless constable? Is it some friend of yours you want to protect?'

'Letter?'

'The constable showed me. He's gratified at it.'

Still keeping his back to Tim, Ernie said, 'I hope you don't imply anything. What do I look for, Shea? I look for a joyous bridge opening in a year of great promise. Do you understand?'

'I don't try to push anyone into a corner.'

'Oh but you do. You are accepted as a citizen, but still you look to upset the damned balance. You can't be a smartalec without people latching on. People aren't stupid, you know!'

'Oh, the letters in the *Argus*. Can a fellow lose his name so easily? A hero one month, a gouger in another. Generous in January, traitorous in February.'

'A man can lose everything,' said Ernie, 'very easily. We all live on a knife-edge.'

He simply walked away. Then: I'll write them a letter, Tim resolved. I'll swear a bloody affidavit drawn up by Sheridan. Those letters aren't mine.

So he had a strategy, and for the sake of his peace anyhow he fixed his mind back on Missy, who was another matter, her own.

* * *

He limped around to the Kempsey Hotel, trying as he went not to look like an enemy of the shire. But outside Savage's, Borger the vocal cow-cocky stood by his wagon. He strode up to Tim, took him fraternally by the elbow, and spoke in a low voice. 'I have to commend you on your letters to the *Argus*. Masterly, old feller. Those buggers might have the battalions, but we've still got them beaten when it comes to turn of phrase and genuine prophetic fire.'

'Holy God,' said Tim. His ankle was in a bad way now too, bulging over his shoe. 'I didn't write those damn letters. I don't have any grievance I want to express in public against Britain. I am not like you.'

'No, old son, I know,' said Borger, not believing him. '*Australis* did it. A good feller, that *Australis*! And from Central. Who else from Central . . .'

Borger continued to caress his elbow. Were people watching?

'I'll tell you what, Tim. There are two men in this valley with the education and passion to write those letters. They both spoke out at the public meeting of the so-called Patriotic Fund. What two fellers are they, Tim? One is me. But I didn't write the things, I wish I bloody had. The other, Tim, is a feller who keeps a store.'

'No. Don't go around town telling people these things.'

'I tell them only to those who understand certain things. That we may have a destiny other than that of the British army in South Africa.'

This promise alarmed Tim. Borger wasn't secretive at all. He was a talker. An enthusiast.

'Please, please,' said Tim. 'I have a business and a third child coming.'

'I understand. What a society where a man can have his trade snatched away for these kinds of reasons! But I wanted to say just this. Thank you, Tim. You're a hero to me.'

Borger sauntering away now towards the front of the emporium which was just opening its doors.

Tim called, 'The last bastard that said I was a hero took his business from me a week ago!'

Borger waved his hand and smiled, 'Of course, of course. It's what they did to Napper Tandy, Robert Emmett. Ned Kelly, for that matter. You've got my business from here on.'

He disappeared into the emporium. If not for the sharpness of Missy's visitation, Tim would by now have been totally put off in his attempt to speak to the captain of *Burrawong*. But he kept on, though his brushes with bloody Ernie and Borger made him tentative in the entryway of the Hotel Kempsey. A maid came out of the dining room to intercept him – a little as if he were an intruder.

'Is Captain Reid at breakfast?' Tim asked her.

She was an English girl, he could tell as soon as she spoke, and sounded very pleasant. Must be new, not part of the politics of the place.

'Aw, he's up on the verandah, writing his letters.'

Her *up* was *oop*. It was his experiences that English people who said *oop* were honest creatures. The oop-sayers achieved no more credit with the big people than did North Corkers.

When he went upstairs, he found that the captain was not on the verandah, but someone was humming 'Oft in the Stilly Night' in the men's bathrooms. Tim looked in. The captain was giving himself another shave. It was known that he visited a woman in West. Would she now inspect him for fleas?

He saw Tim in the mirror and stopped his scraping.

'Can I help you?' he asked coldly. The manner of command.

'Captain Reid,' said Tim. Wondering himself why he sounded so bloody genial. 'My wife travelled up with you from Sydney on *Burrawong* last week. Quite a fuss, eh?'

'Quite a fuss. Too much of one.' Now he continued to shave. 'Going back and forth to the ship by drogher! I hope they don't put us through quarantine every time we make the New Entrance.'

'If they do, we of the Macleay are put to inconvenience.'

He knew the captain would like such a sentiment.

'That's what I tell people,' murmured the captain, caressing his jawline with the blade. 'There are enough complaints already,' he said. 'How did your wife find steerage?'

'She was a saloon passenger,' said Tim. 'Travelled with Mrs Arnold down, with her emigrant sister back.'

'Ah, yes,' said the captain. 'If she left something aboard, you know, the North Coast Steamship Navigation Company office is in Smith Street.'

'Oh, yes, I know that. I wanted to ask about another passenger. She would have come about the New Year.'

'Not many passengers ever at the turning of the year,' said Captain Reid reflectively.

'A friend of mine tells me he saw a lad from *Burrawong*. Fresh-faced, wearing a blazer from a good school.'

'There was an effeminate sort of boy, yes, just after New Year's. Visiting relatives in the Upper Macleay. A saloon cabin to himself. Kept quiet, as you'd expect. Sick all the time, I'm told.'

'What was his name?'

'A fanciful one. Alastair. Alain. Some name like that.'

These names, even though male and assumed for the voyage, went through Tim like light through a pane. Something potent was released. Its retreat left him lightened. He put weight on his bad ankle to remain upright.

The captain lowered his razor and considered Tim.

'Are you all right?'

Someone must be told and the captain was *there*, fit to approach Hanney without being bullied. 'It's the girl who died at Mrs Mulroney's. It's the woman they call Missy, taking the ship as a boy. You *must* go to the police and tell them. For example, the boy's voice. What was the voice like?'

'Well-modulated for that matter. But it wasn't the girl in question.'

'Please, go and tell the sergeant.'

'I don't think I want to involve myself too much with the civil authorities. What can they make of a well-modulated voice?'

'Was it English, Scottish, Irish? Was she really the sort of talker she appeared to be or was she bunging an accent on? Those are some of the things they could follow.'

'I think you're leaping to conclusions. The boy was a boy.'

He was, very nearly, proud of the force of Missy's performance.

'Listen,' said Captain Reid, 'I was treated to the sight of that young woman earlier than most people, and it was not one of my passengers.'

'When you last saw it, your mind wouldn't have been set up

to compare the features with your schoolboy's. I urge you to look again!'

Reid said nothing for a time and, as if he might consider using it as a weapon, slowly washed his razor. When he did speak he sounded pretty ruminative. 'You're a bloody nuisance with all this. What's wrong with you? You've got a bloody bug in your mind about this woman! It's a bloody impertinence that you should want me to take a cab to West to waste time with those great clod-hopping gendarmes! My company doesn't want me doing excessive things in any case. They get a hard enough hammering from the Macleay rags.'

Tim however still struggling to sound desperately reasonable. 'Some Macleay men – at least one of them – want her to go unnamed. It might be mere bush vanity in him. Would you for Christ's sake consider doing what I ask so that girl can be put to rest?'

'No, I bloody well wouldn't. They *have* the criminal Mulroney. I am a sailor, sir, who spent twenty-two years on the Singapore–Batavia run. I've seen shipmates drowned and fished them up as such inhuman lumps of rot that I became convinced rot is all. There are no ghosts to be appeased or settled. By your tone and accent you're a superstitious man. When you talk about this girl, you see her as languishing somewhere. But whoever she was, she's nothing now. She is nothing. Believe me.'

Captain Reid finished with his work and gauged himself in the mirror, sliding a hand along his jawline. Smooth as a baby's arse.

'Your wife travelled saloon, you said?' It had occurred to Captain Reid that he ought to be polite to men who paid for saloon passages.

'She and her sister.'

'Well, please don't think for a second that my convictions make me a less moral man. It makes me a *more* moral man. As the whole Macleay knows and is always saying – *Burrawong* is a difficult and somewhat older vessel. All the more reason to treasure my passengers' lives, since life is everything and beyond is nothing. As it stands, the whole population, if you read the *Argus*, thinks I'm deliberately trying anyhow to spread the plague and enlarge the population of the deceased. So I wish to live quietly while I'm here. Good morning. I'm going to my room.'

For a moment, Tim had an urge to get in his way, but that would have convinced the captain he was a weird fellow.

Reid went indoors. Tim loitered a while, above the thoroughfare, seeing men open stores and put out goods. The old Jewish jeweller who spoke with a cockney accent put his trays of unaffordable wonders in the window. Missy might look in there, yearning for the gaudiness of ordinary days.

In the window of Savage's stood a sign which said, 'WE CAN SUPPLY YOU WITH PRE-PLAGUE GOODS!'

One sign of Bandy's seriousness as a herbalist. If he were as fly as Savage's, he would by now have bottled a herbal specific against the plague. But a sensible fellow like Bandy knew you could gamble with the colic, but better not dice with plague.

T. Shea – General Store couldn't advertise pre-plague goods. Not with a post-plague wife and sister-in-law on the premises.

Back home, Mamie stood in front of the store, beaming. Plump Kitty inside, leaning against the door frame which led into the residence. She'd been waiting for him.

'Timothy, could we have a talk?' she asked.

He knew the trouble he was in, and why. She did not humble him in front of her sister, however. She was proving herself an equable partner in his decaying universe.

They went into the living room with its clock and ottoman and its bookcase: the *London Illustrated News*, *The Standard Book of Great British Poets*, *Chamber's Encyclopedia* And dimness.

'Tim, here's a further bill from Staines and Gould. Three months unpaid. You intend to pay it?'

'I meant to tell you. I paid off Truscott and Lowe and we're all square there. But I had an inspector from the Colonial Secretary's. The bugger was policing the early closing business. He fined me fifteen quid for selling him sugar and shortbread.'

Beneath a frown, Kitty's features bunched. 'You didn't tell me that!'

'Well, there was plenty of other stuff to relay, wasn't there? Johnny's head . . . This inspector turned up smiling and well-dressed and saying his wife was having a tea party . . .'

'The bloody Good Templars sent him,' Kitty concluded at once. 'Those bastards! You put yourself forward, didn't you? The Patriotic Fund meeting. Have to talk up like that criminal uncle of yours.'

'Not criminal. *Political*. But not me. A farmer called Borger puts himself forward. Not me.'

'But when you speak last, you see, Timmy, people remember. It's the worst bloody talent on earth you have.'

They stood together there by the ottoman sofa, which was used only when worthies like the Burkes came to town. Yet this was the core of the household, the core of what was treasured and at threat.

'I see too in the *Argus* you gave an entire thirty bob to bushfire relief.'

'Had to. For business and compassion.'

'No. For vaunting bloody pride! That's what. Recklessness and vanity. So speak to people about this. How else do you propose we pay the bill I have in my hand?'

'I have a number of outstandings. I will send Joe O'Neill out to ask for them. It should be a change for our customers and a good introduction to Australia for Joe.'

'Go yourself. Joe's no persuader, for God's sake.'

The notice of meeting at the Good Templars stood over him and the anger of Ernie bloody Malcolm. Too complicated to recount. He felt the weight of his unutterable fragility as he stood in the doorway, halfway between his store and his home fire.

'If you leave this bill another month,' said practical Kitty, 'they'll send the bailiffs.'

'I know, I know,' he told her. He wished between partners in life there could be an instant passage of mind, so that all the threatening news received in her absence could be in a second transferred to her. It was not totally deceit that made him a liar, it was the difficulty of exact translation.

'Do you think Joe O'Neill will take Mamie off our hands soon?'

'You're very quick to get rid of my sister.'

'No. Your sister is very welcome. It just seemed . . .'

'My sister will never attach herself to a wet item like Joey O'Neill. Why do you think she's in the front of the store? She's hoping for something better. She's not hoping for the world. But at least she's hoping for something better than Joe bloody O'Neill.'

He gathered himself to squeeze the truth out. 'I have to tell you this. Our future may depend on a motion presently before the Patriotic Fund. To make a list of the disloyal.'

'Oh, Jesus,' she said. She knew somehow that he could so readily be described as disloyal by those who sought to depict him that way. She had married a man who could so handily be a butt. Done it knowingly. Hard to see what possessed her. Love, of course, whatever that entailed.

'We will have to leave the bill another week,' he told her.

'The outstandings?' she said. 'Our useless clients. You'll just have to hit them hard, Timmy. I can't go out in this condition putting a scare in them, but dear Jesus I'll do it as soon as this child's born.' She seemed to thrust forward a little of the belly made by the child. A claim. At the end of all the dancing, shouting, stout-drinking of the Kennas, a hardhead. 'I know you. *Jesus stand in the way of anyone thinking I want to be paid for what I supply!* Talk to the Malcolms again, then. Find them in the morning before Mrs Malcolm can get near the bottle.'

'She didn't always drink. She has become a shadow.'

Kitty laughed to herself. It was half vengeance. 'She can't talk Alfred Lord T by the hour any longer. Poor ninny. She liked you in the way I do, but couldn't get the message over!'

He began to laugh, shaking his head. She knew that in this world *they* were wedded, and he was gratified by her knowledge. But she understood his taste for literature and betterment and all that. Not that in New South Wales he hadn't got into the way of all manner of slang and flash talk and saying *bugger* to everything. But he betrayed the voice of the aspirer in what he'd said at the Good Templars!

'We can't have the Malcolms' sort of people leaving us,' she told him flatly, the fun over, her hands folded on her risen abdomen.

From the store, Mamie appeared. 'There's a woman been talking to me from the door. She told me, the old whore, that she doesn't mean any harm. She'll be back with you as soon as the plague proves out.'

'Jesus,' said Tim. 'Rank superstition.'

He thought of the sign in Savage's window. He really should try a similar sign in his own window.

Mamie smiled at her sister and winked. 'We're totally assured of two customers. Joe O'Neill and Mr Habash.'

Once Joe O'Neill was collected by his uncle and aunt from Toorooka, he found it was a long ride into town to court Mamie.

Joe was also finding the patterns of Australian farming harder than those of the Irish. Encouraged by the late arriving sun and the sluggish seasons, Irish farmers often slept late. But Joe O'Neill's Toorooka uncle's Jerseys bellowed for milking at first light, like everyone else's in New South Wales. The rich mudflats were heavy ploughing too. So not even Mamie's tantalisations could keep Joe awake all the time after he rode to town in the evenings. Joe would even forget to bring his banjo, though Annie thought it the cleverest thing on earth. But if he drank stout before dinner – and he always did – his head lolled at the table. When Bandy was there, Joe would try bravely to be awake.

It was an old story: an uncle in the Macleay bringing out from Ireland, England, Scotland, Wales and sometimes Germany a nephew to become a slave-by-kinship. So was Australia populated. A bright fellow like Joe would sicken of it, get a small acreage of his own or even inherit his uncle's, and repeat the eternal story, bringing out in twenty years' time another sister's son to labour in Toorooka. Or perhaps Joe might get sick of bush life and move to town and be a haulier like Tim. When that time came, he would certainly marry Mamie. A saving if Kitty was looking for one, a marriage to be encouraged.

Mamie would say to Joe coolly as he nodded, 'You should bring the cart to town with you. Less likely to fall off a cart while you're sleeping than off a horse.'

Tim felt he had been given a short, near-happy season of adjournment. He'd collected some money from his humbler customers but not spoken to Winnie Malcolm yet, for the loyal vote still a week or more off.

Obdurate Captain Reid had earlier today walked along Smith Creek to catch his drogher downriver to his ship. Men in the street stopped and reflected on the captain as he passed. He was going back to the plague city and bore watching. Tim found himself looking at the man in a different light too. A man not to blame, of course, but stubborn, possessed by what was called invincible ignorance. Believing only in extinction and putrefaction. Sailed off leaving Missy in the same limbo as ever. And Tim in similar postponement too – between mixed fortunes of one kind and another.

Now Mamie's mention of the cart struck Tim as a chance to declare a holiday such as events called for. To speed as well the unavoidable bush marriage – no matter what the women said – between Mamie and Joe.

'Get the cart from your uncle on Sunday and we'll all go to Crescent Head,' Tim told Joe. 'Your cart and mine.'

'With our mad horse?' said Kitty, kindling at the idea though. 'Bring your banjo, for God's sake, Joe.'

Tim felt immediately enlivened. The Crescent Head jaunt was a journey he did for new arrivals. Had done it for Kitty seven years ago, for her sister Molly in the days Old Burke was courting her. And now he had Mamie and Joe, and – as promised – the orphaned Lucy. In return for the jaunt Lucy might feel appeased and desist from urging Johnny to high points.

'It's the grandest place,' said Kitty. 'The grandest beach.'

'We saw some long, long beaches on the way up in that rat ship,' said Mamie.

'Different to see them from the land side,' Tim argued. 'Different to see them from the Big Nobby at Crescent.'

'Beach to the north, I swear,' Kitty corroborated, kindly helping him and gesturing with her plump right arm. 'Beach to the south. Neither of them ends.'

'They *must* end,' said peevish Mamie. She suspected Tim's impulse to set her up with Joe.

'I'll ask the old man,' said Joe in an intrepid voice, since he saw the chance too.

The night waited, and the matter of Missy in abeyance, Reid gone, Ernie resistant, his own letters to the Commissioner trumped by Ernie's. He had tried every avenue. Wouldn't *she* in her waiting for the name to break, for her tragedy to be entitled and lodged and forgotten, indulge his modest demand for a holiday?

'So get the dray off the old fellow then,' Tim urged with a surge of temporary joy. This weekend. The last golden sabbath. He felt heady about it.

'I have a little something to tell you,' said Kitty, lying on her back, a small reddish-complexioned knoll in a white night dress without sleeves. His familiar of the night. A rock in his dreams. One day, far in another century, they would turn to dust together on the hill below the hospital in West. They would not travel around in flasks in constables' saddlebags. These were the assurances which arose from lying beside Kitty.

'No displays of temper,' she warned him.

'Why would I display temper?'

'Why? You don't know yourself very well.' A little dreamy laugh started up over her lips. 'Mr Habash will accompany us to Crescent Head. Mamie asked him.'

Some anger slithered up through him and out across the floor.

'I bloody well thought I was in charge of asking people.'

A repeat of laughter, partly a soft belch, from Kitty. 'Mamie wants a different picnic from the one you planned.'

'Dear Heaven, her stunts. I just want to go to Crescent Head.'

'So do we all.' She reached out her hand. 'I'm going to *your* picnic. Me and Annie. And Johnny of course.'

'I promised to take the Rochester orphan.'

'Some of us will be at your picnic then, Tim. Others of the buggers will be at Mamie's.'

'All right, I don't mind Habash any more.' But he minded Mamie.

'Neither do I, as a matter of fact. Shall we say one Our Father and three Hails for the conversion of the infidel or for the repose of lost souls.' It was a joke about Habash.

'Bugger the infidel,' said Tim.

He wondered though what did Bandy Habash and his infidel father and brother do on their Saturdays in Forth Street, Kempsey, New South Wales? Facing the East. Sitting on mats.

What did they say, so far from their home? To what torrents or rivers of sand did they compare the Macleay.

On the Sunday morning of the picnic, at the early Mass, Father Bruggy happened to speak of the Holy Name and the common abuse of it on low tongues.

'Ireland is a Catholic nation,' he said, 'and possesses a strong sense of the Ten Commandments. But there are two vices the Irish immigrant brings to New South Wales. The one, drunkenness – which shall be the subject of another sermon. The other – the undue invocation of the name of Our Lord and of his Blessed Mother. My English brother, Father McCambridge, comments on the fact that the Holy Name is most under threat from those who most honour it, the Irish emigrant to these shores. Here, his looseness with the Divine Name combines exactly with a colonial looseness of expression in general. I must warn Irish newcomers of their tendency to contribute to the general laxness of colonial, Australian expression. I would urge men to join the Holy Name Sodality, whose purpose is to stamp out the misuse of the Divine Name . . .'

Kitty was muttering at Tim. 'Takes an Englishman to remind us of all this. Put the Holy Name up on a shelf and rent it out for day-to-day use!'

Father Bruggy said that the Holy Name Sodality would meet at the end of Mass.

'Devil you'll join them!' Kitty told him. When she chose to obey priests she did it thoroughly. But she was discerning on the matter. Fortunately he lacked the inclination to stay behind.

After Mass, Mother Imelda and the other nuns observed a short thanksgiving period – as did their boarders perforce – and then rose and genuflected and processed out of the church. Their boarders in trim clothes and shining faces, behind them. Little Lucy Rochester amongst the boarders with her clenched features and her glowing eyes. The reformed climber. The repentant imperiller.

As already arranged, Mother Imelda brought Lucy to the Sheas. She nodded to Kitty and dragged Tim imperiously by the elbow a little way distant from the group. He could hear Annie say, 'That's Lucy, Mama. Lucy. She lives with the nuns.'

'The child,' Imelda murmured to Tim, 'has listened intently to everything, and Sister Philomena is astounded by her grasp of Christian Doctrine.'

Tim groaned – perhaps aloud. He knew what would now be said. 'She wishes to take instruction as a Catholic.'

Tim flinched. He had a duty by Albert. 'You're sure, Mother, she isn't just trying to please you?'

'Mr Shea, I have watched this occur with other children of Protestant parents. Give me some credit! I can sniff out what is genuine and what is merely opportune.'

'Her father's so recently dead, and he would not like this.'

'If our faith means anything, Mr Shea, it means he is now in possession of the *real* facts and is at peace.'

'Well, as much as I trust your discernment, Mother . . . Perhaps she should wait a little while. That's what I think.' Imelda staring him down. He shrugged, touched his hat. 'I'll talk to her on our picnic.'

Mamie had filled a hamper, and it sat in the dray along with a basketful of ale and a number of blankets. Joe and Mamie, shadowed by Johnny, who for some reason liked Joe and was quiet in his presence, climbed into Joe's uncle's plain yellow farm cart. It too carried an ample basket of ale.

Tim went and lifted Kitty up to the seat behind Pee Dee. Lucy and Annie were already in the dray, talking. Yet so hard as ever to hear what Lucy said!

All around, the carts of other communicants of St Joseph's Kempsey were pulling away from the church. Young men on ponies raced each other like young men of any communion at any time. Men with pipes in their hands who waited outside Kelty's – Kelty's opened up to certain Romans after Mass on Sundays, despite the licensing laws – took off their hats and waved to Tim. Did they also think he'd written the *Australis* letters and provoked bitter Billy Thurmond to his Patriotic Fund motion?

In Elbow Street in West, they encountered an astounding and ominous sight. The postmaster was out in the spare block beside the Post Office. With an axe, he was chopping through the timber uprights of the closed shooting gallery. The postmaster a mad-eyed Scot named MacAllen, and he paused and wiped his brow and nodded to Tim. 'The Shire won't take action. I've complained and complained about lads shooting away to all hours of the evening. Armenian bugger who runs the place is only squatting on this land anyhow.'

'Fair enough,' called Tim. Though secretly he was a little surprised by this kind of lawlessness in an official. MacAllen said, 'My wife sits up worrying about the children and the Sydney plague, and all we can hear is bang, bang, bang!'

'Very trying,' called Kitty, turning her short body with difficulty towards the postmaster, but then covering a laugh with her lace-gloved hand.

'Better to agree with a man with an axe,' she muttered to Tim.

As the postmaster applied himself again, the sheet of corrugated iron which had roofed the gallery fell like thunder. The postmaster stepped back and was pleased.

They rolled on, convinced that this might be a good day to be away from the town.

At the Central punt in Smith Street, Bandy was waiting for them, smiling. On the same grey he'd been riding the day of Albert Rochester's tragedy, and the night of the illicit ride.

'Good morning, Sheas and Miss Kenna and Mr O'Neill. Prayers completed, the day now belongs to a totally decent picnic!'

Tim looked to the cart behind, because he was curious to see how Mamie reacted to this fulsome sentiment of Bandy's. She was rolling her eyes at O'Neill and laughing. Yet it did not seem to be in total mockery.

Annie touched Tim's arm from the back of the cart where she sat on a pile of rugs with the white-frocked Lucy. 'Bandy Habash is funny,' she sagely told him.

The exhilaration of being on the deck of a punt, all in a party, observing the thickness of fertile soil in the banks, the splendid mountains too bluely distant to show their burnt trunks.

They landed in East, Bandy leading his biddable grey and at the same time hauling Pee Dee by the bit, while Tim hallo-ed and urged. The road followed for a little way the path he and Bandy had taken to the plague camp. But went past the turnoff for a mile before itself veering back to the coast, becoming a sandy, claggy track. Ahead, between them and the sea, lay a huge mountain, Dulcangui. Covered with grey-green trees and displaying gnarls of sandstone, it rose up out of the low ground like a threat. When they reached the rise, the road now became a cutting through the mountain's rock. Kitty took over the reins of the Shea wagon. Tim and Lucy got down to walk. Bandy himself dismounted from the grey after making a number of experimental canters up and down the stony slope. Then he put Annie in the saddle, a place that seemed to please her very much, and began to lead the way up Dulcangui.

'Watch out for snakes!' cried Tim. For he did not want the grey shying with Annie in its saddle.

To make the ascent, Tim walked level with Pee Dee's neck, grabbing him by the harness to hold him to the mountain. After Pee Dee had shaken his head the required number of times to satisfy the Horse Union's idea of bloody-mindedness in a beast, he allowed Kitty at the reins to gee him up the first section of road. Rocks and saplings designed for impaling lay all the way down the murderous slope which fell away from the side of the track.

Mamie strode past Tim and Lucy, her neat knees ploughing away beneath the fabric of her white dress. A bit of an athlete, this one. She went ahead and walked and talked with Annie and Habash, while Joe O'Neill, alone except for Johnny and at the rear, learned to urge his uncle's cart up this severe track.

In country like this, the Patriotic Fund seemed barely a dent on human contentment. Yet Tim could hear Pee Dee snorting, the bugger. Just to make things interesting. Kitty tugged at him with her now-bare, red little hands and uttered both soothing and threatening non-words to get him over the hill.

Lucy beside him. The little would-be Papist. How horrified the Primitive Methodists would be.

'Well, you want to be a convert, do you?' he asked the child.

'Yes.' She walked with the gait of a grown woman.

'You wouldn't do that just to please the nuns, eh? You can't please them. I know it because I'm their grocer.'

He could tell by her up-tilted gaze that she knew it too. They were hungry goddesses.

'You'll have to remember,' said Tim, 'that your little brother at Mrs Sutter's won't be with you in this.'

Typical of her, she said nothing.

'Well, do you think he'd mind?'

'He's too young,' she told him. 'This is a business for me.'

'Why do you want to do it though?'

'I want to have God. But I want the angels too.'

'Wouldn't the other people let you have angels?'

'I want the Blessed Mother too.'

'You *are* an ambitious little woman, aren't you?'

'I want a Blessed Mother.'

A reasonable and pitiable desire in an orphan, he thought. He took one of the lollies he was keeping for the children out of his pocket and slipped it into her hand.

'I'll tell you this. Don't do it too easily. And don't do it to please anyone. Because you're stuck with it for life then and people think the worse of you. Suspect you of all sorts of things they don't suspect you of if you stayed Primitive Methodist.'

'I know. But.'

'*But*. But you have the angels and the saints?'

'Yes,' said Lucy. 'There's lots of them.'

'Some people consider that a problem.'

Kitty on the reins and Tim at the halter dragged Pee Dee and the cart around a last wall of rock, and now this was the top. A vast glitter of sea could be seen from up here. Its line broken only by Crescent Head's two famous headlands – the Little Nobby and the Big.

Down again towards the paperback swamps which lay between Dulcangui and the ocean. Bandy let Lucy lead the grey and came back to help control Pee Dee. Pee Dee fussy on the stony downslope. Mamie climbed up beside Kitty and took a hand at the reins. You could hear the bottles jiggling in their baskets. Before they got to the bottom, two in the hamper on Joe O'Neill's cart exploded.

Meanwhile, Lucy and Johnny, who had abandoned poor Joe for the greater excitement of the vanguard, between them led the grey down onto the corduroy road across the swamp to the sea. In the grey's saddle, Annie still sat. Entering into a fair imitation of her kingdom.

The picnic place finally chosen was on a sward above the surf at the bottom of the Little Nobby. They could look out over the sea and then across a small saltwater creek to the twelve miles of Front Beach. Mamie was enthused by this vigorous bright sight and was soon knee-deep in the creek with the children. Johnny, shirt off, began splashing round as he did in the river, but his strokes were interrupted by the shallowness of the creek and the playful current. Tim waded in too, his trousers rolled up. Standing still you could see mullet swim by. Annie, Johnny, Lucy kept trying to catch them in their hands.

Ashore Kitty lay on her back on a rug and under a parasol, pointing the unborn Shea child straight at the arc of blue sky. Near her, Joe O'Neill began smoking reflectively and plunking his banjo. The tune 'Bold Phelim Brady' was raggedly released into the air. His boots were still on. Perhaps he had an inlander's fear of the water. When Tim waded ashore, Joe and he began opening beer with flourishes. After the rough trip, the stuff fizzed out of the necks of the bottles.

'Porter, Mrs Shea?' asked Joe, putting a long glass of frothy stout in Kitty's outreaching hand.

'Oh, dear,' sighed Kitty. 'As lovely as you'll get.'

Meanwhile Bandy took the saddle off his grey's back. Steam rose gently from the crushed, damp hair. Tim was surprised to see Bandy take his shirt and pants off too, so that now he wore only a singlet and his long, white linen breeches. The singlet was low-cut and revealed in part a smooth, brown, hairless chest. Arms not like the arms of men from Europe. Both smaller and yet more sinewy. He jumped on the grey's back and urged it gently into the creek. It went placidly, standing to its belly in the water, seeming content amongst the little waves. Bandy turning to throw a salute to the shallows where Mamie and the children were prancing and yelling and trying to grab mullet.

Lucy now with her skirts tucked in her knickers looked more a child and less of a witness than he'd ever seen. Though sometimes she would cup up a palm full of saltwater and study it.

Having crossed the creek, Bandy put the grey into a gallop on the firm sand below the tidemark along Front Beach. All this looked splendid to Tim, half-naked Bandy leaned down to the grey mane, the lovely mare shattering its own reflection in the wet sand, and thundering away.

Whereas Pee Dee was up along the slope, turned out of the traces and eating grass as if he'd never go back to work again.

'You bugger, you're for the knackers,' Tim casually called to Pee Dee, who disdained to stop devouring the hillside.

At last, for love's sake, Joe O'Neill took his big boots off and rolled his trousers and went and stood in the rim of the creek. Kitty must have been able to see this from her lying position. 'Look out for them sharks, Joe,' she murmured.

They ate a drowsy lunch – sardines and cornbeef, beer and ginger beer. Chewing heartily, Mamie looked across to the larger headland, smooth and green and momentous. It took up a whole quarter of the sky.

'We'll be climbing that big feller there?'

He could see the children's eyes flick towards the Big Nobby. Not a question that it invited you!

'You and Joe can go up there after lunch,' said Tim. It was the right sort of physical feature for courting. It demanded that hands be reached to each other. But he didn't want mad Johnny up there.

'What can you see from the top?'

'The whole coastline of New South Wales,' said Kitty dreamily. 'At a total sweep. And the air. A lens, you see. The air like a bloody telescope.'

'Can we go, Papa?' asked Johnny bolt upright like a jack rabbit, on his knees. More than ready for high places again, the little ruffian.

'I'll take you over the creek to the beach,' said Tim. 'Mr Habash might take his grey again and you can ride. But not gallop, son, not gallop. I know you.'

'But can't the children come?' asked Mamie. It was as if she did not want to be left alone with Joe. 'We can all keep an eye. You'll be good won't you, Lucy?'

Lucy looked up at her levelly. 'I learned my lesson,' said Lucy in a way which implied canings and made everyone laugh.

Something entirely convincing about Lucy swayed Tim, as did the size of the day. He remembered too the gradual, accommodating lines of the Big Nobby.

'Then I'll go too,' said Tim. 'I'll keep an eagle eye out. And you, Bandy. You come too if you would, and watch these little blackguards.'

He felt sorry for Joe, the corner of whose mouth conveyed disappointment. Mamie was a bugger of a tease.

'But first the tea,' said Bandy. He had made a fire a little way down on the creek. He now went and fetched the excellent tea he had brewed. Mamie stood up and asked to see into the billy he was carrying.

'There's tree leaves in that tea,' she complained.

'That's gum leaves,' said Tim. 'Australians make their tea with gum leaves thrown in. When there's a tree handy.'

So, it struck him now: Bandy was by habit an Australian.

They drank plenty of this tea to ready themselves for their thirsty climb. When they were finished, Tim wanting to get up there and down and have it over, they left Kitty lying on a blanket in scant shadow, with her parasol leaned across her face to give double shade. A strong sea breeze cooled her and played with the tassels of the parasol.

On the flanks on the great whale-like Big Nobby, whorls of tussocky grass made the climb easy. You stepped from one knot of grass to another. Step by step, like climbing a pyramid. Johnny kept racing ahead and looking down like a gazelle from some nest of grass. But Lucy mounted the headland beside Tim, whose hand was held by Annie. So they rose up the green slope quite easily, Joe O'Neill chattering away, to the domed top of the thing.

Bandy seemed to take care to be up there first, not it appeared for rivalry's sake but as if he too wanted to prevent any madness in Johnny. As Tim and Annie rose higher on the great headland, they began to pick up the welcome southerly on their brows. Tim finished the climb with Annie on his back, since the child did not believe in wearing herself out. All the others were waiting on top for them, looking south, Mamie exclaiming at what could be seen. Joe had a wrestle-hold on Johnny, and Johnny struggled in it, laughing. Lucy stood soberly there like one of the adult party.

Arriving and dropping Annie so that she could take up her normal august posture, Tim saw Back Beach and its wild surf stretching away to Point Plummer, Racecourse Beach, etc, etc.

You could have seen Port Macquarie except that the day's haze blurred the scene about twenty miles south.

'Now you don't see a sight like that,' said Mamie, 'anywhere on the Cork or Kerry coast.'

'Because it's always wrapped in mist there,' murmured Joe.

From here it could be seen that the headland on which they stood had two tops, this one and another further to the south. In between, a green saddle with grass and little thickets of native shrubs. Beneath the saddle a partially seen great rock wall fell into the sea, which grew plum-coloured in the shadow of the black stone. You could hear and partly see the ocean raging down there, making caves. Of course there was no way, having got here, the party would choose not to walk on into the saddle towards the other, lower dome. Finding a way past the spiky banksias, and so to the Big Nobby's second summit. From there they would, of course, be able to look from safety directly down into the turmoil of rock and sea below.

'No shy-acking then, Johnny,' Tim called out. He didn't utter any warnings to Lucy. For she seemed a changed child. She knew about witnessing angels.

As they walked down into the saddle, dragging their feet through clumps of button grass, the Big Nobby maintained its gradual character. Not like cliffs elsewhere – not a case of grass running sharply to the definite and dramatic precipice, and then the sudden fall. You knew that somewhere to their left the black cliff began. But here, because of the headland's gentle angle and its thick grass tufts, each one a rung of its massive ladder, there was no sense that you could topple and roll.

'Prickly, prickly,' said Annie as they reached the thickets, flapping her long-fingered hands at him, pleading to be picked up. She had those delicate fingers utterly unlike Kitty's. They came from his sister Helen, who'd married the newspaper editor in Brooklyn.

He lifted her and followed the path the others had taken. These strange, olive green banksia bushes with their black cones. Splits in the cones like eyes and mouths. 'Look,' said Tim, holding one of the cones. 'The Banksia Man. He's an evil little fellow.'

Annie threw herself about in his arms with fake shudders.

They came back up out of the banksias to Big Nobby's grassy

southern crest. Ah yes, you could see down to where the grasses grew steeper and the rock layers began and the hungry surf worked away. A number of birds wheeled around the semi-circle of this rock wall. It seemed to Tim to be the mad energy of the waves that kept them up, since none of them flapped their wings. A little way up from the wall above the sea, a sea-eagle considered a dive. A sharp, pearly, commanding shape with black wingtips.

'That one there's a sea-eagle,' he told the others. 'When they dive, they bloody dive.'

'This is the place,' said Mamie. 'You could have a tea-house up here.'

'A pub perhaps,' amended Joe O'Neill, who was sure to crack more ale once they got down. Lucy stood beside Joe and on the other side of him, still quiet from respect for this soon-to-be uncle, Johnny. Good. They were still. They watched the sea-eagle. Its circles had them hypnotised. It had authority over the air. It put the frenzied children in their place.

'Will you carry me down like you carried me up, papa?' asked Annie ceremoniously, at his side.

'To walk will be good for your little legs.'

'I don't think that's true. My little legs don't agree.'

He heard Mamie laughing. The sea-eagle banked and Tim took a new sense of it, that it was no mere natural wonder of some kind. A sudden gust came up to them as if the bird had manufactured it for them with its banked wings. Tim felt the stirred air all around him. The damned wheeling thing had command of the day. Its very ease, he felt at once, was a frightful temptation and the young should not be exposed . . .

He heard Mamie shriek, and Habash cry, 'Stop this!'

Somehow the bird had by its malign circling and its sending a breeze engendered something unspoken but at once mutual between Lucy and Johnny. In all their campaigns, had they ever exchanged a word? If they had, no one had heard it. They planned it as if by fishing in each other's mind.

This was their venture now. They were running down the incline of the headland, their hands clasped. Johnny could be heard laughing in between Joe's shouting, but Lucy was silent. It was such an inviting slope, and from some angles you found it hard to imagine or give credence to the drop, the indented face below, the Nobby's true, black sting. So piteously confident were they of their impunity, that seeing them you were possessed by an absolute panic of pity. Pity could be heard in the way everybody howled.

Now they all followed – Bandy, Joe, Mamie. Then himself, dropping Annie's hand, since she could be trusted. All the party running with their heels thrust forward to avail themselves of the holding power of the grass. All yelling direly. Pleas not to be remembered afterwards word by word. Simply a general, frantic, fatherly pleading of the two little buggers running hand in hand. Ahead the feverish sapphire sea, and a sky of acid blue. Tim feeling his ankle yell at this strange usage as he ran madly towards the gulf. The younger men and the one young woman still ahead of him, all helplessly shrieking. *Noooooooooooo!* So steep now where the children were, and Johnny leaning back, Tim saw with hope, but Lucy thrusting skinny shoulders forward. Welcoming the fall. And still hands locked. Soon they would go flying over together. This beat the stern of *Terara*. This beat the Angelus tower. This so clearly a venue worthy of their shared will that he cursed himself for allowing anyone but Mamie and Joe to approach this climb.

But when the result seemed obvious, Johnny simply sat on a tussock. The grasp was as easily broken as that. Lucy sailed out alone. Shrilling but not with terror. And vocal now she had taken to the air. So close to the fall of the cliff was everyone that they saw only the first liberated segment of her fall. Tim continued down the awful grade and yanked Johnny upright by his collar. Johnny's face was ghastly. *He* had been playing. Had expected her to sit too after the joke had been played out. *Look, we are reformed! You only thought we were playing the old games!*

Nonetheless, Tim couldn't stop himself striking the boy on the head in a kind of horror and gratefulness. Bandy was working energetically around the rim, the only one not screaming and exclaiming. He wanted a better view. To see if Lucy was frolicking or fluttering in and out on the waves in that chaos down there. Everyone, whimpering and pleading, worked their way around the edge as Bandy had, so that they could see into the cauldron.

'There is nothing,' Bandy yelled against the wind. 'Nothing to be seen.' The hugh masses of white there contained none of Lucy's whiteness or white fabric. She had been swallowed.

Above them, Annie – who had had the best view – was wailing for him to come back.

It was Bandy's idea to rush down the hill and alert Crescent Head's four families of fishermen. Tim followed, arriving back down to the bottom with stark-eyed Johnny and with Annie just in time to see Bandy and two fishermen put out in a rowboat from the creek.

Kitty was standing, frowning at the boat. She turned. 'How could this happen?' she asked in reproach.

'How could it be bloody stopped?' Tim howled so furiously that both children began to sob.

By Bandy's later report, the fishermen rowed him around right up as close as the surf would let them to the face of Big Nobby's cliff. They were so long coming back that Joe, Mamie and Tim climbed the Nobby again and looked down on them. You could understand why such a scrap had been devoured without trace. Such a bullying, sucking, rending sea. So much chagrined. Bandy could be seen down there, standing in the dory, agilely shifting his stance at each swell.

The boat returned to Front Beach in late afternoon, and by then Tim and the others were in place to give it a bleak welcome. The offspring of Port Macquarie convicts, these Crescent Head fishermen. The younger fisherman came to speak to them. His father utterly leathered and browned, but Viking blue eyes glittering in there amongst the creases, kept quiet.

'See, a kiddy like that. Would be taken straight down. Tumbled over and torn out by water getting away. Straight out to sea. Only a long way out there would she be thrown up again, see. Ought to come up on Back Beach in the long run.'

The rugged fish-takers and eaters didn't want demented people from town hanging around to spoil with questions a tranquil evening meal. And because they knew it was no one's child who had fallen into the gulf, they were very honest about the chances.

'Could she be crying for us somewhere on a beach?' asked Tim.

'No, she's drowned. You can bet on that. She drowned, and nothing to be done about it.'

After midnight, Tim woke so vastly angry and walked so heavily up and down the bedroom in his bare feet, hoping his fury would wake Kitty. It had of course been a dreadful journey home over Dulcangui, with Annie gone tearfully asleep in Kitty's arms on the blanket in the back of the cart and Johnny still and staring. In their trance of surprise and grief, their suspicion that there was something further to be done they hadn't done, they did not once, these two queenly folk Kitty and Annie, complain of the roughness of the mountain or the jolting of the corduroy road through the paperbark swamps.

There had been a comedy, an awful one given the history of the day. Unsupervised, Pee Dee had made a feast of cunjevoi root which lay along the banks of the creek at Crescent Head. The root was succulent and poison, and most livestock had the sense to avoid it. Not Pee Dee, and it had got to his bowels. Mamie had had to sit beside Tim with an opened parasol while Pee Dee blurted, farted, and bucked his way up and down Dulcangui.

'Bandy,' said Tim as they crossed the Macleay by punt. 'Could I leave you to take a note to the priest? That Bruggy feller? He'll tell Imelda.'

Strange not to ask Joe, but in this tragedy Bandy seemed more trustworthy.

'I will do that,' said Bandy, bowing a little in the saddle. Shaking his head. No one could believe the day. The brain had to be shaken into accepting it.

Tim knew he needed to face the police, the sharper civil priesthood, the real binders and loosers. They would certainly be confused into their normal suspicions if he and Bandy presented themselves as joint reporters of Lucy Rochester's supposed drowning. But he himself would be less ashamed somehow to face the constables than the priests.

'You send me though I am not a Christian,' Bandy remarked.

'You're a better poor bugger than most Christians, and if you give him ten bob for two Masses I'll repay you tonight out of the cash box.'

After making town Tim and Joe had found the younger constable minding the station, the one who had no grievance yet, and he had taken their deposition without showing any tendency to define blame.

'You can ask the nuns,' said Tim. 'Always given to climbing things. Mad on heights.'

As if he had not killed her by keeping her out of his house.

And now he woke enraged over that.

And of course she woke, sitting up awkwardly, using an elbow, and watching him stamp around.

'Timmy, what is it?' she cried.

'*I* would take her in!' he accused her. 'I would bloody take her in. But she couldn't be fitted for Kennas. This is something fairly regular on the Macleay. Jerseyville pub could not be fitted either. For the sake of Kennas. Kennas marrying, Kennas arriving, Kennas suiting them-bloody-selves!'

Kitty looked appalled, but he could see with a perverse further annoyance that she didn't intend to fight the matter. 'Oh Jesus, Tim. Not all that at this moment. We all feel badly enough.'

'I should have stood up. I should have stood up to your sister. But she wanted everyone on that mountain for the vanity of teasing the hell out of poor Joe.'

'It's not Mamie's fault, Tim. Be a sensible fellow.'

'So mother and father departed from Lucy. Mrs Sutter wouldn't give her the time of day. We hived her off on Imelda. No wonder the poor brat took to the air like a bird!'

Kitty struggled to an upright stance now and came towards him. Seeing this fraught little woman, he wondered how she could ever have been considered beloved, this hard creature who hadn't room for orphans. Who had wheedled him into having no room.

'Our own child will be cursed, you bloody know!' he told her. 'That child you have there. Bloody cursed!'

Kitty so nakedly alarmed. She moved in and tried to embrace him. He fought her off.

'No, no,' he yelled. 'Facts are facts!'

He still hoped she would combat him, that there could be

mutual screaming this intolerable night. But she was both so measured and so frightened of him.

'Timmy, listen to me. I am too busy giving life to one child without carrying the blame for another. None of us took her there from ill will. She was at Crescent Head as a kindness.'

'Then she was killed with bloody kindness. A pretty miserable bloody kindness.'

'I won't have this, Timmy! You're going mad in front of my eyes. Pull back, for Jesus' sake.'

He thrust his long, long finger at her. 'We will not be let off this, Kitty. We will not be forgiven this.'

With a strange exaltation he saw how he distressed her. Her face bunched in pain. Good! Bloody good! Did the world operate for her convenience? Did the tides of pain flow to suit her awful, freckled, pushing clan?

'Oh God!' she roared.

He hoped that Mamie on the back verandah would be awakened and suffer for all this. Taking children to a precipice so they could watch her play off Bandy against Joe O'Neill.

Yet he had not thought it likely that Kitty would so easily accept his condemnation, take it upon her frame. Which now looked far too small and too much at risk. Her face cracked and an awful cry came out.

'For mercy's sake don't judge me, Timmy! The world's full of orphans, but they don't go flying off cliffs!'

Her cries seemed to raise an echo somewhere else in the house, an outburst on a higher, weirder pitch.

'Johnny,' he told his wife.

He left Kitty, turning into the corridor and so into the room where Johnny was sitting up in his sleep wailing, while Annie, who had been jolted awake by everyone's rage, complaints, defences, uttered more usual sobs. Kitty went to comfort her daughter while Tim shook Johnny back to the world and said the usual, blessed things.

'All right, Johnny darling. You are here with Papa. You didn't fly off.'

But Lucy had of course, and no one could get beyond that.

'You see, you see,' Kitty called to him as she caressed Annie to sleep. 'John stayed, he's here, here. No earthly reason she couldn't have been. Here on solid ground. No reason.'

Staying indeed seemed at once to Tim the most important achievement miscreant Johnny had ever been responsible for. *Staying* proved his innocence of real malice. It had been a joke to him. He *had* sat down at the end. While Lucy flew off seriously and with intent.

Now that Johnny was fully awake he had nothing to say to his father but sat rocking in his arms. 'I'll stay with him,' Tim told Kitty. He looked at her dim, night shape. His beloved accomplice. It was all certain and fixed and nothing could be done. Between them and in concert with others they had encouraged Lucy to embrace the thin air.

Kitty said, 'You're the one who must rest, Tim. You'll only grow madder still.'

'Bugger it, woman!' he warned her, and so when drowsiness overcame Annie, Kitty went off. Johnny leaned into Tim's arms and began to sleep with a few complaining moans. How unfair to the child it had been to begin screaming at night. He saw now that attaching blame was an exercise best pursued in morning calm. They would need to watch John and ensure Lucy had not done for him, for young John, the thrower at cricket stumps, the circus performer.

Un-sleeping Tim held Johnny in the dismal hours and for the sake of his own much-needed stillness of mind he began to think of certain protocols of the living which must somehow be attended to.

First of all, he went and pulled on a shirt, his drawers faintly yellowed in the Macleay's muddy water in which the women washed them, grey coat and pants. Old hat with the required sweat around the band. Ruined forever in shape by too much rain followed by too much sun. But part of the habit worn in the valley of the living.

12

The business day would have started before anyone got from Crescent Head with fish and news, good, bad, nil. So put a saddle on Pee Dee and ride him to the dawn Mass. Imelda and the Waterford nuns and some of the boarders were there, praying for the lost child. On a plinth, the Angel Gabriel flourished a trident at the serpents and ministers of hell. Had Lucy taken a special note of his plaster wings? She wouldn't have been tempted by them if Albert had lived, and taken her to the Primitive Methodists.

Imelda walked down the aisle towards him. He stood to meet the big nun. She leaned towards him and her breath smelled of communion wafers and almonds. She asked him if he had any hope.

'No,' he said. 'The poor child fell into the total maelstrom.'

He felt nothing while telling her. No anger at all now. How curious. No anger against Lucy, Kitty, Mamie. No blame against Imelda pointing Lucy to Gabriel's wings.

Imelda said, 'I spent summers by the sea when I was a child.'

Tim tried to discern the child in that huge face.

'Are you familiar with Mullaghmore?'

'No, Mother.'

'I know enough to believe that we should perhaps reconcile ourselves to God's will. I'll convert the rest of her school fees to Masses to be said either for her safety or eternal rest.'

He would have welcomed even fifteen bob of that money heartily. But so profane to think like that.

'Yes,' he said. 'For Lucy by name.'

'By name, yes,' she said. Putting her hand to his elbow briefly to ensure that he would stay upright.

'You see,' she said. 'Remember the Angelus tower? She is a very hard child to predict.'

All right, he would have said, except that it would soil Lucy's memory. *You win that bloody argument!*

As he moved out of the church, he was astonished and consoled to see Bandy in the rear row, kneeling very neatly. A formal Muslim in the house of the infidel.

Bandy the sole hero in all this. Innocent in all Mamie's little dramas. He was the one who had taken the fishing boat to where Lucy had entered battling waves which hissed like acid. Bandy raised a tear-streaked seraphic face to him.

'Come outside,' Tim told him.

Out into the morning's velvet, fraternal air. Bandy, Tim noticed, had not shaven. The features of the satiny upturned face seemed a little swollen with earnestness.

'Have you slept, Bandy?'

Bandy bowed his head. 'I waited here. I didn't wish to go anywhere else.'

'Here? *Here?*'

'I saw at once that I possessed no other home.'

'But your father's home . . .?'

Bandy stared up at the top of the Angelus tower where Johnny and Lucy had shared their high hazy view. 'I have to tell you, Mr Shea, that I am the newest Christian of all – at least in my desire. I am a fallible creature with my sins written on my forehead. But I have felt God's breath, and where it lists in the valley of the Macleay. It lists to the Christ rather than to the Prophet. Hearing the wind, I have decided not so much to turn myself around as to increase my store.'

'Oh God, Bandy. What are you saying? A change of faith? It won't make any difference to the Turf Club.'

His gaze still on the apex of the tower, Bandy sighed. 'No, Mr Shea. Please don't do me that injustice. I heard the wind, old chap. When I visited the priest's house here to tell them of Lucy's accident, the woman who maintains the house asked me to wait. And I waited, and in my waiting was confident of what I had been taught in childhood, that Jesus was a prophet but not the final one. The priest stayed inside, as if knowing that my mind could be turned. And as I stood there I felt a wind blowing from within the house, from the very centre of things. It pushed against my brow. All around, in Kemp Street, nothing happening. But here at the priest's door a blast!'

Bandy burned with his story.

'Like you I am used to doorways, to waiting, to receiving the odour of the house and the currents a house contains. Often curious smells, Mr Shea. Made up of God knows what. Bad secrets and failures here and there. But this door was so different, this house. A mighty breeze, Mr Shea. Blasting away at me.'

'It's a big, old, comfortless place,' explained Tim.

'No, no,' insisted Bandy, shaking off Tim's blunt explanations. 'More than that, old chap. As that wind washed over me, I knew at once that Jesus was more than prophet, was the living Son of God. It was so clear to me, Mr Shea. Christ the Son of God. The man I was waiting to see might well be perhaps nothing more than a hawker like me. Except for this, this serious truth which had washed over my face and skin, bathed and baptised me. And I was ready and thirsty for it after the awful day we had suffered. Ready to be refreshed, Timothy, and made anew. I am not a *servant* of the valley. I am its citizen.'

'But you always have been.'

'Not quite,' said Bandy with a tired smile. 'But now I felt that my blood was your blood, Mr Shea, and that we were both brothers in redemption. I have become one with you, old chap. I am, to quote Father Bruggy, taking instruction in the faith.'

Bruggy. Consumptive Bruggy.

'What will your father say of this move?'

'It will be a sadness for my father. He will say this to me. *You would not do it if they threatened to shoot you. So why do you do it for the sake of a breeze?*'

'I think that's a bloody good question, Bandy.'

'I pray with a fresh voice. A fresh voice which the Great Virgin has never heard before.'

The idea washed into Tim and gave him a sudden colour of hope. But it came to his tongue as irony and laughter. 'At least they won't be able to say you're a Fenian, son. Fenians come a bit pinker than you.'

A sulphur-crested cockatoo, a big, robust bird, tore through the air at the corner of Tim's sight. It arrested and shocked him with its brilliant white, its splendid yellow comb. It joined others of its species in a tall gum tree in the paddock across the road. A tree so adorned always looked as if its branches were hung with white and yellow silk.

There was something about this brightness this morning which caused Tim to sag and weep. Bandy was forced to hold him up.

'Tim, Tim,' said Bandy. 'We must go to our daily work, though in grief and weariness.' He freed a hand and indicated the sky, the Angelus tower, the Celtic cross atop the church and the school. 'We must be borne up and consoled by all this.'

Drinking tea at the dining room table, Mamie and Kitty looked wan.

'You went to Mass?' asked Mamie.

Considering her, he felt no enmity. No admiration either. Not for her vanity. But Lord, the hell had been shaken out of it!

'A lot of people were there,' said Tim. But he did not mention Bandy. With sleep and in time, Bandy might change his attitude.

'I must go,' said Mamie. 'I must go too. I must go to the Rosary tonight.'

Become a nun while you're at it and leave a space here for orphans.

'Will you excuse me,' he asked, forcing a little sociable smile. 'I have a letter to write.'

Kitty looked so pale. 'Don't work too hard, Tim,' she sighed.

Johnny and Annie still slept. An hour to store-opening. He found the inkwell in the living room and the special paper and sat at the table with the formal lamp on it. Rarely lit, this one, painted glass. A shepherdess with a bodice. French. Visits by Old Burke might warrant lighting this special lamp.

He began to write a letter.

'TO WHOM IT MAY CONCERN'

The WHOM, he knew very well, was Ernie. Ernie who had chosen to be aggrieved with him. Ernie who had wanted a ceremony and citizenry unspoiled by the Missy affair. But it was impossible that Ernie actually *knew* the girl. Unthinkable that the spouse of divine Winnie . . . Well not impossible, but unlikely. Missy simply a shire scandal so huge no one talked about it. They wished to cover it up with regiments, to diminish it to scale beside the proposed Central-to-East bridge.

'TO WHOM IT MAY CONCERN

'This stands for my willingness to declare upon oath that I am not the author of the *Australis* letters or any other letters appearing in the newspapers of the Macleay. I am willing to swear an affidavit to this effect before any Justice of the Peace the Patriotic Fund may wish to name. I make this solemn assertion in the hope that the Patriotic Fund, set up to preserve the values of our society, will take care not to cause reckless harm to any man's business.

Yours . . .'

When he re-read it the letter reeked to him of the willing, peasant cleverness which marred his family and made it so uneasy on earth. Yet he felt as well so guiltily consoled by finishing this testimony. Would Lucy forgive the small joy he felt in repairing this one wall? In re-making the little world out of a pond of ink when she had taken on the huge ocean?

He knew in his blood that she wasn't coming back soon or late. She would lie punishingly far out beyond the surf. Not for days either. It would be decades he would need to wait and wait.

His affirmation and pledge sat now in an envelope in his breast pocket in readiness for an early call on Winnie and Ernie Malcolm.

To the dining room door beyond which Kitty and her sister sat, soberly drinking their tea and discussing in hushed voices. While staring at the door jamb, he stated his intentions. 'I'll be back in time for opening,' he said. He creaked out an oblique smile.

Kitty drew his gaze, and her frown and her clannishness now seemed beautiful to him. Small, deliciously indented lips. A network of sisters too. For what he'd ranted about at night now had a new light on it.

'It's just business,' he told her.

He put Pee Dee in his traces. Pee Dee recovered from his comic spasm.

'Off to Winnie's,' he told the horse. 'It's for her intercession.' Hail, Holy Queen, sister of Alfred Lord T . . . Wife to Ernie, the Buddha of the Macleay. If Ernie not in then on to his office. Had Missy ever seen something of Ernie? If so, how, when, where?

No, Ernie was a citizen not a lover. It was simply this: Ernie did not want promising Kempsey burdened with Missy's name.

A few morning people in the streets of mauve dust. They did not seem to be electrified by the news from Crescent Head. Two saw-millers walked down Belgrave Street carrying tucker bags, their children with them, running and returning. He hauled at Pee Dee's reins a bit, secretly examining the men as they passed, and saw at once – or so he thought – that they would respond wistfully to the Rochester orphan. The only rage at her death came from him. 'Sad, sad,' they would say. 'Poor little thing . . .' The little doll-like tragedy would sit in the corner of their rooms for a week or so. Small-boned. Meagre. Fading.

And Mrs Sutter to be visited and Hector to be consoled this endless day!

He turned Pee Dee out of Elbow and into River Street. At Ernie's place he was slow in tethering Pee Dee, at last putting his forehead against the horse's neck.

'Well, your tucker depends on this, old feller.'

Pee Dee took no account of this peculiarly human frailty. His air was that of someone who had an inheritance in another place.

Tim chose the side path and went to the back of the house. There was no activity about the cookhouse, he noticed. No smoke from the chimney, no fragrance of breakfast-kindling wood. Were the Malcolms not up?

He knocked at the opened back door but Primrose did not come. Straining his head around the jamb, he saw the curtained place where Primrose slept. She was there. In the bed. Because her breathing could be heard.

'Oh, the big feller,' she sang. 'With the money purse.'

Staring into the depths of the house, he was startled to see immobile Winnie regarding him narrowly from the door of the dining room.

'Oh,' he said. 'Mrs Malcolm.'

'Is it you again?' she asked, in a tone which implied she did not seem to be sure who it was. A sad deterioration. She too was falling down some slope. She wore an evening jacket and a long loose muslin dress. Long, long strands of hair had come unbraided. In the crook of her right arm, she carried her black cat.

'I wondered was Ernie in?'

'Ernie's gone all night. A *contretemps*. His favourite servant, mind you, has a fever.'

She nodded towards the curtained space.

'I'll go and see him at his office then.'

'No need. Come in, come in for God's sake. Whatever you wanted. Drawing room. Drawing room.'

'I can't stay long,' said Tim.

He followed her along the hallway into a vast drawing room. Three settees, lamps, a roll top desk, a bookcase. A distant table, with china stacked on it. A flash dinner set gleaming there.

'My husband brought home a gift,' said Winnie, 'and as so often happens it triggered disputation. Perhaps if you see him when you go on to visit him, you could tell him I need him to come home again?'

A certain moisture appeared in her eyes and she flushed. The cat remained strangely quiet in the crook of her arm.

'Yes, I'll do that for you,' said Tim. 'Perhaps something you could do for me. People think I write these letters, that I'm political. I wondered could you speak to Ernie for me? I swear I wrote no letters.'

'And you will speak for me, Tim? Is that the bargain? Tennyson speaks for Daley? Daley speaks for Tennyson? "So I triumphed ere my passion, sweeping thro' me, left me dry, Left me with a palsey-ed heart and left me with a jaundiced eye." That's what Tennyson says.'

'It's a nice set of china, as far as I can tell from this distance,' said Tim, abashed, and unable to quote a thing in this contest of rhymes. 'I'm sure Ernie will be home soon, but I'll tell him if I'm lucky enough to see him.'

'"Home they brought her warrior dead,"' said Winnie on a streak of verse, '"Nor uttered cry:
'"All her maidens, watching said,
'"She must weep or she will die."'
'It'll be all right,' said Tim.

He wanted to be off. He wanted to find Ernie, who would probably be irritable after a night spent in the Commercial, or perhaps on the floor of his office. But he must be spoken to direct.

'I've taken a vow now, Tim,' said Winnie Malcolm. 'No more verse. No more verse. This is Kempsey after all. And Ernie is Ernie. The china from David Jones is the limit of grand things.'

'Is that cat well?'

She closed her eyes and her mouth slackened.

'It seems sick.'

She laughed and squeezed her teary eyes up and seemed to squeeze the poor cat as well. Six months ago he'd thought her the most abstractly beautiful woman on earth.

'I'll ask him not to ruin you, Tim. You ask him not to ruin me in return.'

'If you'll ask him calmly, he must take notice of you.'

'A kind of notice,' she said, beginning to shudder. 'A kind of notice. Do you know my cat's name? Its name is Electra.'

It seemed an overly classical name for a Macleay mouser.

She shook her head. 'Ernie calls it Kitty. So your fat little wife and your brats, Mr Shea! You're worried for them?'

'Extremely so, Mrs Malcolm. I have given people good credit and am given little credit myself.'

'I must stand by you and thank you, Tim, for all the poetry. There is something you can do for me. Would you kindly post this letter? I am not well enough to go out and do it myself.'

She gave him a thick and odd-sized envelope. Something stiff had been wadded in it. He knew it was un-gallant to read the address, so maintaining custody of the eyes he put it into the side pocket of his coat, his breast pocket being already occupied by his solemn declaration.

'Have no concern,' he said. 'It'll be attended to today.'

'The letter not to be mentioned to Ernie, though.'

Oh God, she was making a conspirator of him. And if Ernie discovered this . . . Well!

'All right,' he admitted. 'Everything is in confidence between you and me. If I post this letter, I never posted it. All right? Is that our understanding?'

She moved the seemingly sick cat into the crook of her left elbow and hauled Tim to herself without warning, kissing him wetly and lushly on the lips. This was an experience nothing like what he had once envisaged and – with one side of his nature – expected.

Before he could disengage himself, he heard behind him someone enter and commence gasping. The sound of outrage? Bloody Ernie! he surmised.

But battling Mrs Malcolm away, he saw it was Primrose emerged from the corridor. Looking at him from broiled eyes. 'Oh the white feller,' she announced. 'Fire on his bloody head!'

'Dear God, Winnie,' said Tim. 'She is very sick.'

Primrose slid to the floor and lay on her side, wheezing. Something landed up from another realm.

'Oh,' he said. 'Oh dear Jesus. This is not plague, is it?'

'Don't be a ninny, Shea. It is purely influenza.'

'Does Ernie know?'

'She had nothing more than a cough at teatime yesterday.'

The *Argus* and the *Chronicle* were unanimous in the matter of sudden onset.

'I must fetch Dr Erson.'

'Oh, you arrange my affairs? Yet want me to speak for you!'

'Let me find a rug for Primrose.'

'Yes. Make free of my house, Mr Shea. Go on. Do whatever you like.'

Out through a wide door and across the lobby, he found a bedroom but kept custody of his eyes as if he were being observed by Ernie and would need to justify himself. If it were simple influenza, what a fool he would be! People could rave from a mixture of influenza and laudanum. People could see fire about the heads of others.

When he came back with the rug from the base of the Malcolm bed, he was pleased to see Winnie Malcolm seated. She had lain the cat, purring and gagging by turns, on the ground.

'Look,' said Tim. 'It is shedding.' There was a trail of black hairs where the thing writhed.

Winnie laughed awfully. She drew herself up in a theatrical posture. 'Then you must do something, Shea! Men of action and decision. "Bury the Great Duke, With an Empire's Lamentation!" Holy God in Heaven, what a laughable crew!'

'Wait here, Winnie. Sit still till I fetch Erson.'

'How did you know Erson's our physician?' asked Winnie.

'I'm a prophet, Mrs Malcolm.'

She shook her head at this silly claim.

He chose to rush out by the corridor, the dining room, pantry, back verandah. Hustling through the side garden with its rose trellises, he inspected his shirt inside his coat, fearful of some sudden infestation. He did not have time for a proper survey. He removed Pee Dee's feed bag, climbed aboard, took the brake off and screamed, 'Yoa!' at the horse while desperately shaking the reins. Pee Dee broke out into a grudging canter.

'You are an utter uncooperative bastard!' Tim screamed at him.

The horse began to trot all at once. 'Good fellow,' sang Tim. 'Good fellow!'

The downhill slope helped. So, reaching Dr Erson's surgery. Leaving the horse and jogging in panic-stricken, Mrs Malcolm's mad spittle-ridden kiss sitting in his mouth. There were women and children waiting on chairs. He jiggled a little bell on a table in the centre of the room and Mrs Erson came in from the hallway. He muttered a request to see the doctor on a pressing matter. She frowned but was unwilling to disturb her husband. Yet Tim did not want to utter the word in the room where people waited with daily twinges to see the doctor. How could *plague* safely be spoken? Later he would not be sure how he managed to speak and achieve these things. He remembered being taken to the surgery and telling Erson of the series of signs he'd had in Ernie's house. And Erson frowning away, a cloud crossing his face. Tim was after all the man who'd ridden to the plague camp, the man too foolish to shoot an unruly horse. He should be the subject of reports from other people, you could see Erson thinking. He should not be reporting on others.

Even as he spoke, Tim was very taken with this question too

– how would Ernie Malcolm let him off the hooks of credit and repute if he recklessly called doctors to the house? If Primrose had flu, the cat distemper, Winnie merely gin?

Tim thanked the doctor for hearing him out and said he would continue with the day's work. There were many to be seen about yesterday's tragedy.

'No,' said Erson. 'Tim, listen, you must return to Malcolms' for now.'

'I have a day's work,' Tim protested. 'And a letter to post.'

'No, I beg you, Tim. Go back to the Malcolms' for the moment, until we see. I can't imagine you'll be kept long. But you are what is called a contact now.'

Tim flinched at this idea. That house in West on Showground Hill. It seemed a possible sepulchre to him.

'So go back there for now,' Erson said. 'Just until we are sure. This is likely just a fever. But if it were not, you could kill your wife and children and other citizens with a mere visit.'

'I understand,' Tim insisted, flinching. Did Erson believe what others said and expect anarchy of him? 'I am as reasonable as the next fellow.'

'I am pleased to hear that, since the police have extraordinary power in this matter.'

In all bloody matters. Yet how dismal he felt, how lost.

Erson began writing. Then offering Tim a note. 'One thing you can do, Tim. I must go *quam primum* to the Malcolms'. But you could take this to Ernie. Don't be tempted to stop on the way, and don't stand too close to people. I trust you in this. If, as we hope, it's nothing, you'll be home by night.'

So Dr Erson to the Malcolm house, Tim to Ernie's office in Smith Street. By Clyde Street to avoid a sight of the store, to avoid being tempted to call to Kitty, or to be delayed by a palavering Offhand or Habash. Into Smith Street by the back route, far from the Post Office. He abandoned Pee Dee and the cart, ran up the stairs at the side of Ernie's office block and so presented himself at a non-infective distance from the desk of flash, robust Miss Pollack of East, Ernie's secretary. Perhaps Miss Pollack was the trouble between Ernie and Winnie.

A matter of great urgency, he told her. Bugger the mistrust

on her face. 'Dr Erson wants to see Mr Ernie Malcolm immediately at home.' Just watch her now abandon haughtiness for dismay.

She went inside, and then Ernie himself appeared in the door of his office, his brow lowered, lips pushed forward, ready to ward off Fenian ambushes and pleas.

'You needn't put on any sort of face, Ernie,' Tim told him. 'There's sickness in your house.'

'Winnie?' he asked as if he already expected it and was half-pleased it had come.

'Primrose at the moment.'

'A sickness, Mr Shea?'

'Erson's gone up there to put a name to it. You and I have to go too.'

'You? Why so?'

'Here's a note from Dr Erson. I am what he calls a contact, Ernie. You would be too. Better not to argue but to go.'

Ernie read the page Erson had written and at once briskly fetched his coat and hat, as if he had no unfinished business at all. He did not speak to Miss Pollack as he left.

Tim and Ernie joined now in a mutual rush for the Showground Hill. Urging Pee Dee, Tim arrived in sight of Ernie, who had drawn up beside the doctor's neat pony cart. Saying nothing at all in farewell to his horse, Tim walked freely through the central gate and so entered the house by the front door. He could see and hear Mrs Malcolm sneezing hectically, jolting the dazed cat she cradled.

Tim and Ernie stood separate by the drawing room door and watched the kneeling Dr Erson attend to Primrose. As the doctor raised his head, Tim saw with alarm that he wore a white linen mask and white gloves, and this highly serious combination was somehow more shocking than if it had been spotted in one of the town's other two more sombre, less musical physicians.

'You must lay down that cat, Mrs Malcolm,' Dr Erson told Winnie through his mask. Tim thought he sounded a little dismayed, as if a sick cat and a fevered black woman were for the moment beyond his powers of containment.

'Tim, fetch me another cushion from the sofa,' he called. As

Tim took the cushion and approached Primrose, Erson reached his arm for it in an exaggerated way.

'Thank you, Tim,' called cracked tragic Winnie, stifling another sneeze, and clumsily winking. A reference perhaps to the letter. 'It's just as well you're here.'

It was fortunate therefore Erson had other tasks for Ernie, sent him off to call over the garden fence, asking his neighbour loudly to send his two boys, the Woodbury twins, for the police and the district ambulance. With the physician's eyes tracking him, Tim followed Ernie as far as the back door, and watched from there. Contemplating whether to flee. And so carry plague to Kitty.

Tim returned to the living room. Erson got up from Primrose's side, and murmured to him. 'Cannot pretend it isn't serious, Tim. No reason you should develop the disease though. You have not had close contact. Nothing to do other than wait out quarantine. Seven to perhaps ten days I fear.'

'Dear God,' Tim said. Seven days would ruin him. But he was appalled too that Winnie Malcolm had kissed him so moistly for so long. Did that make him a close contact? Closer than Ernie who perhaps hadn't been kissed for some time? How would a man confess that sort of distinction to Erson?

Caught so deep in this poisonous house, he covered his mouth with his hand for a time. That could not however be kept up.

Ernie was waiting outside in the front garden now. Tim could see him pacing, pausing by bushes he seemed to find unfamiliar. Someone else's garden. Winnie's.

'Are you making any headway with Primrose, Dr Erson?' said Winnie, her nose snuffling.

Erson looked at Tim. Primrose's gasping, you would have throught, was evidence enough. 'She is very ill,' he told Winnie. 'We'll leave her here on the floor for the moment. For her comfort.'

Winnie intoned, '"She only said, My life is dreary,
'"He cometh not, she said
'"She said, I am aweary, aweary.
'"I would that I were dead."'

'That's Alfred Lord Tennyson, isn't it?' asked Erson.

'My dearest mother died of an extreme fever,' said Winnie. 'Far away, you know. Melbourne. Do you remember that? The typhus outbreak of the Eighties? You may have heard of it. Doctors told my father it was remarkable for striking down some of the better types of people.'

'I've read of it,' said Erson, frowning down at Primrose. But you knew straight away he hadn't really read of it.

Winnie said, 'My mother was out shopping with her maid in Melbourne when caught by one of those quite terrible summer storms which bring the temperature falling. The maid insisted on running into some hovel in the city and coming out with an aunt's coat. My mother was grateful for it even though the garment wasn't of the cleanest. We surmised it was then she suffered the fatal lice bite.'

Still nursing the cat, Winnie began to shed gentle tears, no frenzy in them. An orphan modestly requiring of God the causes of extreme events.

'The fatal bite,' she reflected. 'You know, I didn't like Primrose. Ernie's choice. I wish her no harm but do not like her. Do you think God is mocking me now, Dr Erson?'

She seemed at that moment just about ready to fall. Erson seized on this helplessness of hers. 'Sit down now in that tall-backed chair, dear lady. That's exactly right. I would like you to place that cat of yours on the floor at your feet.'

In both respects – to Tim's surprise – she obeyed him. Erson rose and walked towards her then, making hushing sounds until her tears ceased. He did not approach too closely though. Looking down, he surveyed from his full height the cat and its patchy coat.

'Make her some tea, Tim,' asked the physician through his mask. 'Could you do that?'

Tim moved to do it. Wishing to prove his promptness to the doctor who thought him suspect for visiting the plague camp and failing to send Pee Dee to the knackers. But before going, Tim stepped up close to the doctor. 'I was hugged and much breathed on by Mrs Malcolm,' he confided. 'Not her fault of course – you see how she is.'

Erson shook his head. 'God, Tim, you're quite a lad,' he said softly.

Tim feared he'd betrayed Winnie somehow. 'No, I was kissed when she was upset. I didn't choose it, and she didn't either in this awful distress. Something disordered in her, you see.'

Erson looked at Tim with something far too much like pleading. 'Come with me then. I'll have you gargle. It might be of some use.'

Leaving drowsing Winnie and Primrose, they went out the back and found the fire in the cookhouse was out. And so no tea. For who had the spare intent to get a fire going in the stove on such a morning. The doctor took what seemed to be carbolic from his bag and mixed some with cold water from the tank. Wrigglers in it just like the last water he'd drunk at the Malcolms', but the carbolic made them frantic.

Erson watched Tim gargle and spit by the cookhouse door. He seemed still to be weighing Tim. To hell with that!

'I haven't caused this, you know,' Tim told the doctor. 'And I was kissed and held firmly. All against my will.'

But he remembered what some could describe as earlier desire, and his face burned.

Erson said, 'I don't so much want to be here, deciding on you one way or another. But you were the one who came to me. You could have gone to Dr Casement or Dr Gabriel, but came to me!'

'But now we need to be quarantined. Not you though?'

Erson's eyes above the mask considered him in sorrow. That was worse than anger. 'I will not go home again from the hospital until your quarantine period is done with. The other Macleay doctors will look after my normal patients. I will be on call for you alone. I shall need to be bathed and my clothes fumigated just as with you, Tim.'

Nothing to be said then. Nothing to be hoped for. Except Tim did say, 'I didn't understand. You'll find me a good patient.'

They returned to the living room where Winnie drowsed and Primrose raved. Fragments of words came out. Or perhaps the other, half-remembered language.

Outside in the garden, Ernie had stopped pacing. Through the windows it could be seen that Hanney had arrived on a police mount. He was dressed not as Tim had seen him emerge from the Armidale Road an age past – not in cavalryman's breeches, but in the usual dusty navy blue. Erson rushed across the room and lowered his mask with his white glove to call orders through an opened pane.

'Please, Ernie. Come inside now. Constable, don't you come in but wait there.'

Hanney paused on the garden path and saw Tim behind Erson. Tim didn't doubt he'd been spotted. It was clear in the slow triumph of the constable, the way he shook his head. Not surprised to see Shea his humiliator in the matter of plague camps. Now at the plague's centre. He stepped a few paces closer, took his hat off and watched hard.

'That's Shea the grocer in there?' he called. The presumption of guilt. Suspicion confirmed. And so on.

Erson cried, 'Exactly,' before adjusting his mask. Hanney stared a little longer. Looking on Tim as familiar and instigator to all the tragedies – Albert, Missy, Lucy, and now perhaps, the worst of all.

'Thank you, constable,' cried Doctor Erson. 'You could wait by the gate for the district ambulance!'

Meanwhile Ernie stepped listlessly up onto the verandah. The far-off river could be seen violet behind him. He paused on the verandah and came in then, opening and closing the door, and appeared in the living room. Self-imprisoned on his hearth.

Watching him now, Tim felt an enlarged sense of damnation, of the separation of Hanney's normal dusty police blue from his own grey cloth coat.

All the unmade and unmakeable calls – Kitty, Mrs Sutter, Hector, customers – in turn itching in him. Ernie called to his wife. 'Are you feeling not too badly, dear?'

But Winnie did not answer, though you could hear her shifting in her chair. Dr Erson had crossed the living room to approach the corner table. He picked up one of the china plates and inspected it.

'Winnie's new set,' cried Ernie, and when Erson did nothing more than nod, Ernie turned to Tim. 'What were you doing here anyhow? Drumming up business or pouring the bloody gin into a man's wife?'

'I asked your wife to intercede for me. Tell you that I'd asked for nothing more than to be paid. Three months' credit is enough,

Ernie. And while we are bloody at it, I have written a statement I wanted to deliver to you.'

He took the letter pleading his innocence from his breast pocket. But remembered he was meant to keep his distance.

'I wish to give Ernie this letter,' Tim told Erson.

'Hold on to it for now,' murmured the doctor, putting one of the plates down.

Seven days' quarantine. There would be time to talk to Ernie.

'So china, eh?' Dr Erson asked.

'Yes,' said Ernie. 'A present for my wife.'

'A peace offering,' murmured Mrs Malcolm to herself. 'A dove. An olive branch.'

'Just settle down, dear,' weary Ernie advised her.

'China,' said Dr Erson. 'From China by way of David Jones. And it came in a crate?'

'Yes. Very flash.'

'The ungrateful wife!' said Winnie Malcolm theatrically.

'I did find a deceased rat in the the crate,' Ernie confessed. 'Took it out and threw it to the back of the yard. However, found it bloody dragged back into the house by that cat. I took it finally and properly burned it.'

At the mention of the cat, Winnie Malcolm bent to pick the creature up again.

'No, Mrs Malcolm,' Erson cried out.

'You can't get plague from a cat, can you?' Ernie asked in a pathetic husbandly voice. 'Your cat may be very ill, dear,' he explained to Winnie without waiting for Erson's answer.

Dr Erson's grimness of movement. No longer that of the matinee actor. He took off gloves already perhaps sullied by contact with Primrose, and felt Winnie's brow and the glands under her jaws, and then her underarms. After vanishing to wash his hands like a modern physician, he returned and repeated his medical exercises with Ernie and then Tim. Tim had had to try to read the doctor's eyes as the other two victims were gauged and handled, but now he felt Erson's masterly cool fingers probing at his armpits. They were somehow a sacrament of comfort.

Outside, beyond the gate, pulled by two draught horses and

greeted by Constable Hanney, the Macleay's white ambulance wagon turned up, putting a fullstop to Tim's attempt to make peace with Dr Erson. Two men got down, tying white linen masks around their noses and mouths as they came towards the door, and dragging white gloves onto their hands. The world entire, it seemed now, knew that he and Primrose, Ernie and Winnie could not be safely touched. How astonishing an idea in a place like New South Wales, a modern colony, a land of promise.

Dr Erson opened the door to the men, and they came in in official boots, ordinary men raised to authority by their masks. In their hands they carried a rolled-up stretcher. Failed farmers reduced to carrying out the mercies of the ambulance.

'Take the cat,' Dr Erson murmured through his mask. 'Wring its neck. Watch yourself. It may have plague fleas. Then the stretcher for the black woman. Wrap her up well.'

Tim shook his head. How did I manage to be here, at the end of the world, on a remote river, in a bushweek town on precisely the right morning to incur this risk?

Primrose protesting at their presence in her own language. The Gaelic of the Yarrahappini of the Macleay. One of the ambulance men wearing heavy gauntlet gloves now and lifting the cat from Winnie's feet and gingerly holding it at most of his arm's length.

'Poor cat, poor cat!' murmured Winnie. She stood up and made a noise of protest. Dr Erson rushed to hold her back by the shoulders, and she begged to know, 'Has the rot gone so far?'

'Kitty will follow,' called Ernie. As Winnie had predicted, he did not use the flasher Greek name Electra. 'The cat will come behind.'

'Is the dumb universe spoiled too?' cried Winnie.

A fine question, Tim thought, deserving a better audience.

'No, be at ease, Mrs Malcolm,' he cried.

One of the ambulance men, carrying a sealskin sack, proof against fleas, passed through the garden towards the wagon. Winnie thank Christ not alert enough to see that. The fellow hung the bag from a hook on the side of the wagon. Back in the house then to rejoin his mate.

As the two ruined farmers lifted the black woman from the ground, Ernie stepped forward overtaken by sudden anguish. 'I have a very important meeting to attend tonight,' he told Erson.

Above the linen mask, Dr Erson looked at him. 'Ernie, this is grievous indeed. There are no meetings for us at the moment. Your associates would not thank you for coming amongst them, and will postpone the meeting anyhow on the advice of the sanitation officer.'

'And we are most endangered?' Ernie asked.

'You are most endangered, sad to say, Ernie.'

'Bloody hell then,' said Ernie, looked at Tim, and laughed.

Winnie paid more attention than he did as her un-liked servant was borne away.

The ambulance waiting, Ernie packed a bag of clothing each for himself and Winnie. From the living room he could be heard sighing as he chose items. Packing not for some brave voyage on *Burrawong* but for a meaner one in the white wagon.

Each item would need to be fumigated at the hospital, said Dr Erson, so certain as to what would be done. There must have been secret meetings between the physicians and sanitation officer to plan how these affairs would be managed. From the hallway he encouraged Ernie and Winnie, who had now joined her husband in the packing. Ernie's muttered directions and Winnie's sudden raised voice marked the work of sorting garment from garment. In the dreary air, Tim stood by astounded and dismal.

When the Malcolms were ready and had emerged from their room, Tim moved to pick up Winnie's bag, but the two men in masks were back. One of them offered to carry it at the rear of the promenade out of the house. As they all gathered themselves to leave, neither Winnie nor Ernie seemed to look back. Winnie won't be returning, Tim thought. She will go back to her Melbourne.

Here now on the garden path, the procession still in good order. Erson at the head, the man who knew their chances best, and Winnie, hair unbrushed, assisted – contrary to the rules of keeping distance – by Ernie, who toted his own portmanteau.

From far up the fence, Hanney watched. Safe from exhalations or fleas or whatever it was which made up the curse. In lazy delight he waved a hand at Tim. No chance he would lose this bit of the contest. If plague were in Tim, then Hanney would consider it an utter and personal victory, a knock-out punch, a besting. Tim Shea clean bowled – Hanney!

The man not burdened with Winnie's port swung open the back door of the ambulance, then stepped down to allow the rest of the party to mount, the doctor first. In the soft brown light of the interior, Primrose had been lain on a broad bench far forward.

Dr Erson directed the seating. The Malcolms on a bench running down one side of the wagon – 'You and Winnie should really sit apart as hard as that might be.' He pointed Tim to the bench on the other side, a position near the door.

This was the side where Primrose lay, but at a more than safe distance forward. Tim squinted up the length of the wagon to where she had been lodged on her stretcher and thought that in this umber air Primrose looked uneven in colour. Still she murmured, engaged in some horrid argument.

Erson stepped out to travel in the front with the ambulance fellows, and Tim sat last of all and the door was closed. Winnie and Ernie opposite him, lit through the canvas-covered windows. Against the rules, Ernie reached for and held Winnie's hand at what would in normal times be thought a comic distance. Tim's finest, imperious customers. The spacious couple who had descended the gangplank of *Terara* on picnic day.

The door now bolted from outside. Erson could be heard instructing Constable Hanney on returning Pee Dee and the cart to *T. Shea – General Store*.

'Tell the Shea woman not to be concerned,' Tim heard Erson tell Hanney. How could *this* constable be depended on not to twist the news in some way?

'Don't play with the message, Hanney!' Tim called, but the warning sounded weirdly muffled in here.

'Why would I have to, Tim?' Hanney cried.

Outside. In no way a contact. Lucky bugger.

Behind the huge bungalow which was the Macleay District

Hospital lay a barracks-like wooden building which had been the first hospital. People knew it as the loony house, since it was fitted out as a place to hold those lonely spirits who went mad up and down the river and needed to await shipment to the asylums of Sydney. Therefore it was set up with heavy wooden doors layered with steel, and barred windows.

Now it would be the Macleay's quarantine.

The nurse to whom Tim had once delivered the body of Albert Rochester waited in the opened doorway of this isolation ward. Though she wore a mask, he could tell her by her forehead and eyes. At the top of the stairs, she stood aside as the ambulance men carried Primrose in. Then she addressed the rest of the party. Inside, she asked, could they kindly undress and put on gowns provided. Masks of white cotton would be found in the small dispensary and were to be worn whenever possible within ten feet of other patients. Future health depended on that. After close contacts with other patients, the masks were to be dropped in a bucket she would point out and new ones could be taken from the dispensary. In between, hands were to be strictly washed with carbolic soap. The clothing they were wearing at the moment would be fumigated – that was the best policy – and they would be supplied with clothing from their suitcases once that too had been fumigated.

She came down the stairs and took Winnie's arm. 'Is that her portmanteau?' she asked the man carrying Mrs Malcolm's bag. She did not wait for an answer but led Winnie up the steps. 'You have a fever, dear,' she said. 'Possibly just a cold.'

'Have you seen my cat, miss?' Winnie asked.

'I think the fellows are looking after it.'

Dr Erson himself led the men upstairs, past the door lined with metal. Its flakes of paint and indentations made Tim's soul creak with melancholy. He could taste despair brownly on his tongue. Into a comfortless yellow corridor of tongue-and-groove timber. Erson addressed Ernie and Tim. 'That is your bathroom there. Are you aware of Sister Raymond? She is a brave young woman who has volunteered to attend to plague cases.'

'Oh, Jesus,' said Tim. 'At least take my receipt and cash books from my top pocket. My wife will need them.' He thought too of his letters. Winnie's un-posted one as well.

Ahead, Sister Raymond said through her mask, 'Of course, of course. All that.'

Dr Erson said, 'Place them by the door, Tim. We shall fumigate them and get them to your wife.'

Tim doubled back and laid the books by the door. Love letters to Kitty in a sense. But not enough joy in them.

Past three other doors down the corridor, a large whitewashed ward waited for him and Ernie to share. Camp beds set out. Two barred windows and the camp beds strictly separate and adorned with a scaffolding for mosquito nets. No nets were in place however, since mosquitoes were rarely found on top of this hill. All boards scrubbed. A place designed for perishing.

Everyone who wore a mask very busy now. Erson and the nurse discussing near the kitchen: refining their minds on the whole regulation of these perhaps-sufferers of bubonic. From the door of the large ward, Tim heard the two masked men clattering about, sloshing tubs of water into baths somewhere closer to the door, toting other heavy things elsewhere.

Then, Tim saw, they exited through the iron-girt door and brought back commodes. Thunder-boxes, shafts and handles affixed either side for carrying night soil away. They put such a contraption in a pantry across from the kitchen, for use by Ernie and Tim. What a divine punishment for political opponents: to have to share a shouse seat and smell each other's water.

A second thunder machine. Located far down the corridor for use by the women.

In the men's bathroom two tubs of steaming water waited, reeking of carbolic. Tim could smell the fragrance. One of the men came to the door of the ward and told him and Ernie to undress and lay out by the door the contents of their pockets, and any books and newspapers they had with them. Imagine, the letter returned to Winnie.

If it were a plaguey letter, the damage had already been done. He had already held it in his hands. Instead of putting it out, as he did all his other effects, including a wallet and the black Rosary his mother Anne had given him for his emigration, he slipped Winnie's letter under his mattress.

Going to the bathroom, he was instructed to dip himself into one of the carbolic baths. Watched by the ambulance men, Tim unclothed, looking down at the auburn hair of his chest and legs and wondering why the failed and masked dairy farmers didn't laugh.

Taking off his shirt across the bathroom – more than ten feet, Tim was pleased to see – Ernie revealed himself a chunk of a man. Certainly an ale-y belly, but grafted onto a body built for labour. Four square like the Army at Waterloo, hurrah! Gingery hair marked his heart and his prick and connected the two. So this is the boy Winnie had taken into her garden.

'For a breeze of morning moves,
And the planet of Love is on high,
Beginning to faint in the light that she loves
On a bed of daffodil sky . . .'

He wondered was he already fevered? All this Tennyson he'd read for Winnie's sake washing up casually in his brain now.

Scalding in the tub, and something in the water burning at his skin. As long as the plague was scoured out by these means!

Opposite him, Ernie plunged his body into the tub with a sigh. Across the hallway in the women's bathroom, Sister Raymond could be heard advising Winnie towards the hot water and soap.

'Take the bath, darling,' Ernie called musically from his own tub of water. 'It's for your good.'

He turned a tormented face to Tim and whispered, 'She's been hugging that bloody, flea-bitten cat half the night. Thank Christ though she always kept her distance from Primrose.'

Seen through the partially opened bathroom door, the ambulance fellows had begun working in the corridor, piling clothing into a wicker tub, Primrose's night dress, Mrs Malcolm's chemise, his own shirt and drawers all tumbled in there promiscuously with Ernie's tie and butterfly collar. The collected wealth of those infested.

'He left her nothing but a failed business,' people would say wisely as they watched poor little Kitty.

From the women's bathroom, they could hear Sister Raymond saying, 'Let me inspect you there, dear, to look for broken skin.'

Tim rose too, covering his privates with a freckled hand. Then to one of the white wraps which hung on the wall. He folded himself into it. His long feet stared bluely up at him. Flippers fit for a slab, he thought.

'Ernie,' he asked, 'will your friends still blacklist me if I get the plague?'

Ernie shook his head and rose up urgently from his bathwater, his stub of a prick showing. Slug and angel of mercy.

'Poor Winnie,' Ernie said, his arse to Tim now as he gathered himself into a wrap. 'What you call my friends . . . various of the Patriotic Fund gentlemen . . . I can't undo the sort of work they've done on people already. As soon as you were suspected, Tim, they started writing off letters to the Sydney suppliers. You know, warning them your credit isn't good. Your social credit as much as anything.'

Tim was struck still in his white shroud. Come on, Ernie! Was that possible? Something relayed so offhandedly. The ordinary power to ruin a man. On his big feet, Tim could say nothing. His tongue an orb of leather. You couldn't pick the poisoned world apart with such a silly instrument.

'Your little store has a pretty hard row to hoe now,' Ernie stated. 'I don't approve of that sort of thing, Tim. A little campaign, without warning a man. Easy to get going though, don't you see? But more so if a fellow is a bit behind on his payments and a bit strained for the ready.'

This knowledge couldn't be contained. He knew that in this garment you could not exercise a rage properly, but that itself fed the rage. He rushed white-robed Ernie and pushed him up against the grooves of the wall.

'In that case, Ernie, God damn you! You've as good as murdered me, your whole murdering bunch!'

Ernie however wouldn't give Tim the joy Tim wanted from him, the rage he could have punished. Wouldn't even try. Ernie's eyes slid sideways. He seemed too melancholy to be hit.

'Come, Tim. You're not a solid sort, you've got to admit. Though I suppose the flea bites us both with equal venom. I could have forgiven even the dunning of Winnie.'

Tim stopped pushing so hard. You couldn't push against such a pale talker.

'But those *Australis* letters, Tim. Baylor picked them at once. Boils down to this. A man who renounces his own society . . .

who lies there at its heart pretending to patriotism . . . what can that fellow bloody well expect, Tim? What could *you* bloody well expect?'

Anger revived and Tim pushed Ernie back in place after all. 'But I am not the sodding man.'

'Whatever you say, Tim. Everyone knows. It would have gone better for you had you appended your bloody name in the first place. Had the courage to do that . . . By the way, Tim, we are meant to be wearing masks aren't we? Up this close.'

Tim let Ernie go and walked across the room. Just as well too, he decided then. Before Erson took any further false notion of him. 'I suppose *that* was part of the bloody plan also then? That bloody inspector.'

'People like Billy Thurmond are very energetic. They meet like-minded visitors to the Good Templars and guide them to the people *they* would like to see punished.'

Ernie sighed, and Tim knew it was not just because the plague had him hostage. But on top of that he had changed in a month. At all recent encounters, there'd been no real enthusiasm in Ernie. No fuming rage even when he pretended there was. No hectic affection. *Take the bath, darling. It's for your good.*

All his enthusiasm had been spent in writing that glowing letter about Hanney.

Not waiting for any further Ernie clarifications, Tim opened the door of the bathroom. It was – based on Ernie's recent information – an even more venomous world, and what he saw now stood as evidence. Under Sister Raymond's directions Winnie, barefoot in a white gown, staggered down the corridor.

'He said, "She has a lovely face,"' Tim remembered.

'"God in his mercy lend her grace,

'"The Lady of Shalott."'

Mrs Winnie Malcolm guided to a room further along than Primrose's, and casually declaring, 'I have a dreadful head-ache.'

'Oh, yes,' called Ernie soothingly over Tim's shoulder. 'But it may be from what you've taken.'

Winnie said nothing in rebuttal.

Ernie and Tim then were to share the third, big space. The men's ward, for companionable madmen. Ernie sitting on his camp bed, his naked knees showing through the shroud-like cloth.

Soon one of the men in white brought in Tim's fumigated effects and put them on a chair – watch, the letter offering the Patriotic Fund an affidavit, the blackthorn rosary beads his mother had given him when his trunk was packed and waiting for the charabanc to come for it and him. Oh migration, oh!

Carried habitually, these beads. Not honoured by as much use as his present fix would seem to warrant.

A negligible little pile of possessions was brought in and put on the chair near Ernie's bed. Tim touched the big rosary beads above his cot. No need to be guarded about any of that any more. Murder revived in his heart with the sight of the beads. He imagined himself mad and purple with plague riding naked to Pola Creek and breathing on Billy Thurmond's family.

The as-yet-unworn mask someone had placed on the deal chair by his bed depressed him, but he was cheered when a port-manteau packed by Kitty was delivered late in the day. Tim opened it gratefully and began to dress, a man reassuming his skin. Nothing smelled of fumigation – these came from Kitty's uninfected household. A modest joy in that fact. His better pants and coat. Underdrawers and a singlet which smelled of sun and soap. Small aspects of her care – folded against the singlet for wearing around the neck a scapular, two patches of brown cloth connected by cord. A note in her hand said: 'We all cry for you, Timmy. But soon soon I don't doubt it! Saint Anthony's scapula guards against plage and influenza.' Every Kenna family misspelling delicious to him. Then today's *Argus*, Saturday's unfinished *Chronicle*. So touching. Kitty knew he liked newspapers.

Added to the note, 'Poor child still not found so must commit her to mercy, Tim.'

Across the room Ernie sighed and rose. His mask was in his hand. He seemed embarrassed by it. 'You have reading matter, Shea. Perhaps when you're finished with them . . . I wonder has the singing doctor seen fit to fumigate them. For now, I must visit poor old Winnie, as unwelcome as a man might be.'

Still in his white garment and on his white little blocks of feet, he went off to keep his marital post. He was on safe ground. For the nurse wouldn't let him stand too close to his wife.

In the *Chronicle*, as Kitty had foreshadowed, news of no news of Lucy. Tim was now guilty to realise that in this pressing hour he had half-forgotten her. 'Crescent Head fisherman Mr Eric Dick says that the drowned child, who fell from Crescent Head's Big Nobby during a picnic on Sunday, should by now have been found in the vicinity, unless caught by the stronger Pacific coastal current . . .' How Lucy would have embraced that stronger current! Sought its hand and let it make her a journeyer. While I am justly made to serve the plague's time.

Page eight, the third *Australis* letter.

'Sir,

'The year progresses, and since the British garrisons in South Africa still go unrelieved, and since they like us must be wearying of all the talk of the much-praised British mettle, I am forced to reflect further and in the frankest terms so far on our colonial situation. I do so as the valour of the Australian Mounted Bushmen is sacrificed by clumsy British generals in bungled attempts to relieve those garrisons.

'As all this occurs to our disadvantage, we nonetheless take the Constitution of our infant Nation off to London, to have it ticked and amended by a Colonial Secretary in Whitehall, who is not one of us and who has no understanding of what we are, or of the equality and independence which are the better side of what we are. Could you imagine Jefferson and Washington submitting the Constitution of the United States to the scrutiny of Lord North? They would laugh at you if you suggested it, those great democrats! How is it that even approaching Nationhood we lack the confidence to seek only one assent alone to what we should be? That is: our own assent?

'Until we do that, there will be many follies like the follies of South Africa. Until we do that, we will need to seek leave in perpetuity of aristocratic dolts in Whitehall who will arrange matters for the convenience of the Mother rather than the welfare of the Child.

'I trust that fair-minded citizens will see that my three letters are a good and reasonable summary of an Australian democratic position, one taken irrespective of race and sect. In the spirit of that, I am, forever and with just pride,

Yours, etc.

Australis'

'Oh, Holy Christ,' Tim whispered. *Reasonable* citizens! In a town where people wrote off to the supply houses in Sydney, saying you were done for. Reasonable bloody citizens!

Masked Ernie wandered in again, glum, and slumped down on his cot.

'Not allowed close to her. She has a cold and looks a little flushed. Primrose, though, not well at all. The glands show black under her chin.'

Poor Primrose then. Winnie wouldn't weep for her, and Ernie wasn't likely to.

Tim knew Winnie's letter lay beneath his mattress, but he had his useless statement of innocence beside his bed. No use giving it to Ernie now. Ernie was out of the debate. Perhaps use the back of the sheet to write to Kitty. As soon as he felt the first fever. Not till then would he know what to say.

A restless grief for Lucy had grown in him again. He tried to contain and soothe it with print. He shook out his *Argus* – Ernie could bloody whistle for the *Chronicle*, though reading the Offhand might improve his mental habits. Tim leafed past the serials full of genteel fairness and simple maps of the world. He began to read how New South Wales had defeated South Australia outright in the Sheffield Shield cricket in Adelaide. Where, reports said, plague had also made its landing.

At mid-afternoon, when the isolation ward was quiet and masked Ernie across the room and Winnie Malcolm further down the hallway seemed to be asleep, he decided to pick up his own white mask, tying it at the back, all like a well-ordered patient, and went down the corridor to the door of Primrose's room. Sister Raymond, however, intercepted him at the door, forbidding him with her huge eyes.

'I wanted to see what it was like,' Tim explained. 'The poor woman . . . she's had no company.'

'She's not aware of that, Mr Shea. The struggle is extreme.'

Patches of supremely black skin now in Primrose's half-black face. What townsperson, very aged these days, maybe under the sod, had taken his lust up the river to Primrose's black mother. A quart bottle of port handed over as the contractual grounds for Primrose's mixed blood. She had white relatives in town who did not know of her. Didn't know that their blood went to make the plague's first target.

An awful struggle for Primrose. Her chin stretched up above a mumpy neck. Sister Raymond put a wet cloth on her forehead, dribbled some water across her mouth.

'It feels so normal, all this, don't you agree?' Tim asked. 'So usual?'

Albert Rochester normal across Pee Dee's shoulders with a bag over his head.

In the humidity of mid-afternoon the thunderstorm, still standard in this late summer, struck the hospital hill. Three o'clock. Beneath the thunder Tim, gone to Primrose's door again, witnessed the last weak seizures. In spite of nature's bombast and the fury of rain on the roof, there was no sense of a great culminating tragedy. Tim in fact felt he was there yet not there, witnessing from another place. In the spiritless moment, in the ward wilfully empty of human decoration, fitful pieces of old prayers and funeral verses spilled over his lips but reached no proper conclusion. And yet while distant, still too real, too actual.

Behind the cold glass of his own fear he saw something to be admired. Sister Raymond stood up to make a healthy distance though not ten feet between herself and the half-caste and took off her mask so that Primrose could pass with the sight of a human face. He knew at once he had never given Lucy such a thing. He'd given her an anxious face, a dutiful, solicitous, guilty face. But nothing as frank as this.

The struggles ended as simply as you could wish. Primrose exemplary and quick at the end.

Her recent employers the Malcolms slumbered. Their suitcases of fumigated clothes lay by now at the foot of their beds so that like Tim they could dress as usual inhabitants when they woke.

But they still slept as the two men came down the corridor past Tim and lifted Primrose up and out without ceremony and straight away.

'Make way, Tim,' said Sister Raymond.

'Call the Malcolms,' he suggested.

'No. Not now.'

'You won't burn her?' Tim found himself softly pleading as the ambulance fellows carried Primrose fairly delicately to the door.

'Doctor will see her,' said the nurse.

'Where will she go?'

'Consecrated ground, Tim.'

'Where? Where consecrated?'

He might in fact need to share her space with her, Primrose, Ernie, Winnie, Shea. Somewhere, haphazardly and uncritically, he and Primrose might be free with each other's limbs.

Sister Raymond's huge eyes over the restored mask, brown with some selfless, calm, sisterly virtue. 'You do want to know things, Mr Shea. In consecrated ground. The edge of West Kempsey cemetery.'

'A common pit?'

'Tim!' the sister warned him. But in times of epidemic, he knew, it was a matter of common pits, not individual resting places. Common pits and quicklime. The rumour of Primrose's girlhood, let alone all the uncelebrated dinners and ironing she had done for the Malcolms, would be resigned to the fast work of that pit.

For superstition's rather than medicine's sake, mask off now, thrown into a bucket of carbolic and water. Hands washed in carbolic. New mask fetched for coming use from the pile in the small room named the dispensary. No need yet to put it on. No close contact planned. But performing these small duties very comforting.

Back in the ward where Ernie slept, he took down the thorn beads and applied himself to reciting one of the Sorrowful Mysteries. *Jesus Is Crowned with Thorns*. Hands trembling, beads likely to fall. Under his whispers, Primrose and her handlers crossed the garden outside and vanished past the window. Out to sea with Lucy and the narwhals.

He would choose that, though. To voyage with lucky Lucy. Rather than be with Primrose.

Later, while he read, Sister Raymond could be heard arguing

soothingly down the corridor with an awakened Mrs Malcolm. Winnie crying, 'But I must see her!'

For something to say, Sister Raymond advised Winnie to wait for Doctor who would be here soon. Across the room Ernie writhed in his shallow afternoon slumber. Sister Raymond came in holding up a hand to signify that Tim should sit still.

'Mr Malcolm, Mr Malcolm,' said Sister Raymond. Ernie sat up in his white gown.

'I regret to tell you that your wife has a fever.'

'Oh dear God!' said Ernie. 'She isn't ready for this.' He sat up. 'We have a reconciliation still to make . . .'

'Come and see her. I have dressed her in one of her own nightgowns.'

Ernie reached for his pile of fumigated clothes, but then covered his face with his hands and was defeated by the prospect of dressing.

'I'll manage it soon,' he promised.

'Yes, but be quick.'

The accountant gathered himself and picked up a limp, fumigated white shirt with a high collar, rushed into his brown pants without bothering with drawers, and hauled on a pair of oxfords without socks.

'Dear, sweet God,' he murmured softly, catching Tim's eye. 'It's all too quick by half, Tim. Where's the bloody time for a resolution?'

Then he sat on his cot again.

'Could be just a simple fever,' Tim kept saying. How could you believe bloody Ernie would have looked so affecting? Recklessly shaking his square head. Tears spilling from his eyes.

'I have put a fresh mask there for you to wear when you're ready, Mr Malcolm,' Sister Raymond told him.

'Dear God, these masks,' said Ernie. 'We are punished, we are punished.'

Tim stood as if to help Ernie by example, and Ernie painfully stood but then got going quickly towards the door.

'Wait for me,' the nurse called. In big masterful shoes she pursued him.

Winnie's letter was certainly infested, then. He'd leave it where it was pending events. On his own, Tim spent a little time regarding Ernie's watch-chain, which had flopped on the floor. With its array of civic medallions, scarlet, blue, gold, green, white, it resembled a brilliant snake. Ernie's public skin sloughed off there while the poor bugger went in sockless pain to see his wife.

'Fatherless children,' he murmured aloud.

Annie uselessly earnest once she was fatherless, and turning suspicious. Johnny rushing down the precipices of the new century with every Lucy Rochester he could find. Seven-months-pregnant wife. Left with a barren store, a store from which the credit had run out. Kitty would fight, of course, but the idea of her undertaking this struggle seemed to him poignant beyond bearing. Old Burke might be sparingly kind, in a cold, cautionary way, saying what a fool her husband had been. Joey O'Neill would be more generous in spirit, he and Mamie supporting the children. But they'd all become a bread-and-dripping clan. No roast potatoes or leg of lamb or sago and custard as he and Kitty had grown accustomed to. O'Neill wasn't fashioned for wealth.

Winnie not designed either for this silly plague, this paltry, plain affair in the old prison of Macleay lunatics. She was devised by temperament and by her lean and elegant bones to invite Death wistfully, to intend it. Not to be jumped on, nor ambushed like this.

'I have been half in love with easeful death,
Called him soft names in many a mused rhyme.'

Young Keats the poet who melted like snow. Winnie entitled to do the very same. Her poets had promised her that. Bloody Alfred Lord had promised it.

'Death closes all: But something ere the end,
Some work of noble note, may yet be done, Not unbecoming men that strove with gods . . .'

Bullshit.

I should expose the bloody poets, Tim promised himself. That's the letter I'll write to the *Chronicle*! For Ernie's sake, but for Winnie's above all. For she'd believed them. Believed the posturers, the death-flirtatious buggers, and here she was in a plague ward amongst gum trees.

He took a decision to get up and follow the direction Ernie had taken. No mask on, since with Sister Raymond on duty no closeness could be hoped for. Following the corridor he reached a point from which he could see into Winnie Malcolm's room. Nothing there that was up to the high level of Tennyson. The plainness of it all brought that instant sting of grief. Winnie very flushed, her face unencumbered and open, since she was beyond protecting . . . Seeing Ernie, and pushing at him with her fists. Ernie stepping back, uttering through the linen gag he wore un-poetical, forlorn sobs, moist in the wrong way for grandeur. But truly mourning also, poor fellow. Not the sort of sound normal to a mongrel pillar of the bush.

Sister Raymond soothed mewling Winnie with a wet cloth, holding her by the shoulder and persuading her to drink the second half of a cup of something – bromide, laudanum, God knows what. Something Lethean, Tim hoped. To make her serene. How could Ernie, whose duty was to love her, restrain himself at such a time?

'Now sit down by the door, Mr Malcolm, if you don't mind,' said the nurse, forcing the dose over Winnie's lips.

Splendid Winnie Malcolm grew quieter – weakness and the drug curtailed the low drama, loosened her face, made it serene. On his chair, Ernie raked the backs of his hands with his nails and said at last so much, so many appeals to God and mercy, that Sister Raymond looked at him with something less than patience.

'Now we must be calm. Do you want us to have to bring more and more nurses?'

'No, no,' Ernie agreed. 'But it's too bloody cruel.'

'And it must be borne,' said Sister Raymond.

'I'm not afraid of bearing things,' Ernie claimed like a child on the edge of some darkness.

All the thwarting of Tim's letter to the Commissioner, all the betrayal over accounts and all the useless urgings to loyalty and valour meant nothing now to Tim. At this hour, Ernie presented himself as a plain animal in grief.

And this large young woman who commanded them. Be thankful at least for her. She would not permit florid deaths. They were under a duty, he and Ernie, to grieve and be fearful in an orderly manner. Theatre on their parts would only drag in more nurses or masked attendants and spread the peril too broadly.

*　　*　　*

In the early dusk, as Tim sat on his cot in the men's ward, one of the white-coated men went by unmasked in the garden. Idly moving amongst the rhododendrons. Sun-leathered, about Tim's age. Tim swore he'd never become such a man if lucky enough to live on. He'd get work hauling, cutting or milking rather than this. The fellow looked aimless, glancing up at the highest branches of a red gum. No doubt he and his mate paid a margin for plague duty, for waiting in their hut in the garden and carrying food and medicine back and forth, carrying the thunder-boxes. Carrying Primrose. But what margin would be worth it? And were they scared too? They certainly maintained a distance and didn't swap their names with him and Ernie. Men with a memory of labour so fierce that they'd rather now be paid to hang around for the plague's pleasure.

Soon after this sighting, he heard both attendants came along the path to the armoured door. They talked as they advanced. 'Lost half the bloody herd,' Tim heard one of them say. Unlocking the barracks, they came in carrying trays of corned beef, potatoes, split peas, sago pudding. Their gloves, brilliant white, looked delicate on their big hands. Tim watched from his doorway as they put the four meals down on the table in the little kitchen by the door, and one of them went to get the teapot while the other began to trim and light the hurricane lamps. This lamplighter saw Tim approaching, held up a hand to keep him at a safe distance, and asked, 'Feeling all right at this stage, Tim?'

'Thanks. It's a bugger but I'm perfectly well so far.'

'Saw you walloping the cricket ball at Toorooka. Bloody good innings.'

'Ah yes,' said Tim gratefully. 'My son's a great chucker of the ball, did you notice?'

The lamp-trimmer nodded in his mask. 'Fires upriver did for me. Lost half the bloody herd.'

But still no offer of his name. The other one went out again and came back with the teapot. Then both men left, locking the door. 'Dinner,' Tim called as melodiously as he could down the corridor. Past the closed door beyond which Primrose had perished.

Entering the kitchen with Ernie, Sister Raymond took off her mask and then Ernie's, stripped off her gloves, threw everything into the bucket of carbolic and water. She washed her hands with the prescribed carbolic soap – Tim watched all this, this antiseptic rite – and ate her meal quickly, standing at the kitchen bench, her back to Tim and Ernie.

'The corned beef will make us thirsty,' Ernie plaintively announced at the end of the table. He ate little before fetching a fresh mask without having to be told to, and returning to his station on the chair in the room along the corridor. Tim and Ernie plague-trained in less than day by this rigorous nurse.

'Don't go up close though,' Sister Raymond called after the accountant.

Not feeling entitled to crowd in on Ernie and Winnie, Tim loitered on his side in the male ward. The men could be heard coming in to take away the remnants for burning or burial. Tim could hear them chinking the plain china together as they exited.

He wondered were there sick half-castes and spiritual women in Grafton, Lismore, Bellingen, Taree? Or was the plague particular to this valley and to Sydney? If the latter, were they writing him up as a 'contact' in the *Sydney Morning Herald*?

How sweet if released from here to make himself in a new town, taking *definite* account that everywhere there were Billy Thurmonds, M. M. Chances, Ernie Malcolms to be courted and reassured. Everywhere Lucy Rochesters looking for the sea or lost parents. He must give them a place at table too, no matter what Kitty told him about new-arriving Kennas. But within those limits, re-making yourself. Talk to Old Burke about a loan for a pub. Then, be a harder man! Meagher the publican had learned to be hard. Not to return cash to drunkards' wives.

In darkness the new visitor was rapping on the door of the plague barracks, and then opened it with his key. Dr Erson. Erson went by down the corridor in his fresh houndstooth suit.

The doctor could soon be heard discussing Winnie's vital signs with demented Ernie. Tim waited. Winnie, Winnie. Erson came back past Tim's door on his way to the dispensary. Some energetic washing went on there, hands were flapped about in the carbolic. When he walked in again to visit Tim, he looked perhaps tired. Perhaps fearful. He had his gloves off to feel the pulse in Tim's wrist and placed the back of his hand against Tim's forehead, but then put them on again to feel the glands under the chin and the arms and in the groin. He asked about joint pains and fever.

'Be kind to our friend Malcolm,' he murmured then to Tim. 'We have hope for his wife, but . . .' The doctor looked steadily at him now. 'The bubonic plague in the Macleay. Not possible says my every instinct. We must insist shipments to the Macleay are all unpacked and directly fumigated. That's the only way. Perhaps you could mention that should people like Offhand ask you.' The doctor sighed to indicate the beginning of reflectiveness. 'The plague returns at the end of a startling century and in a new location. To remind us that even here we are dust.'

'Winnie Malcolm was my most esteemed customer,' said Tim. 'The joy went out of her though at some stage.'

'This is nothing to do with joy,' the doctor reminded him. 'This is a matter of minute organisms entering the blood.'

Finished his inspection, Erson said, 'I have every hope you might come out of here on your own legs, Tim.'

But he sounded too much like a punter assessing odds.

'Have you heard? Has the girl been found yet at Crescent Head?'

But Tim knew it was her nature to be lost for good.

'No word on that, Tim. But let me tell you, you have room in your head to deal with only one problem. Plague. So with the rest of us.'

Tim must write a letter for his parents. In the event and when the first fever comes and after the one to Kitty. What would they think of New South Wales if they heard of his death from plague here in the Macleay? They would think *barbarous*, *Asian place*. They would consider him an unfortunate exile. They would never know how he loved all this, the mad antipodean river.

'You are having a hard year,' said Erson.

Under the doctor's loving yet mistrusting gaze, Tim said nothing. Too complicated a remark to answer.

Finished with him, Erson stood up and took on the air of a tired, ordinary man leaving to take his day's dinner, looking for the oblivion of his bed.

Ernie asleep still. Only his shoes off, waiting by his bed for the night walk to Winnie. Sister Raymond had placed fresh white gloves and a fresh mask on Ernie's camp bed. Tools for making his farewells.

'I fear thy kisses, gentle maiden,
Thou needest not fear mine.'

Sister Raymond had issued her orders. 'It would be good, Tim, if you stuck to your ward and even to your cot.' She must know he had an impulse to go and show Winnie his face.

Taking the beads down from the mosquito net bracket, he dosed himself asleep with the repeated, numb *Aves*. First Sorrowful Mystery, *Jesus in the Garden of Gethsemane*. Let this cup pass from me. And if it does, then the other cups to be drunk, the ones waiting for him in Belgrave Street, at Templars' Hall, off Crescent Head, in Hanney's care.

Ernie with lost-looking eyes and Sister Raymond standing over him, Tim was shaken awake at midnight.

'Ring the bell at the kitchen door,' said Sister Raymond. 'When the orderlies come, ask for tea.'

She was brightly awake. The emergency blazed in her eyes.

As Tim waited for the metal-strengthened door to be opened, masked Ernie staggered towards him along the corridor.

'She is very bad, she is very bad. And no conversation possible either, Tim.'

One of the ambulance men unlocked the outer door.

'Sister Raymond would like some tea brought.'

'Oh, Jesus,' said the ambulance man, rubbing his brow.

But he came back with the teapot quicker than Tim expected.

'Likely to need us again?' he asked from behind the linen.

'Yes,' said Tim. 'I think it's likely.'

'All right, all right,' said the man, as if someone had been harrying him. He went out and locked the door.

After the normal hygiene, Tim poured out the tea in the kitchen, putting plenty of sugar into Ernie's. He took it out to Ernie, who was pacing in the hall, and then began carrying a mug towards Sister Raymond when she emerged from the sickroom.

'Prepare yourself, Ernie. Wear the gloves.'

Ernie put his cup on the floor and went off for what might be farewells.

'Do you want tea yourself?' Tim asked the nurse.

'You could leave it by the door in the hallway.'

Carrying the nurse's tea and setting it by Winnie's door, Tim saw Ernie lay his covered mouth to Winnie's unknowing forehead. Sister Raymond then sent him across the room, where at last he lay down on the bare boards like someone doing penance.

Tim, not permitted to join the tragedy but dazed by it anyhow, returned to his cot, slept two haunted hours in his own bed, but woke at the first lightening of the sky. He heard a hammering at the door – the orderlies with breakfast. Sister Raymond answered them, and his mask dutifully in place, Tim helped her carry the bucket of porridge in. When he and Sister Raymond returned towards Winnie's room, they met Ernie emerging crazed.

Tim, who had not gone to caress Winnie, now clasped plain Ernie in his arms. Erson couldn't have asked for more giving of comfort: may in fact have asked for less. You could hear Ernie's plaintive hiccoughs. But no rasp of breath and no noise at all could be heard from lovely, poetical Winnie Malcolm.

The solid feel of Ernie. The thick cage of his bones. Tim had to continue to hold and caress him as the orderlies came and covered her totally and briskly carried her out.

'She will have all the appropriate rites,' Sister Raymond, frowning and pale now, promised Ernie in passing and in the hope of calming him.

Tim and Ernie clumsily following the procession to the door. As the ambulance men worked the stretcher down the stairs, Sister Raymond said, 'Let's close the door now. We have to close it at once.'

Her large, burly, country hands shut them in. Could it be, though? Could Winnie, so august on the shopping mornings of the past years, be crept out so casually? By men whose ordinary leather boots could be heard on the plain wooden steps?

Ernie reared up, trying not only to escape Tim's clasp. Trying to disappear through the space in his own ribs, and roaring with the loss.

'I must give him something,' Sister Raymond called across the storm of Ernie's misery.

She went to the dispensary. Tim felt very lonely, struggling with heavy-breathing Ernie. He found himself, as with children, uttering useless things – 'Settle yourself, Ernie,' and, 'She felt nothing, she was far away.' But he wasn't himself a mere witness. His own eyes streamed. Sister Raymond brought out some murky fluid for Ernie. 'Best to get him to sit on his cot,' suggested the weary nurse.

Tim wrestled blocky, crazed civic Ernie into the big ward, and could only sit him down by sitting down himself as well. The camp cot felt it might collapse under their weight.

She snatched Ernie's mask away and forced the drug in over his lips. Splashes of brown fluid fell from the process onto Tim's shirt.

'Damn and bugger you!' yelled Ernie now. But he gave up wrestling with Tim, who stood up and went halfway across the room and surveyed him. Ernie began to grieve in a more orderly way now, doubled over in grief.

Outside curlews and currawongs were everywhere raucous, disclosing as always the fresh day. Bullying the town awake, accompanying the dairy farmer and his lank wife and children back from the milking shed to the porridge pot in the kitchen. Unlyrical, practical birds. Galahs and the rosellas beautiful though, and frequent in the Macleay. The white cockatoos with their crests of sulphur.

'. . . but as when
The Bird of Wonder dies, the maiden phoenix,
Her ashes new-create another heir
As great in admiration as herself.'

Poetry had died with Winnie. No maiden phoenixes newcreating themselves here in West. Only the limepit.

As Tim wept, Sister Raymond came up and took off her glove and put a hand to Tim's forehead.

'What can you feel with that?'

Ernie was quiet in his cot against the far wall, but Tim took up the grieving for him. And the nurse's touch so welcome that Tim wished to raise his hand too and grab her fingers.

She said, 'While Ernie rests, I must rest too until the doctor comes. I've had no sleep.'

'Yes,' Tim assented, composing himself.

The nurse closed their door on them, as a sign that she wanted no intrusions.

Not long gone when Ernie sat up again. He stripped his gloves off and let them fall to the floor, where they sat on splayed fingers. He picked up his watch and watch-chain and – as if to destroy time, hurled them to the floor.

'Go easy there, Ernie, old feller,' Tim advised him.

'You're a bloody peasant, Tim,' Ernie complained.

Tim felt nothing but weariness. A swimmer without a stroke left in him. Kitty on the shore, frowning out to sea, could not be reached.

'You're right, Ernie. Go very kindly to sleep, will you?'

'Winnie in your store, Tim. Your eyes were out on bloody sticks. Peasant bloody wonder . . .'

'Winnie is a splendid woman,' said Tim, choosing wilfully to speak about her as a presence. 'You'd blame me more if I didn't know that. Now please. You'll disturb the poor nurse.'

'I suppose you think she's a lady too, you stupid bushweek dolt?' The opiate had brought out aggression in Ernie. It was said to do that. The patient went best ignored.

'I have been so lucky with beautiful women,' said Ernie. But his luck made him wail for half a minute. 'You think Winnie's a noble spirit, don't you, Tim? Winnie bloody Lady Guinevere? Reads poetry and yearns for refinement, and doesn't get it in her poor bloody husband! Her old man though, her father the Brighton alderman, gave her piss-elegant old mum a social disease. And he . . . he was just one of those plain Melbourne fellows who killed himself when their shares went bust at the end of the boom. Didn't tell you that I bet, not while she was buying the bloody bickies! Half bloody Melbourne offed itself in those days. Country's never bloody recovered till now! *Melbourne's Australia's elegant city*, she'd say. Palaver. Melbourne's a city of bloody horrors. Above all for the Belle of Brighton, Miss Winnie! Clapped mother, shot father!'

Tim managed to sit up straight preparatory to going across the room. But whether to hit or soothe Ernie was the question. Ernie's pupils as huge as a cat's now, Tim saw. His features were dissolving. Coming apart in his own sea. He wailed and wailed, and Tim eased him down. Sleep came to him suddenly, at a gulp.

Now Tim took Winnie's letter out from beneath his mattress. It constituted a small risk beside having been kissed. The envelope was addressed to the Solicitor General of New South Wales, Macquarie Street, Sydney. It was easy to justify opening the thing – thereby, he argued with himself, he would know best how to protect Winnie, to champion her intentions.

He discovered a photograph backed by stiff cardboard. Missy looked clearly and knowingly at him from this picture. He looked again – he knew from the cricket match that care had to be taken with this identification. Missy. Not some child-woman from up or down the river. But Missy, dressed in a boy's school uniform. She stood full length, and a banner over a painted scene behind her said, *Tyler's Touring Company*. Indented across the top was the slogan: *Miss Florence Meades in her Noted Role as Young Arthur*. Her firmset shoulders were a fair imitation of a boy's.

'Miss Florence Meades,' said Tim. The name was out. It escaped the barred room. It sat in the trees. That plain and essential name.

Miss Florence Meades – it seemed – was one of those young actresses who made a speciality of playing smartalec, mischievous boys from the best schools. She would have made a fine Desdemona though as well, Tim thought.

Some inscription in the bottom corner had been obscured by scratchy lines of ink. It had been deliberately and permanently rendered unreadable. On the back of the cardboard, in pencil in a cursive hand was written: *Miss Meades is the young woman found deceased in the Macleay.*

The handwriting was probably a disguised version of poor Winnie's.

Ernie cried out in his sleep, as well he might. 'Criminal,' said Tim to the vacant day. 'Criminal.'

After one more calm survey, Tim returned the picture to its envelope, the whole thing to the breast pocket of his coat, where it sat beside his re-pocketed and useless statement of innocence. Winnie had scraped Ernie's name out, had been uselessly loyal even in her fury. Did this doped lump of guts on the other cot across the room deserve such delicacy, a right to be harboured so kindly?

He knew the routine. He went and washed his hands with the carbolic soap which scoured the flesh. The name he had found would be released more widely than in a plague ward. It would cow the guilty everywhere, he promised himself.

Dr Erson came later in the day, letting himself in with his key. At his shoulder, a refreshed Sister Raymond looked at Tim with clear eyes above her mask.

'Has Mr Malcolm taken it calmly?' Erson wanted to know.

'He's spoken in his sleep a lot,' said Tim.

He raised his chin so that the doctor could feel his glands. The name was out. Tim rejoiced secretly. Young Arthur was released from the glass.

'You have no swellings or fever, it seems,' said Dr Erson almost in admiration. 'Your pulse is normal. I approve of that, Tim, and would be grateful if you maintained it.'

A little irony in the doctor's eyes.

'I intend to do that,' said Tim.

But Ernie refused to awaken to be chastised, and the more Tim waited, looking across the room at Ernie's homely shape, the less scandalised Tim felt and the more an air of pity and forgiveness took over in the room. He was sure he knew where it came from. The Communion of Saints. Winnie and Florence Meades, Primrose and Lucy and Albert Rochester. The lenient dead.

It did not come from him. He was determined to punish Ernie at an early or late date, whichever proved more advisable.

In the coming time, Tim would wake at intervals with imagined fevers. Four or more times a night the frenzied awakening. In the first gulping moment his hand would race to his underjaw, his underarm. Feeling for the swelling. 'Rock hard,' as Sister Raymond had sadly declared, feeling beneath Mrs Malcolm's chin.

Dreams of resting like a peasant beneath a huge tower, one of those great stone cylinders monks had built a thousand years ago on the Cork and Kerry coast as shelters from the Vikings. His tower the eternity of Kitty's widowhood. The coldness of its stone entered his kidneys. Is that a shiver? Am I hot, or is it just night-fear?

Winnie the quietly dead, the softly remembered. More notably, the named Missy, Florence Meades and Young Arthur, had grown inactive at last in his brain. She did not step in through the bars to harry him.

If he woke after first light, there would be sudden, chancy joy. His mind would rub over the smoothed-out, recalculated odds of his chances of rising living out of quarantine.

According to newspapers left by Kitty or her messenger Habash at the hospital later in the week, fishermen at Crescent Head had been attracted by a stench beneath the Big Nobby and had thought it might be Lucy. It proved to be the body of a rare narwhal which had been thrown up on the rocks by the tide.

So Lucy still evasive. Not willing to present herself. Placed at the peak of the ocean she could see and judge him. And by staying out to sea and putting sombre questions, she had turned the Muslim jockey round to the valley's most visible theology, the one that had the presbytery, the two-storey convent, the boarders two-by-two, the Angelus tower.

Sister Raymond dosed Ernie to the point of incoherence these days. Barely a finished sentence escaped him. Yet once or twice a surge of mad animation. One night Tim awoke to hear Sister Raymond shouting and her bell clanging, calling the orderlies from their hut in the grounds. Tim, in his shirt and drawers, ran into the corridor and then the recently fumigated room where Winnie had died earlier in the week, and where the nurse still slept. Ernie in a night dress two-thirds luminous from moonlight, standing over the nurse's cot. Tim grabbed him from behind. His body felt to Tim like a warmed boulder.

'I just wanted to touch your face,' Ernie yelled.

One of the orderlies volunteered to spread his swag on the boards in the corridor against the arousal of further childlike desires in Ernie. Yet despite this molestation, Sister Raymond nursed him lovingly. To be fair to Ernie, it was easy to see how – child to mother – he could seek her out in the night.

At last she began to take Ernie for walks in the garden. She made sure that Tim knew he was welcome to accompany them, since Ernie had an old man's stagger and no conversation. Through the scattered gum trees she led the masked two of them towards the edge of the unregenerate bush fringing the Warwick Racecourse and the cemetery. Primrose and Winnie had taken this path, but no one else walked here and the blowflies distracted the party from its grief. Afternoon sweat showed at the points of Sister Raymond's cheeks and under her veil on her brow. Ernie content in his drugged state, a man willing to be mutely unhappy, one who had half-forgotten the causes of his misery.

The progress was slow.

'Does Mr Kerridge the stonemason know that if spared I'll be needing to see him?' Ernie asked suddenly one afternoon while he and Tim and Sister Raymond returned through the straggle of saplings into the garden and up to the old mad barracks.

'I've already sent a message,' said Sister Raymond, but like one who probably hadn't.

'I want something that will draw all the town's attention to this tragic thing,' said Ernie.

Meanwhile, Tim could tell Doctor Erson was beginning to feel less despair, and touched their glands and their brows more jovially with each day. 'Lucky chaps it isn't typhus or some such. Quarantine of ten days after the last death is considered utterly adequate for plague. The Black Death doesn't hang about the place being subtle.'

Late in that quarantine time, Ernie suddenly showed himself to be more clear-headed. Up he got, looking for one of his clean, fumigated shirts, and the white and yellow tie he'd been wearing the day the emergency had begun. For the first time he picked up his watch and its medallioned fob. Time had become once again of some interest to him. As Tim watched him from across the room, he put on his jacket to go walking with Sister Raymond.

'Can we go to the grave?' he asked as they neared the cemetery.

'We can't go too close,' said Sister Raymond wearily.

'You think I'll be unruly,' Ernie smiled sadly. 'I won't be unruly. I want to visit it. Like any mourning husband.'

'So I have a promise from you?' asked Sister Raymond. 'You won't get distressed.'

'Certainly I won't.'

They headed off to their right, downhill, amongst Australia's own go-to-hell, deliberately unpleasing and perennial shrubs. Hardy, dull olive in colour. Lean, canny branches. Perhaps they grew in Eden before God even knew. Perhaps they came after the

Fall. The cemetery lay ahead, the lost town of Macleay people, beneath its collection of Celtic crosses and broken columns, its occasional standing marble angel.

The first thing they came to, on the hospital side of the informal cemetery fence, was the grave. Covered not only with earth but with planks, as if it were not yet fully filled in. Still a chance that one or two more might need to be put there. Tim saw Ernie's face bunch and grow piteous.

'On the edge of a cemetery, and in quicklime! Like someone bloody hanged! Like Mrs Mulroney!'

Sobs started out of him again. Mrs Mulroney hadn't been hanged yet, had she? The name Florence Meades was needed for her trial.

'Poor Winnie's dignity taken away,' moaned Ernie. Ernie said, 'If she had not been so kind in nursing Primrose and the bloody cat!'

Even on the seventh evening since Winnie's death, night came on with its acid dread and fidgets and false fevers, and Kitty's remembered visage seemed a lost hope yet again. Dr Erson calmer, sagely taking pulses, feeling for fevers without expecting to find them. As Sister Raymond looked on like one unlikely to be required to offer consolation.

Before he left for the night, Erson turned to Tim and said, 'Mr Shea, I must congratulate you on your technical survival of the plague.'

Tim asked, 'Technical?'

'Well,' said Dr Erson, seeming to be enjoying himself at last, to think himself a real wag, 'should you develop the signs tonight, you would be entitled to feel discriminated against by the odds. As it is, I've told your friends and relatives to greet you both at the front of the hospital at three o'clock tomorrow afternoon.'

A strange berserk joy in this promise of reunion. Like school-masters all at once lenient at the year's end, the orderlies left the barracks door unlocked until nine o'clock, and Tim wandered in the garden and sat for a time on a bench, looking up at what was so brightly evident. Venus, Orion – that's a good one, with his tail, his sword, his handle. The Southern Cross, emblem of migration. People crowding up to the taffrail somewhere in the Indian Ocean. The navigation officer pointing upwards. *There, there.*

Ernie came out, no longer masked, sat near him on a bench and lit a cigarette. A widower. He too looked upwards.

'Winnie, are you there?' He sighed and puffed. 'Answer came there bloody none.'

Despicable, pitiful Ernie. Had he ever invoked the stars for Missy? Now he concentrated on the humbler glowing star of the cigarette end, which he held before him at chin level.

'You've been a white man to me, Tim, through all this.'

'It's a pity you didn't know me, Ernie, before your mob wrote their letters to supply houses.'

Ernie murmured, 'I bloody told you. I take no pride in over-zealous business like that.'

'Will you write me a reference? Will you break with your friends and say I'm an honest fellow? Now we're in the land of the living, Ernie?'

Ernie thought awhile. 'You say that, Tim. Not all of us really with the living though. Not all.'

Albert, Lucy, Missy, Primrose, Winnie. The holy, diverse ever-present departed.

'Ernie, I see the signs of mending in you. You've put on your bright medals again, haven't you. You'll want to be a father of our city. West, Central, East.'

'Tim. It's all hollowness . . .'

'The injustice that's been done me and others. Is that hollow, Ernie?'

'Come to me, Tim, then, when I go back to the dreary bloody desk, the dreary bloody office. I'll see what I can do for you. You've been a white man . . .'

But Tim could taste stale reality on his tongue. The same nonsense, saving and beginning. And then the lies, the contentions, the same ruinous enthusiasms. In the earth, solely Kitty, the thought of Kitty, did not weary him. Apart from that, a hemispheric weariness from here down the huge coast and over limitless water and ice to the South Pole. Weariness across the snow there like a stale yellow light.

Turning a shoulder, Ernie withdrew himself. He was looking at the piercing stars again.

Sullen afternoon for Tim's and Ernie's release. Bulky, plum-blue clouds conspired above the mountains and casually threatened the valley. They would bring a great gush of air behind them, a great coolness. At such an hour as this Lazarus had emerged. Under such biblical clouds.

Carrying their portmanteaus. They had still not exchanged names with the ambulance men. But having thanked them earnestly, Tim and Ernie walked around the side of the building like two workmates going off a shift. At the end of their imprisonment, short in time but intense in content, they moved edgily, unused to the outer world.

Rounding the side of the verandah where he had unloaded poor Albert, Tim saw first someone who meant least. M. M. Chance, standing by his sulky under the big Morton Bay fig at the front of the hospital. Waiting for his bereaved friend. Ernie walked to him like a soldier surrendering, Chance reaching a hand out, drawing Ernie back to the community's daily offices. Over his shoulder, Ernie looked across at Tim, as if what terrified him most was that Chance would lift him into the vehicle and cart him away.

'You're welcome to stay with Mrs Chance and me until you're steady again,' said Mr Chance.

'Mrs Chance has been reassured by Dr Erson about the plague?' asked Ernie.

'She's an educated woman,' said M. M. 'She knows you don't get the plague from people looking at you.'

Kitty and the children were beyond the gates standing by the gold and blue *T. Shea – General Store* dray. Pee Dee, the old fool, his bag on, deigning to wait, not to back the cart through the hospital fence. And familiar horses of a different order waited a little further down the hill – Bandy's grey and his beautiful roan, and by their heads, side by side with reins in their hands, stood Bandy and Mamie. Mamie had ridden up here on the roan. It had a woman's saddle on it. Tim was tickled somehow by the idea of his sister-in-law the horsewoman. What a goer, that Mamie!

By the dray, Kitty waited, grinning a big, criminal grin. He gave himself up to the first huge embrace, the children taking a part at the edges. Kitty's mouth full of affection and warm spittle, and her face moist.

'I knew that scapular would see you out, Tim,' she wetly cried, and delight and hope and terror went through him and brought out his tears . . .

'Are we broke yet?' he asked her.

'It's a mixed bag. I'll certainly be telling you.'

'I am a victim of injustice,' Tim confided to her.

'But the fleas didn't bite you, so let it go at that.'

He did let it go at that, let his limbs hang, and her arms encircled him at the elbows. When strength returned he lifted Annie, whose face was full of a terrible confidence in his immortality. Johnny kept a distance.

Meanwhile Bandy and Mamie closed in together. Their unison seemed strange. They smiled foolishly.

'Give your congratulations to the engaged couple,' Kitty told him.

'Is this so?' Tim asked. He felt a surge of outrage but a kind of innocence in Bandy's face chastened Tim when it came to expressing outrage.

'Bandy is accepting instruction as a Catholic,' said Mamie blithely.

'Well,' said Tim. 'Well. I'd heard that earlier on.'

'Wish them every happiness, you miserable old bugger,' said Kitty. 'The happiness we have.'

'Oh, I do, of course I do,' said Tim. 'You don't come out of the plague hospital for the purpose of cursing people.'

'I should hope bloody not.' Kitty was laughing. She who had always been at home to Bandy.

'I will be a very obedient husband,' Bandy told him. 'I will give up the reckless expense of racehorses.'

'Don't make rash promises,' said Tim. 'Just because you're getting married.'

Though he'd meant it in strict terms, everyone seemed to find it hilarious.

'God you're such an individual, Tim,' said Kitty.

'I'd like some black tea with rum in it and a large lump of fruit cake. Does our present condition permit such luxuries?'

'Buckets of tea. Pounds of cake!'

Both Kenna sisters uttered their totally individual laugh.

'Wild horses!' cried Tim though. For a sulky was thundering up the hill out of West. He could see it was driven along by his friend the Offhand, and seated in it by his side, holding her hat, was the little wisp of widow with whom rumour associated him. The rumour publicly declared today in this stormy light.

Offhand, pink-faced from the rush, drew the sulky up and tied the reins to a gum tree on the far side of the road. Rough old road which led to the upriver demesne of Old Burke, to Comara, and in the end, by breakneck escarpments to Armidale. As the Offhand came running across the road, Kitty and Mamie and the children stood back, so clearly was Tim in the Offhand's sights. He drew Tim aside without apology.

'There is nothing to say,' Tim warned him. 'No bloody tales of the plague ward. Except there isn't any Boer War in there. And let me tell you, the plague keeps different bloody lists than at Templars' bloody Hall.'

Panting Offhand held his hands up. 'You are entitled to your chagrin. But I'm talking to you for the last time, Tim. My fiancée Mrs Flitch has agreed to marry me, as women will – it's typically when my affairs are at their worst. I have no job, Tim. I have been dismissed by the management board of the Macleay *Chronicle*. *Australis*, you see. I wrote those letters off to the *Argus* for a joke. Regretted them straight after the first one, when people began to attribute them to you. I laid low though, thinking, damage is done! Might as well finish with my rodomontade, might as well cover the canon of my concerns. Then I kept postponing the confession, Tim. Hit me if you want.'

It's always your friends who do you the worst harm. Tim would need to pretend to be furious, when what he felt was weariness. 'I don't bloody well want to hit you. A hit isn't enough.'

'Tim, Tim,' murmured the Offhand and looked very ill. 'Let's at least part friends. The fact is I am emigrating to America. I have a sister there. San Francisco and Oakland are excellent newspaper towns, I am told. If mistakes made in the rest of the world are unknown in Australia – just ask half the doctors on this coastline if that's not true, half the older men married to younger women too – the converse is that mistakes made in Australia are unknown in the wider world! I go with a reference as to my editorial competence, and with little else. The editorial board are very happy to foist me onto the Americans. They say I'm too puckish for the bush.'

Tim whistled to himself.

'Puckish? They say *you* were puckish. I wish they'd say that about me, I wish they wrote my crimes so bloody low. They say *I'm* so despicable that they need to write to the supply houses and cancel my credit! You're sent off with a reference. I'm on my own.'

'Oh, I've written a full confession which shall appear, and an exhortation to sanity. Last Tuesday, Tim, the news came that Ladysmith had been relieved. The British column had at last broken through to rescue the gritty garrison, et cetera, et cetera. Now you would have thought that the gentlemen of the Patriotic Fund would have danced in the streets of Central. But no such thing. An ordinary day of business. No giddiness, no great municipal gasps of relief! They still smoke their pipes and clang their cash boxes and milk their bloody cows! I've written this in my last piece. It is already composited. Might do some good.'

'I hope to Christ you didn't mention me!'

'Ah, you think I have a poison touch, don't you, Tim. No, though I do mention certain businesses in the Macleay district which have been singled out, and so forth. But Tim, let me say, for any harm I've done you, please accept this.'

He took an envelope from his vest pocket and pushed it into Tim's hands. 'There's fifteen pounds in there. It'll pay for some things.'

'No,' Tim said. 'I can't take this.'

But the Offhand had skipped backwards, waving his hands. Already making for his sulky and Mrs Flitch. 'Won't take it back, Tim,' he called.

He untethered and jumped aboard his vehicle so fast that for Tim to chase him to argue would have been out of kilter with this afternoon, this plain plague resurrection on which the first grand drops of rain were beginning to fall.

Tim went to Kitty flapping his arms like a helpless bird.

'Fifteen quid,' he told her.

'All contributions welcome,' she said, grinning, reaching up and drawing him down towards her breasts, her paunch. Their child readying itself in secrecy. He noticed Johnny staring now, an unlikely, still gaze.

'He has not been himself,' said Kitty.

In the world again, he did not like the counter so much, did not like to stand there at the mercy of whatever person entered. It had in any case proved an unwise procedure in the past. Women to whom he made deliveries now were of course possessed by a fear that he had not been long enough in quarantine. They would call out from deep in the house, 'Just wait, Mr Shea. Wait in the yard. I shall leave the money on the back step, and then you can come up and collect it.' Was Ernie finding the same, and in his grief did he care? Did people look fearfully at pages he had audited and passed his finger down.

In the residence dining room one mid-afternoon, a conference was called around the table. Kitty casually assembled it. He noticed how sure she was that the omens had lifted from him, how exultant to have him back, certified by Erson. He and Kitty sat together at the top of the table. At the side of the table Bandy and Mamie sat, Mamie with a languid hand on her fiancé's forearm.

'Bandy's been reading Irish history now,' said Mamie, and Bandy – not wanting to be showy with his knowledge – murmured, 'The plantations of Ireland. Cromwell crying, "To Connaught or to Hell!"'

He was such a willing enthusiast for his new fidelity, his new systems of loves.

'We need to circumvent the hatred they have always had for us,' said Bandy like a Fenian. 'Your wife and I, Tim, have devised an arrangement.'

'From here on, the accounts at the supply houses will be in Bandy's name,' Kitty explained. 'He'll receive the bills and underwrite them, though we'll pay them. I think it's generous in a big way and that he's a total white man.'

'Not in exact terms,' said Tim, and everyone laughed.

Kitty said, 'See, we have that safety net. Bandy's our long stop.'

Bandy beamed diagonally across the table at Tim. The services he had been threatening to offer Tim from the start, the system of generosity, was now in place, and Tim and Kitty such poor beggars they couldn't refuse it all. And gratitude was the only right emotion. But Tim felt resentment. Even of Mamie, so recently landed and now with an edge on her sister.

'Ernie Malcolm promised me a reference,' he said, and the three of them, the two sisters and Bandy, looked at each other and pursed their lips at his gullibility.

'We are a family now,' said Kitty. 'A wonderful thing to have the strength of it behind a person.'

She caressed Tim's shoulder, an indulgent caress. As if she believed his quarantine, the daily fear of plague which had occupied him in the old barracks, had left him incapable for the time being.

Bandy and Mamie rode together to Benediction of the Blessed Sacrament, Father Bruggy in his golden cope raising up the species of bread which masked the substance of Christ. In a gold monstrance for the adoration of the engaged couple.

Thanksgiving. Thanksgiving for the sparing of Tim and the discovery of each other. Plus thanks for the conversion of the infidel. Mamie's charm had done what the Crusaders couldn't.

At these times, the children asleep, Kitty and Tim were left alone at the big sandsoaped table, the broad surface of their marriage.

'You don't say much,' said Kitty. 'What do you think of Bandy? As regards Mamie, is what I mean.'

'I think it could be recklessness. To have a Muslim father-in-law. And what about poor bloody Joe?'

'Oh, someone will get sick of seeing Joe stand around calf-eyed and marry him just for the chance of educating him. That's how it happened with you.'

'A just point,' Tim said. He stood up to pour Kitty more tea. *Tay*, she called it, like a peasant. But that hadn't stopped her understanding the way things went in New South Wales.

She asked, 'What would you think if I told you Bandy's already put up cash? That I'd borrowed the whole of our debt from Bandy? The little feller's rolling in it, you know. A wealthy young man, not a drinker. No women to spend money on. No children. And seems to think we are his relatives.'

'I'd say I don't want to depend on him.' In fact he felt the beginning of tears. Have I travelled so far to be someone's tenant all over again?

Kitty shrugged, reached for his wrist, and put her head on its side. 'It's happened, I'm afraid. We signed an agreement letter. Something had to be arranged, darling. Something had to be managed! Be angry if you have to be.'

But he couldn't manage anger. Anger was for those lucky buggers who had some power left. 'Dear God! Was this before or after Mamie agreed to marry the little individual?'

'Fair play, Timmy! Do you think I'd sell my own sister? Only the bloody nobility do that sort of thing. No. She always thought he was Christmas. I mean, Tim, can you see Mamie lying still for being an item of sale?'

'I thought she was just pretending to like the hawker, see. Just to get at Joe.'

Kitty shook her head with such energy. 'From the first time he came into the plague camp, down the river selling things. From that time, she thought he was Christmas.'

'So how much did you borrow, Kitty?'

'It was a full two hundred pounds.'

Again, it was too large a sum to remonstrate over. All he did was drink his tea with its rum lacing. He'd need a lot more rum. 'Bloody mad,' he then said sombrely. Yet he felt both exhilarated too, as well as tethered. 'We are bound to the little fellow for eternity.' He uttered it like a matter of fact. 'But two hundred. Why did you need so much, for God's sake?'

'Because. I have bought Elliott's old store in East.'

He stood up without knowing it. East! There was joy in that idea. The river between him and his Central foolishness. The idea of the river sliced through him now, dividing him, putting all that was foul on the further bank.

'Jesus, is this really true?'

'We'll primp the place up. Great deal more space than here. When the bridge opens . . . well, we'll be on the pig's back!'

All too much, too fast! In a rush, the tide ran out and left him stranded.

'Did you think I'd be dead?' he asked. 'And you'd never have to account to me?'

She wouldn't answer and her cheeks reddened, bringing forth a freckle or two. She rose from the table, waddled inside, came back with a large dossier of documents and slung them down in front of him. 'I kept this for you, Tim. Read this and don't insult me.'

He fingered the dossier. A marvel how much had been done in a period of quarantine. Her arts of business let free by his absence. There wasn't any question about that.

'Though you'd be much better to wait till morning before addressing the details,' she advised him.

Tim wanted to know. He felt indeed too tired, even a little sore-headed for business.

'How much interest is the little Punjabi asking?'

'There is no interest. He says it is a crime to charge interest to members of his family. He wants repayment and a tenth part in the business, that's all.'

In East, though, they would draw on the populations of Dock Flat and Pola Creek as well as on flasher residences on Rudder's Hill. It was an idea! Again the waters commenced to run and he was excited in spite of himself.

Before they went to bed, he visited his sleeping son and daughter. Annie's cheek, and the scar line on Johnny's head. Johnny still slept like someone concentrating for a dive. He'd been chastened, said Kitty, and spoke in his sleep. Each day perhaps half his soul went down the cliff with Lucy's.

He touched the boy's head. 'We are going to East,' he whispered.

He saw one day, while passing the creamery in Smith Street, Ernie Malcolm in a dove-grey suit, somehow apt for the season of mourning, passing down the pavement and entering the staircase to his offices. The *Argus* had carried a piece, 'BRAVE SURVIVOR, MR E. MALCOLM BACK AT DESK.' The gist was that Ernie had chosen to lose himself in his accounting.

So at last Ernie had been declared brave in his own right, and as senselessly as Tim had first been.

Tim had imagined unleashing the girl's name the second after his release from the plague ward. But a Saturday and Sunday followed his release, and so he had secreted Winnie's envelope with the photograph of boy-impersonating Missy in the *London Illustrated News*, the 1891 edition with the flood marks and the views of Uganda ceded to Britain by Germany in exchange for Heligoland. Having lived and been returned to the great turbulence of events, he was too stupefied for the first few days, but by late on the Sabbath he had begun practising a false hand on scraps of paper. Because he must write his own letter, as he saw it. Winnie was not here to rescue Missy. He was the living rescuer.

It began to strike him too that he needed to retain Missy's picture with Winnie's contrived handwriting on the back.

On Monday morning he wrote his letter on some Aberdeen Line notepaper he'd been keeping since his emigration voyage more than ten years back. The moist Macleay air had by now spotted its creaminess with little discs of brownish stain.

The letter said that the Commissioner of Police for New South Wales, situated in Sydney, who sought a name in the Mulroney case, should enquire from Tyler's Theatrical Company, presently touring somewhere in the Australian colonies or perhaps in New Zealand. He said what the young performer's name was, and added that she seemed to have a repute for playing the role of Young Arthur. He posted this communication in its staged hand at Central Post Office, together with Kitty's renewal of subscription to *The Messenger of the Sacred Heart*, the Sheas' credit being at least better with that divine organ of mercy than it was with Truscott and Lowe.

Missy's name would be uttered at the Mulroneys' trial, and the order of things thus restored. He had at last a sense that Missy was now a redeemed vacancy. His dreams were a jangled mess of things from the plague hospital, and he was content that they should be. Missy no longer entered. Her plain name had saved him, and he had taken her as far as could be expected of ordinary flesh. There was still a distance which she could perhaps take him. For that reason he had retained her photograph.

The affianced Mamie, walking over to Savage's Emporium on some business for Kitty, ran into her sister from up the river, Mrs Molly Burke. Molly had come to town with her husband and daughter, and without rushing to report to their relatives in the general store or to introduce Old Burke to the new immigrant, they had taken rooms at the Commercial. Though the two sisters embraced, Mamie later said there was something about the meeting which did not measure up. It did not resemble the previously imagined reunion of Mamie with the grandest and most successful Kenna.

That evening the Sheas, Mamie and the children were eating a normal meal when Old Burke and Molly *did* appear at the back door. Molly was chastened, embarrassed at having been seen to creep into town.

'We thought you were worried about Timmy and the plague,' Kitty remarked, winking. They had not heard about it though, and now were informed – chiefly by Kitty and Mamie. All Tim did was hold his hands up and say, 'Clean bill of health.'

'Not here on pleasant business,' Old Burke growled through his clenched pipe. Sitting at table and humbly accepting tea, it didn't seem as if he was going to be infallible on any subject at all tonight. They sat severely apart, Old Burke and the Molly he had so strenuously courted in the store. They were not a united camp. This fact at once paired, allied and reconciled Mamie and Molly. Molly's hand reached out to Mamie's wrist, wriggled it.

'So, my little sister,' said Molly. 'Here!'

'No other place,' said Mamie. 'And very glad I came.'

But the sisterly jollity still seemed forced and silences intervened. Some sorrow had overtaken Molly. She did not even comment on what she must surely by now know – that her sister was engaged to the hawker.

'Look, might as well say it,' Old Burke soon announced. 'We are putting Molly and Ellen on the boat. That's the situation. I expect it to go no further than your ears, but Ellen has conceived.'

He shook his head and wiped his eyes.

'Some lop-eared boundary rider from Comara,' he said.

'How long?' breathed Kitty. Tim wanted to know too. Could it have been when the girl was in his care? Was this too on his slate?

'Seems to've been some time in December last,' said Molly.

All the women exchanged glances. They knew the perils, the hair's-breadth nature of things. Was Flo or Missy present in the room to gaze quietly down on the constant risks of womanhood revealed here?

Molly said, 'Thank God for Croydon.'

Tim realised she meant a suburb of the great capital down the coast.

'That's Saint Anthony's Home for Fallen Girls at Croydon we're taking her to,' Molly explained to her newcomer sister.

'So you're going to Sydney?' asked Kitty. 'With the plague raging there?'

'Well, you did,' Molly told her a little testily. 'Would you have Ellen stay on at Pee Dee until she shows, and bring her to town then?'

'Where is she now?' asked Mamie.

'She is in her room at the Commercial,' said Old Burke. 'On retreat. Reading a devotional book as she should have done earlier. Flirtatious, you see. She's flirtatious by nature.'

He glanced at Molly. He blamed his young wife for some of it, for a lack of gravity.

'Well, Jesus,' Kitty protested, 'women *are*. Need to be too. To get you bloody crowd going.'

Molly sat back in her chair. She looked very tired. 'Ask us the questions you've got to ask us,' she told them. 'Who's the father, for example?'

'Well,' said Old Burke, supplying the answer for his wife to get it done with. 'She won't say. And I remarked to her, does this mean there is more than one blackguard? And instead of a clear answer, I get tears.'

Molly said, 'I'm glad I was there at Pee Dee. Men can take a hectoring approach.'

'And a bloody man is behind this,' said Kitty, lightening the discussion with wise and emphatic shakes of the head. 'There's only one Virgin Birth. The story's used up.'

Both the other women laughed guiltily at this blasphemy from Kitty. Old Burke looked at Kitty with amazement.

'She's foolishly protecting her lover,' said Molly with a twisted mouth.

'Don't dignify him with a word like *lover*,' growled Old Burke. 'He's a brute and a bloody ram.'

As if Old Burke had never ridden high. But this was an awful and wilful scandal, Tim could see.

Old Burke said, 'God, she flirts even with that Indian bastard, what's his name? Haberdash? Molly herself's no better.'

Mamie instantly flushed. No delays in the Kenna crowd showing their feelings. 'I have news on that,' said Mamie. 'I am engaged to Mr Habash and don't appreciate wordplay on his name, Mr Burke.'

Molly lowered her fine eyes. She hadn't been told after all. Old Burke paused in gouging away at his pipe.

'Mr Habash is receiving instruction in the Faith,' Mamie added.

Molly wiped at a sudden sweat on her upper lip. 'He's hung around all of us, you know,' she scoffed, wanting to draw blood. 'Until he found someone simple-minded enough.'

There was jealousy here. It betrayed Molly into letting on to things she wouldn't let on to in her normal wisdom. Jealousy of the hawker!

'Well, thank you,' Mamie said, flaming. 'That's a grand estimation of me . . .'

But she stopped there because Old Burke threw his pipe down on the plate before him.

'You bloody Kenna women have gone utterly astray in your bloody minds!' he yelled.

The outburst brought a little silence at first. But it was a rope thrown to the sisters. Molly decided to sit forward and grab it. 'So my family are to take the blame for this tragedy? For spoiling your daughter?'

She blazed and it was not all rage at Old Burke. But he served as the first victim and deserved to as well, the old fool. Molly would punish him at length later as well. He'd be treated to the turned shoulder at night when she got back to Pee Dee.

Old Burke could foresee this and became more plaintive. 'I just think there's an air of conspiracy gets going when women are together.' He'd widened the accusation from just the Kenna girls to the whole gender. 'It isn't always for the best, you know.'

The three women frowned communally at him. Of course this was Mamie's first meeting with Old Burke. Old Burke was Molly's fortune, the rumour which had brought Mamie through the Atlantic, the Indian, the Southern Ocean and up the Pacific coast into the Macleay. She had given Old Burke and Molly as an excuse for her migration. It was what Red and Mrs Kenna had used to soothe their aged tears. This dismal old cow-cocky!

Molly ignored him and spoke to her sisters. 'She reckons she'll raise the child herself in Sydney.'

'All bloody well,' said Old Burke. 'But she's bloody young to pass off as a widow!'

'We will give her every support,' said Molly.

'Goes without saying,' muttered Old Burke.

'She has made it totally clear to me . . . totally clear,' Molly asserted, 'that she will not marry for this cause. Whoever it is . . . the fellow, she won't say. And she has made it clear that she won't marry.'

'She's been to confession and the sacraments,' growled Old Burke, as if this had a bearing on her decision.

Molly nodded. 'That was this morning. And we're off on *Burrawong* tomorrow, she and I. By all accounts, it's fumigated to the last square inch. We'll have to walk the deck pretending we're overtaken by an urge to see the Sydney autumn fashions.'

'It's too bloody believable in her case,' said Old Burke. 'Believable she would get an urge like that!'

Tim remembered how well despite their arguments the girl had minded his children. 'Give her my warmest wishes,' he said. 'And tell her if she should need anything . . .'

'Yes,' Kitty said, finishing his sentence. 'She mustn't hesitate.'

All the party looked at each other understandingly. They thought his quarantine had left him clumsy, put his social timing off.

'But can't we go and see her, Molly?' Kitty asked. 'Mamie and myself? Sure we could see her. She might be embarrassed by Tim. But Mamie and me . . .'

Molly said of course. Then she turned back to Mamie. 'Sister, do you love this Habash?'

'What an idiot question! I could put the darling little fellow in my pocket and walk the earth's highways with him.'

'And do you trust him?'

'He's a bloody scamp and a charmer. But he has taken to instruction like Cardinal Newman!'

Molly looked aged, and shook her head.

'Then God bless you both!'

Everyone but Old Burke could read what all this was. She would not be able to flirt with Bandy when next he came to Pee Dee. The bush was narrowing in on her.

The visit to Ellen was arranged for that evening, and Molly and Old Burke got up to leave. As they went through the house and store towards Belgrave Street, Old Burke hung back a second.

'Fellows tell me you've been hugely political, Tim,' he commented with the usual above-human-folly frown.

'It's nonsense,' Tim told him.

'No. Be careful. You don't think you're political, but you bloody are by nature. Keep clear of it all. None of it's worth a toss. Land is the whole story.'

Blood came to Tim's face. 'Tell *them*, bugger it!' He pointed off indefinitely towards the powerful and complicated town. 'Tell your flash friends to let me live.'

Old Burke stared dolefully. 'I think your troubles have got to you, Tim. It might be the start of an education.'

The self-important old streak of misery went and joined Molly, who waited for him by the pavement.

'Thank God I don't have to ask you for favours,' cried Tim after him.

Molly looked away, but Kitty laughed.

The visit to Ellen was made and Mamie and Kitty came back home to drink tea with a look of mutual placation, of the old sisterly unity, on their faces.

'She really won't name the feller,' said Molly. 'Says if she does Old Burke will force a marriage.'

Both sisters seemed disappointed by this. They wanted to know for knowing's sake as well. They could have been savage to him in the street when he came to town.

Next morning, a drogher took the Burke women off with Captain Reid and the other passengers, up the river to where *Burrawong* had moored. Tim's letter travelled by the same ship. Captain Reid had already announced in the *Argus* that *Burrawong* was fitted with new anti-rat hawsers of the kind which had been developed to combat the plague in Calcutta two years before. They had come to the North Coast Steamship Navigation Company too late for lovely Winnie.

A full week after his release from quarantine, Tim sent Bandy to the hospital with a basket of puddings and biscuits for Sister Raymond, and then himself resolutely took from the bookcase the envelope with the inscribed photograph of Miss Florence Meades playing Young Arthur, put it in his breast pocket, decided not to wear a tie, and walked down Smith Street past the curtained Southern Cross Billiard Rooms, the Greek cafe, the Good Templars', and took to the stairwell – beside Holt's Ladies' Fashions – to Ernie Malcolm's office.

At the head of the stairs, Miss Pollack, from the Rudder's Hill Pollacks in East, still kept Ernie's outer office.

He told her he wanted to see Ernie.

'Could I have your name, sir?' she asked in her bush-flash, piss-elegant manner. Her parents would be his future customers with any luck, but he was tired of dancing around people.

'Tim Shea,' said Tim. 'I was in plague quarantine with Ernie and his wife.' Watch it or I'll breathe on you! he implied.

And she *was* chastened by such a pronouncement, and went

and spoke to Ernie, who then appeared haggard in his dove-grey suit at the door of his office, looked out and said, 'Oh, yes, Tim. Could you hold hard a few moments?'

As Ernie spoke his eyes darted around towards unseen things in the office. His manner said, 'Expect nothing.' Then he near-closed the door on his visitor.

Some minutes passed, but Tim would not take the seat Miss Pollack recommended to him. He wanted Ernie to get a sense of a restless presence in his outer office, and indeed Ernie seemed to, coming to the door at last and wearily murmuring, 'Yes, Tim,' ushering him in then with a slack hand.

From Ernie's office you got a view of the butter factory and the laneway leading to *Burrawong*'s berth at Central wharf, left vacant – or else taken up by droghers – through the influence of plague. The walls of Ernie's office were covered with bright certificates, some of them from Melbourne, from municipal councils there. An apostle of service all along Australia's south-east coast.

'Sit, sit, sit,' sighed Ernie, gesturing to the visitor's chair, going behind his desk which was covered by files, the ramparts behind which he defended himself against gusts of disabling loss and accusation. He looked once out of the window to the river, but then faced Tim.

'Ward mates, Tim, eh?'

There seemed to be great weariness not so much in the eyes as in the lower face, in a hang-dogginess there.

'You have no bad effects from all that?' asked Ernie.

'No,' said Tim. 'Since I had no credit before, and I still have none.'

'Oh, yes,' said Ernie, staring out at the river again for an answer. 'Have you thought of going to Queensland, Tim? It's said to be full of opportunity up there for people of your type.'

'My type? What is my bloody type?'

Ernie shrugged. 'You take pretty quick offence at a man who means you no harm at all.'

'You yourself mentioned a reference when we were together in that place.'

'Yes, Tim. A random impulse of generosity.'

'Yes. But it had the features of an undertaking, Ernie.'

'Let me tell you it won't do you any good. Your credit is shot through the head for some time yet. A solitary reference from me, even if I appended all my honorary secretaryships, would not cut sufficient ice for you, Tim. I must tell you this frankly.'

It was probably the case. All his charitable vanities, all his fussiness about asking for bills to be paid. It had ended with him being swept from the business map of the Macleay.

'What about for my wife then?'

'What, Tim?'

'What if you wrote a reference – to my dictation if you don't mind – for my wife?'

'You want your wife to be your boss?'

It was what on reflection he wanted: the humble arrangement by which he'd be disciplined and saved. Better than depending on a future brother-in-law.

He said that. 'Bloody sight nicer than the alternatives, Ernie.'

'But I don't know your wife. I think you should just go, actually. Declare your true situation. Leave the business to be picked over by creditors. Queensland, Tim. That's the go.'

Tim sat back. He was content for the moment with the strong tide of his blood.

'Why don't *you* go to bloody Queensland, Ernie?'

'I am, despite everything, settled in here.' Ernie pointed to his walls of certificates. 'These are the signs of the man I am. Bereaved, Tim. But solid.' He leaned forward, a man to be congratulated.

At once Tim took from his breast pocket the envelope with the photograph of Missy as a boy. He took the picture out and held it up. Ernie stared at it.

'You notice,' said Tim, 'Winnie was careful that you should be saved. She scratched out the inscription. She wrote on the back, but named no one except the girl. Who badly needed to be named.'

Ernie stared at him and had the grace to cover his eyes with his left hand.

'How did you bloody get it?'

'She asked me to post it. But we were quarantined first.'

'You're right, Tim,' Ernie murmured very calmly. 'Winnie very loyal.'

'I just want some reasonable help,' Tim reminded him.

But Ernie raised his head and seemed to begin arguing with an unseen audience. 'Tyler's Touring Company. Premier British Touring Group. From triumphs in New Zealand and before that Fiji, before that again America! Acclaimed in California. Travelling players. Jesus, travelling! Grand repute. Crowned bloody heads. By appointment to the court of. *Young Arthur*. Tyler's Touring Company. She came to the house as Young Arthur, wearing actor's rags from the Tyler Company. Asked for me and Winnie. Primrose said we were not there. Winnie didn't actually meet her. Poor bloody Primose did the turning of her away. But Winnie watching from deep inside the house thought straight away, *That's an actress playing a boy*. And it was, of course. Astounded that dolt of a sailor Reid didn't spot it straight off. The role of Young Arthur famous on three continents. Tyler's a company, of course, you'd never find touring a bushweek place like this! Cities! Golden harbours.' Ernie stood up. 'I'd no idea at all Winnie found the picture.' He shook his head. 'Only safe thing with women is to have *no* secrets.'

Tim put the picture away in its envelope and looked up at standing Ernie.

'For an ugly bastard I have known beautiful women,' Ernie told him, his eyes softened and glistening.

'This was a girl though, Ernie.'

Ernie said, 'I know that. Met her when I was doing audits for North Coast Cane Company. Big trip to bloody Sydney, Tim. A party at the Hotel Australia. Next day she and I drove out to Watson's Bay and looked over the cliff. Should've bloody jumped. I was proud, Tim. So bloody proud. Thought I was bloody Christmas. Young Arthur. Utter enchantment, but didn't touch her. Some other bastard touched her. Some other bastard got to her core.'

'Did you tell Winnie that?'

'Wouldn't believe me. Anyhow, Ernie wasn't home, was he? On Showground Hill when Flo called there. Since we were friends for bloody life – she'd said so – you would have thought she would have come down to the office in Central, would have gone there first, much closer to the boat. Maybe . . . well, I thought she might have wanted to claim

me, cause trouble between Winnie and . . . So she went up to
the house, and she might have been tired all at once. She'd
gotten Mrs Mulroney's address from someone. Addresses like
that shared amongst women in the know. Actresses and so on.
Must've got overwhelmed from the sea journey. The strangeness
.of bloody Kempsey. Sort of blackness of its tone. Dullness. I
don't know. Defeated anyway. And straight to Mrs Mulroney.
No names. Bloody huge final pain. Face in a flask. *Do you know
this poor bloody girl? I know her, I know her, constable. Her name is
poor bloody Flo.'*

Flo? What an ordinary tag for something all the elements of
earth and sky strained so long to produce. Name of a barmaid.
Name of an actress. *Flo*. Now may your servant depart. At the
sounding of that ordinary, bush town, bush week, jovial name.
Name from a picnic to Watson's Bay. Name of laughter and half
a glass of gin after the play. Flo, bloody Flo.

Ernie said, '*Have you seen this woman, Mr Malcolm? Doesn't look
familiar, constable*. My sweet little actress. What does that prick
Ernie Malcolm think? He thinks the harm's done already. He
cries out and bites his knuckles in private, in his office, behind
the door. Harm's done and can't be unravelled by a pillar of
society coming forward and saying, *I took Flo to Watson's Bay.
Flo came here to let me know*. No need for me to say that with
a big bullet-headed idiot like Hanney making notes and bloody
sniffing. I wrote a letter to keep him on that particular job, the
hopeless bastard.'

Committing Missy to her dreary route with Constable Hanney!
That was a crime, but by his tormented face, Ernie had already
discovered the fact for himself.

'No use telling anyone the truth that I never touched the girl.
Winnie knew I wanted to touch. *The world is too much with us*,
says Winnie. I can't explain the excitement, Tim, when I heard
of Albert Rochester and the rescue. And Habash talking like a
fountain, praising you. Can't explain the excitement. Thinking,
raise a hero in Flo's name. Bring him forward, let Flo fall into the
shadow. Open the bridge and fill the passageway with a screen of
bloody heroes. Winnie knew straight away what I was up to, and
so we had it out. Over your bravery, Tim. Over Albert Rochester's
remains, the great marriage brawl. Things never went well again.

A sober woman. A bloody gin fiend in a week flat! Bloody took to it with a passion!'

Ernie shook his head and sat again. 'What can you do with that photograph there?'

'I don't want to do too much, Ernie. The thing is, I've come to the furthest place in the world. If I'm pushed out, it's the bloody void for me. Not Queensland, do you understand? The bloody void.'

'I can resist any story you spread, Tim. I have plenty of friends.'

'Do they include a new editor of the *Chronicle*, whoever that may be? Winnie spoke to me, Ernie. Passed the photograph to *me*. It has to be used for purposes she would approve of.'

They both speculated in silence on this.

'If I yield to you on this, you'll be back with that picture every week.'

'Only if my customers are warned off, and my suppliers. You know me well enough, Ernie. What I desire is a peaceful life.'

'I never wanted anything but a peaceful life for you, Tim. Until you started to write those things.'

Tim shook his head. 'If you still believe I wrote them, watch for the Offhand's letter of apology.'

Ernie Malcolm shrugged. 'Purposes Winnie would approve,' he said.

'Write me the letter of recommendation. Or rather, write Kitty one.'

Ernie inhaled and reached for a sheet of correspondence paper.

The letter Ernie and Tim devised, and took to have typed out on Ernie's huge typewriter by Miss Pollack, read well enough.

'To Whom it May Concern:
'Dear Sir,
'This to introduce to you Mrs Katherine Shea of Belgrave Street, Kempsey, an exemplary member of the community. When her husband's business fell into unfortunate debt, she acquitted the total amount as soon as she knew about it. I have no hesitation in recommending her to you on the grounds of her business ability, her high moral values, and

her reliability in commercial matters. I do so in the highest terms possible.

> Mr E. V. Malcolm,
> Justice of the Peace.'

Beneath Miss Pollack's long fingers, the letter of rescue bloomed. And though Tim might have inherited Bandy as a brother-in-law, fellow believer and shareholder, he had avoided having him as master. His master was Kitty, and he was at peace.

Returning to *T. Shea – General Store*, Tim made a detour to the bridge, where its planking rose out over the water and threw a shade over the river bank. Here he tore Winnie's envelope and Missy's photograph to pieces and floated them downstream. The river would obscure with its silt every fragment.

Missy now was indefinitely blended with her ancestors.

The Close

As the Australian autumn brought in temperate air, the Macleay newspapers let people know that Mr Bandy Habash had bought the large Clarence River drapery store previously owned by Mr F. O. Bentley. This gave Bandy instantly a place in New South Wales Northern Rivers society, and Mamie told Tim and Kitty that since Mr F. O. Bentley was a member of the Grafton Jockey Club, he had been disposed to write Bandy a letter of introduction to the more junior Macleay Turf Club.

As a result, on a day in late April, the Shea family attended the running of the Macleay Autumn Cup. M. M. Chance's four-year-old Dasher was beaten into second place by five lengths, finishing behind Mr B. Habash's roan, Strong Medicine, ridden by the owner. Later, a delighted Mr Habash and his fiancée Miss Mamie Kenna were photographed with the Autumn Cup Bandy had garnered. Mrs Kitty Shea, towards the end of her term, applauded the event from a camp stool set up on the tray of the delivery dray.

Coastal steamers, though still forced to moor at New Entrance, had brought in members of the racing fraternity from other parts of the North Coast. *Burrawong* had also brought in punters from Sydney, as well as a small number of regular passengers, Mrs Molly Burke amongst them. She went through a restrained reunion with her husband and told him that under pressure from the Provincial of the Sisters of the Sacred Heart at Randwick, a cousin of Old Burke's, young Ellen had at last uttered in tears the name of the father of the child she was carrying.

As Bandy Habash emerged out of the prize ring, smiling in jockey silks of green and blue, to be congratulated by Tim Shea, Mr Burke of Pee Dee station, whom Tim had not known to be present at the race meeting, launched himself at Bandy and felled him with a furious blow. Restrained by a combination of constables and citizens, Mr Burke would not state what his reason for this attack was. Mr Habash for his part said he would not press charges.

Later that day, after a conversation with her sister Kitty to which Tim was not a party, Mamie Kenna broke off her engagement to Mr Habash. To some people's surprise, Mr Habash – not yet departed for the Clarence River – consoled himself with the observances of the Catholic Church – first confession, then the Rosary, Benediction, and daily Mass. Habash also made a number of appeals for help to Tim Shea, but though more sympathetic than some saw as proper Tim told him that nothing could be said to the sisters.

The week before the Macleay River Bridge connecting West and Central to East was opened, the British garrison of Mafeking, besieged by the Boers for longer than Kempsey had been besieged by plague, was relieved by a British flying column. No British garrisons were hostage any more in the world. Things had been restored to their accustomed balance. A procession was held in Belgrave Street and down Smith. That was the end of the serious drum beating, and Tim Shea was pleased. It would be another year before Tim Shea would need to frown down upon reports in the *Chronicle* of General Kitchener's sweeping clearance of the Boer population, of the burning of farms, of the crowding of Boer families into 'camps of refuge', or as the Spanish called them, 'concentration camps'.

So, in the autumn of Bandy's victory in the Macleay Cup and the British victory of Mafeking, a conviction of civilisation restored ran in the veins of all the citizens of the Shire of the Macleay. The white thwarts of the bridge stood as high as Lucy's Angelus tower. Blackbutt planking was broad enough for any herd crossing to the markets in West, and the pathway had been fitted with bays to allow citizens to shelter as the herds came over.

The opening of the bridge was marked by a regatta to which Captain Reid of the *Burrawong* had been invited to contribute that now rarely seen vessel. *Burrawong*, however, despite its new rat-proof hawsers and its weekly fumigation at Darling Harbour, was not allowed to moor at Central wharf after honouring the bridge. It was required to retreat to its accustomed quarantine station inside the New Entrance. Captain Reid nonetheless ingratiated himself with the populace by carrying every flag in *Burrawong*'s lockers. The high colour could not be allowed to obscure the reality that plague still sought a landfall everywhere, and that cases were still occurring around the shores of Sydney Harbour.

The regatta and the opening of the bridge were observed from their own segment of river bank by Mr and Mrs Tim Shea, their children Johnny and Annie and the new-born infant, Maude. Mamie Kenna and Joe O'Neill were also in the group. They sat apart, although a friendliness was growing between them.

Some of the conversation at the bridge opening concerned the life sentence Mr and Mrs Mulroney received for the manslaughter of the young English actress Flo Meades. Amongst the notables, Ernie Malcolm made a brief reappearance. People were cheered to see him, though noticed that these days he stood back a bit.

But Bandy Habash was not at all visible in Kempsey for the civic event linking Central with East. Tim Shea knew he had already gone to Sydney to see Ellen Burke, and now lay low in town, wearing a scapular provided him by Mrs Kitty Shea, who still secretly spoke to him.

He had left a letter for Mamie, which she read, retained, but did not reply to.

'Dearest Woman,

'I appeal to you as one who has only recently seen Salvation's light. I was guilty of extreme sins within your own family, but they were the sins of a man unredeemed, a man in darkness, an infidel who thought those who dwelt in Light were infidels. I have now drunk at the Fountainhead, I now dwell in Radiance, and my past crimes have no bearing on my present life or intentions.

'My life is turned utterly, like the face of a flower, to the Divine light of your face. I have tried to expiate my sin with Ellen Burke and will speak to her and will of course forever support her child. It is she who has chosen not to take me as a husband and will now seek her independent fortune in Sydney. To that fortune, I shall make appropriate contributions.

'You are my lodestone, and if you would only, dear woman, return to our former arrangement, you will never have cause to doubt my devotion.

Yours forever and ever, *in saecula saeculorum*,
Bandy Habash'

Many small craft speckled the river for the bridge opening, including one rowed by two ten-year-olds, Eddie and Ronald Sage. This rowboat, through too much shy-acking on the part of the children on board, capsized. The Sage boys' younger sister Doris was thrown into the tide and gave Johnny Shea, who had already been playing in the shallows, wavering towards the depths but strangely obedient to his parents' edict that he should not swim out amongst the boats, a pretext to go out into the depths to save her.

Eventually, on the recommendation of Mr Ernie Malcolm, Secretary of the Humane Society, Macleay branch, Johnny Shea was awarded the Silver Medal of the Society for saving the Sage child. It was acknowledged by his parents that this award was very good for the child.

From the day after the bridge opening, one of the busiest transitters was Tim Shea, transporting his household goods to the newly purchased store in East by dray. The signwriter did the place out in blue and gold, and the lettering said *K. Shea – General Store*. No one seemed to refer much to this change, or persecute Tim about it. For by then it was generally acknowledged that Tim Shea wasn't the dangerous fellow some had earlier claimed him to be.